The Lady and the Lawman

The Kincaid Family Series

Joyce Brandon

DIVERSIONBOOKS

Also by Joyce Brandon

After Eden

The Kincaid Family Series
The Lady and the Robber Baron
The Lady and the Outlaw
Adobe Palace

Diversion Books
A Division of Diversion Publishing Corp.
443 Park Avenue South, Suite 1008
New York, New York 10016
www.DiversionBooks.com

For more information, email info@diversionbooks.com

First Diversion Books edition July 2015.
Print ISBN: 978-1-68230-245-3
eBook ISBN: 978-1-62681-903-0

Novels are always about relationships, so this book is lovingly dedicated to my husband, John C. Brandon (1922-2005), and our children, Robert Kevin Firestine, Suzanne Lonelle Satragni, John Lee Brandon (1948-2010), and Brian Mark Brandon. From these five precious seeds—along with their spouses, ex-spouses, children, step-children, grandchildren, and step-grandchildren—have come countless plots and subplots. Also to my brother, Charlie Miller; my sister, Ann Hall; my double-cousin, Dap Gene Parker; my foster daughter, Kristina Lynn Wilson; my step-father Joe L. Shannon; and my grandchildren in order of their appearance: Thomas Madison, Brittany Carter, Rebecka Davis, Dylan Zapf, and Caleb Zapf in Suzie's family; Brandi Firestine, Tyson Freer, Brittan Freer, Holly Beck, and Takoda Freer in Bob's family; Santos Sanchez, Nicholas Sanchez, Stephanie Sanchez, and Dominic Sanchez in Mark's family; James Wilson, Jeffery Wilson, Isaac Paradise, and Jeffery Wilson Jr. in Kristina's family; and Katie Fairburn in John Lee's family. I am very grateful to each and every one of you.

CHAPTER ONE

Thursday, March 11, 1880

Hostile men lined both sides of the street in the small border town. With one foot on the ground, the other on the bottom step of the stagecoach, Angie hesitated and looked at the man called Shotgun.

"Don't worry none, ma'am. 'Tain't you they're after. It's him," he said, tilting his head to the south.

Angie tried to peer around the stagecoach, but its wide body and the way it angled in toward the buildings obstructed her view. "Who?"

Displaying crooked tobacco-stained teeth, Shotgun grinned and cut a plug off his chewing tobacco. "*Hombre de verdad*, the grissel heels call him. The man with the lethal eyes."

"Where?"

"Don't look behind you, ma'am. 'Tain't a sight for the likes of yourself."

Angie turned immediately and walked around the heavily laden stagecoach. Her bicycle hung on the back of the wagon. She had seven items of luggage, including valises, a camera wagon, and camera boxes, but the bicycle caused the most complaint among the men who loaded and unloaded the stage. As if this one safety bicycle threatened the horse in its own domain.

Coming down the middle of the wide, deeply rutted road, a long line of horses—manned and unmanned—kicked up a red cloud that settled slowly over the faded wooden buildings on both sides of the street. Angie frowned. Not one lethal eye in sight. Each rider's face seemed lost under dirt, beard stubble, and the shadow of a wide-brimmed hat.

Then she saw the reason for the consternation and hostility on the faces of the townspeople. From the third rider back, almost every other horse carried a body or two tied over the saddle.

"What happened?"

"Reckon *he* happened. *Hombre de verdad*. Reckon he caught up to that passel of hot iron *hombres* running a maverick factory along the border."

Angie had been gone from the territory for four years but knew he meant rustlers. Grissel heels were old-timers.

The ragged column, led by a wide-shouldered man on a big chestnut, moved steadily forward. Angie counted seventeen riders and twenty-three bodies. Dead men hung across saddles like bags of dirty laundry. One man—taller than the others and draped across a squatty, black and white piebald mare—dangled one arm precariously in front of the horse's back hoof. Angie expected the horse to step on the man's hand, but each time the horse's hoof came down, the hand was a scant inch ahead of it. Blood ran down the side of the man's face and into his hair.

Death confused Angie. Part of her wanted to get closer to those rigid bodies and part of her was horrified and wanted only to look away, to be sick. As a child she had poked and prodded a dead wren as if its little stiff body could explain the secret of death. Part of her still wanted to run over and examine that gangling dead man—to lift his head and look into his eyes in the hope that some answer would be there.

Clutching her throat, lest she throw up, Angie turned to Shotgun. "Which one is *hombre de verdad?*"

"Ridin' point. The lanky feller straddling the big chestnut."

Angie tried to see beneath the trail dust this man who aroused such hostility but saw only dirt, beard stubble, and the distorting effects of deep, slanting shadows.

"Would you get my crate down," she asked, her gaze still fixed on the column of men—alive and dead. "That one." Angie pointed from memory at the spot where the Scenographe—a small lightweight camera with a walking stick tripod, relatively easy to assemble and shoot with—lay strapped to the top of the stage. She yearned for the Hale but feared Shotgun's good humor, such as it was, could not be stretched to unloading a wagon, tripod, and a big, heavy camera.

Shotgun popped the plug of tobacco into his mouth and laboriously climbed back up onto the stagecoach.

"How long will we be here?" she asked.

"Couple of hours anyways, until they either sober up the driver or find another one."

She hoped they sobered up the doctor as well. Angie had ridden in with an army doctor who took furtive nips from his flask, three soldiers who snored, and a heavyset woman who asked questions that Angie could not answer in an acceptable manner. Angie had no children or husband to testify to her womanliness. She had no chaperon to attest to her virtuousness. She was on the Arizona-Mexico border in a little dust mote called Nogales, assigned there by questionable publishers—notorious for their woman's suffrage efforts. Angie had failed every test of respectability the stout woman put forth. She'd suspected that even her brown traveling gown and bonnet didn't have a reputable enough look to it. Perhaps the rust ruching on the collar displayed a penchant for frivolous adornment or a lack of sincerity.

The riders drew almost even with the stagecoach.

"How can he kill all those men and get away with it? He did kill them?" she asked.

"Him or his helpers. Them's riders from the Stokey ranch, the Bar S. Kincaid gets away with jest about any danged thing he wants. He's the law in these here parts."

"The law?"

"Arizona ranger. The worst son of a bi…bi…biscuit you'd ever want to lock horns with."

Angie took the box that Shotgun handed down to her and stepped back inside the stagecoach so she could sit down, unpack the camera, and assemble it on its tripod. Shotgun was probably trying to impress her. Westerners had an almost irresistible urge to haze pilgrims, to dazzle them with slang and nonchalance. He could not know she had grown up on this miserable frontier.

Camera assembled, Angie climbed out. The rangers stopped their horses on the east side of the road. A northeast wind, so slight as to go unnoticed until this moment, carried the sickly sweet smell of the dead men to Angie's nostrils. Grimacing, fighting the almost irresistible buckling of her knees, Angie carried the Scenographe to a spot upwind that afforded a view of the rangers and the men lining the sidewalk in front of the saloon.

Townsmen on the west side crossed the road to stand shoulder-to-shoulder with their friends. No one spoke, but the tension was so thick she smelled it the way she had smelled lightning as a child. Angie knew—by riding into town this way, loaded down with what must be dead friends and relatives of these townsmen—the ranger had issued a challenge and drawn the line.

Silent, curious men glared at Kincaid. Kincaid looked from face to face, lifted off his tan-colored hat to reveal damp black hair—mashed down but so wiry it was already springing up—and dragged his shirt-sleeve across his forehead. A fine Sharps rifle nestled in his saddle sheath. A forty-five rode low on his thigh. Tied down for action, Laramee would say.

"Hotter'n blazes out there," Kincaid said sociably, running his fingers through his stiff hair. He had one of those raspy voices that some men had, and the sound of it, so unexpectedly rich and attractive, eased down inside Angie like warm liquid.

Up close and with his hat off, Kincaid made a striking picture: tall and rangy and a little slope-shouldered, his blue denim breeches tucked into dusty knee-high black boots, he looked hewn from mahogany. Some Moorish ancestor had surely altered his family tree.

To her keen artist's eye, his brick-brown face hid more than it showed. As an avid student of human form, Angie was fascinated by the energy he exuded. His careful, amiable facade reminded her of a pile of embers that concealed its smoldering heat inside.

Men grumbled in low tones, but the lawman ignored the buzz. He turned to the man sitting the sorrel next to him.

"Take the bodies of Stokey's men over to the church and put 'em in the shade. Dump the rustlers on the sidewalk. And leave 'em there."

An angry murmur from the crowd caused Angie to duck under the cape and peer through the lens of the Scenographe. A fight was about to erupt. Kincaid had sixteen men with him. Close to fifty men stood on the sidewalk. She focused on Kincaid—tall and lithe in the saddle—tripped the shutter, pulled out the plate, and shoved it into the plate holder she had hung around her neck.

Kincaid turned and looked at her for the first time. Angie brushed hair out of her eyes. She had taken her bonnet off, and the cape had a way of working the hairs loose so they frayed out around her face.

"What are you doing?" he asked. A smile twinkled in his eyes.

"Me?"

"Yes, ma'am, you."

"I'm taking pictures."

"For what?"

"For a picture book of the Arizona Territory."

The smile moved down to his mouth and created inch-long dimples at the corners. Kincaid's finely sculpted features fit together in an appealing, thoroughly masculine face dominated by expressive black brows and piercing blue eyes with the luminosity of stained glass windows. He had the kind of smile—probably learned at a young age—that could mask anything or promise the world.

Kincaid shook his head. "So you're that famous George Barnard I've heard so much about," he drawled, bringing a leg up and crossing it over his saddle so he could lean his elbow on it. Laramee had a habit of sitting the saddle like that on occasion, usually when he was fooling around or tired.

Angie flushed with a combination of emotions. She wasn't a George Barnard yet, but she would be. Barnard had become famous for his hallmark photographs of the Civil War. He impressed Angie far more than Kincaid could guess, because Barnard had taken his pictures before the gelatine dry plate process was invented. He had to coat his plate in the field, take his picture, and then develop his plate immediately. He had to cart far more equipment with him, including a portable dark tent.

"Well, ma'am, I sure wouldn't want to interfere with history being recorded, but do you think you could wait till I've had a bath, a shave, and maybe a cold beer before you take my picture?"

Angie slid a treated plate out of the box, loaded it into the camera, and smiled. "If the men at Valley Forge had insisted on waiting for a hot bath and a cup of coffee before they were photographed, Mr. Kincaid, our country would have lost a very valuable part of its heritage to vanity."

Apparently amused by Angie's standing up to the ranger, men on the sidewalk chuckled. Kincaid grinned, then laughed, and everyone joined in.

When the uproar subsided a little, the man beside Kincaid said, "See, Lieutenant, that's what's been holding us back. Your danged vanity." That caused another round of laughter, then someone remembered the dead men, and a hush fell over the crowd.

"Well, snap away then, ma'am. Shore wouldn't want to cheat this territory of its heritage." He started to dismount.

"Why are you dumping those poor, unfortunate men on the sidewalk?" Angie asked loudly. Her voice shook with emotion as she viewed the bodies draped over the tired-looking horses.

The smile died away. With a grimace Kincaid settled back into the saddle, which creaked in the sudden silence following her remark. For one moment he looked utterly bleak. "I had to watch 'em die, ma'am," he said tersely, his voice loud enough for all to hear. "Now they can see 'em dead. Maybe some youngster swinging too wide a loop'll get the message."

As if daring them to protest, Kincaid's steely blue eyes swept the faces of the men lined up on the sidewalk. No one spoke up. The townspeople looked at one another, at Angie, and at the dead men, but no one looked at Kincaid.

• • •

Hardly an hour had gone by, barely time to drink a cold sarsaparilla and take a birdbath in a bowl of water, but Kincaid had gotten into more trouble, Angie reflected. He was about to engage in a gunfight with a man he hadn't even known an hour ago—if rumor could be trusted.

And she was going to photograph it. Angie adjusted the heavy, awkward Hale camera on its wagon tripod and glanced back at the lawman who leaned against the building across the street from her.

Angie had prevailed upon Shotgun to unload the Hale. Assembled, the Hale sat atop a tripod screwed onto a miniature flatbed wagon. She had designed the wagon herself and hired a carpenter to build it. They had tinkered with the design until she'd gotten exactly what she wanted.

She had chosen the Hale in spite of its awkwardness and bulk because it alone could cover the size area she needed to capture the whole scene and to provide the size pictures she wanted for the book. And it had a faster shutter—one-thirtieth of a second exposure instead of the slower one twenty-fifth of a second on the Scenographe.

Generally a shooting would not have occasioned much interest from Angie. Personally, she held violence in low regard, but when she'd been commissioned by *Trumbull and Maxwell's Weekly* to take the photographs for a picture book of the Arizona Territory and its pioneering inhabitants, she'd altered her views. Now every event in Arizona took on new meaning.

Johnny Winchester, the man Kincaid waited for, was rumored to have seventeen notches on his gun handle—not counting greasers or Indians. Winchester waited in the saloon at the end of the rutted road.

Angie glanced at the saloon and prayed Winchester wouldn't come out yet. She wanted to get both gunmen in one picture. She was gambling on Kincaid being the winner. She'd angle the camera to get a front view of Winchester. Both cameras should have been set up, but it was too late. Kincaid looked impatient enough to drag Winchester outside right now.

She had exposed four plates of Kincaid, carefully noncommittal, in slightly different poses, as he waited. Now the ranger stepped out into the sun and looked up the street at the saloon. Angie took a profile shot of him. At the click of the shutter Kincaid's sturdy head swung back around, and he narrowed his eyes at her. Piercing and hard, his gaze flicked over her, and the distinctive heat of anxiety that had crept into her earlier flooded her again. In that instant Angie understood his nickname. She lifted the corners of her lips to signal her good intentions, raised her hands in surrender, and stepped away from her camera. The ranger quirked one corner of his mouth in a wry look of grim satisfaction and dismissed her. Angie flushed at the realization that she had backed down so easily.

• • •

Using both hands, Lance cocked his Stetson down over his eyes to block out the sun's glare. Sweat trickled down the middle of his chest. It was as hot as a fire in a pepper mill, but he was used to heat. Weren't for the heat, he wouldn't know he was in Arizona.

Except for the pesky photographer—one of those big-eyed, idealistic young women, thin and fragile of limb and intensely purposeful of spirit—a skinny red-haired kid, and a small brown dog chasing its own tail, the street, tracked by a thousand deep ruts, simmered, vacant under the blazing sun.

Lance looked back at the girl. A big-eyed skinny girl could almost always get and keep his attention, no matter how busy he was. The girl's pale blond hair was pulled back in a bun on her slim neck. A light film of wispy hairs framed her face. She kept ducking under the black cape and popping out. Each time her hair looked a little more frayed. What was a pretty little thing like her doing pulling a contraption like that in a place like this? She'd look more at home lifting a crystal goblet in Delmonico's or Sherry's in New York City.

Three half-drunk prospectors stepped out onto the sidewalk in front of the tobacco store. From inside the nearest store, men placed bets on the gunfight. No matter which way it went, someone would be the better for it.

Farther south, in an upstairs room of the town's only two-story building, Ben Thompson waited. Motionless, rifle across his knees, Ben watched every movement on the street below. He and Cal McNulty had driven the wagon into Nogales to find Kincaid. They were part of Kincaid's band of six rangers working out of a chuck-wagon office that rolled around the countryside, poking and prying, flushing out whiskey peddlers, bootleggers, horse thieves, and rustlers. The wagon served as their traveling headquarters—office, arsenal, kitchen, and jail. They had wired McNamara to let him know where they were, and McNamara had fired back a telegram saying to tell Kincaid when he came back from Mexico how pissed McNamara was with him. McNamara always assumed the worst when Kincaid got near the border. And he was usually right. Lines on paper didn't mean much to Kincaid. He'd just swear he didn't know where the hell he was, and there weren't many men who'd call him on it. Except McNamara always seemed to know what was going on. Probably right this minute the Scot was having a conniption fit, what with one of his best men about to get shot at.

"Who the hell is this Johnny Winchester?" Cal asked, interrupting Ben's train of thought.

Keeping an eye on the street below, Ben spat a stream of tobacco out the window. "He's a murdering coyote who's trying to make a name for hisself," Ben said, his voice gruff. "The stories about Winchester are wilder than a marshtigget in May. Probably the only thing about 'em that's true is that Winchester has kilt every two-bit cowpoke who stood up to him. But when it comes to shootin' straight, I ain't seen Kincaid's beat."

Ben blew a speck of dust off the oily perfection of his thirty-thirty's blue steel barrel. "What I don't understand is why a slick like Winchester has a following like a camptown reverend. What do ya s'pose he does to make the calico queens throw themselves at his feet the way they do? Seems like a pure waste of womanpower to me."

"Just goes to show some women ain't got the sense God gave a pomegranate, some men neither," Cal McNulty said, shaking his head. "Where's Winchester from anyways?"

"Nobody knows. From hell, I s'pect. Some folks say he's the devil hisself."

Cal was perplexed. "Why the hell don't we stop this thing? What do we tell McNamara if Kincaid gets kilt?" McNamara headed up the ranger unit. He purely resented his men getting killed for no good reason.

"Tell him the best lie we can think of, that we didn't get here till later after the gunfight," Ben said. "The lieutenant ordered us to stand aside." That explained everything to his satisfaction. Except Ben had no idea why Winchester had chosen Kincaid. The lieutenant had practically eaten crow in the saloon in front of fifty men to avoid a fight.

"I think we ought to stop it anyways," Cal grumbled.

"We'll likely stop it," Ben said, "right after the lieutenant kills the bastard."

The young woman, obviously engrossed in her apparatus, leaned unselfconsciously over the camera, unaware or unconcerned with the image she projected to Lance's keen eyes. Her absorption triggered a sense of peacefulness in Lance. She adjusted a knob here and a screw there. Her great dark eyes bobbed up and peered at him, an object to be photographed. Ordinarily he would have approached her to chat a little, but he was exhausted from watching men die who shouldn't have had to die. Gun duels were a waste of time and manpower. And he particularly disliked tramping through horse apples and cow patties to get shot at.

He had heard in the saloon that she wouldn't be in Nogales except the stagecoach had gotten lost. The driver was drunk and took the wrong fork in the road, so here she was. He didn't blame her for making a living. But he hoped his family didn't see the pictures. Especially if he got killed. He didn't want his mother staring at a picture of him lying in the dirt of this damned, weasely little stink-hole. The thought of it caused the back of his mouth to taste of grit.

Lance's right hand twitched. Johnny Winchester had goaded him into this gunfight. He and Winchester had no history of mutual animosity, no special reason to want to kill each other. Lance had never seen the man before today. But he wasn't surprised. Men got squirrelly in the heat.

He felt squirrelly himself. He and twenty riders from the Stokey ranch had chased rustlers half the night and ridden all morning. Only sixteen strong this morning, they had brought in the bodies of five of Stokey's riders and eighteen rustlers who had hightailed it across the border with a few hundred head of Bill Stokey's immigrant cattle. Rather than surrender and hang, the rustlers had fought to the death. Lance did not relish the thought of killing Winchester today. And he did not relish hearing McNamara yell at him for crossing the border.

Nothing moved on the wide, dusty boulevard. Even the photographer was still, her blond head hidden under the black cape doing whatever it was she did under there. He liked the thought that she was paying so much attention to him, but he didn't like her being in the road. Sometimes bullets went astray. He'd sure hate to see her get shot.

If he was smart, he'd stand his ground and make Winchester tramp through the horse turds to get to him. But he'd always been too damned impatient for his own good. His father had said once, *Lance wants to plant a tree in the morning and saw planks by nightfall.* Apparently today wouldn't be any different. Lance picked a rut he liked and started to walk.

Cal nervously fingered his rifle. Kincaid walked as if he were pissed about something. Puffs of yellow dust rose off his heels. "You sure the lieutenant can beat Winchester?"

Ben wanted to reassure Cal, but something stopped him. In the saloon he had seen Winchester up close. The man's eyes had about as much expression as a stainless-steel spoon, except for that one instant when he'd seen Kincaid. Then something had moved in the killer's eyes, something that wasn't there the next time Ben had looked. It had reminded him of a weasel poking its head out of a hole on the prairie one second and disappearing the next. Left him wondering if he'd really seen what he thought he'd seen. And wishing he hadn't seen it, if he had.

"I don't like this," Cal said, spitting out the window.

With shaking fingers Angie grabbed the wagon tongue and moved her camera alongside to stay even with Kincaid. Her heavy plate holder banged on her hip, but she ignored it. Her wagon clattered and bumped over ruts. Dust rose on the still air. Sweat trickled down her belly. Kincaid stopped. Angie glanced from Kincaid to the saloon where Winchester waited. She leveled her wagon by rocking the handle until the wheels settled into a better position.

The batwing doors swung open, and Angie straightened. A tall man, about forty years old, dressed in a black frock coat and white shirt with string tie, stepped out onto the sidewalk. He put on a buff-colored hat and stamped his feet. Hands on hips, he surveyed the town for a moment and then stepped out into the road. A dozen men poured out of the saloon behind him. A smile appeared on Winchester's somber face and disappeared as quickly as it had come.

Angie trembled. It had started. Her hands went damp with fear. Kincaid glanced over at her, and her heart thumped so hard it hurt. Angie was glad she hadn't known Kincaid before. The fear for him would be unbearable. Somewhere, some wife, mother, or sister would be devastated by his death. She didn't even know him and yet she, too, felt she would be devastated if it happened.

Winchester started to walk. Kincaid followed suit. They were a hundred yards apart, closing rapidly. Kincaid walked faster than Winchester. In panic Angie pulled her wagon alongside, praying she would have time to check her focus after they stopped. Or would they shoot while they walked?

• • •

Johnny ambled forward slowly, carefully, enjoying his thoughts. Kincaid had been a thorn in his side long enough. Too long. The thought of killing the son of a bitch who had killed Sid and Morris exhilarated him.

Then Winchester stopped abruptly. Kincaid stopped. They were less than twenty feet apart. If Kincaid was scared, it didn't show. Johnny waited while the photographer scampered around that silly wagon-camera contraption. He wanted to be sure she got her picture. He wanted the world to see Kincaid get his comeuppance. Johnny knew he could take Kincaid. He knew it in his gut. Kincaid was about to be a dead man.

The girl popped under the black cloth behind her camera. He gave her a few seconds.

"Go for your gun," Johnny said softly.

Angie peered through the lens. She had both men framed in her camera. Both of them! In profile. Her heart raced in her chest. She tripped the shutter, ripped out the plate, and put in another. She could not believe her luck. Both men crouched slightly, in that bent-knee posture of attack. Both men looked intense and at the same time relaxed, as if they knew they could handle whatever came next. Angie's heart thudded against her chest. She said a small prayer for Kincaid. And for herself. She was about to take the picture of her career.

Upstairs, Thompson waited and sweated. Sweat trickled down his chest and back and beaded on his forehead. He wiped his brow with his sleeve. Kincaid would wait for the signal in Winchester's eyes…

It must have come. Their hands moved in unison, flashing downward.

A split-second apart, both guns spurted flame.

Too stunned to move, cursing quietly and automatically, Thompson watched in disbelief as Kincaid was knocked backward by the force of Winchester's bullet. Winchester stumbled, spun around, and fell. Cautiously men stepped out of the buildings. Thompson stood up. His rifle clattered to the floor.

Ben and Cal ran out of the room and down the stairs.

• • •

Kincaid fell, and Angie abandoned her camera to run to his side. She flashed a look toward Winchester, but only to assure herself that he was no longer a threat.

Angie knelt beside Kincaid, and gunsmoke stung her nostrils. Kincaid's eyes seemed to focus and find her face, then seemed to lose focus. And as if his body were reacting to his injury, a starburst, like an explosion of light in a tiny, dark tube, flashed deep inside his pupils. The starburst happened again, another split-second only, but it registered inside her like Morse code. Her body comprehended that flash at some deep level and responded with a flood of pure compassion.

Angie swore she had seen into Kincaid's soul. She swayed, near to fainting. Others crowded around them.

Lance blinked. His eyes blurred into focus. The photographer knelt beside him. She looked stricken. Lance steadied her with his right hand, then touched his side where the bullet had entered. His hand came up bloody. Fortunately he felt no pain—yet.

The girl's face, pale and riveted on his, reflected so much fear for him, so much compassion in her eloquent brown eyes that Lance felt a sudden urge to protect her.

The crowd nearly blocked out the sky. A familiar voice yelled over the murmuring strangers. "Let me through."

Ben Thompson and Cal McNulty pushed their way through to Lance's side. Relieved to see familiar faces, Lance grinned at his sidekicks. Though obviously rattled, Ben and Cal were good men. They just needed direction.

"I thought I told you to plug that so-and-so," Lance growled at Ben.

Knowing Kincaid had done nothing of the sort and grateful for Kincaid's attempt to steady him, Ben knelt beside his fallen lieutenant. Ben forced his eyes away from the spreading bloodstain and followed his lieutenant's lead. He made his own comment cool and hopefully steady. "McNamara's gonna be mad."

Lance smiled. "When he sees me, he'll probably talk a blood blister on a rawhide boot."

The men's reckless exchange surprised Angie, and she laughed and sobbed at the same time. Tears streamed down her cheeks. She wiped her eyes, embarrassed at what he was sure was an unaccustomed display of public emotion. Lance wanted to reward her compassion and humanity in some way. He couldn't do that, but he might be able to lighten her load momentarily.

"Ben, take a look at my back," he said.

Ben turned him carefully and peered at his back.

"Did I fall in cow patties?"

Caught off guard, the girl fell again into her nearly hysterical little laugh-sob. Others in the crowd joined in. "Nope, seemed to of missed all your chances for that honor," Ben said.

Lance winked at the girl. "Sure glad he didn't ruin my day. How about getting me in out of the sun? I want to get my beauty rest in private."

"Get back!" Ben yelled at the crowd. "Which way to the doc's office?"

A man's voice answered. "We ain't got a regular doc, but they's a army doc over at the telegraph office. Came in on that stage that got lost. Over thataway!"

Angie watched in silence as they carried Kincaid down the road and up the few steps to the telegraph office. She wanted to follow but felt reluctant to intrude on his privacy. They disappeared inside, and she walked back to her camera wagon.

A boy ran up, panting. "Ma'am. The stage is leaving."

Angie sighed. Her heart still pounded madly. It had all ended too suddenly for her. She hadn't adjusted to the fact that it was over. "Thank you. I'll be right there."

"You need help? I could pull your wagon for you?"

"Why, yes, thank you. I do feel a bit shaky."

The boy, all freckles and sandy brown hair, pulled the wagon. Angie glanced at the telegraph office. She wanted to see how Kincaid was or do something for him, but there was no time.

She walked to the stagecoach on rubbery legs, dismantled the camera and packed it into its cushioned box, folded the tripod, and supervised as the driver loaded it all back onto the top of the stagecoach. He muttered into his filthy whiskers about the size of the load she'd toted, but, since she'd paid extra, he couldn't refuse to accept it.

The stage started to roll, and Angie leaned back and closed her eyes. They were not so crowded now, because the doctor had stayed behind to take care of Kincaid. That caused her another pang. No man, wounded as Kincaid was, should have to rely on a drunk.

Angie's head pounded. She should have stayed in Boston.

The stage passed the telegraph office where Kincaid lay inside on the counter, and Angie leaned out and waved. Kincaid didn't see her, but the sight of him lying on the counter caused a warm rush of emotion, almost like the heat from a furnace door suddenly opened, to flush upward from the base of her spine.

One of the men who had carried Kincaid waved at her. Angie sat back, closed her eyes, and prayed that he would recover. She remembered the way his eyes had looked immediately after he was shot, and this time the message projected from his eyes into her awareness made a picture in her head—for one split-second only—of a very young boy, hurt, and momentarily confused. For the rest of her days she would remember that look, that split-second of total unmasking and pure human-to-human contact.

The stage bounced along for hours before Angie recovered enough to think of anything else. Then she realized once more that she was going home. When Angie left Durango four years ago she had vowed she would never go back, but that was before she discovered the national obsession with the frontier. Pictures of anything at all from what easterners called the Wild West were as good as gold. The picture book would establish her reputation and make her some money. It had already made it possible for her to make this trip and to see a historic gunfight, one that would go down in history, thanks to her camera—if her plates came out. *Please don't let him die.*

The stage lurched and sent her flying into the man next to her. They both apologized, and she settled back. Soon she would see Laramee and Sarah. When her parents died and left the fifty-thousand-acre ranch to her brother, Laramee, and two thousand dollars to her, Angie had felt disinherited. She had gone east to attend school and vowed she wouldn't come back. Laramee knew she was hurt, and he had told her the will didn't make a difference, the ranch was as much hers as his, but it made a difference to her. She had been disinherited. Nothing could soften that blow. In spite and in pain she had left. She believed that if her parents had wanted her to live with Laramee, they should have made her his partner instead of his poor relation.

Ben Thompson and Cal McNulty waited on the steps outside the telegraph office. The stagecoach rumbled past. Big-eyed and solemn, the young woman leaned out the window and waved at them. Cal waved back. Finally the doctor came outside. Thin, blond, and seedy, his middle-aged face was red with the flush of alcohol. "You friends of his?"

"Yeah. He gonna pull through?"

"Maybe. The bullet went in at an angle. His kidney may not have been hit directly, but it ain't going to be worth a damn if he gets infected. I'll have to take the bullet out. Can you get a wagon so's we can take him to Fort Lowell? Do it here, I'm going to have to use a can opener."

"We got a wagon." Thompson spit into the dirt. "Can I see him?"

"Sure."

Kincaid lay on the counter. A young, sallow-faced man worked at his desk as cool as if a man weren't bleeding in front of him.

Thompson stopped beside his lieutenant.

Kincaid grimaced. "Winchester ain't so fast."

In spite of his chagrin, Thompson laughed. "You're lying there halfway fit for a coffin, boy."

"I feel about fifty pounds heavier. You sure he only shot me once?"

"The doc wants us to take you to Fort Lowell so's he can take the bullet out…"

"Did I hit that bastard?"

"Yeah. Must not a been dead center—his friends helped him walk away. They rode out about twenty minutes ago. We didn't try to stop 'em. They'll be easy to catch though."

The truth was that after Ben saw his leader fall he was so shocked he couldn't get his back up to fight. The spunk went out of him like air out of a bellows.

Kincaid nodded.

Ben looked around for a spittoon. Finding none, he spat on the floor. That got the kid's attention. "Picked a fine day for it—no sleep and all."

Lance grimaced. "He called me every name in the book. Had to either fight or crawl…"

"And you're too damned grouchy to crawl. You ain't been fit to live with since you been back. Anybody you want me to notify?" Kincaid had gone east to see his folks. He went every year, and every year when he came back he was testy as a stallion with a burr under his saddle. Ben couldn't figure out why he went if it made him so cranky. He'd heard that Kincaid's pap wasn't too happy with him and ragged him about coming into the family business, but he didn't know anything about that. Kincaid didn't talk about it. McNamara had let slip once that Kincaid came from a family of swells, but it didn't bother Ben. Kincaid pulled his own weight. He didn't shirk like some men Ben could name.

"I want you to be real careful not to notify anybody. Is that understood?" Kincaid growled, his eyes bright with pain and stubbornness.

"That's the way you want it, that's the way it'll be."

Kincaid nodded. "Get me to Fort Lowell. I'll stay there after the doc gets the bullet out until I'm strong enough to ride back. I can recuperate there as well as in Phoenix."

That way he wouldn't have to explain to Yoshio, and Yoshio wouldn't be tempted to wire his parents whom he had seen in New York two weeks ago. Less than two weeks actually—Sam had graduated March first—and every one of his parents' fears had been realized, except he wasn't dead yet. His father's patience with him was already strained to the breaking point. No sense pushing him too far. He would let them know—after he was fully recovered—and not a minute sooner.

Angie Logan stepped off the stage in Durango and looked around at the dreary, bustling little town—a sprawling warthog of a town—that didn't know how vulgar and dear it looked to her. She had lived there for fifteen years. Her parents lay in the cemetery outside of town. Her dearest friend still lived here. And her brother. A flood of emotion welled up in her. For one moment she thought she would cry.

A blue-clad Chinese, one lone pigtail hanging down the center of his back, balanced baskets from the ends of a bamboo pole draped over his shoulders as he threaded his way through pedestrian traffic on the sidewalk. His back bowed under enormous loads of laundry in the two swinging baskets. He ducked his head and lifted his cone-shaped bamboo hat as he passed Angie.

Excited by the prospect of capturing the picturesque Chinese on film, she glanced around at the stagecoach. Her cameras were all boxed on top. By the time she talked that crusty driver into getting one of them down for her, the Chinese would be gone. Drat.

"Welcome to Chinese Durango." Tall and blond, smiling his laconic, familiar, devil-may-care smile, her brother stepped out of the shade of the Butterfield Stagecoach Company's awning and into the street.

"Laramee!" Her glad cry caused him to grin. He was sunburned, boyish, and vigorous. Red-blond hairs glistened on his forearms below the turned-up cuffs of his red-checked shirt.

Practically before he made it off the sidewalk, she was in his embrace, her own slim arms tight around his neck. The smell of him—sweat and leather and horses—assaulted her nose. A thousand memories flooded her. Tears stung her eyes.

"Good thing you're not glad to see me," he drawled.

"Let me look at you!" Angie cried. "Oh, you are still the handsomest man in the world! Did you tell Sarah I was coming?"

From the shade of the building Sarah stepped close to Laramee. "You were so busy looking at him you didn't see me."

"Sarah!" Angie abandoned Laramee to fly into Sarah's arms. "I'm so glad to see you."

They hugged, and Angie looked from Sarah to Laramee, trying to tell if they had made any progress in their maddeningly slow courtship. By reading between the lines and comparing versions of Sarah's frequent and Laramee's not so frequent letters and, now, seeing the frustrated, challenging glint in Laramee's eyes as he looked at Sarah, Angie guessed that nothing had changed: every time Laramee pushed, Sarah fled. Sarah was one year younger than Angie, barely twenty-one, an old maid in the West, where girls married as young as fifteen. But emotionally she was much younger. She had a soft, round figure, a wide, square jaw, and a generous mouth that gave her face a sulky, gypsy look, except softer. Her green eyes, now filled with tears, completely lacked the craftiness Angie had gotten so used to seeing back east in the eyes of self-conscious young ladies of *society*. Angie hugged Sarah hard, a little stunned at how much she had missed her.

"You been behavin' yourself, little sister?" Laramee drawled.

Angie laughed. "Not when I had a choice. But I have had a good time. I knew that's what you'd want me to do," she said, grinning at the look of delighted chagrin on Laramee's face.

Laramee looked at the stagecoach, still loaded down after the other passengers had departed. "See you haven't changed much. Good thing you weren't born a blamed terrapin, the stuff you carry with you."

Sight of her equipment and boxes reminded Angie of what she'd just experienced. "I saw a gunfight in Nogales. It was awful. And a miracle I happened to be there at the right time. I hope my plates come out. A lawman got shot…"

Angie turned and took Laramee's arm. "So tell me everything," she said, changing the subject, taking Sarah's arm as well. "What are we doing?"

Laramee grinned. "I don't know about you two, but looks like I'm going to unload a stagecoach for an hour or so. Where'd you get this contraption?" he asked, turning to receive the bicycle the driver handed down.

Angie laughed. "This is my safety bicycle. They're wonderful transportation, and they don't eat much grass. I paid ten dollars for it in Boston." It was one of the first with fairly equal sized wheels and air-filled tires. Earlier models had enormous front wheels and tiny back wheels.

Sarah wiped her tears with a quick hand. "How do you keep it from falling over?"

"I'll show you how to ride it later. Let's go inside. It's hot enough out here to fry eggs."

Angie and Sarah turned to walk inside. Sarah looked guiltily at Laramee. "I talked Cort into buying me a newspaper," she said hesitantly.

Angie stopped. "I can't believe it. Cort?"

Sarah's lush lips closed in on themselves; she shrugged in embarrassment.

Angie made a wry face. She had forgotten how defensive Sarah could be about her good-for-nothing father. Shame that she had trampled on Sarah's sensitive feelings in front of Laramee made Angie flush. Sarah would defend Cort no matter what. "When did this happen? The newspaper?" she asked.

"Three weeks ago. I've been so busy I haven't had time to write—" Sarah stopped and glanced at Laramee to see if he was getting mad. They walked into the hotel lobby. Laramee stayed outside to load Angie's things into his buggy.

Sarah pulled Angie inside. "I want you to be my partner. To help me run it. I'm practically working night and day. I can't pay you a lot to start, but I can trade you the upstairs floor for your photography studio and pay something."

"I might not stay in Durango very long."

"It doesn't matter. It's yours as long as you stay. Besides, I might not need help forever. Just to get me started."

"Are you getting along with Laramee?" Angie asked.

Sarah sniffed. She was so glad to see Angie. She had been sure she never would again. "I'm sort of a boil, one he can't lance. I just keep coming back." Sarah's voice broke. She half-laughed, half-sobbed.

Filled with love and sympathy and confusion, Angie pulled Sarah close and hugged her. Laramee loved Sarah, that was apparent from his letters and the sight of him with Sarah. And Sarah loved Laramee. That was just as apparent. How could this be so difficult? Of course, she herself had never been in love. Maybe it was harder than it looked. Angie started to speak, but Sarah shushed her, nodding at Laramee walking inside to join them. Sarah squeezed Angie's hand. Apparently Sarah still tried to protect Laramee from anything that would upset him. Her own experience with Laramee told her it was better to upset him right away and get it over with.

"You're not trying to talk her into working in that blamed little newspaper office, are you?"

Sarah seemed to shrink. Angie frowned at Laramee. He had seen that look any number of times when their parents were alive. When he was young, Isadora Logan had perfected that look to silence him in church.

Grimacing, Laramee shook his head. "She'll think about it," he said grimly. Angie kept quiet. Poor Laramee. He labored under the incorrect assumption she had come home to live on his ranch with him.

An hour later Angie and Laramee bounced along in the surrey on their way out to the Boxer brand. The Logan ranch boxed in a good part of the Santa Cruz River. If anyone had water, Logan had water.

On the north end of Durango, Rio Street teemed with Chinese. Crowded together, their tiny rooms looked more like honeycombs than living quarters. An open door revealed smoke-blackened walls and ceiling and floorspace crowded with tables, beds, and chairs; clothes mounded in corners. The urge to unpack one of her cameras was strong.

"What are so many Chinese doing here?"

"Damned if I know. Most of 'em drifted in to work in the copper mine. The rest do laundry or something," Laramee said grimly. "They're treading on thin ice though."

"Why?"

Farther north, she saw the reason. Almost a dozen houses dotted the meadow near the creek. One, off to itself, had the round windows and exotic, curving rooftrees unique to Chinese architecture.

"Did you sell this land?"

"I did not."

"But..."

"They built without asking," he growled. "We were busy with spring roundup. Next time I came into town..."

"What are you going to do about it?" she asked as the surrey bounced and jostled in the deeply rutted road.

"Not a hell of lot, unless they try to build another house. They're paying rent now. I'd do a lot more except I don't expect 'em to stay long, and I can use the money. The copper mine is almost played out. Once that's gone, I'm hoping they'll drift away."

Glancing at her brother's angry face, Angie felt sure the warning had been clearly stated in language anyone could understand. Laramee did not mince words.

Almost to the creek, Angie looked back. Thin, sloe-eyed, barefoot Chinese children had followed them.

"Stop, Laramee."

"Blame," Laramee growled, but he stopped. Only a fool argued with a skunk, a mule, or a woman. Angie unpacked the Scenographe and climbed down from the surrey. Enchanted by her camera, the children posed, giggling and eager as any children she had ever seen. She took as many pictures as she had plates. Reluctantly she climbed back into the surrey.

Near the creek a slender Chinese girl knelt in a small pagoda-like structure. Her hands over her face, she cried so hard her shoulders shook. Adorned with red flowers, her shiny black hair was pulled into a decorative knot on the side of her neck. Her red sheath shimmered in the sunlight, making Angie wonder about the differences she detected between this young woman and the Chinese closer to town.

She vowed she would stop and talk to the girl next time she had an opportunity. Glancing at Laramee, Angie wondered if the girl had anything to do with her hotheaded brother's not evicting them the minute he discovered the buildings.

Yoshio unwrapped the *Phoenix Expositor* and spread it carefully on the kitchen table. When his master was away from home, Yoshio saved the newspapers so Kincaid-san could look them over on his return.

Yoshio had learned most of his English from Kincaid-san, who had taught him the rudiments and then turned him over to a young bank clerk recovering from a gunshot wound and needing to earn extra money.

One headline mentioned efforts by national labor leaders to force Congress to repeal the Burlingame Treaty, which allowed Chinese to immigrate to America and its territories. Yoshio shook his head. Being Japanese was as dangerous now as being Chinese. White men did not discriminate between two Oriental races. Kincaid-san had saved his life during an anti-Chinese riot in San Francisco, and after his wounds healed, Yoshio had become Kincaid-san's house-boy.

Leaning over the table, one finger holding his spectacles in place, Yoshio idly scanned the front page. A headline leapt out at him: RANGER WOUNDED IN GUN BATTLE. His heart beginning to pound, Yoshio found Kincaid-san's name and read quickly until he came to the part where it stated that Lance Kincaid was recovering at Fort Lowell from his wound. Hands shaking, Yoshio lifted the paper, read it again, and then ran out of the house, not bothering to close the front door.

The wire arrived at ten in the morning. Mrs. Lillian carried it into the sitting room where Elizabeth lay on the sofa recovering from a late night of dancing at Alva Vanderbilt's spring social. Elizabeth sat up and frowned. She took the envelope, glanced from it to Mrs. Lillian, then opened it and read it slowly. With a small cry she handed the telegram to Lillian. Mrs. Lillian read it quickly.

Elizabeth sank back into the velveteen sofa.

Mrs. Lillian laid the telegram on the sideboard. Her hand trembled. "Mr. Kincaid may insist upon going to Phoenix."

Elizabeth put her hand to her forehead. "And Samantha, too, no doubt."

Samantha had left the town house only yesterday and had moved into the Bricewood to be near the shops. She was going to London for the summer season. Elizabeth had planned a lavish party shipboard before the sailing of Samantha's Cunard liner.

Chantry would be in his office. The Kincaids had one of the few telephones in New York City. "Shall I ring Mr. Chantry and Samantha? She will undoubtedly still be at the Bricewood. I expect Mr. K. will be in his office."

"Yes, please." Elizabeth buried her face in her hands and cried.

CHAPTER TWO

Thursday, March 18, 1880

"Thanks, Sabbath," Angie said, shading her eyes against the bright sunlight.

Sabbath Turk, her brown-skinned Indian escort, was clearly reluctant to leave her. "Laramee say Sabbath take you to newspaperhouse."

"I know, but I want to talk to the young lady over there," she said, gesturing with a slim hand toward the Chinese girl she had seen a week before. "I'll be fine, Sabbath."

Without waiting for him to leave, Angie turned Pumpkin and walked the mare slowly toward the girl who again knelt before the shrine in the small pagoda. Angie dismounted and waited at a respectful distance.

Shortly, the girl touched her forehead to the floor and scooted back until outside the small structure. Dressed in a royal blue sheath, probably silk, that reached from a high-necked mandarin collar to slim ankles, the girl was lovely. Though she did not appear to have seen Angie, anger smoldered in her black eyes.

"Excuse me," Angie said softly.

"Oh!" The girl jumped, startled.

"I'm sorry. I didn't mean to scare you. Do you speak English?" Angie asked.

"Yes."

The sullen reply made Angie wonder if she had intruded in some unforgivable way or at an inappropriate time.

"Last week I saw you crying…I'm sorry to intrude, but I wondered if there is anything I can do to help?"

Black eyes blazed with anger. "Unless you can destroy *fan quai*, you cannot help me."

Taken aback at the harsh tone, Angie blinked. "What is *fan quai?*"

"*Fan quai*, foreign devils, white men!"

Angie suppressed a smile. "You are angry at white men? All of them?"

Lily shook her head. "Sometimes," she said defiantly. "But now only the ones who killed my three cousins."

Instantly contrite, Angie's smile faded. "I'm sorry. How did they die?" she asked, remembering the gunfight last week. Had Kincaid survived?

Lily turned away quickly, ashamed she had exposed herself to this white stranger and had spoken in the forbidden tongue of anger. "I grieve for my honorable cousins. There is nothing anyone can do. I thank thee for thy concern."

Though charmed by the girl's genteel speech, Angie persisted. "How were they killed?"

A frown creased Lily's wide, perfect forehead. "I know not. They were murdered by *fan quai*. When I try to talk to my honorable father about it, he becomes angry with me." Her smooth chin quivered. "He will not speak of it."

"I'm sorry. I had no idea."

"I, too, am sorry." Lily flushed and bowed her head. "When I am angry I fill up inside with blackness in the same way a rotten apple fills with worms." She shuddered. "Slimy worms gnaw at my insides until I spill over with rage..."

"Or tears..."

Lily nodded.

"You speak very well, your English."

Lily shrugged. "I was an interpreter at the American Embassy. My father was an attaché in Hong Kong."

"Why would you leave that to come here?"

Lily sighed. "There is much unrest in China, much revolt, many starving. My father lost ancestral lands and the family's home in the last revolt, took the job at the embassy, then it closed temporarily...they said it would be temporary. We waited..." She shrugged. "We had no choice."

"What is your name?"

"Lily."

"I'm Angie. Angie Logan. Your family name?"

"Liang. Liang Lily."

"Oh, it's backwards..."

"Or thine is..."

"Touché!" Angie said, enjoying the first glimmer of amusement she had seen in Lily's dark eyes.

"Is this an English word, *touché?*"

"It means that your point was well taken. It's French."

"Thank thee for thy interest. I feel better now."

They talked for an hour. Lily was seventeen and an only child.

"Among Chinese," Lily whispered, glancing at the house twenty yards away as if she were about to be caught in some mischief, "to have a girl child is considered misfortune. To have no other children, is a tragedy. To have an only child, female and disobedient, is a curse of great magnitude."

"Are you disobedient?"

Lily shrugged. "I cannot help myself. There are books this high of rules," she said, measuring higher than her head. "My mind refuses to contain so many rules. And so I spend a great deal of time in penance."

"Here? In the pagoda?"

Lily nodded. "To contemplate my honorable ancestors. To teach me obedience..." Lily sighed with dejection, then brightened. "When I was little, sometimes my mother would talk-story for me. I learned better when she would talk-story."

"Tell me one of the stories."

A smile played on her lovely features. "My honorable mother talks-story better than I. My favorite is about the red that lightning gave to the world." Lily stopped, flushed, realizing that, to this modern young white woman, a Chinese story about ghosts, spirits, and demons would seem childish and stupid. Logan Angie would be horrified to learn how superstitious Chinese were. How could she tell this golden clear-eyed young lady about red spirit money for the dead?

"The story is very long and complicated, and I remember it not," she lied, "but red is both lucky and strong. In blood, roses, poppies, rubies, feathers, even peonies. That is why I search so hard for the red flowers for my hair." She touched the red desert lily pinned in her black hair.

"May I take your picture?" Angie asked on impulse. The Scenographe with its walking stick tripod stuck out of a confiscated rifle sheath on Pumpkin's saddle.

"If you like."

"You're not afraid?"

"What is there to fear from a camera?"

Angie flushed. She had heard stories of Indian tribes who feared cameras. Apparently the Chinese were not superstitious. Angie took Lily's picture and promised to bring her a copy next time she came this way. Angie mounted her horse and waved. She rode quickly toward town and vowed she would talk to Laramee about the murders.

At dinner that night Angie asked about Lily's cousins.

"How'd you find out about that?"

"Lily told me." Quickly Angie explained about Lily, Joy, Mei-ling and

Third Uncle. "How did they die?" she persisted.

"Blamed if I know. Story I heard was that a young Chinese gal raised a stink about one of the men that died, else no one would of known anything about it. Those Chinese are sneaky devils. I heard they tried to bury 'em without saying anything to anybody. Someone turned it in to Ramo, and he asked a few questions. Didn't turn up anything though. 'Course, he ain't one to work overly hard or stick too close to the truth, either, unless there's a fine involved."

"Is that all? Three men die, and no one does anything?"

Laramee leaned back in his chair. "Whoever killed 'em must have scared those chinks pretty bad to shut 'em up. Almost nothing shuts them up." He shook his head in chagrin. "I think Chung Tu had 'em killed."

"Who's Chung Tu?"

"Looks like a little bitty dried apple to me. He's got a pigtail down to his ankles, and he wears the prettiest silk skirts I ever seen. Supposed to be the head chink. He keeps all those celestials tied up real close like with the emperor back in China, sees to it they don't choose up wrong sides or some such."

"Is Ramo still looking for their killer?"

"If the killer can be found in a bottle of Kansas City beer, I reckon he's looking hard. Been some pretty hot days. Ramo ain't one to strain himself."

"Sam? Is that you?"

Samantha leaned close to Lance. "Yes, darling, it's me."

Darling? Lance closed his eyes. It *was* Sam or a vision of Sam. Perhaps he was dead. Perhaps that ride *had* killed him. But would he hurt so? His jaws ached. His head ached. A rat gnawed at his side, rooting in tender flesh. He remembered riding in that damned bumpy wagon and drinking whiskey from a bottle Ben offered him. The whiskey had burned with promise. Unfortunately the gnawing subsided only a little, and the bleeding started up again. He had decided he'd better stop drinking. If he had to throw up it would kill him.

Lance opened his eyes. Samantha's lovely, familiar eyes—wide and blue and soft, so intent with feminine purpose and concern for his welfare—caused his heart to beat faster and increased the pain in his head. She leaned over him and wiped his forehead with a cool rag. Behind her, his bureau gleamed in the sunlight. So he had made it home. He remembered a telegram from Yoshio saying his father waited in Phoenix. How had he found out? How had Yoshio known where to find him? And how had Sam gotten here?

"How did you..."

"I came as soon as I heard. I've been here a week. I thought you would never wake up. Oh, Lance, darling, I've been so scared..." Her beautiful face crumpled at the mouth. Tears rolled down her cheeks. From infant to young debutante, that was the way she cried: her mouth folded in on itself and tears flowed. He had teased her about that when they were younger. That she couldn't cry if her mouth was open. She hadn't called him darling then. She'd hit him hard. He'd carried a bruise on his arm for a week.

So he had been home a week...

"How are you?"

"I feel," he started to lie, "...like hell. Would have been easier to die, probably less trouble for everyone, and a damned sight less painful."

"Oh, God, Lance don't talk like that."

Sam had never been much addicted to reality. She'd prefer he say something soothing rather than the truth...

Mrs. Lillian walked into the room, surprising Lance further. "Well, our invalid is awake at last." After fifty-five years of living with the Kincaids in England, New York, Texas, and occasionally France, her Danish accent was still detectable in her slightly gravelly voice.

Lance pulled at his covers. "The whole family come?"

Samantha placed her soft hand on his forehead. "No, Aunt 'Lizbeth couldn't get away. She had already sent out invitations to her spring ball. She has insisted on a daily wire to keep in touch. Uncle Chantry is in town taking care of that now. So far, every wire has been pretty much the same. STILL UNCONSCIOUS. STILL ALIVE. WILL SEND MORE LATER. Oh, Lance, I am so happy to see you awake and alive!"

Lance swallowed. "Could I have some water?"

Sam poured a glass of water from the pitcher on his nightstand. Lance drank it and dozed. When he woke, his father stood beside his bed.

"Well," Chantry said, his usually deep baritone gruff.

"Dad."

A pulse sounded in Lance's head. His father looked like hell, his face haggard. Deep circles under his eyes made him look older, almost fragile. The sight was too much for Lance. Overcome with emotion, he closed his eyes, swallowed.

"Sorry I caused so much..."

Chantry gripped Lance's wrist for a moment. His son was awake. He would live. Emotion swelled in him. His throat and forehead ached with it. Lizzie would be so relieved. The whole family would. "You rest, son. That's an order. You hear me? Rest. I'm going to send another wire to your mother." He turned and walked out of the room.

Angie spent the second week gathering what she needed to assemble her studio over *The Tea Time News* office. Her other trunk and the perambulator tent came, and she unpacked her darkroom equipment so she would not be wholly dependent upon the tent. In the field it was wonderful because she could wheel it around and develop her prints as she took them if she wanted. She didn't have to wait to see her pictures. It saved a lot of anxiety, wondering if she'd captured what she had wanted to capture, but it was small and hot and close and one more thing to worry about.

Her big Lewis camera—it took eight-by-ten-inch portraits—survived the trip atop the stagecoach in excellent condition. She set that up in the studio. The Scenographe, a small collapsible bellows camera, went everywhere with her because it was lightweight. The Eastman was left in its box. Her studio appeared quite workable. She parked the wagon equipped with the Hale camera beside the door and propped the Scenographe near it. Two choices were ready at all times.

Angie told Laramee her plans at breakfast the next morning.

"That's not a real newspaper," he growled. "It's just some blamed toy Cort bought her to keep her from marrying me."

Angie laughed. "It's a society paper now, but, once we learn how to do that, we'll expand it to include news as well."

"We already got a newspaper. Don't need another one."

"Do you agree with everything Harry Sloan prints? Is he so fair-minded and so in tune with your philosophies that you want everyone in town agreeing with him?"

Laramee frowned. There had been times he had been so mad at Sloan, steam tooted out his ears. He had taken that blamed rag and thrown it in the fire. He leaned back in his chair.

"Guess I can't blame you for not wanting to stay on the ranch. Hell, it don't surprise me. Any woman gets a taste of doing something she likes ain't gonna have any trouble giving up ranchin'." Laramee spoke stark truth.

Being back here for one week after spending years away had resolved all her conflict about her parents' wills. Rising before cockcrow to endless toil—supervising household help, boiling mountains of dirty clothes over an open fire, tending the vegetable garden and the household livestock, feeding and slaughtering chickens, finding eggs wherever the setting hens laid them, coaxing water out of a rusty pump, and cooking at least two meals a day for upward of fifty men was spirit- and back-breaking. She appreciated her lost inheritance. Laramee was more than welcome to the ranch, stretching from a few miles north of the Papago Indian reservation to ten miles south of the ponderosa pine forests on the plateau. The Boxer brand, all fifty thousand acres, had been acquired by Lindsay Daniel Logan from the last living relative of a man who claimed to have bought a Spanish land grant from a dying Spaniard. More likely the man had dealt the fatal blow himself.

"You be careful in that town, you hear?" Laramee growled. Durango had tripled in size since Angie left. It had become a home for drifters and cardsharps.

"I will."

Laramee's concern and confusion were evident. Angie wanted to hug him. They disagreed on every subject, but he loved her. Seeing the proof of it surprised her. They had fought so growing up. She went to the stove and scraped the last of the eggs onto his plate. "You're too thin," she said.

Laramee glanced quickly at Angie. "You sound like Mama." Their parents had died seven years before. The ditch bank had collapsed under the buckboard's wheels, sending it tumbling over an embankment. They were pinned under the wagon and died before help reached them.

"I did, didn't I?"

Laramee grinned. "Shore did. Maybe there's hope after all."

Angie rode into town that afternoon. She rented the house that Hank and Amy Fairchild had lived in until Amy's baby was born and they moved to San Xavier del Bac. The house was small—two bedrooms, a parlor, and a kitchen big enough for an eating table, stove, and icebox. Its nicest feature was a big front porch that looked out on the desert. The Fairchilds had left behind a big iron stove, icebox, two beds with corn shuck mattresses, and a rocking chair. They had intended to send for their furniture when they got settled, but they had died from smallpox about a month after they left. Angie bought a feather mattress, a bureau, and two small tables.

She rode out to the ranch to tell Laramee. He shook his head in consternation, but he and Sabbath loaded everything including her bedroom furniture into the wagon. Angie stopped Laramee. "Are you sure about this? I mean, the will left the ranch to you. That includes the house and furniture…"

Laramee shrugged. "It's mine. I guess I can give it away if I want to."

"You don't have to do that." Angie squinted at him, embarrassed. Laramee had sent her a check every month she'd been back east, and she was sure that many times it had been at great personal expense. She had asked him to stop, but he hadn't. He'd known or guessed she wasn't earning enough taking pictures to stay in school.

"Reckon I know that. If you want to come back for a visit, there'll still be the folks' room you can use. You'll be more comfortable with your own things around."

Angie would have hugged him, but he turned away too quickly.

She developed the pictures of the ranger the day she got everything in place. She was too tired to start anything else, but her curiosity hounded her into developing them.

Mercilessly revealing, the pictures showed more about the ranger than she had seen that day. In one picture he looked tired, in another curious, in yet another cranky. But in all of them he exuded that smoldering energy and intense concentration she had sensed in him. One picture drew her back to it. He faced the camera with a look which, though itself carefully noncommittal, reminded her of that one moment after he had been shot, that one split-second when she had thought she saw…what? His narrowed eyes looked directly into the camera. The deep smile lines on either side of his mouth were extremely expressive. He looked like a man capable of anything. Of tenderness or of strength, of killing a man in a dusty road or of taking a bullet in the side and joking with other men, of winking at her. Her throat constricted. The small worm, the one he had installed in her the first time she heard him speak, moved. Angie quickly set that picture aside.

Mrs. Lillian stopped in the doorway. "Well, you look much better today."

Lance pulled the covers up over his waist and struggled into a sitting position. Running his hands through his dark hair, he had the grumpy look of a small boy just waking from a long sleep. Always a loner, Lance had had the silver spoon shoved by force into his unwilling mouth. Predictably he had rebelled. More at home in the bunkhouse than in the mansion, he had coped as best he could. In Paris he had escaped to the stables. While the family learned drawing-room French, he perfected French obscenities.

Lance watched as she walked around the room, opening the drapes and letting in fresh air. Last night Samantha had said that Mrs. Lillian was going to celebrate her seventieth birthday next January. She didn't look that old. Her step was still light and graceful, with none of the plodding, painful movements of old women.

Stopping by the bed, Mrs. Lillian put her hand on his forehead. "How do you feel?"

"Better, Mrs. L."

Lillian Thorvaldsen smiled at the title. Two generations of Kincaid children had called her Mrs. L. or Mrs. Lillian. She'd never married, but the Kincaid children gave her the honorary title because they said it wouldn't look right—an unmarried woman having so many children. She first came into the house as a fourteen-year-old *au pair*. When Lance's father began to talk, the elder Duchess of Twombley, matriarch of the Kincaid estate, directed Chantry to call her Miss Thorvaldsen. He had failed in pronunciation so charmingly that even the fearsome Lady Twombley had relented.

"How is everyone?"

Mrs. Lillian smiled. "Samantha is in fine spirits. She went to town to wire your mother."

The look on his face was cautious. "Did she say anything?" His husky voice dropped lower, almost broke at the end of the sentence.

Mrs. Lillian fluffed his pillows and straightened. She was tempted to torment him, but the strained look on his face stopped her. Though they were not related, Lance and Samantha had been raised as brother and sister. Now she was out of school and determined that Lance would marry her. It would be difficult for Lance to refuse her anything. No doubt she was pressuring him to set a date.

"Tell me about this Arizona," she said, sitting down beside him. "What do you do here?"

"You mean before half of New York decided to visit me?" he asked, smiling at the way his life had changed.

Lance talked, and Lillian listened. She weighed what she knew about him against the frustrated complaints of Chantry and Elizabeth about his seeming wildness, and his unwillingness to marry and provide them with grandchildren.

Lance paused.

"So you enjoy this hard work?"

"Yes, ma'am. There are whole communities of people out here at the mercy of men who kill for no good reason. They take a man's life, his livelihood, his family—and they don't care. They laugh about it. They seem to feel they have a right to destroy because they can."

Searching his eyes, Mrs. Lillian knew that Lance would talk so earnestly with no one but her. He dearly loved his parents, but they would never hear him speak so unguardedly.

"You have undergone terrible hardships, and you have survived. You are not bitter."

"No, ma'am. I'm thankful to be alive. People out here need protection. They're dependent on an almost nonexistent law and trapped by fear and lack of mobility. A man loses a horse, he could die from it. He trusts the wrong man, it could cost him his life."

He feels this strongly, this calling. And yet, she sensed a deep change in her favorite charge. *He trusts the wrong man, it could cost him his life. He means himself.* But when had he stopped trusting? The obvious answer was when Lucinda died, but after a moment's reflection, Lillian knew that wasn't true. Lance had stopped trusting after his estrangement from Gilbert Lee, the same time that he stopped taking flowers to Lucinda's grave, only days before he sailed for San Francisco and began his travels through the wilderness.

Gilbert Lee—half white, half Chinese—had been like a brother to Lance. They had been closer in many ways than Lance and his brothers. Until something had happened between Gilbert and Lance that drove a wedge between Lance and the wisdom of his feelings, something that had alienated him from family and self. It surprised her that she hadn't realized this before.

Lillian spent an hour talking with Lance. To her, the time with him was a gift from heaven. At the end of it, she reached out and patted his hand. "I want to ask a favor," she said.

"Anything, you know that, Mrs. Lillian. As long as it does not entail my getting married tomorrow, buying the house next door to my parents, and presenting Samantha with my father's grandchild." He smiled easily, innocent of everything except wanting to please her. The tension she had sensed in him when she mentioned Samantha was gone. He looked younger, more relaxed.

"When you are up and about again, I want you to find Gilbert Lee," she said.

His eyes, usually as clear as bluebells on a sunny day, clouded and filled with resistance. He looked away from her. "I can't. I don't know where he is." His tone was gruff.

"That is precisely, young man, why I chose the word *find*," she said, patting his warm hand.

"Yes, ma'am," he said, looking sheepish. "The West is a couple thousand miles square." He sighed, slanting a look at her to see if she was impressed with his excuse. "Do I look like a divining rod?"

"A good bit, yes. You are strong and intuitive and almost as blind as a stick."

Lance grinned.

"When you find Gilbert, I want you to forgive him for whatever you two fought about. Or I will die a miserable old woman."

The teasing laughter died in Lance's eyes. "I can't do that." Though he was totally unprepared to contemplate Mrs. Lillian's death, even in jest, he could not forgive Gil.

To say that Lance loved Mrs. Lillian was a gross understatement. He could not remember a time when Mrs. Lillian had not been in his life. Most of his early childhood memories were of Mrs. Lillian. She had been his primary source of comfort. His mother was a wonderful woman, but her life-style and social position were not conducive to spending much time with children. Elizabeth and Chantry Kincaid attended almost nightly social events that often kept them up until dawn. Engaged in her daily toilet for hours, Elizabeth rarely showed herself until early afternoon. Then she received callers and entertained guests for tea and chatted until the evening meal. After dinner the children were sent off to bed. When Lance and his brothers and sisters rose at six each day, they were greeted by Mrs. Lillian's warm smile.

"Do not look so stricken, Lance," Mrs. Lillian interrupted. "At the moment I have no intention of dying. I wanted only to impress upon you how truly important your reconciliation with Gilbert Lee is to me."

CHAPTER THREE

Saturday, March 20, 1880

Sarah, Laramee, and Angie worked steadily until Angie's new home sparkled with care and organization. Laramee collapsed into the rocking chair. Angie pulled one of the kitchen chairs into the parlor and positioned it behind Sarah, who gratefully sank down into it.

"It looks wonderful," Angie sighed, sitting down on the floor, her back to the wall.

"I'll bring one of the sofas in next time I come."

"You don't have to do that."

"Blame! Then I won't."

"All right." Angie laughed. "Bring it."

Sarah beamed at Laramee.

"Might bring two sofas," he muttered, pleased.

As good as his word, on Saturday Laramee brought the sofa, two of their mother's best lamps, her sewing machine, ironing board, and iron, a sack of lye for the outhouse, and miscellaneous supplies Angie wouldn't have asked for but was thrilled to get.

At the side of the house Angie was planting a small vegetable garden. She had tended a corner plot in Boston when she visited with her cousins Virginia and Tennessee, and had enjoyed it.

"What are you planting?" Laramee asked, scowling at the short rows she had laid out in the sandy soil.

"Beans, tomatoes, corn, squash, peas."

"Better plant some melons."

"How come?"

"So when all that stuff dies from the heat, you'll have something to eat."

"I'm not going to let it die."

Laramee grinned. "How's it going at *The Tea Time News?*" he asked, his eyes restlessly scanning the desert between Angie's house and town for sight of Sarah.

"We're learning a lot. We haven't put out our first issue yet, but we're getting close."

"Didn't know there was much to it," Laramee grunted.

"There isn't if you know what you're doing, which we do not."

"Anything like calving one of the heifers?"

Angie laughed. "Maybe. Once we get everything in the right place, it should happen about like that."

Laramee offered her a ride into town. He loaded her bicycle in the back of the buckboard and then drove northeast. Durango was northwest from her house. Angie resisted the urge to question her brother. Near the copper mine, the ore crusher was loud and smelly. Sulphur fumes from the roasting furnace made Angie gag. "Why did you come this way? You know I hate that smell."

"Hold your horses, girl. I wanna see something," he said. He drove the buckboard to a spot under a tree upwind of the plant and stopped.

"What?"

Laramee shook his head, and Angie knew that attempts to extract information from him before he was ready to talk would be useless. Within minutes a mob of white men walking six abreast appeared on the dusty road. Jack Smith was the only one she recognized. They stopped in front of the mine office, little more than a shed, and yelled for John Copley, the mine operator, to *get his butt out here.* Copley walked outside, wiping his greasy hand on his pants leg. He still carried the wrench he'd been using on a rusty water pipe.

Copley looked over the mob. "What you boys want?"

From the back a man yelled, "We want you to quit hiring them damned China boys and put white men to work."

Copley nodded. "You all looking for work, are you?"

"Jack is."

"You want me to fire all my Chinese and hire one man?" Copley shook his head. "Don't make sense to me."

"You refusing?" one man demanded.

Copley eyed the crowd. They had all worked for Copley at some time in the past—four Civil War veterans, two Irish and three German immigrants, a Mormon, two atheists, a drunk, and a Paiute. They were hardworking, hard-brawling men but short on common sense. Beneath floppy hats with brims twisted into each man's idea of fashion, every eye watched Copley. "I'll give Jack a job if'n he wants it, but he's got to work."

"You saying a white man can't outwork a chink?"

"Ain't saying nothing except that he's got to pull his weight," Copley said stubbornly. The men pushed Jack forward.

"Rest of you get on back to town. I'll take him on." Copley led Jack toward the mine shaft. Slowly the crowd turned and walked back toward town.

Angie looked at Laramee. "Did you know what they were going to do?"

"Sure. Everybody in town knew."

"Why didn't you tell me? I could have taken pictures of it."

"Didn't think of it."

Angie asked Atillo at the livery stable to keep her informed of any news about the mine. Three days later she heard from Atillo that Jack Smith hadn't showed up for work. He had lasted a day and a half. According to Atillo, Jack claimed that Copley favored the chinks and near worked him to death. A gang of men formed in the saloon and marched off in the direction of the copper mine. Angie grabbed her Scenographe—the wagon would be too slow to pull, rented a surrey from Atillo, and followed them. This time Copley came out with a shotgun draped over his left arm.

"What you boys want this time?"

"We ain't gonna tolerate the way you treated Jack Smith," a man in the front yelled. Other men added their voices in a chorus of agreement.

Angie stood up on the seat of the surrey, steadied her camera on its partially spread tripod, and took a picture of Copley surrounded by angry townsmen.

"Hell, I didn't even expect him to keep up. I'd a kept him on if he'd a just quit pulling swigs off his bottle. He was so drunk he couldn't stand up. I ain't going to ask good men to carry him while they work. Anyone who's ever worked beside a Chinese can tell you no white man can keep up with 'em. They may be small, but they're tough as cat gut."

"That's a damned lie!"

A man in the back sent a rock sailing over the heads of the crowd. It barely missed Copley. He stepped inside the shed and yelled for them to get going before he sent for Marshal Ramo.

Angie took a picture of Copley inside the shed as he peered out at the yelling mob. She climbed down and ran around to the side and took another picture of the mob from Copley's point of view.

Sarah drove up in a borrowed buggy, leapt down, and ran around behind Angie. "Have you been here long?"

"Long enough," Angie said, grinning.

Sarah watched the crowd and Angie, working efficiently and quietly, completely unnoticed by the men she photographed. Angie was so professional, so quietly self-contained, that within days of her arrival in Durango, after the novelty of seeing a woman photographer had worn off, the men had accepted her and her picture taking without any more comment than a pretty woman alone would elicit.

"Sure wish we could print some of your pictures in *The Tea Time News*. Wouldn't that be something?" Sarah whispered.

Angie wished that too. The newspaper was dependent on line drawings. They could cut a picture from a wood block and make prints of it, but so far no newspaper press could reproduce an actual photograph.

The next day Angie went back to the mine to interview Copley for the narrative portion of her picture book.

"I taken Jack Smith on, and I would a taken another, but…" Copley stopped talking. Angie glanced up and followed his gaze. A crowd of white men reined their horses and dismounted beside the entrance to the mine shaft. From her vantage point near the shed, Angie could see down into the mine shaft. The quitting whistle blew to announce the shift change. Chinese workmen dropped their pickaxes. Tiredly they walked toward the mouth of the tunnel.

Squinting against the bright light, three Chinese, the first to reach topside, paused to rest.

Angie didn't like the looks of the white men. They spelled trouble to her. She grabbed up the Scenographe and left Copley standing there with his mouth still open. Outside, she hurriedly spread the camera's tripod legs and focused on the horsemen.

As she ducked under the cape, one of the riders nudged his horse into a walk. As he rode toward the Chinese, he took out his rope, shook it out, and started to swing a wide loop over his head. Before the Chinese could react, he dropped the loop over their heads, tied the rope around his saddle horn, and kicked his claybank gelding into a canter.

Angie focused on the three Chinese, snared in the rope, and snapped her shutter. The three Chinese were jerked off their feet and dragged. White men yelled and hooted. Angie changed plates and snapped off another shot.

Screaming and waving their pickaxes, enraged Chinese ran up the incline, spilled out of the mineshaft, and charged the mounted riders, who drew their guns and fired into the mass of shouting Orientals. Angie took pictures as fast as she could reload her camera. Five Chinese were shot before the riders spurred their horses into a run back toward town.

Angie followed the Chinese back to their apartments on the north end of Rio Street. Two slim Chinese in sloping reed sedge hats and baggy cotton pants carried a dead comrade to his front door. Others helped the wounded or carried them. Women saw them coming and ran outside. One woman recognized the dead man, threw herself on his body, and cried. Her mouth formed a near perfect circle, tears ran down her cheeks, but no sound escaped her throat.

Angie clicked the shutter. Another woman recognized her wounded husband and let out a wail of anguish. Children cried. Angry men and women crowded around and yelled in high-pitched, singsong Chinese. Angie took pictures until she ran out of plates. Amid the clamor and the grieving, no one noticed her.

Finally, overcome with her own emotion, she slipped away and walked blindly back toward the newspaper office. On the sidewalk in front of the Baquero, she stopped to wipe her eyes. Inside, men drank and talked about how they wanted to kill every chink in town. Angie leaned against the wall until her strength returned and then walked tiredly back to *The Tea Time News*.

Inside the door, she leaned against the door jamb. "We have to do something," she said, rubbing her back. The Scenographe was heavier than it looked. The plate holder around her neck weighed enough by itself to make her ache.

"What happened?" Sarah asked, looking up from the tray of lead type.

Angie recounted her tale of the slaughter, the grieving Chinese, and the lingering resentment brewing at the Baquero. By the time she finished her story, her breathing had returned to normal.

"What can *we* do?" Sarah asked.

"I don't know," Angie said. "But we have to think of something. People are dying. We're about to have a war on our hands."

Angie stewed for about two hours, then she walked down the block and across the street to the jail. Marshal Ramo sat at his desk. His thin face had a permanent sardonic look to it as if he were about to make some sly remark or laugh at something that wasn't funny.

"Marshal Ramo, what do you intend to do about the Chinese who were killed?" Angie challenged.

Ramo came to his feet in a caricature of politeness.

"Well, I'm not about to bury 'em. They got friends and relatives to take care of that."

"I mean about the men who killed them."

"They was killed by a mob."

"But they were all recognizable. Everyone in town knows who was in that mob. I have pictures of the killers."

"Maybe so, but ain't nobody coming forward to make a complaint."

"Murder is against the law," Angie said, her voice breaking with emotion. "No one has to make a formal complaint."

"Maybe not, but I can't arrest the whole town. Besides, it was self-defense from what I heard. Them chinks boiled out of that mine shaft and all over those men like stink on sh…shinola. Ain't no law against self-defense. You show me them pictures and I might jest go up there and arrest them chinks for attacking innocent men riding past that mine."

"Ohhh!"

"Why don't you jest settle yourself into your studio and spend your time taking pictures of younguns and their mamas? You shouldn't be running around trying to tell menfolks how to run this town."

That evening Angie developed her photographs from the day's events. What she saw sickened her. She sat down at the table and wrote a letter to the territorial Governor.

> Dear Governor Frémont,
>
> Chinese are being slaughtered like cattle. Today a dozen white men rode up to the copper mine, roped three Chinese and dragged them behind a horse until they were half dead. Their countrymen tried to save them, and five of them were shot down like dogs.
>
> Our local marshal blatantly refuses to stop the killing or to prosecute the criminals responsible. I have photographs of the killers, and Marshal Ramo merely brushes me aside.
>
> The Chinese are arming themselves. Please send soldiers immediately, before this town and the people in it become victims of a race war.

She signed it A. B. Logan, enclosed three photographs of the wounded Chinese, sealed the envelope, and walked over to the *Gazette* office to ask Harry Sloan where to mail it. She mailed the letter and felt better. Help was on the way.

• • •

In the weeks that followed, Angie barely had time to work on her picture book. She painted a sign in bold letters, ANGELA LOGAN, PHOTOGRAPHER, and Laramee hung half out the window and nailed it up under the double windows of the upstairs studio. Almost the minute the sign went up people started walking into the office. When Ramo told her to limit her practice to taking pictures of women and children, she had decided in anger that she would do no such thing. But in spite of what she wanted, she had a steady stream of people who wanted to sit for portraits, and she was too tenderhearted to turn them away. Quite apart from the pure wonder of the photographic images, these hardy frontier folk seemed to feel a profound need to capture themselves and their children on paper. April turned into May and still no answer from the governor.

On the morning of May 6, when she wanted to be out scouting the town for more interesting pictures, Angie peered through the lens at a young, sunburned woman and her gaunt husband.

"Smile," Angie coaxed. "Say 'pumpernickel.' Say 'I'm going home.'"

Nothing worked. The woman's mournful look did not respond to coaxing. Beneath the heavy black cape, Angie was so hot steam was probably rising from her. She gave up trying to get the young woman to smile, snapped the picture, and stepped out from under the hot canvas cape.

"All done. The photographs will be ready next week."

The girl, no more than seventeen or eighteen, looked shyly at her husband. "Your mama will be so happy to get a picture of you, Rad."

"What about your mama? She's been writing to us and writing to us. She wants one for her, and one for your sisters and brothers, and one for your grandma. I reckon even if we had twenty pictures we'd have people complaining because they didn't get one."

"I sure wish we could of had one of the baby before we buried it."

"Now, now. Don't you start a-crying again. We'll get you another baby."

"I'm going to have its picture took right away."

On Thursday, Angie and Sarah put out their first newspaper. They had designed the content specifically for women. They wrote stories of interest to women, printed recipes, remedies for common maladies, covered social events, and had a section in which they printed items about children. Angie interviewed the teacher at the school and printed a comment about each student. She took samples of their work: poetry, a line drawing, a good sentence out of a homework assignment, and anything a child wanted to give her. Angie wrote stories and Sarah set the type. Together they printed the sheets and paid Atillo to run around town selling the papers for two cents each.

Two hours after the first newspaper hit the streets, a woman walked into the office.

"I need five more of them newspapers," she said.

Angie glanced quickly at Sarah. "Five?"

"Yes, please. I think I've got some pennies here." She rummaged in her reticule, brought up two nickels between a grubby finger and thumb, and blushed.

"I hope you'll excuse my dirty hands. I was working in the garden when I seen that newspaper with a little story about my Johnny. I wanted to send that newspaper to my folks back home. I ran down here afore they done sold out."

Angie walked to the back of the office for five copies of the paper. Sarah took the woman's money and put it in their cash box, a new cigar box city clerk Charlie Miller had given them.

The woman turned to leave the shop. Atillo waited for her to go and then stepped inside. "I need more papers."

Sarah grabbed Angie and twirled her around in a bear hug. "We did it!"

On Friday, Marshal Ramo stopped Angie on the sidewalk.

"Thought you might like to hear the news. A chink took advantage of an eight-year-old Chinese girl. I arrested him and put him in jail. Don't personally think he's gonna stay there too long. Now that's something you ought to have a picture of. I told you they was different…Ain't like real people."

Angie ran for her camera. After she had photographed the man, who looked more confused than vicious, she ran for her bicycle and pedaled up to see Lily.

"The marshal thinks the townsmen are going to hang him. He doesn't look guilty to me."

Lily took Angie to the Chinese lawgiver who listened patiently as Lily interpreted Angie's story. Sadly he shook his head. Lily turned back to Angie. "There is nothing he can do. This is a very serious offense among Chinese."

"Well, he could at least find out if it's true, couldn't he?"

• • •

That evening, unwilling to go home for fear the jailed Chinese man would come to harm, Angie watched the jail from the window of *The Tea Time News*. Shortly after eight o'clock two dozen enraged white men stormed the jail.

"Turn that filthy chink over to us."

"Yeah! We know what to do with his kind!"

One man waved a rope. "We'll hang that bastard before he comes after one of our kids."

The crowd surged forward. Ramo and Smalley slipped out the back door of the jail.

One of the rioters stopped in his tracks. "Hey! What's that?"

He pointed toward the north. A crowd of Chinese walked down the sidewalk toward the jail. "They're coming to save the man who raped one of their own kids!"

"Filthy celestials!"

"Filthy chinks!"

The white men started toward the Chinese.

"Hold on, there!" the man leading the Chinese yelled at the crowd in front of the jail. Dressed in western garb—on closer inspection—the man was Dr. Amberg. Men stopped in their tracks. Every eye turned toward Amberg, soundly respected in the community.

"What are you doing with them?" an angry white man yelled.

"There's been a misunderstanding. The girl's father came to me tonight and asked me to check his daughter. I did, and the girl is fine. She came home with a dollar. Her mama asked her where she got it, and the girl told her. Mama thought the man had paid her daughter for a favor. Mama raised a stink, and Ramo arrested the man, but it was just a misunderstanding. The girl was supposed to take the dollar to her daddy to pay back a loan. Mama didn't know that."

"Shit!"

Men grumbled, but they walked slowly back to the saloon. Ramo slipped back into the jail and released his prisoner.

Angie breathed a sigh of relief. That one event had turned out well, but Durango remained a powder keg ready to go off. Angie prayed that the governor would act quickly on her request to send the military. Why hadn't he responded?

• • •

Lance Kincaid walked slowly into Captain McNamara's office. McNamara barked orders at a young man Lance knew only slightly. Undaunted, the recruit waited politely for McNamara to finish his tirade.

"When I tell you to track a stolen bangtail and bring it back, I don't mean for you to track it into a saloon, up the stairs, and into one of the bedrooms."

"Yes, sir. Is that all, sir?"

"No, Jenkins, that is not all. How the hell did you explain to the mayor, lying in bed with that whore, what the hell you were doing riding a horse into his rented room?"

"I told him I was following a stolen horse, sir."

"Stolen horse, my ass. I heard you had a crush on that whore, what was her name?"

"Liz Fish."

"Liz Fish." McNamara sighed and waved the young man away. "Get the hell out of here. I can't take any more. But you better leave that gal alone, you hear me?"

Jenkins turned, looked at Lance, grinned as if to say *I got him all warmed up for you*, and sauntered out the door.

McNamara shook his head, motioned Lance into his office, and stood to shake hands across his battered, wooden desk. "Kid's getting wilder and younger every day. Soon I'll be running a nursery school." His own hair was snow white. His face was a ruddy pink that had resisted tanning. A retired military officer, he was now a shopkeeper who earned extra money acting as captain for the rangers. A hip injury kept him off a horse, or he would have been riding with them.

"Up and around, huh?"

"Yes, sir."

"I'm surprised to see you up so soon. I would have gotten over there to see you, but my leg's acting up again. Hurts like hell when I walk. Your parents still in town?"

"My father is leaving on Monday. My mother didn't make the trip."

"How's your side?"

"Better."

"You ready to ride?"

"Depends on who you ask. Probably ready to ride nice and slow."

"Good. I've got a slow one for you. You know Duarte?"

They had been through this before. McNamara either couldn't remember or didn't want to acknowledge Durango, a town halfway between Tucson and Phoenix on the Santa Cruz River. He always referred to it as Duarte, a small town in Mexico.

"Durango?"

"Some chinks are causing trouble all over town. I want you to go down there and straighten 'em out. Shouldn't tax you too strenuously."

McNamara tossed him a letter. "Your friend, John Stapleton, brought this over. Guess he figures we don't have enough to do what with rustlers, gamblers, prostitutes, whiskey peddlers, Indians, and claim jumpers." John was secretary of state for the territory. In actuality, he did more toward running the territory than Governor Frémont did. McNamara sighed heavily and sat back. Lance read the letter and filed the rancher's name in his memory. He'd heard of Logan; he ran a few thousand steers west of the Santa Cruz River.

"How was John?"

"Acting horny as a goat in rut and looking slick as spit. He asked about you."

John was a career politician noted around town for his frequent visits to the various whorehouses. He and Lance had attended law school together. John had visited him twice while he was laid up. Usually they argued about women. This time they had argued about Governor Frémont. John wanted to use Frémont's term as governor to launch his own campaign. Frémont, still somewhat famous as the Pathfinder, was more concerned now with education of the territory's young people. According to John, Frémont had mellowed considerably, almost to the point of being useless to other politicians. Lance stood up to leave.

"Take your time, Kincaid. See your parents off. Don't rip anything loose."

Lance grunted. He felt in more danger from Samantha nursing him than he would be from an angry mob.

Laramee cleaned his plate for the second time and leaned back. "Dang good chow. Glad you can still cook."

He glanced around Angie's kitchen and sat up straight. "Oh, I forgot to give you this," he said, fishing a crumpled letter out of his shirt pocket. Expecting a reply from the governor, Angie quickly opened the letter and read it.

But this letter was from her cousins, Tennessee Maxwell and Virginia Trumbull, owners of the newspaper she worked for back east and the ones who had commissioned her to take photographs for a picture book of the west. They were in Phoenix to organize a local chapter of the national woman's suffrage movement. They wanted her to join them in Phoenix to photograph the demonstration they had planned. They expected the demonstration to receive in-depth treatment in her picture book.

Their interest in Arizona was obvious. Folks were talking about statehood. Women leaders wanted the territory to go into the Union as the first state to give women the vote. In the territories, men were so happy to have women with them that they gave women anything they wanted. Wyoming Territory had given women the vote in '69. National feminist leaders had decided to bring pressure to bear in Arizona toward that same end.

Laramee pushed his chair back from the table. He had ridden in to have dinner with Angie and to try to see Sarah. Angie passed the letter to Laramee. He read it and shook his head. "Blame," he grumbled.

Angie laughed. "You remember Tennessee and Virginia, don't you?"

"I'm not likely to forget those two." One summer the Logans had visited the Trumbulls in Mississippi. Warning them all to stay put, the parents left the children in the buckboard while they went into the general store. Tennessee tossed Laramee's hat out onto the sidewalk. When he scampered out to get it before the wind or another child took it, the girls wouldn't let him back in. Lindsay Logan came out and stripped a limb from a nearby peach tree and gave Laramee's legs a fit.

"I reckon by the look in your eye you're gonna go."

Angie grinned.

Laramee shook his head, his mouth set in a look that clearly said she was just being stubborn.

Angie shook her head, mimicking his expression. "Some folks might think it stubborn to insist on ranching in this godforsaken place. Mexican bandits ride across the border every night to steal cattle and horses. Indians leave the reservations and get drunk and kill settlers. Streams dry up after every rain. Rattlesnakes try to crawl in bed with you..."

Laramee cocked an eye at Angie. She was definitely in a horn-tossing mood.

"Mama warned us about those damned Trumbulls. They never was any blamed good."

Their mother had, once they were older, made some critical remarks about her sister Elsie's choice of a husband. Isadora had never liked Silas Trumbull. He'd had too many liberal ideas to suit Isadora. Elsie had run away from home to marry him: a lazy-eyed, lanky northerner more at home in a saloon than behind a plow. He'd sired a baby every fourteen months or so until Elsie died of the fever. The kids had raised themselves, taking care of Silas as best they could in the process. Isadora had claimed to be scandalized by everything about Silas. Angie had overheard Silas telling her father that he thought 'Dora was turning sour on him. He had recommended Lindsay keep her a little busier in bed. Lindsay had coughed in embarrassment. Even at twelve Angie had known what Silas meant about her mother. Isadora had been a little self-righteous.

"Don't you start on Tennessee and Virginia. They are intelligent, hardworking, honest, and well-respected women..."

"Sure, if you don't mind smut peddlers," Laramee said, quirking his eyebrows at her.

"They are not smut peddlers," Angie said stoutly. Tennessee and Virginia *were* publishers of a radical feminist newspaper, *Trumbull and Maxwell's Weekly*, in Cambridge, Massachusetts. At one time in the '70s her cousins had been the most talked-about feminists in America. The *Weekly* advocated socialism, free love, and spiritualism, but free love was a long way from smut. And the *Weekly* had been the first newspaper in America to print the *Communist Manifesto*. Angie personally thought that linking Communism to the woman's movement had done more to damage Communism than to help women.

"Well, dammit, you could at least wait until I marry Sarah. What if you get her so het up about women voting and this blamed little newspaper that she decides not to marry me at all?"

Angie laughed. At least Laramee was being honest with her now. He wasn't trying to pretend that he had only her happiness in mind when he asked her to give up something she wanted to do.

"Time and tide wait for no man."

Laramee grunted. "I'm just supposed to let you run wild all over creation?"

"Yes. I'm going to chase every man in Phoenix, bed the slow ones, and trap and skin the fast ones. What else would I do?"

"All right. All right." Laramee laughed.

"Regardless of what you think about Tennessee and Virginia, they have never encouraged me to be irresponsible."

"Now that is the biggest piece of horse hocky I've ever heard of," he said firmly. "Women votin'..."

Angie no longer listened. In her mind she was already en route to Phoenix. Which camera would be best for the demonstration? The Scenographe was lighter, but it took only four-by-five-inch pictures.

Better to take the camera George Eastman had given her. She'd have to unmount the Hale and mount the Eastman. It used six-by-eight-inch plates, and she could change them more quickly.

Her beau during her last two years at the Mount Holyoke Seminary for Young Ladies of Talent in South Hadley, Massachusetts, had introduced Angie to George Eastman. James Madison Pierce had attended the Institute of Technology in Boston and had encouraged Angie's interest in photography. Eastman had recently invented a machine for coating the glass plates used in cameras. When he and Angie first met, he'd been so impressed by her earnestness, he had given her one of his first experimental cameras to field-test.

By the time she left South Hadley, Eastman was on the brink of perfecting flexible roll film. He estimated that roll film would be an actuality by 1884 at the latest. Then he could produce a lightweight camera for under twenty-five dollars. Angie wished her mentor's inventions were already available, so the day after tomorrow she wouldn't be dragging thirty pounds of equipment some incalculable distance. Her cousins were perfectly capable of organizing things that only the stoutest could survive.

"I hope you don't regret this," Laramee muttered.

Angie lifted her chin. "Liar."

Propriety firmly on his side, Laramee picked up a toothpick and proceeded to clean his teeth.

At the stagecoach Angie hugged Laramee hard. He didn't want her to go, but he had stayed overnight to help her load her equipment and drive her into town. He could have let her do it by herself.

"I love you," she whispered to his neck. He smelled exactly like their father had always smelled. To hug Laramee was to be transported back in time.

"You be careful, you hear?"

"I will. All I'm going to do is photograph a carefully orchestrated demonstration."

The stage arrived in Phoenix at three-thirty in the afternoon. Angie hired the driver to help her pull her wagonload of equipment and carry her portmanteau to the hotel. She washed the dust of the trip off and then ventured downstairs to find her cousins. Just as she stepped out onto the sidewalk, she saw them: two tall, large-boned women with erect bearing and smiling faces.

Angie rushed forward and threw herself into their outstretched arms. "I'm so happy to see you here, Cousins."

"We wouldn't miss this moment for the world. If Arizona comes in as a woman's suffrage state, it'll be a feather in our cap."

"I should say so. Where are you staying?"

"The Orlando."

"I asked at the desk. They didn't know..."

"I shouldn't wonder. The young man was so beguiled by Tennessee, he was tongue-tied."

"He did rather fancy me, didn't he? Perhaps I may decide to settle here. Phoenix doesn't seem half bad."

Angie didn't bother to explain to her cousins that any woman who breathed could have fifty men at her beck and call in Phoenix. Virginia and Tennessee had worked in what many members of the woman's suffrage movement had deemed unsavory careers. Starting life in extreme poverty, they had worked in a medical road show, been clairvoyants and stockbrokers, and now were publishers. Because of their public stance on free love, they had been denounced even inside the woman's movement. Virginia would have been expelled entirely but for Elizabeth Cady Stanton, who defended her with words that had gone down in history. *Women have crucified the Mary Wollstonecrafts, the Fanny Wrights, the George Sands of all ages...Let us end this ignoble record and henceforth stand by womanhood. If this present woman must be crucified, let men drive the spikes.*

They dined in the hotel dining room. Their entrance, understated as it was, silenced the entire roomful of men. Word had spread. As they seated themselves, the noise level slowly increased again. Tennessee and Virginia ate with gusto. Too excited to eat much, Angie picked at her food. Her cousins finished and sat back, satisfied and smiling. Tennessee, the younger sister, slipped Angie an envelope. "The latest thing off the press," she said, smiling.

While at school Angie had visited her cousins in Cambridge at every opportunity and had received regular copies of their *Weekly*. To protect their younger cousin's tender reputation, they had mailed the *Weekly* in a plain brown envelope. Half her dormitory read it to relieve their anxieties. The sexual stirrings of young women of her day were, of necessity, so hidden and shameful that few could admit to stirrings, much less loss of virginity, even to themselves. Most young women had been so carefully protected from information about men that they were exceedingly easy targets for them.

Angie chatted at length with Virginia and Tennessee about the family and how each of their mutual friends and acquaintances was doing. By nine o'clock Angie drooped and the women adjourned, eagerly anticipating the next day's events.

May 10 dawned clear and cold. Pulling her camera wagon behind her, Angie marched down the main street of Phoenix with fifty-five angry women. Loaded down with plate holders, Virginia and Tennessee trudged along beside her. All of the protesters seemed in excellent spirits.

The women of Phoenix had come to demand redress for the mayor's acerbic comments. He had insulted womankind as a whole by his statement that *women, with their limited mentality, must needs be protected from the rigors of the voting process.* In actuality, what the mayor had said was no different from the opinions of most men—Laramee had said worse—but his comment had been reported in an eastern newspaper, and the woman's suffrage movement had targeted the mayor.

Dressed in black to symbolize their mourning about the state of ignorance and servility to which they had been condemned by social training and custom, the women marched down the middle of Main Street singing "The Battle Hymn of the Republic." Exhilarated and singing loudly, Angie felt a special kinship with these strangers and her cousins. She no longer noticed the weight of the wagon behind her.

"This is the place," a female voice yelled. At this signal, women spilled around Angie and charged forward into the mayor's yard. They shouted for him to come out and face them.

In a town of two thousand, over fifty women had turned out to protest the affront to their mentality as a gender. Angie was willing to bet a golden eagle that she wouldn't have been able to find fifty women in South Hadley who would have gotten up early in the morning for anything short of a visit by Queen Victoria. Frontier women were a hardier breed than easterners. Western women worked shoulder to shoulder with their men. Usually men thought twice about making belittling remarks where a woman could hear them—simple politeness. Apparently the mayor had forgotten himself.

The mayor offered no retraction. Instead, dozens of volunteer deputy marshals armed with sticks and some of them on horseback came toward the women from behind his house.

The women jeered at the ragtag volunteers.

Angie positioned her camera.

From the sidelines a man with a railroader's megaphone ordered the women to "clear the yard and return to your homes and your babies." One woman answered this request with a tomato that sailed through the air and landed on the speaker's chest, spilling seeds and pulp on his frock coat. Tomatoes were not easy to come by. Raised and protected at great personal expense from worms, birds, and jackrabbits, they were expensive artillery.

Enraged, the marshal ordered his volunteers to clear the yard.

The men shifted uneasily, obviously well aware that these were still women, and therefore a relatively scarce commodity in Phoenix.

Angie squinted through the lens at the spot where she expected the two lines to come together. The men, clubs raised, began their advance. A barrage of ripe tomatoes and uncooked eggs sailed across the short distance and found targets. Yelling their rage, covering their heads against the endless stream of soft or brittle missiles, the blinded men stumbled into the silent, determined ranks of the women.

Smacked in the eye with an egg, a man on horseback struck the nearest woman with his stick. Angie captured the act of violence on film. Seeing the camera, the man turned his horse and bore down on Angie, knocking the wagon over; her camera and tripod toppled to the ground. Using swear words Laramee had taught her by example, Angie grabbed the man by the foot, twisted it as hard as she could, and dragged him off his horse. On the way down he cursed and grappled her to the ground.

Chantry Kincaid, II, leaned out the window of the elegant brougham, purchased to transport himself, Samantha, and Mrs. Lillian from the end of the railroad to Phoenix, and watched for a moment. "Is this the sort of thing you do? Ride down on women tramping on somebody's yard?" he asked, turning to his son, who sat forward in his seat to watch.

Disdaining the bait being dangled before him, Lance chuckled. "No, sir. Compared to this, I lead a relatively mundane existence," he said, shaking his head at the pandemonium that had erupted on the lawn two blocks from his house. He and his father had been on their way to the post office when the riot started. It was Lance's second trip to the business section of town since being wounded almost six weeks earlier.

"Mundane, huh?" the elder Kincaid demanded gruffly. "Your humility causes you to speak less than truth. I have made certain contacts and talked to a number of people since we've been in Arizona. They tell me you're one of the three deadliest gunfighters west of Austin…"

For Chantry Kincaid to claim that he had certain contacts was like the commander-in-chief of the United States Army to say he had a few soldiers. Lance didn't believe for a moment that he had just learned his information. "Isn't this a case of the pot calling the kettle black? You were no saint when you were my age, Father. I'm a lawman. I take whatever action is necessary. I don't kill men who don't demand to be killed. My job is to take wanted men in for trial. Some men can predict the outcome and choose to avoid a lengthy trial. Can't blame a man for not wanting to die of throat trouble…"

Lance scowled. The real problem was not the one they talked about. His father didn't give a damn how many men he killed in the line of duty. He cared only that his son had chosen to be an Arizona ranger rather than to join Kincaid Enterprises, Inc., as corporate attorney and to marry Samantha Regier. If he would join his brother Chane or his father, as his younger brother Stuart would do after his graduation from Harvard, all would be forgiven.

"Dammit, I don't care about them. I care that my son could get himself killed. You're a *Kincaid*. Let some other damn fool get shot at! You were raised a gentleman! You have one of the finest educations money can buy! You could be engaged to one of the most beautiful young women in the United States. All you have to do is say the word."

On the lawn the two lines advanced on each other, ready to engage. Women reached into their bags and pockets. "I grew up with Sam dogging my tracks. She's more like a little sister to me…"

"Bullshit!" the elder Kincaid said gruffly. "No woman who looks like Samantha Regier can seem like a sister to a red-blooded man. Most families intermarry. Look at the royal families of all the monarchies. She isn't even related to you."

"I grew up with her. I'm closer to her than to Maggie."

Kincaid eyed his son suspiciously. "You haven't been hanging around with those damned Englishmen have you?"

Lance threw back his head; laughter, deep-throated and masculine, burst out. English himself, his father didn't notice the incongruity in his statement.

Chantry rubbed his chin, dismissing the idea that Lance, however unsatisfactorily employed, could prefer the company of men over women. His son had reacted with obvious desire to a number of women in New York City. And they had reacted to him.

Eyeing the fine figure of masculinity across from him, the clean profile, the thick black Kincaid hair that framed a rugged, handsome face, Chantry felt a surge of pride. According to Samantha, who had a tendency to romanticize everything related to Lance, his son's most outstanding feature was his eyes: *fire-and-brimstone eyes*, Samantha called them. *When he's angry, they're like a blue norther brewing in near-black storm clouds over the Texas plain. When he smiles, they're like heat shimmering off a flat desert rock.*

Chantry grunted. Sitting in a near sprawl on the elegant cushions, his son's body radiated energy. His fire-and-brimstone eyes narrowed at something outside. Lance's years on the frontier had hardened him into strapping manhood, so it hadn't all been for naught. In New York he had cut an elegant figure in a tailored silk dinner jacket and fitted trousers. Lance could do more with a look than most men could with money and flowers. A lifted eyebrow, lowered eyelids, a shrug—God knows what he did—but it called attention to a sensitivity that seemed only to enhance his rugged masculinity. After only a week women all over the city had been abuzz about Lance Kincaid. Lizzie had been filled with pride. And surprised. Apparently his reputation as a gunfighter, which she hated, had affected the young women almost as much as his wealth and physical attractiveness.

But Lizzie had her heart set on marrying Lance to Samantha. Lizzie and Lillian had raised Sam since she was four. Her parents had died when the ship they were taking back to England sank in a howling winter storm. Imelda Regier had been Elizabeth's second cousin and dearest friend. Samantha had had other relatives, but none who wanted to be bothered with a child whose parents' wills had provided that her wealth be held in an inviolate trust until her twenty-first birthday. Caring for her would be without monetary reward. Imelda had known her family well enough to accomplish her wish that should anything happen to her and her husband, Samantha would be raised by Elizabeth and Chantry.

From the time Samantha was four years old and Lance ten, Sam had adored Lance. In spite of his protests. Lance loved Sam. He had protected her with fierce devotion all the years they were growing up together.

Just as no gentleman was complete without his horse, in Chantry's eyes no son was complete without his wife. His oldest son, Chane, appeared doomed to a lengthy bachelorhood; he was immovable. Stuart was still a mite young, but Lance had no good excuse. He was twenty-eight years old. From Chantry's viewpoint, by the time a man had passed the quarter-century mark, he should have a wife and be renowned for more than the smartness of his turnouts and the gloss, speed, and style of his carriage horses. Lance was widely renowned, but the danger of his calling kept his mother in a constant state of agitation. Lizzie did not handle anxiety well.

Chantry was accustomed to getting his own way. With a word, he could sway leaders in positions of great power, but he was frustrated before his son's indifference. If he mentioned how wasteful it was to forego the privilege of his birthright, Lance would lift an expressive black brow in a sardonic smile and tell him that his many years of training had not been wasted. He rode constantly in his job. But being a ranger in Arizona was not equivalent even to being in the cavalry, the elite of the armed forces and the proper place for the aristocracy if military service could not be avoided.

Second son of a destitute English duke and deprived of inheritance by the law of primogeniture, Chantry had clawed his way up from poverty. His hard work entitled his sons to certain advantages. He would not, without a struggle, allow any one of them to forego those advantages.

"It's time you gave up this nonsense and came home," Chantry said, his voice reflecting the fear enhanced by Lance's recent injury.

Lance glanced at his father and knew why his father had stayed long after he was needed. "Did you promise Mother you would bring me back with you?"

Chantry pulled in his chin. "I did not," he lied.

Chagrined at his father's extended scrutiny, Lance crossed his long legs and stared at his boots. He had enjoyed the last month: the closeness with his father, the time with Samantha, the long chats with Mrs. Lillian, the knowledge that, anytime he wanted, he could walk downstairs and find one of them there, eager to spend a few moments with him.

This last month had changed him in some inexplicable way. Part of him dreaded his family's departure almost as much as he was sure they had dreaded his when he left New York more than two months before.

Lance looked out the window at the continuing melee and wondered why the coachman remained still, but he said nothing. He felt no inclination to get involved.

On the lawn fifty feet away from them, a young woman pulled a man off his horse. In turn, he tackled her and knocked her to her knees. Irritated, Lance leaned forward to open the door of the carriage, but before he could, a young man apparently on the ruffian's side threw himself on top of the man and dragged him off the girl.

Relieved, Lance leaned back. The girl sat up and straightened her hat, and Lance felt an odd sense of disquiet. He knew her. That was the girl who had taken his photograph in Nogales…

"Are you all right?" his father demanded, green eyes sparkling like bottle glass in the sun.

Lance nodded. "Fine, sir. Why do you ask?"

"You look pale. If this is unpleasant for you…"

His words trailed off as if Lance were somehow deficient if he found the scene unpleasant.

Stubbornly Lance nodded. "I do find it unpleasant, sir. It is too easy to imagine my mother or Buffy or Maggie or Samantha out there being chased by those bullies."

Chantry followed his son's gaze and saw the girl. Anger suffused her face with warm color as she picked up parts of her camera. The resemblance was unmistakable—the same pale wheat hair and willow-slender young body as Lucinda. Rage flushed into Chantry Kincaid. If not for Lucinda, Lance would be working beside his brother and father instead of risking his life in a wilderness.

There had been a time in Chantry's life that money had seemed most important to him, but watching his children grow and mature had changed that gradually—almost imperceptibly—until now, without having voiced it, he knew that the only thing that mattered to him was that the people he loved—Lance, Chane, Stuart, Buffy, Margaret, Samantha, and Elizabeth—be safe and happy and healthy. He wanted his son safe and happy—now.

"When are you going to make it official with Sam?"

Uncomfortable, Lance shifted on his seat. His father pinned him with a piercing look.

"You could propose before she leaves Phoenix."

"I don't think Sam is ready to get married."

"Hogwash! Have you asked her?"

"She's a busy woman…"

"She's a *beautiful* woman. Beautiful women are always busy. That doesn't keep them from marrying."

"She's just finished school. She has her grand tour this summer." Lance shrugged. He wasn't handling this well at all. Everyone had known for years that he and Sam would marry. It was not an unpleasant thought to him. He loved Sam. She was beautiful, heartbreakingly vulnerable where he was concerned, and entirely feminine. But Lance didn't like being pushed.

The pandemonium had reached its peak in the mayor's yard. The din of horses screaming and voices raised in angry protest was loud and urgent. The women were giving as good as they got.

Chantry leaned back in the seat and glanced at his son's stubborn face. If not for Lucinda's death, Lance would not have tracked down her murderers, killed them, and rejected his heritage. He damn sure wouldn't be running around the country avenging one wrong after another.

"Maybe you could announce your engagement before Sam's trip to Europe. Then your mother would have a good excuse to throw that party she's been building up to."

"Mother doesn't need an excuse to throw a party." Lance had turned restless. "I think I'll walk to the post office," he said, reaching for the door handle.

"You want to see that girl, don't you?"

Startled, Lance flushed. "And if I do?" His usually husky voice had dropped down even lower, raspier.

"You'll regret it. She'll look enough like Lucinda to open old wounds, and she'll be different enough to disappoint you."

Lance let his hand drop away from the door handle. His father was wrong. Lucinda was dead. He started to tell his father that he knew the young woman, but he didn't need to prove anything to anybody. "Then why the hell don't we get this thing moving…sir?"

There was a harshness in his expression that caused Chantry Kincaid to look hard at his son. His handsome face was tense. His blue eyes, so like Lizzie's, were shuttered against him. Chantry rapped on the underside of the carriage, and the coachman overhead slapped the reins and yelled at the carriage horses to *giddyup!*

The brougham leapt forward. Lance settled back in the deep plush seats. Outside, a woman yelled, and Lance glanced in that direction. A buxom woman, taller and more statuesque than the man she pummeled, hit the man again, wiped her hands, and then turned him and sent him flying with a well-placed high heeled slipper into the seat of his pants.

Lance recognized Virginia Trumbull. He opened the door of the carriage and leapt out of the rolling vehicle.

"What the hell?" Chantry yelled and rapped on the underside of the carriage roof. The driver slowed the brougham.

"I know those women," Lance said, running alongside. "I have to help them. I'll meet you in town."

Shaking his head, Chantry signaled the driver. No good would come of this, but there was nothing he could do about it now. Lance would have to learn this lesson the hard way.

• • •

Lance lifted Angie up from the grass and helped her retrieve the parts of her camera.

"I don't know why I'm doing this. You don't look like you need help," he said.

Virginia walked over and knelt down to help. She flashed Angie a wicked grin. "We just destroyed our last chance for a date tonight, and he thinks we don't need him. Why, Lance darling," she said, faking a southern accent, "little old Virginia has needs your pappy hasn't even told you about."

Before Lance could think up a reply, a man barreled out of the melee and stumbled backward into the middle of Virginia, who toppled toward Angie. The man was followed shortly by Tennessee, grinning a wicked grin and winding up another haymaker in case the unfortunate man woke up.

Lance picked the man off Virginia, helped her and Angie to their feet.

"Are you all right?" Lance asked, looking at Angie.

"Is *she* all right?" Virginia wailed. "I was the one that bastard fell on."

Someone fired a shotgun into the air. Men and women stopped in midswing. "Gentlemen, draw your sidearms. We're placing these women under arrest," the marshal yelled.

Men drew their guns. A deputy marshal stalked over and placed Angie under arrest. Some women ran; others stood their ground.

Angie, Tennessee, Virginia, and a dozen others were loaded into a cart. Arrested. Laramee would surely judge this as proof that he had been right about Tennessee and Virginia.

Angie watched Kincaid until the cart turned a corner. The marshal carted them down the main street of Phoenix like witches on their way to the woodpile. People stepped out of stores to watch and cheer.

"You know Kincaid?" Angie asked over the racket.

"Lance Kincaid?" Virginia asked innocently. "Why, darling, everyone knows Lance Kincaid."

"Lance Kincaid has broken more hearts than the crash of '69. Surely you're not interested in him."

Tennessee piped in. "Of course, she's not. Our Angie's much too smart for anything so foolish."

"Well," Virginia sighed in mock resignation. "Of course, darling, he does have that smile. He could sell dead horses to the cavalry. Even

Angie, as smart as she is, might be intrigued."

Angie threw up her hands.

At the jail, the marshal gave them a good tongue-lashing and let them go. Undaunted, Virginia and Tennessee completed arrangements for their planned victory party. They distributed fliers printed the day before and invited any and everyone to join them that night at seven. They hired a fiddler and hoped they would get enough people together for a couple of cotillions.

CHAPTER FOUR

Monday evening, May 10, 1880

Angie spied the lawman across the room. She raised her hand and waved. He narrowed his eyes at her, looked behind him to be sure it was him she meant, and then started across the room.

The celebration at the schoolhouse on the east side of Phoenix was crowded with men and women who laughed and danced as if they might never have the opportunity again.

Tennessee had struck up an alliance with one of the men who had changed sides during the melee. Dressed in a scoop-necked foulard gown that displayed her fine breasts to their best advantage, she appeared in excellent spirits. "The men of Phoenix certainly know how to turn out for an unpopular cause," she said.

Virginia shook her head. "Men would turn out for rattlesnake bite if you promised them liquor and women too."

Slowly the lawman made his way through the crowd and eased himself into position behind Virginia. He slipped an arm around Virginia's waist; she turned, saw him, and let out an exclamation. "Lance, *darling*! My *God*. I thought you were *dead*. I didn't believe my eyes this afternoon."

She flung her arms around him and he was soundly hugged against Virginia's ample bosom. Quirking an expressive eyebrow, he glanced over Virginia's shoulder and smiled at Angie.

Virginia held him at arm's length and beamed. "Lance Kincaid. What a fine, swashbuckling lawman you've turned into. Ten years ago I'd have thought you didn't stand a chance among true badmen, about like a jackrabbit in a pack of lobo wolves, but just look at you."

"You'd have been right," Kincaid admitted.

Tennessee laughed and poked Angie with her elbow. "Lance was the quiet sort when he was young. Mama always said it was the quiet ones you have to look out for. She never worried about me. I talked too much. She always said she'd know what I was doing before I did it."

Clean-shaven and without his Stetson, the ranger was a man of contradictions. Dressed in a blue serge English lounge suit, the mark of a gentleman, he exuded dangerous masculine charm. The skin of his dark, handsome, sturdy neck seemed to chafe in resentment against the high, starched white collar.

Angie was so pleased to see him again she could barely contain her happiness.

Tennessee turned to Angie. "Have you two met, formally, that is?"

"Why no. I suppose not."

"Then by all means let me take credit for this auspicious occasion. Lance Kincaid, our cousin, Angie Logan."

Hopelessly intrigued by this time, Angie offered her hand. "Are you fully recovered?" she asked.

His smooth, ruddy-brown hand, warmer and more alive than any hand Angie had ever touched, closed over hers and jolted every nerve in her body. Touching him confirmed every impression she had had of him. As he touched her the warm light in his eyes seemed to waver in mild panic for a second, but on second thought, she was sure she only imagined it.

"Except for my pride. Did your pictures come out?"

"You've photographed him? My, doesn't our cousin work fast," Tennessee said, smiling archly at Angie.

"I watched Mr. Kincaid once when he was working."

Kincaid laughed. "*You* were the only one working. The Territory doesn't pay me to get shot. Did that on my own time."

"I'm glad you survived," she said. Joy bubbled in her.

Tennessee pinched Kincaid's cheek. "You handsome devil. Did you ever get married?"

"How could I? I kept remembering what you said about the marriage contract being an assumption that the community could regulate human instincts better than an individual could..."

"Why, bless your heart, darling. I should have known no one could regulate your natural instincts," Tennessee said, dropping into a parody of western dialect.

Lance looked meaningfully at Angie. "Well I wouldn't go so far as to say that no one...Are you married, Miss Logan?"

"Do I look like a fool, Mr. Kincaid? Marriage is a sorry bargain for a woman."

"How so?" Kincaid asked.

"Unless a woman has a penchant for enforced prostitution."

Virginia coughed in surprise. Tennessee howled. "I think she's gone you one better, Sister." Virginia, in spite of her usual taciturn nature, was the official spokesman for the *Weekly*.

"Enforced prostitution?" Kincaid asked, ignoring Tennessee and Virginia. The sisters were capable of anything, they routinely dared and even enticed men into calling them names that would make a muleskinner shudder. It was part of their methodology. They endeavored to prove by example that labels were only words, that women could live their lives with or without society's blessing. These two famous feminists routinely printed men's insults to them in their newspaper. Lance expected them to do and say the most outrageous things, but he hadn't expected it from their young cousin, in spite of her spunk and her obvious ambition.

Angie Logan lifted her chin and looked Lance square in the eye. "Marriage is actually worse. For a scrap of paper that may or may not guarantee her food and shelter, a woman is expected to relinquish control of her body to a man. I hardly think it is a fair bargain."

Merriment danced in Kincaid's eyes.

Angie endured as much of his teasing attention as she could, then relented. "Of course I'm sure there must be instances where a wife does not merely submit."

"We can only hope," Kincaid said dryly.

"Hear, hear!" Tennessee injected. "I think you should let Angie speak at the next convention, Sister. She would wake up those preening sissies who look down their prudish noses at our philosophy of free love."

"Angie speaks blunt truth in all candor, and that is most admirable. A wife who submits to sexual intercourse against her wishes or desires, virtually commits suicide. I soundly denounce the law that gives a husband legal ownership of his wife's body. I shall most definitely bring it up at the next convention."

Angie's head fairly buzzed. Under Kincaid's influence she had publicly espoused a doctrine that surprised her as much as him. Now, whether fortunately or unfortunately, she had aligned herself solidly with her cousins, perhaps even bested them in their radical ideology. Angie wasn't sure how she felt about her new role as self-professed radical. Until this moment she had strenuously avoided politics.

Tennessee picked up the thread of conversation again, and Angie retreated. It was apparent Virginia, Tennessee, and Kincaid had moved in adjacent or overlapping circles at some very stimulating, though distant times. Tennessee asked numerous provocative questions about Colette, Maggie, Buffy, Latitia, Elizabeth, Lillian, and Samantha. Kincaid answered with witty but unrevealing comments—his appealing, whiskey-tinged voice as intimate and unsettling as it had been in Nogales. With equal ease he spoke as precisely as the proverbial Philadelphia lawyer or with as much mischievous irreverence as the most illiterate rangehand ever to see the inside of a bunkhouse.

His magnetic blue eyes smiled at Angie frequently, deliberately including her in their conversation to prevent her from wandering off.

Angie bubbled with joy and unaccustomed shyness. Perhaps she had mooned over Kincaid's pictures too long or too frequently. Countless questions flitted through her head, but she had no opportunity to ask them. On closer inspection, she recognized no identifiable accent or twang in Kincaid's pleasingly raspy voice—rather a number of possibilities: English? Upstate New Yorker? Even on occasion a languid, drawling quality that reminded her of the wranglers on Laramee's ranch. Texan? She had thought so in Nogales, but the wit and poise he exhibited in talking to Virginia and parrying thrusts with Tennessee were not bred on a cockleburr outfit in west Texas.

Tiny currents of energy passed between Angie and Kincaid. Up close, there was a certain angular set to his jaw and chin, a certain richness of coloring that could not be captured in a brown-toned tint, a certain swell and curve to his lips that made Angie's fingers itch to touch him.

As if he knew her thoughts, he glanced into her eyes and paralyzed some vital part of her that should have warned her away but could not. That lingering shiver of emotion aroused first in Nogales flamed up again.

Angie glanced away from Kincaid and back at Tennessee, who said, "But of course none of the foregoing prohibits volunteer efforts at bridging the lamentable gulf between men and women." They all laughed; the moment passed. Tennessee launched into a monologue about her alcoholic ex-husband who periodically returned home so she could nurse him back to health.

In unguarded moments a certain healthy arrogance sparkled in Kincaid's eyes. He was intelligent and handsome and knew it. There was no sign of insecurity in his eyes, even though he had fallen in combat, so to speak. No sign now that his soul had signaled hers. She had imagined it after all.

"I rue the day I met that man," Tennessee ended jokingly. "When I am seventy, I will still be taking him in."

Another couple drifted into their assemblage, vying for Virginia and Tennessee's attention, and Kincaid deftly cut Angie out of the noisy circle and steered her toward the punch bowl. The power she had sensed in him from a distance, the power that had made her step away from her camera when he scowled at her, stirred something deep inside her. She looked up into his eyes and then quickly away. In spite of his playfulness, singular resolute masculinity in the blue depths warned Angie that he was not a man to trifle with. *Touch me at your own risk.*

"Where did you meet my cousins?" she asked as his warm hand on her waist guided her through the clamorous, jostling crowd. She turned and faced him.

"In Cambridge. They had just started their *Weekly* when I entered law school." Kincaid's smoky voice mesmerized Angie.

"You're an attorney?"

"I swore off. How did your pictures come out?"

"They're wonderful," she said, maintaining her composure with difficulty.

Kincaid rubbed his chin.

"You had a beard in Nogales, didn't you?"

"A few days stubble…"

"You look different…"

"I am grateful for that." He didn't ever want to look or feel the way he had that day. He didn't even want to remember. He focused instead on the coral color of Angie's cheeks and the tiny smattering of precise coral freckles that looked like paint flecks sprinkled across her nose. Her skin was radiant, her cheeks smooth as alabaster. She was beautiful.

"This is the first time I've seen you without your camera. Do you dance?" he asked.

"I love dancing actually, but I'm not very good at it."

Lance absorbed her glance reluctantly. Angie Logan. This fragile beauty with vivid, flashing dark eyes and shining, wheat-colored hair made his hands long to touch her.

The fiddle started up with a low, catchy whine. Kincaid swept Angie into his arms and into the rhythm of the waltz. As if he sensed the sudden racing of her pulse, something happened in his eyes and Angie grew dizzy with wondering how it would feel if Kincaid kissed her, if his brick-brown hands pulled her hard against him, and his mouth…his smooth, richly colored mouth…

"You dance very well," he said.

"Which are you, Mr. Kincaid? The slick barrister who can hold his own with my notorious cousins? Or the saddle scab I saw in Nogales?"

"Which are you, Miss Logan? The young modern who thinks marriage a sorry bargain for a woman? Or the soft, sweet, feminine woman who cried when I got shot?"

"Touché."

They waltzed in silence for a moment.

"Lance," he said softly. "My name is Lance. A young woman with your speed and refinement should be able to handle a first name with no problem."

Angie adopted a southern accent. "Why, I declare, Lance dahling, but you sound downright embittahed."

Lance dropped into a lazy Texas drawl. "Naw. I plumb admire slick-tawking womenfolks. Some fellers thank it's downright scandless, but I reckon it ain't no more scandless to tawk up a storm than it is to shoot up a town on a Saturday night."

"Are you implying I am all talk?" she bristled, dropping the dialect.

"I am suggesting that you may have a surprise in store for yourself, Miss Logan," he said, just as formally.

"The capacity for compassion does not necessarily preclude the ability to act with good sense."

"Perhaps not, but I have some experience with women, and if emotion does not preclude sagacity, it is apparent to me that the two rarely cohabit. Let's say the one encourages lapses in the other, Miss Logan."

"Angie," she said sweetly. "My name is Angie. A straight-shooter like you should be able to stride fearlessly past such false modesty."

"You are absolutely ravishing, Angie." His voice had dropped the teasing dialect, and his eyes no longer twinkled with merriment.

Caught off guard, Angie blinked. Her waist tingled beneath his warm hand. As he gazed down into her eyes, his hand tightened and pulled her against him for one, two, three beats of the music. Through her gown and his trousers, momentarily, breathlessly, she felt the heat of his thighs, the swell of his manhood.

An imperceptible movement of his expressive, black brows and the look in his narrowed eyes was now humorously cynical, agreeably mocking. "What are you going to do next? Serve time for assaulting an officer of the law?"

The attractive raspiness of his voice quickened her pulse. "The marshal scolded us and let us go."

"He'll probably be sorry about that." With her hair combed and carefully in place, she had an intelligent, mobile face and large golden brown eyes, snappingly alert and almost too sensitive. He could see everything in them, everything. He should take care not to get involved with her.

Pleased with his recovery so far, Lance was grateful that he could dance without pain but equally chagrined that his body responded a little too vigorously to Angie Logan. It had been a long time since he had wanted one particular woman—a long time since he had experienced anything except his body's dark, anonymous passion. It was exhilarating… and a warning.

Angie concentrated on the movements of the dance. Kincaid guided her with a masterful touch. His body radiated heat. Her body tingled, as if her blood had become inflamed in some inexplicable way. Probably because she was so glad to find him alive and well. That uncertainty had weighed on her.

Lance liked Angie Logan's mouth. She had one of those sensuous upper lips that didn't quite let her mouth close. "Do you live in Phoenix?" he asked, momentarily ignoring the warnings.

"No. I…" Angie started to answer, but the dance ended. Men stomped and yelled, drowning out her answer. Kincaid led her back to her cousins. Tennessee, also affected by Kincaid, engaged him in conversation.

They were interrupted by a tremulous, prettily uncertain Samantha Regier. Tennessee and Virginia exclaimed over her for several moments, then Samantha turned her gaze on Lance and Angie.

"Angela?" Samantha's eyes widened even further. "Is that you?"

"I never expected to see you here in Phoenix," Angie said.

"I came because Lance was shot. You remember Lance? He was my guest at commencement…"

"You remember I was sick and I missed all the festivities." The part about being sick was a lie. Angie was never sick; she merely hated formal parties. She wouldn't have come to this evening's get together except her cousins insisted. "I was sorry to miss your valedictory speech. I heard it was wonderful."

Kincaid—quietly exuding masculine power and impatience—watched Angie. His eyes sparkled with humor, as if he knew she'd just lied. The knowledge flustered her further.

"Thank you. But I wrote a better speech than I delivered," Samantha said, embarrassed.

Angie denied that possibility vehemently. Samantha was the daughter of an English lord and the most beautiful woman in Angie's class: delicate, Dresden-doll features, coal-black hair, and the creamiest ivory skin imaginable. She had clear blue eyes and perfect rose petal lips. Tight at the midriff and snug over the hips, her fashionable gown flared into alternating flounces of pink satin and cream lace. Draped over a slender, sensuous body that made Angie feel boyish by comparison, the gown artfully emphasized Samantha's beauty. Angie could have forgiven Samantha such physical perfection if she had not been the smartest woman in school, graduating at the top of her class.

Samantha chatted with Angie as if they had been the best of friends in school, but of course, Samantha could do no less. She was so thoroughly well bred that she certainly could not tell Kincaid in public that Angie Logan was an eccentric. Or that she had trudged around the campus with her back bowed by a heavy plate holder and pulled a camera on a silly little wagon.

Angie resented Kincaid suddenly. She sensed something selfish and eager in herself that had never existed before. She would be glad to be away from him. Unfortunately Samantha's arrival had stimulated a new round of exchanges.

"How do you like Arizona Territory?" Virginia asked.

"The desert is fascinating. I have walked into it every day, and each time I find something new to marvel at. The skies are beautiful. I love the sunsets. The air is so clean, compared to New York. Actually, it's a lot like Texas."

"Which doesn't say much for Texas," Lance said, grinning.

To Angie, Samantha's careful listing of positive accolades about Arizona sounded more like a young woman hedging her bets so that the man of her dreams could not elude her. Poor Samantha. If she wanted Kincaid, it was apparent she would have to take him on his terms. Angie's earlier pronouncement about signing her body over for a marriage certificate hardly applied to this union. Samantha looked like a young woman who would surrender all to her mate. Somehow such eagerness irritated Angie.

After a polite interval, Samantha slipped her dainty, white fingers into the crook of Lance Kincaid's arm and apologized for "borrowing" him. Kincaid nodded at Angie. His eyelids lowered for a fraction of a second, and a sudden warmth flooded inside her belly. Angie swallowed, lifted her chin slightly, perhaps drunkenly, she couldn't be sure, and Kincaid allowed himself to be towed to safety.

Blinking, Angie sat down in a corner to get control of her nerves. In all of her twenty-two years, no man had ever affected her in that way. By the time she regained her composure and stood up, Kincaid and Samantha had gone.

They went out to dinner—a large, boisterous, merry group of

women—and finally Virginia and Tennessee announced they were ready to retire.

The two cousins walked Angie to her hotel room. Virginia reminded her that their *Weekly* would monitor the progress in Arizona. "Would you accept the presidency of the territorial chapter?"

"No thank you, Cousin. I plan to be back in Cambridge practically before you are," Angie reminded her, sounding a little too twinkly for her own taste. The long day had taken its toll.

Virginia hugged Angie good night. "Get a good night's sleep. Don't lie there and dream about Kincaid."

"If he's so wonderful why hasn't one of you caught him by now?" Angie asked.

Tennessee's face arranged itself in a scowl. "Would you marry someone who lies, cheats, and is unfaithful?"

"No, I would not."

"Well," Tennessee sighed. "Neither would Kincaid."

Angie joined them in a laugh.

"Kincaid does look changed, though, doesn't he?" Tennessee asked Virginia.

"Ah yes. But he still bleeds for 'Cinda. I saw that in the way he looked at our little Angie."

"Who is 'Cinda?" Angie asked.

Tennessee yawned and stretched her arms over her head. "Sometime when we have nothing better to do, ask me and I'll tell you all about Kincaid," she said. "But now I am tired." She yawned elaborately.

Virginia shook her head and patted Angie. "Don't let her tease you unmercifully about Kincaid. No man is as fascinating as Tennessee finds him."

"You would be wise to forget him," Tennessee said sagely. "Just put Kincaid out of your mind. He's a man, and as wonderful as they are, God bless them, men are nothing but trouble."

Angie bit back her questions about Kincaid. She would get no satisfaction from her cousins. Besides, Kincaid was obviously and quite satisfactorily taken. Their paths would probably never cross again.

Tuesday, May 11, 1880

"Let me stay," Samantha pressed. She slipped her arms around Lance's waist, careful not to jab into his left side.

Lance closed his eyes. He knew how hard it was for her to ask.

"Every Regier since the sixteenth century has taken a grand tour." He teased her, pretending he didn't know she meant tonight. "The Czar of Russia is probably waiting for you this minute, wondering what the hell has happened to the Regiers. They used to be so dependable. Now—"

"Be serious, Lance Kincaid."

"Am serious. The old boy's probably got men out looking for you."

Samantha felt a rush of loneliness. Usually his teasing would pull her out of any bad mood, but uncharacteristic tears welled in her eyes. She turned away quickly and pretended to fold a shirt carelessly thrown on his four-poster bed. Lance was still lost to her.

"Hey," Lance said softly.

Angry, Samantha turned to face him. "It isn't fair! I have loved you all my life, and some woman who doesn't even deserve you can die one day and destroy you." She turned away, filled with bitterness at how Lucinda's death had ravaged Lance Kincaid's life. "I hate her! I hate her!"

"What are you talking about?"

"Lucinda!"

Sighing, Lance pulled Samantha back into his arms. "I cannot understand why everyone persists in thinking about 'Cinda. She's been dead six years…"

"Not to you!" Samantha flounced onto his bed. "Suppose I decide to go to New York and have a passionate, scandalous love affair with Chane? How would you like that?"

"You'd have to stand in line. Last time I was there Chane was as busy as a man ought to get."

Samantha threw herself across the bed. "If I hadn't loved you forever, I would hate you." Sobs racked her slim body.

Half surprised by the vehemence in her rich voice, Lance scowled. Heiress to one of the most massive fortunes in England and one of the most beautiful women he had ever seen, Samantha Regier cried like an orphan calf that had been run too hard and jerked around too much. Feeling like hell, Lance walked over to the bed, pulled her up into his arms, and smoothed her heavy mane of shiny black hair back from her damp face.

"I love you, Sam, but I'm not ready for marriage. Truth is, you're not either. Maybe by the time we are, you'll be enough of a stranger so it wouldn't seem like sleeping with my sister."

Samantha sniffed, and pain spread throughout her chest. He had seen her once a year for the past six years, and apparently it hadn't helped. "I wish I didn't love you," she said softly, miserably. All her life she had been blessed with wealth and impoverished in the ways that mattered most. No frivolous extravagance had ever been denied her. Only the truly important things—like her parents and the man she loved.

The loss of her parents, both of whom she had loved with the needy passion of a four-year-old, remained like a gaping chasm in her life. Even though Aunt 'Lizbeth and Uncle Chantry loved her, part of her yearned for her parents and could not be completely satisfied. When she thought about them, her chest ached with a sad, sweet pain. To blot it out, she lifted her chin. "I need you, Lance. I'll be the perfect wife to you. No one can love you as much as I do."

Lance looked at her tense face and remembered the nights he had sat by four-year-old Samantha's bed and let her clutch his hand while she cried herself to sleep, her thin voice periodically whimpering, "I want my mommy. Please take me to her. Please make her come back. I want my mommy."

He hadn't been able to comfort her then either.

Lance felt helpless. "If I make you miserable now, think how bad it would be if we were married," he whispered.

Samantha sniffed and smiled shakily at the truth in his words. She caressed the smooth, dark skin of his face. Beard stubble already pushed through, the short stubble like sandpaper against her fingertips. "Then promise me something," she whispered, mesmerized by the way her body reacted to the feel of him. She felt at peace. Safe and secure and loved.

"What?"

"Promise me you won't fall in love with anyone else. Promise me you won't marry anyone else before I get back."

"I could easily promise that," he said gently, "but I'm not going to. You're emotional now because you're leaving tomorrow, but you're going to be gone a long time. A promise like that would bind you as well as me. No woman should take her grand tour engaged. If I were czar of Russia, I'd make a law to that effect. Any beautiful woman who toured my country and caused my men to fall in love with her, only to find out she was engaged, would be beheaded as many times as necessary."

Samantha laughed. "Probably once would be enough."

She knew she had lost. Lance wouldn't be serious. And he was so stubborn. He pretended, but those dark furies of the spirit that lurked in the depths of him, driving him away from the people who loved him, were still there.

She had known that last night when she saw him with Angie Logan. Samantha wiped her eyes. "Did you know Gil left the university?" She couldn't think about the past without remembering Gil. Lance and Gil had been very close during law school. Something had happened after Lucinda was killed. Neither Gil nor Lance would talk about it. Samantha hated secrets—especially ones six years old. She would have been able to pry the answers from either of Lance's brothers, but with Lance…

Lance shrugged. He had known Gil was teaching at the university, but he hadn't cared. He looked quickly away. "No."

"Are you still angry at him?"

"Where'd he go?"

"West. What is so wonderful about this place? Every man worth having goes west. I heard he was going to visit relatives. Do you know where they live?"

"No idea."

"Yes, you do."

Lance shook his head. "He told me years ago that his friend was going to California or one of the territories. I don't remember where. That was a long time ago." Lance turned away. Gil. His ex-friend. Gil, who had helped murder 'Cinda as surely as the men who actually did it.

"He gave up his position and left at the end of the semester. I'm surprised he didn't visit you."

"The West is not a tunnel. I don't meet everyone who comes this direction."

"You don't have to be mad at me." Samantha sighed. She just couldn't let Lance go. "I know you love me. I will be the best wife in the world. No one could be more loving, loyal, devoted, or passionate. I will be anything you want me to be."

"Sam…"

Samantha's mouth started to crumple around the edges. He pulled her into his arms. Her body vibrated.

"So this is good-bye," she whispered.

Lance lifted her chin. "You can't trick me, Sam. You know the rules…"

Smiling in spite of her pain, Samantha sighed. "No good-byes, no good deaths," she said, repeating a litany that had become a family tradition among the Kincaid youngsters.

"And don't you forget it. You're a Kincaid too. You have to be braver than the bravest, stronger than the strongest."

This was a game they had played many times. It warmed her to play it again. Wiping her eyes, Samantha shook her head in protest. "Not fair. What do you have to be?"

"Meaner than the meanest," he growled.

"You always get the fun part."

"We each do what we're best at. Isn't that fair?" he asked, his teasing eyes drawing the knife out of her heart.

"I guess," she sniffed. "Do you really love me?"

Lance kissed her on the forehead, the nose, the mouth. "Yes. I really, *really* love you."

A long ragged sigh told him she was going to be okay in spite of him. Perhaps it was for the best. In his own way he *had* made a commitment to her. He would marry her unless she found someone else, but it was better not to tell her that. No sense binding her any more than she was.

Tennessee and Virginia walked Angie to the stagecoach. Angie promised to finish her picture book of the West as soon as she could and join them before the end of summer. Staying in Arizona any longer than she had to was insanity.

Angie almost cried when she told them good-bye. She climbed into the stage and sat back, grateful to be wedged in between two soft women. She could sleep.

The desert shimmered under the blazing sun. She loosened her bonnet strings. Part of her had wanted to see Lance Kincaid again in spite of Samantha Regier and her obvious infatuation with the lawman. Angie's face burned to think of it. But it was his fault. He shouldn't have signaled her soul that day in Nogales. If he did…

Lance spent the day with Samantha and his father. Strangely the elder Kincaid loved Arizona. Lance assured him it was because they were having the mildest spring weather since he had been there. Daytime temperatures stayed below ninety, which was unusual.

The next morning Lillian called Yoshio to bring the carriage around. It pleased Chantry that Lance had created a comfortable home with all the amenities. He was not the savage they had all feared he was.

Lance carried the bags out to the coach. He said good-bye to his father and Samantha. She sat in the carriage, looking as pitiful as she had a few days after her parents died.

"I'll see what's keeping Mrs. L. She might need my help."

Lance walked back into the house. Mrs. Lillian chatted with Yoshio. "They're waiting."

Yoshio picked up Samantha's bonnet, forgotten on the sideboard although in plain sight, and ran out to give it to her.

Mrs. Lillian reached out and touched Lance's arm to stop him, noting the throb of tension in him, knowing she had caught him at exactly the right moment. He was vulnerable now, even more so than before.

In spite of his unwillingness to please his family in its hopes and dreams for his future, Lance loved them, and having his father, Samantha, and Mrs. L. go was taking its toll on him. Deep grooves on either side of his mouth were white with strain. His breathing was quick and shallow. He felt Samantha's pain deeply and hated good-byes. They lived in a time of sudden, unexplained deaths. Lance, of all the Kincaid children, knew that each parting could be the last. Lillian had always known it as well. And had acted accordingly. Each time one of her brood left her, she looked into that child's eyes and said I love you instead of good-bye.

Admiring the power and strength she felt in Lance, she hugged him and stepped back. "You are strong and capable. You will make some woman a fine husband."

"Is that a Danish curse you just put on me?"

"Perhaps," she said, enjoying the warm light that kindled in his fine eyes. Sobering, she squeezed his arms. "Have I ever asked you for anything twice before?"

"No, ma'am."

"Would I ask this if it were not important to me?"

"No, ma'am."

She could see him beginning to cry inside. Nothing gave it away on the surface—no tears—but she never looked on the surface. He had never truly cried on the surface. Lance lived deep inside himself.

"Find Gilbert and make your peace with him."

"What if I can't find him?"

"If you set your mind that you want to find him, you will find him. Begin to watch for signs of him. Sooner or later he will let us know where he is. The universe will help you."

Lance was not put off by Mrs. Lillian's presuming to know how the universe worked. He was accustomed to her delvings into the occult. As a child he had accompanied her to various readers, astrologers, palmists, and healers.

"There some urgency?" he asked, filled with dread.

"No and yes. Write to me when you have good news."

"I need a favor in return."

"And what might that be?" she asked, feeling the tension in him, glad to do anything to relieve it.

He wanted to beg her not to die, but he couldn't. It would sound childish and ridiculous. And it wouldn't make a damned bit of difference. "Nothing, Mrs. Lillian. I'll see you next year…"

She pulled his head down and gave him a fierce little hug. "Perhaps sooner than that now that your father has seen Arizona."

CHAPTER FIVE

Saturday, May 15, 1880

Was that a scream?

Angie quieted Pumpkin with her hand and strained to hear a repeat of what had sounded like a scream. Smelling of sweat, leather, and dirt, hot from the ride out to the ranch, the mare stamped and snorted. Dogs barked in the distance. Flies buzzed in the late afternoon air.

Lily was not in the pagoda. Red, blue, and gold paper lanterns fluttered from the roof overhang of Lily's house. The lightweight China house in the distance belonged to Chung Tu. Its exotic curving rooftrees tickled the hot air.

Only moments before, Angie had sent Sabbath Turk back to the ranch. Frowning, she squirmed in the saddle, both impatient and reluctant to continue her ride into town. Sarah would put *The Tea Time News* to bed today, and Angie hadn't finished setting type for the children's section. She should urge Pumpkin forward. Sarah waited for copy. But Angie heard it again. A shrill scream, filled with anger and terror.

Sure of her direction now, Angie kicked Pumpkin's flanks, and the palomino leapt forward. The mare hurtled across the road and around the corner of the house. Lily struggled against a man who had pinned her to the ground.

"Leave her alone!" Angie shouted, and reined Pumpkin.

The man looked around at Angie; surprise contorted his thin face as he recognized her. "Get the hell out of here!" he yelled. "This ain't no place for a white woman."

"Get off her!"

"Mind your own damned business!" He rolled off the girl and stood up. Straightening his clothes, he mumbled something to Lily that Angie couldn't make out.

Lily pulled her tunic down over her breasts and straightened the loose-fitting ankle-length trousers that had become twisted around her shapely legs. She scooted backward, her lovely face reflecting disgust, outrage, and fear.

"Rufe Martin, you should know better than to be over here in the first place," Angie said, settling into her saddle. Martin was a bully, but he would not hurt her or continue his assault on Lily now that he had been found out.

Martin shot a furious glance at Lily, who struggled to her feet. Ignoring Martin, looking beyond him at the new barn, its wood raw and yellow in the sunlight, Lily's face contorted into a scream. Rufe struck Lily with his open hand. She fell backward and sprawled lifeless as a rag doll.

"You bully!" Angie gasped, anger quick and hot in her. "Are you crazy!" She dismounted and ran to Lily's side.

"Just a damned chink," Martin growled. "Don't know why you're getting all het up about a heathen *chinee*," he sneered, furious at being thwarted. He started toward Angie. "Your brother lets you run around buttin' into men's business, does he? You better git 'fore I tell him I seen you here!"

"You come with me, and I will," Angie countered, frightened but unwilling to leave the girl alone with him. She knelt between Lily and Rufe Martin and inspected Lily. The girl appeared unconscious, but she was not bleeding.

Angie had gone to grade school with Martin. He had always been a bully, but as a female, Angie had been immune to his harsher tricks. He had pulled her hair and teased her, but he had never gotten rough with her.

A scuffling sound followed by a sharp exhalation of breath from the direction of the barn caused Angie to whirl toward it. Angrily Martin picked up his hat. "All right, let's get the hell out of here!" He walked toward two horses, a bay and a dun, nipping at spiky tufts of grass. The bay had a botched, unreadable brand on its flank.

"Who's with you?" Angie asked, suddenly realizing the significance of the two horses.

"Nobody. Are you coming or not?"

Angie grabbed her gun out of its saddle holster, darted past Martin, and ran toward the barn. Martin lunged after her. Angie ran inside before he reached her.

Light slanted in through a lone, paneless window. No more than thirty feet square, the inside of the small barn was dim and shadowy. It smelled of new wood, dust, chicken droppings, and hay. Overhead, a chicken clucked and flapped its wings. Straw filtered down through cracks.

A corn crib sat in the middle of the dirt floor. The barn was otherwise empty. Had she imagined that quick sound? An animal perhaps?

Behind her, the barn door slammed shut. Outside, the crossbar dropped into place with a thump, locking the door. Storm shutters slammed over the window, and another crossbar clanked into place, locking the window.

"Rufe Martin, you let me out of here!"

Angie rushed to peer through a wide crack in the wood. Outside, still slumped in the grass, only Lily was in sight. Pumpkin snorted and pawed the dirt. Where was Martin?

Angie checked the walls for a way out. Nothing presented itself. On the other side of the wall, she heard a sloshing sound. The sharp smell of kerosene filtered in to her.

"Let me out, Rufe Martin! You can't get away with this! I know who you are!" she screamed. Smoke and burning resin quickly overwhelmed the barn smells.

Tawny flames leapt and climbed the walls. Smoke filled the barn and burned her eyes. Coughing and blinded, she pounded on the window until her hand felt raw. Tears streamed out of her stinging eyes. She remembered her weapon and lifted the gun over her head. She fired once, then realized she could use her bullets to better advantage. Stung by the smoke, unable to open her eyes, she groped her way to the window and pushed the gun against the wood, where she hoped the crossbar would be. She fired and pounded on the wood and fired again until the hammer clicked on an empty chamber. The window did not budge.

Coughing uncontrollably, Angie fell to her knees and collapsed forward. Beneath the billowing smoke, flames leapt and danced. Pumpkin's sharp screams called to her, and she struggled to stand, but nothing worked. She never should have sent Sabbath Turk back to the ranch. Laramee would be furious with her…

Six men perched on the wooden rails while two others darted and danced around a bucking horse. A lone rider flailed in the saddle. The horse, an enormous white and black speckled stallion, jumped and kicked up with his hindquarters.

Lance groaned in anticipation. Usually this would result in the rider landing on the cantle of the saddle instead of in the seat. Two weeks recovery time—minimum. But this young man, yelling like a wild Indian, found his seat and sunk his spurs into the horse's flanks.

The horse screamed and switched to buck-jumping, plunging, and leaping. When that didn't work, he threw himself against the corral railing. The young man lifted his leg out of the way and rode à la Comanche, clinging to one side like an Indian, until the horse gave up and tried something else. Arching his back, the big horse crawfished, pinwheeled, pitched, and still the cowboy stuck like a burr.

"Haul hell outta that shuck, boy!" one of the fence riders yelled, slapping his thigh with his hat.

"That hoss is gonna warp his backbone!" another one shouted.

"Ride that crow hopper, Laramee!"

Men shouted and waved their hats. Lance stopped Nunca beside the corral. Each man glanced his way, then ignored him.

In the corral the horse sunfished in a circle, then buck-jumped, and the rider, caught off guard, fell into the dirt. Two men grabbed the horse's head, and the wrangler, cursing loudly and creatively, leapt onto its back again.

"That Laramee shore knows how to air his lungs, don't he?" one of the fence riders chortled. "They jest sets on his tongue as easy as a hoss fly riding a mule's ear."

The horse tore loose from its captors and soared up, twisting in midair. Horse and rider crashed to the ground in a heap of sweat, muscle, and dust. The huge convulsing beast rolled over in the dirt. The wrangler leapt nimbly aside, waited until the horse scrambled to its feet then vaulted quickly onto its back again. Truly furious now, the horse lowered its head, shook itself, then stretched out in a run that took him soaring over the far corral fence. Waving his hat, the one called Laramee looked content to settle in for a long run.

"Tight as a new scab, ain't he?" one man admired above the raucous din. Patiently Lance waited for someone to notice him. Finally the young man nearest Lance turned to face him.

"Yes, sir. What can we do for you?"

"I'm looking for A. B. Logan."

The man's eyebrows rose. "A. B. Logan? This be personal or business?" he asked suspiciously.

"Business."

"Business business?"

Puzzled, Lance nodded.

The young man cleared his throat. "You got a name?"

"Yep."

The man flushed. "Mind telling me what it is?"

"Nope."

Flustered, but mindful that with Laramee gone he was host to a stranger in their midst, Walker straightened his shoulders, accepting his role as representative of the Boxer brand with the same reluctance he accepted the other hardships of a cowboy's life. He hesitated to reveal Miss Angie's whereabouts to a stranger, but he knew Sabbath Turk would not allow anyone to bother Miss Angie.

This stranger did not look like the trail trash that occasionally wandered through seeking a free meal and a soft bunk. The penetrating blue eyes beneath the expensive Stetson had none of the shadows or the shiftiness Walker had come to associate with men bellying through the brush ahead of the law. The chestnut gelding between his legs was one of the sleekest, finest-looking horses he had ever seen, so beautiful Walker wanted to reach out and touch him to see if the hide was as silky as it looked. The holster on the stranger's thigh was tied with a slender rawhide strip, possibly indicating a gunman, but, to his credit, his horse was well cared for and rigged with a fine handstitched Texas saddle.

In the final analysis, it was the man's demeanor more than anything else that caused Walker to supply the requested information.

"Went thataway," he said, pointing in the direction of a rutted wagon trail that faded into a vast stretch of gently rolling plain. "Into Durango by way of the Chinese village on the south forty. Down where the creek runs water."

"Much obliged. Name's Kincaid. Lance Kincaid."

The man leaned over and extended a work-roughened hand. Grinning, they shook hands. "Walker's my name," he said. "When you get to Durango, stop in at *The Tea Time News*."

"Much obliged."

Lance stopped where the creek ran water to let Nunca drink. A dozen houses dotted the meadow between the creek and the town. Bold cumulus clouds, pure white against a crisp blue sky, floated in a southeasterly direction. The air smelled of smoke. The meadow as alive with birds and flying insects.

Snorting his satisfaction, Nunca raised his head and walked out of the water.

Bullets fired close together kicked up dirt in front of them. Lance drew his gun and turned Nunca. A small building, previously hidden from view, was in flames. No one moved in the yard. Where had the shots come from?

Without waiting for an answer Lance kicked Nunca into a gallop. Pain from the long ride was like a toothache in his side. High-pitched screams of a terrified horse sounded over the roar of the fire and Nunca's pounding hooves. In the yard a palomino reared and stamped and a young Chinese woman lay as if tossed there. Near the barn a wall of heat drove Lance back. He leapt off Nunca, bent low, and threw the barn door bar out of the way.

A body sprawled in the dirt under the closed window. Engulfed in flames, the roof threatened to fall. Lance took a deep breath and charged into the burning barn. He located arms and flung the body over his shoulder. The body was amazingly light, but fingers of fire shot out from his side. He fled the burning barn and ran until his knees buckled under him, tumbling him and his burden onto the grass.

Behind them the roof crashed down with a roar, sending a shower of flames twenty feet into the air and over the yard, starting dozens of small grass fires. Groaning, Lance struggled into an upright position. Beside him a young woman lay on her back, one slender, tawny arm across her body, the other flung out at her side. Long, shiny wheat-blond hair fanned out around her face. Thick dark lashes lay on soot-streaked cheeks. The pulse in her neck pumped against his fingers. He breathed a sigh of relief.

The palomino walked over and nuzzled her face.

Cool wet lips nipped at Angie's cheek. Hot breath snorted into her ear. Her mind flickered awake. A bell started to clang in the distance. Voices shouted in Chinese. Angie's blurred vision slowly came into focus. Pumpkin leaned over her, her eyes filled with concern.

She patted Pumpkin, who snorted, then walked away to munch at the spiky grass.

Grimacing, the man next to her moved. It was Kincaid, his smooth tan skin rich and ruddy with heat.

"How did I get out?" Angie looked around. In the background, Chinese men, women, and children formed a water brigade. Others had finally noticed the fire. Kincaid's gaze, about to move to Lily's slumped body, paused, searched Angie's face, and a spark of recognition leapt like a flame in his blue eyes, only to be extinguished a second later.

"Angie Logan," he drawled, a grin spreading across his face. "Sure hope you don't mind that I carried you out of there without asking. I figured you'd probably want to get a picture of that roof falling…" His whiskey-tinged tenor was low and raspy. Her heart flip-flopped in her chest.

Angie grinned. "I think I can forgive you."

Lance nodded. He should help her up. Men shouted in the distance. Lance held out his hand to Angie. Her slender hand was warm and small in his. "Are you all right?"

Angie nodded.

Lily struggled up into a sitting position. She saw the barn and screamed. Chinese dropped their buckets and ran to her side.

"What…?" Angie began.

Lance stopped her with his hand. Ignoring the ache in his side, he stood and walked nearer to the Chinese girl, straining to listen over the roar of the fire and the shouts of onlookers. Tears streamed down the girl's cheeks as she alternately cried and gasped out her story. She spoke the Cantonese dialect he had learned from Gil Lee.

Lance walked back to Angie's side. "Did you see her father in the barn?"

Horrified, glancing at the totally consumed barn, Angie shook her head. "You speak Chinese?"

"An odd word here and there. You see anyone inside?"

"No, I thought I heard someone. That's why I went in."

The men had separated into two groups. White men milled around and watched; Chinese passed buckets of water from the well beside the house and threw them on the various small fires that burned in the yard.

A man walked around the burning barn to get a better look, stumbled, and knelt down for a closer inspection. He cried out, "Hey! There's a dead man over here!"

The water brigade disintegrated as people rushed to see who it was.

"Stay here," Lance said.

Ignoring his advice, Angie brushed past him. She elbowed her way through the crowd, saw Rufe Martin sprawled in the grass—his body twisted and boneless—and turned away, sickened and confused. A strong warm hand caught her by the wrist and pulled her away.

"I warned you…"

Expressive and commanding, her forceful brown eyes stopped him. "What?" he asked.

"That man, Rufe Martin, is the one who locked me in the barn. Lily didn't set the fire…who could have?"

"Start at the beginning and tell me what happened."

Angie complied, the words coming in a rush as she remembered. When she stopped, Lance took her elbow and led her toward his horse, away from the crowd.

His hand on the inside of her arm caused a warm tingling sensation to spread through her. Since she'd been home she was accustomed to cowboys too shy and socially inept to even dream of touching her. Kincaid did so as if it were expected. Naturally. As if his touch were nothing special in itself. What was Lance Kincaid doing here in Durango?

"I saw two horses. I asked Rufe about them. He got angry and agreed to leave with me. The bay must have belonged to whoever came here with Rufe."

"Is the horse still here?"

Angie surveyed the yard. The dun was there. "No. That's Martin's dun. The bay's gone."

"Would you know that bay again if you saw it?"

"Maybe. But it was so ordinary…except for a botched brand I noticed. They must have come here together. Why would he kill Rufe?"

Lance shrugged. "Why would he try to kill you? That palomino belong to you?"

Angie nodded.

Lance grinned. "Haven't seen a pumpkin-skinned horse in a long time. What do you call her?"

Angie grimaced. "Pumpkin. I named her when I was ten…"

"What were you doing here? Don't you have someone to keep you out of trouble? We should appoint a committee or something…"

Charmed with the moment and the way his eyes crinkled against the bright sunlight and pulled down slightly at the corners, Angie waved her arm at Laramee's ranch. "This is part of my brother's ranch."

Then Lance understood. This skinny, big-eyed girl, the photographer that kept turning up everywhere he went, was A. B. Logan. *She* had written the letter that brought him here.

"I was expecting a man—a powerful old coot of a cattleman as a matter of fact."

Tiny horizontal lines creased her smooth forehead.

He laughed. "A. B. Logan."

"Governor Frémont sent you? All by yourself?"

Lance nodded. "By way of Captain McNamara…"

Angie shook her head and sighed. "One man? I tell the governor that anti-Chinese sentiment in a town of two thousand has exploded into genocide, and he sends one man? I hope you're as good as they think. You're going to need to be…"

"One town, one man," Lance said. He grinned and touched the brim of his hat.

Angry shouts interrupted them. Men they had forgotten were squared off, whites against Chinese, yelling, waving sticks. Kincaid unsheathed his gun and fired into the air. Startled men turned to face him.

"Get home where you belong! My next bullet is a corpse-maker!"

Angie blinked. Instantly wilder and more aggressive than a rioting mob, Kincaid amazed her. He had gone from loose-limbed and relaxed to smolderingly hostile and threatening. Men stepped back without meaning to. Probably because Kincaid looked as if he had unleashed only a tiny portion of the violence and intensity stored in his sturdy body.

Was he always so volatile? So tightly wound he could explode at a moment's notice? Most men had to build up to such action. At least now she understood the throbbing intensity she sensed in him—it was the pulsation of his fiery, volcanic core. He advanced, and a quiver went through the crowd.

Men grumbled and tried to get up the nerve to defy him. Kincaid fished his badge out of his pocket and flashed it at the crowd.

"These chinks killed Rufe Martin!" a man yelled, waving his stick at the Chinese who backed away from Kincaid.

"I was the first one here," Kincaid growled, waving his gun slightly to clear a path. "Martin's killer left here on a bay horse! You know a Chinese who rides a bay horse, you let me know. Otherwise, get on home! I'll take care of this."

Coupled with Kincaid's brusk impatience, the idea of one of the Chinese, notoriously clumsy around horses, actually riding one was sufficient. Grumbling and intimidated, white men dropped their makeshift weapons and started drifting back toward town in groups of two or three.

Lance strode back to Angie's side. "I'll take you home," he said. He turned her with the firm pressure of his warm hand on her waist.

"I never expected to see you again," she marveled, feeling like a fool for admitting it aloud. What on earth was wrong with her?

"Can't imagine why not. Every time you turn around, I'm there." His eyes sparkled with humor.

Kincaid took her arm and started to lead her away. "What about Lily?" she asked, hanging back.

"She's fine. Her people will take care of her now."

"And later?" Angie persisted. "What if he comes back?"

Kincaid's gaze flicked from her lips to her eyes. He shook his head. "If he'd wanted to kill her, she'd be dead." He took her arm.

Unwilling to give up such an important point, Angie refused to budge. "I'm not going to leave her here to get killed."

Her faint perfume wafted up to his nostrils. Angie Logan defied him and tempted him. His mind should have been working on logical phrases to soothe her, but it wasn't. It wondered if her plump little breasts, so clearly outlined beneath her cotton blouse, would be as tawny-gold as the rest of her skin.

"I don't think the killer will try again today."

Angie ignored Kincaid and walked over to where Lily stood surrounded by Chinese. "Are you okay?"

Lily nodded, but her eyes brimmed with tears. She glanced at the burning barn and her chin crumpled. Angie stepped close and pulled Lily into her arms. "Poor thing." Lily sobbed quietly in her arms. When her tears subsided, Angie loosened her hold on the girl. "I'll come back this evening. Do you need anything?"

Lily shook her head no. Angie hugged Lily again and then rejoined Kincaid. He helped her into her saddle.

The Chinese stood in small groups. Regimented by their loose thigh-length blue tunics and baggy ankle-length blue trousers, they watched in silence as Lance and Angie rode away.

Angie glanced at the pile of smoldering embers that had been the barn and shuddered. Lily's father lay beneath the rubble. Except for Kincaid's arrival, Angie also would have died there…

She rode beside Kincaid slowly because he seemed content with that pace. Grateful to be alive, she stroked Pumpkin.

They rode beneath a large, overhanging oak tree, one of the few in Durango, and then out into the hot sunlight again. Kincaid reined his horse. Angie halted Pumpkin beside him.

On a Saturday afternoon Durango bustled, a busy metropolis. Bare-chested Indians, dusty Chinese miners, hungry prospectors, packers, desperadoes, gamblers, and cowboys walked or rode through the town, heading for one or more of the twenty bawdy houses—saloons, gambling dens, or bordellos—to relieve themselves of their boredom, their sobriety, and their money.

Durango sat on a great natural pathway of commerce. The valuable route from Sonora into the Gila Valley by way of the Santa Cruz River made the town an important stagecoach center. Durango supplied the Papago Indian reservation and Fort Lowell southeast of it.

A reddish dust cloud hung over the busy street. Angie watched the ragged flow of buggies, horses, mules, and wagons, and patted Pumpkin's neck. "I could bring Lily and her mother and their serving girl to my house," she persisted. "They shouldn't stay alone."

Lost in thought, Lance glanced sideways at her. "What?"

"Lily, the Chinese girl…"

"Chinese turn to Chinese in time of trouble."

Angie expelled a frustrated breath. Kincaid was not going to help. She would finish her work at *The Tea Time News* and come back herself.

"I need to check in with the local marshal," he said, his voice husky. "You mind telling me which way I go from here?"

"Marshal Ramo is a crook," she said. "Otherwise I wouldn't have written to Frémont. If you believe anything he tells you…"

Angie understood the look on Kincaid's face and stopped. Kincaid was a man who would listen and draw his own conclusions.

"Follow me." She threaded her horse between the horsemen, the heavy drays, and the rattling buckboards that had flooded into town on this Saturday afternoon.

CHAPTER SIX

Saturday, May 15, 1880

Angie watched Lance dismount, tie his horse, and walk stiffly up the two steps. He stopped at the doorway, his hand on the doorknob.

"I'll be at *The Tea Time News*, just up the street, if you want to stop in…"

Lance gazed into her compelling eyes. He was strongly attracted to Angie, but something, a butterfly brush of foreboding, urged him away from her.

The tiny flutter reminded him of another time. When he was ten years old, he watched Blue Max, his beloved Siamese blue point, walk out the front door. That same light brush of foreboding touched him, almost imperceptibly, and he knew he would never see Max alive again, but a veil dropped between him and that knowledge as if it had not been meant for him. Throughout the day and night his mind hid that information from him. The next morning he found Blue Max dead behind the house, run over by a carriage.

Lance nodded to Angie and stepped into the jail. The place smelled like dirty socks and sour wine. A half-dozen men snored in the row of cells along the back wall. Another man, seated at the desk, glanced up from a newspaper. His glance darted over Kincaid. "Yeah?"

"I'm looking for Marshal Ramo."

"I'm Ramo. Who might you be?"

Lance reached into his shirt pocket and pulled out his badge. He flashed it at Ramo and then dropped it back in. "Lance Kincaid."

Ramo's eyes flashed hatred. Lance ignored his response. Rangers had to expect an occasional hostile local lawman. "Two men were killed on the outskirts of town…"

"The hell you say? You do it?"

He repeated the story Angie had told him about the events at the barn. Mention of the dead man's name jolted Ramo. "You knew Rufe Martin?" Lance asked.

"Hell, yes! Everybody knows old Rufe. Damned shame!"

"He live around here?"

"Stayed at the hotel mostly, hung around the Baquero."

"He work at anything?"

"He did odd jobs. Whatever come up."

A saddletramp. Kincaid waited.

"So what are you doing in Durango?" Ramo asked.

"Looking into the deaths of three Chinese brothers," Lance said, taking a shot in the dark.

Alarmed, Ramo growled, "That's been done." He did not want interference now. "I'll be making an arrest shortly. When you get back to your outfit, tell Frémont we don't need any help from outsiders." Ramo picked up his hat. "I'll take a look-see."

Kincaid left, and Ramo jammed his hat on and headed for the Baquero. Cort Armstrong lounged behind the bar. Ramo motioned him into the back room.

"We got trouble," Ramo said.

"What kinda trouble?" Cort asked, sitting down in the chair behind his desk and putting his feet up on the mahogany.

"A goddamned ranger, that's what."

"So?"

At times like this Ramo hated Armstrong. Cort had a habit of acting so damned knowledgeable. You could sneak up behind him and set him on fire, and he'd pretend he knew what you were doing all the time. Cort's judgment was as faulty as Union honor, but he'd flat out die before he'd admit it.

"Someone killed Rufe Martin. It happened at the chink's place…" It delighted Ramo to be able to surprise Armstrong in this shocking way.

Cort's mouth tightened. "You think it was Johnny?"

"Who else?"

"Anyone recognize him?"

"No. They think Rufe and the chink killed each other, sounds like to me."

"What brought the ranger to Durango?"

"He's here about the three chinks," Ramo said angrily.

"There's more," Cort said, reading Ramo.

"He's the ranger that shot Johnny."

Cort frowned.

It pleased Ramo that Cort's face was showing signs of age and his hairline was creeping back. One day soon Cort'd be paying whores, too, just like the rest of 'em.

"You shouldn't have waited so damned long to spring it. I've told you that before," he said, raising a toothpick to his lips. Cort knew Ramo hadn't sprung it yet because he was scared. He should have done it right away, as soon as the three chinks showed up dead, but he had balked. Now it was getting harder, not easier.

"Easy to see that now," Ramo growled. "So what the hell do we do?"

"You ride over and find out what happened there today." Irritated that their plans were becoming more unwieldy by the moment, Cort stood up. "Hurry back. I want to know what the hell is going on."

Lance took Nunca to the livery stable. He gave detailed instructions about Nunca's care to Atillo, the young Mexican boy on duty, then turned to leave. Angie Logan stepped out of a stall, directly into his path. Her palomino snorted.

"I didn't realize you'd get here so soon. You want to meet my friend, Sarah?"

Lance smiled and followed Angie out into the bright sunlight. Strangely, the reluctance he felt about seeing her again dissolved in her presence. He felt elated and relieved, as if he had already been away from her too long.

On the busy street a slender Chinese man in apricot silk robes stepped from a sedan chair just set down by four unusually sturdy Chinese dressed in the blue fabric worn by Chinese peasants. Sallow and wrinkled, no taller than a twelve-year-old boy, he wore a black silk top hat and large black-rimmed glasses that perched on the tip of his pug nose. His queue hung down to his ankles. A well-manicured hand raised a cigar to his thin lips. In Chinese he spoke to his carriers and walked quickly into the tobacco store next to the livery stable.

"Who's that?" Lance asked.

"Chung Tu. Everyone calls him Tu. He seems to have power among the Chinese."

Lance made a mental note to call on Tu. "How long have people here been stirred up against the Chinese?" he asked, glancing at Angie. She'd washed her face. In the strong sunlight her hair gleamed with golden fire. Thick, dark lashes framed her dark eyes with precise elegance.

"Not too long. When I left three years ago there were only a few Chinese in Durango. Now there are three hundred."

Lance nodded. That matched what he already knew. Initially, before their ranks had begun to swell, Chinese arriving in California and Nevada had been welcomed with tolerance, curiosity, and, on occasion, enthusiasm. They filled a need for laborers and domestics in growing frontier towns.

As their numbers increased, tolerance decreased, particularly among those who saw the Chinese as rivals for jobs. The Chinese worked hard and usually for less pay than whites. Within a few years of their first arrival in the territories, the Chinese had become targets of random, unprovoked violence.

After the Civil War, they'd become scapegoats for the territories' economic troubles. In 1877 part of San Francisco's Chinatown had been destroyed by an angry mob. The same thing happened in Los Angeles, and, on a smaller scale, in other Western towns and cities.

Because they did not intend to stay in America, the Chinese made little effort to learn English or American customs. With their picturesque costumes and pigtails, they were easy targets. Drawn originally by promises of gold, their only reason for coming to America was to make enough money to go back to China and live in prosperity.

At *The Tea Time News*, Sarah was bent over a tray of lead type, her hands black with ink. A formal introduction was Angie's opportunity to watch Kincaid's reaction to Sarah and her voluptuous figure. Nothing untoward happened. Kincaid's blue eyes were polite and admiring, but with as demure a look as any man ever gave a woman.

"Mr. Kincaid is an Arizona ranger. He came in answer to my letter. Sarah owns *The Tea Time News*. Her father owns the Baquero Saloon."

"Oh, you're the one in the pictures," Sarah said, obviously pleased to meet the handsome ranger. She talked over her shoulder and scrubbed the ink off her hands, then took out a box of first aid supplies; she insisted on cleaning Angie's scratches. Though capable of tending her own wounds, Angie surrendered with good grace.

Next to the printing press, Kincaid tilted his chair against the wall, his long legs propped on another chair. He breathed slowly and regularly.

Sarah twisted the warm water out of her washcloth and took Angie's hand in hers. "I know what Del Ramo will claim happened, that the old man was killed by members of the tong."

Lance chuckled. Pain jarred his left side. "How will he explain

Martin's presence there?" he asked, scowling.

Angie rolled her eyes in exasperation. "A coincidence! What else?"

"Who'll believe that?" Sarah countered.

"All the people who believed it when the three Chinese brothers were killed," Angie said, expelling a frustrated breath. "Or pretended to."

Lance smiled at their vehemence. Even aroused, Angie had the tender look of a dark-eyed daisy. There was a curious insouciance and wistfulness about her that intrigued him. He had the feeling that this blond beauty knew instinctively how things worked.

Sarah, with her provocative green eyes and her seductive, gypsy look was softer—more vulnerable. Sarah reminded him of Maggie, who groped her way toward solutions, one mistake at a time.

"So are you going to write an editorial about the injustice of it all?" he asked, smiling.

Angie soaked up Kincaid's attention, and her bottom lip started to tremble. "We can't," Angie said huskily, her anger directed as much at her betraying mouth as at the injustice of Sarah's situation. "Didn't you see the sign?"

Lance chuckled and was instantly sorry he had. Pain knifed upward, reminding him again not to laugh. "That looked like the name of the newspaper, not a policy statement."

"Well, you're wrong. It's a policy statement," Sarah said with embarrassment. "My father made that a condition of ownership. This *is* a society paper."

Lance resisted the urge to shrug. "He may change his mind." The pain in his side needed attention. He decided he'd have a beer—to quench his thirst *and* numb some of his pain—and then check into the hotel.

Kincaid stood up carefully and bid Angie and Sarah good day, fended off Sarah's offers of more hospitality, and started across the busy street to the Baquero.

Angie walked to the window and watched Lance's broad, tapering back as he maneuvered across the road. A warm tingle suffused her chest.

"You didn't tell me you knew him," Sarah said accusingly.

"I didn't?" Angie shrugged. "Well, I don't really *know* him. I just met him once. You knew I had taken pictures of him…"

"When he looked at you, you blushed as red as a desert peony!" Sarah said, watching Angie closely.

"I did not!" Angie said, turning away.

Sarah rushed to hug her. "I didn't mean to embarrass you," Sarah said, feeling slightly elated. Angie had never paid any real attention to any man in Durango as long as she'd known her.

Angie turned to her desk. "Back to work," she sighed.

"We are enjoying enormous success," Sarah said, tapping the ledger. They had printed two editions and sold every copy they printed. Angie's idea for a children's section had made the difference. All a child had to do was scribble a note to *The Tea Time News*, and Angie would find a way to display it to advantage with the child's name, sometimes with the mother's and father's names as well. But could this level of interest be maintained over a period of time? That was the question.

The paper had become instantly popular. Every child so honored had a proud mother who bought numerous copies to mail to her friends and relatives.

Sarah walked to the window. "Angie! Look. A fight!"

Angie grabbed her wagon, parked next to the door, and pulled it outside. Sarah helped her lower the wagon and camera to the road, and they pulled it across deep ruts toward the Baquero.

Grateful to survive the trip across the busy street, Lance walked north on Rio Street to the Baquero and shouldered his way through the swinging doors. The saloon smelled of sawdust, cigarettes, beer, whiskey, sweat, and rum. At the far end of the wide room a lone man plinked on a piano. Clustered around a gambling table and the long bar, men laughed and talked.

Lance was momentarily blinded by the darkened interior after the bright sunlight, and his right arm brushed a man's shoulder.

"Hey!" the man yelled. "Look where the hell you're going!"

Lance allowed his forward momentum to continue for three long strides. He moved easily, without any perceptible sign of tension. He changed direction slightly so that when he stopped and turned to face the man, he could see him and everyone else in the room as well. His back fronted the vacant tables near the street window.

"Sorry." Lance nodded to acknowledge the man—instantly hostile and aggressive—who had turned to face him.

"Clumsy bastard!" The usual saloon sounds died away.

Lance realized his mistake too late. He should have known better than to visit the local bucket of blood. Only a fool would go in a saloon not prepared to fight.

"Don't suppose you would care to join me in a drink?" Lance asked, his tone neutral. His gaze raked over the man dressed, except for the functional Smith & Wesson, like a dandy. Tied with a slender leather thong around his thigh, the gun reassured Lance. Gunmen didn't usually engage in fistfights. At the moment, a gunfight suited him better than trying to protect his sensitive midriff from hammering fists.

The dandy reached over, grabbed one of the ladderback chairs in front of the window, and brought it smashing down over a large brass spittoon. Wood splintered over half the room.

"Guess not," Lance muttered.

A Chinese man carrying an armload of towels stopped abruptly at the door of the saloon, his hooded eyes narrowing as he took in the situation. He stepped back to leave.

"Hey, Smalley, look behind you!" one of the spectators yelled.

Smalley whirled around. The Chinese man smiled an earnest, apologetic smile and mumbled a string of unrecognizable Chinese words. Bowing, he backed away.

"Hop Wo! Where the hell you going?" Smalley growled.

"Come back rater, prease. No lush." Hop Wo bowed again and smiled in apology, his slim body lost in the loose blue tunic that came to his knees. He knelt down beside his bamboo baskets to replace the towels he had been about to deliver.

Cursing, Smalley stepped through the swinging doors and grabbed the Chinese by his shirtfront. To Smalley, all "China boys" were cut from a single mold. The uniformity of their blue garb, Oriental features, single braid, and cussed politeness was so great that one China boy was exactly like the next, but completely unlike anyone else in Durango.

"Who the hell told you to use the front door?" he growled, jerking the man forward.

His slender body limp and resigned, Hop Wo's face reflected no emotion.

"Pigtailed China boys use the back door! You understand that, you slit-eyed bastard? How many times I gotta tell you?" Smalley punctuated his sentences by shaking Hop Wo so hard his head snapped back and forth and his queue lashed around like a snake. Laughing, Smalley threw the Chinese back against the wall. White towels spilled into the grit and dust of the barroom floor.

"Ain't nothing to this critter—just a goddamned hairball been skinned and braided. Don't stand no higher'n a wildcat's ankle…Now look what you done, you clumsy bastard!" Smalley kicked the towels out of his way, skidding them across the grimy floor. "Ought to kick your scrawny ass for that."

Men laughed and shouted lewd comments, egging him on. Grinning, Smalley picked up Hop Wo and hung him on the coat hook on the wall beside the swinging doors. A wild roar of laughter filled the room. Hop Wo kicked and flailed.

Lance sighed. His side ached. Hot fingers of pain spread out around his kidney. He didn't want to get into a fight with this bully, but he couldn't walk away and let the hapless Chinese take the brunt of what he himself had started. "Put him down," Lance said, his voice conversational except for an edge of hardness tightening it.

Smalley stopped laughing. "You hankering to take his place?"

"You willing to die for the sake of brag?" Lance countered.

The men fell quiet suddenly.

Cort Armstrong, owner of the Baquero, grinned. Big, muscular, and a savage fighter, Cort could have stopped the impending fracas if he'd wanted to, but there was something about this gravel-voiced stranger that made him more curious than he was protective of his property. He was eager to see how the stranger would fare, bracing Neville Smalley, who was Ramo's deputy marshal, and, next to Laramee Logan, the toughest brawler this side of Chihuahua.

"Ain't too many lunkhaids willing to die for a scrawny, filthy, chicken-stealing coolie!" Smalley sneered, savoring the fact that this stranger didn't know he was taking on a lawman.

Lance's throat was aching for a swallow of something cold. He was tired and hot. Pain gnawed at his side. "Let the man down."

Two men broke away from the bar and sauntered over to stand on either side of the one called Smalley.

Smalley grinned. "You can't take all three of us."

"Whether you're the only one who dies or one of two or three who die ain't going to make a hell of a lot of difference to you," Lance said, grinning suddenly.

Seth Edwards, standing at the bar next to Cort, pulled his chin whiskers and nodded his head. "Well, I'll be damned if that ain't *hombre de verdad* hisself!" he said in a low whisper.

Frowning, Cort leaned forward. "Who the hell is *hombre de verdad?*"

"That's Mex for the man with the deadly eyes. He's the ranger that brought in those dead rustlers and dumped 'em on the sidewalk in Nogales about a month ago, McNamara's lieutenant...think his name is Kincaid. The one that shot Johnny Winchester."

"You sure?" Cort demanded.

"Sure enough. I seen the story in *The Gazette*. Said Kincaid and Johnny plugged each other and both lived to tell about it. Must not a been much, they're walking around."

Before Cort could decide what to do with this information, Smalley took the matter out of his hands.

"Shit!" Smalley growled. His right hand jabbed out, punching the Chinese in the stomach. The man's knees jerked up, hitting Smalley under the chin. Blood spurted from Smalley's mouth. He staggered back. One of his companions, excited by the blood and activity, put his head down and charged the stranger.

Seeing the man aimed like a battering ram at his midsection, Lance cursed and stepped to the side. Using the man's momentum against him, Lance grabbed him by the scruff of his neck and rammed his head into the wall.

Cursing at the pain the sudden movement cost him, Lance turned in time to see Smalley pick up a chair and smash it across Hop Wo's legs. The crack of bones breaking and a shrill scream of anguish filled the room.

Smalley drew the chair back to strike again.

Kincaid grabbed the chair, along with one of Smalley's hands and tossed chair and man out the door. Smalley landed on the chair, splintering it. Blood spurted out of his nose. He tried to get up, groaned, and fell forward.

Cort watched in amazement. Exultant and savage, Kincaid turned on the other two. He yelled and struck out. Six men wouldn't have been sufficient against him. He used blows that were not like anything Cort had seen before, except that time in San Francisco when two Orientals had demonstrated some crazy way of fighting. Kincaid stepped back to survey his sprawling, senseless attackers.

Cort's eyes narrowed. Kincaid was all horns and rattle. The fight had taken less than a minute.

"Bravo! Bravo!" Sarah and Angie yelled from outside.

Their outburst rankled Cort like a rusty nail in a blister. Sarah had a snootful of rules about how he was supposed to live his life. And while she was careful not to verbalize her ideas, displeasure often shone in her eyes. He hadn't had any peace since he took her on to raise.

The only smart thing he'd ever done was to buy that newspaper. She was so busy now, he enjoyed his freedom without judgment for the first time in ten years. Ed Haskell sold the paper so he could move to San Francisco. Sarah had to ask only once to talk him into buying it for her.

Sudden rage rose up in Cort. His daughter carrying on over a damned Chinaman. Cort's hot Portuguese temper flared, and he slammed his fist onto the bar. "Get the hell back where you belong!" he bellowed.

Embarrassed, Sarah wanted to go inside to speak to her father, but no respectable woman was allowed in a saloon, even if her father owned it. Women could labor at anything they could handle on a farm or a ranch no matter how disgusting or menial. In town they could work as laundresses, teachers, shopkeepers, brewers, photographers, and cooks. A few were tolerated even when they elbowed their way into professions that were traditionally dominated by men. But there were limits.

Angie took two pictures: one of Smalley sprawled on the broken chair and one of Kincaid, carrying the injured Chinese out of the Baquero.

Kincaid put Hop Wo down on the sidewalk. Angie left her camera and knelt beside Hop Wo. "Come help me," Angie pleaded, more to distract Sarah than because she needed help. Blood warmed Angie's fingers and made them slippery. A knot of revulsion moved in her stomach.

"Filthy animal!" Angie hissed, glaring at Neville Smalley sprawled on the sidewalk next to them.

"I'll take care of him," Lance growled.

A crowd started to form around them. Men grumbled their dissatisfaction. Lance stood up, surveyed the angry crowd, and reached into his shirt pocket. He fished out the silver badge. This time he pinned it to his vest.

"Go back to what you were doing!" he yelled.

Cort watched in silent amusement as Andrew Ellington, the town's banker, a man much impressed with his own position and standing in the community, approached Kincaid. Ellington cleared his throat. "Like to talk to you a moment."

His eyes level and patient, holding a look reserved for locals who thought themselves important, Kincaid nodded.

"Name's Andrew Ellington."

"Lance Kincaid." They shook hands.

Cort exchanged a meaningful look with Seth Edwards, who had identified Kincaid. Seth was nodding and smiling.

"Ranger, huh? Well, you can be proud. Fine bunch of men. Doing a good job." Ellington glanced around at the men picking themselves up off the sidewalk. "Nothing can't be rectified, but you've made a small mistake. This man here's our deputy marshal," he said, pointing to Smalley.

Kincaid nodded. "He'll get a fair trial."

Cort could barely contain himself. Ellington's severe face registered shock. His muttonchop whiskers seemed to swell as his expression changed. "You don't understand, Kincaid. I realize you were only doing your job, but you can't go around arresting our deputy. He's a good man. Done a fine job here in Durango."

Kincaid nodded. "I'm sure the judge will take that into account when he sentences him."

Ellington's face flushed. Angry men squeezed out of the Baquero. Kincaid turned away as if the matter were settled. Ellington glowered at Kincaid's back a moment, then he and his two friends pushed past Cort and into the Baquero Saloon.

"He's not going to get away with this," men muttered on all sides, but most of them followed Ellington inside. The rest of the crowd dispersed and wandered into other shops and stores, grumbling their displeasure at the ranger's high-handedness.

Outside, Angie motioned for Atillo. He hurried toward her. Tall and slender, with shoulders already broad and tapering into lean hips, Atillo was half Mexican, half Irish. His father owned the livery stable. Maria, his Mexican mother, had died of smallpox when he was three. Fifteen years old, Atillo had her dark eyes and curly black hair. His face was so richly colored and so handsome that women stared at him without realizing they were.

"Atillo, please fetch Dr. Amberg."

Eager to execute any order from his special friend, Angie Logan, Atillo murmured a soft, "*Sí, señorita*," and turned to comply.

Kincaid stopped him. "Don't bother, *niño*, the Chinese are too smart to use our medical treatment."

Atillo looked to Angie, willing to go in spite of the ranger if she wished it, but Angie shook her head.

Kincaid waved at two Chinese who stood at a respectful distance; they scurried over and knelt down beside the injured man. They whispered excitedly in Chinese, then one of the men unbuttoned his long blue tunic, took it off, and rebuttoned it. They threaded two bamboo poles through the body of the closed shirt to form a makeshift stretcher, then lifted Hop Wo onto it and trotted away.

Cort Armstrong approached Angie. "Can't imagine Laramee Logan is going to appreciate you siding with chinks," he said. "Your brother hates the yellow bastards worse than poison. Can't tell me he don't."

"He does not!" Angie cried.

Cort waved an impatient hand at Angie and rolled his eyes. He looked like he would say more, but Sarah stepped between them.

"Cort…" Sarah begged, her face flaming with color.

"Listen, missy, you may have your own society page, but baby calves don't teach bulls how to graze, and *you* don't tell *me* how to act in public, you got that?"

Angie bit back an angry reply. Sarah and Cort's relationship astounded Angie. She revered her own father and had been loved and adored by him until the day of his death.

Sarah restrained Angie with her glance. Cort Armstrong had fathered Sarah and abandoned her. He returned for her only after her mother had died. Sarah was still grateful, because she couldn't imagine how she would have survived otherwise. But Angie purely hated to see a father abuse his daughter.

Cort stopped yelling and went inside; Sarah's usual rich color receded, leaving her pale. Angie wanted to comfort her, but she knew that Sarah, embarrassed and shaking, would not welcome another public display.

Lance caught Angie Logan's glance. Her lovely eyes held him enthralled for several heartbeats. "Thanks for your help," he finally said.

A tingle quivered her bottom lip. Kincaid nodded at her and turned back to the men on the sidewalk.

Strangely dissatisfied with his gentle dismissal, Angie picked up the wagon tongue and pulled it across the bumpy road. Sarah fell into step beside her.

"I'm glad Laramee wasn't here. He'd have been part of it," Angie said.

"Are you going to the dance tonight?" Sarah asked.

"No. I have things to do tonight. Are you?"

"Laramee will be there," Sarah said, her green eyes suddenly mischievous. "I confess I am not indifferent to seeing him…"

"He's not escorting you?" Angie asked.

"I told him I would try to save him one dance—if he behaves himself."

Sarah was an enigma. Angie had known her for ten years and still understood very little about her. They had been friends since Sarah, a new girl in school, had been assigned the desk next to hers. One day Sarah was looking out the window, daydreaming. The teacher walked up behind her and rapped his cane on her desk. The loud noise, like a pistol shot, terrified Sarah so badly she screamed and fainted, alarming the pompous teacher so badly that he dismissed his class for the day. Angie stayed behind to revive Sarah and take her home. Sarah came down with a heavy cold the next morning and stayed sick for a week. Angie prevailed upon her mother to cook a pot of chicken soup, which Angie delivered. The two girls were inseparable from that time.

"If you fall in love with Lance Kincaid, you can be unhappy like me. Be a nice change for you."

Angie had never been in love with anyone. Every rider who had ever ridden for the Logan Boxer brand had been smitten with her, but she had treated them all like big brothers.

Angie shook her head. "I was spoiled by my father. It'll take one hell of a man to satisfy me," she said, dropping into the vernacular of the cowboy.

"You probably wouldn't be attracted to the wrong man the way I am to your *brother*."

Angie scowled. Laramee was wilder than an Apache warrior and about as predictable, but he was her brother. "You are exceedingly harsh with Laramee…"

"No more so than he deserves." Feeling torn and exposed, Sarah paused. Laramee was the most handsome, appealing man of her acquaintance, but he was a young hothead who would die in a pool of his own blood and break both their hearts. She couldn't think of his inevitable future without bitterness. Unfortunately, even in the face of the future she could still feel the strong tug of his harsh male energy. When Laramee held her in his arms, her heart was powerless to resist him. Her mind still resisted, but only when Laramee wasn't with her.

"Maybe you'll see Kincaid at the social. I'll wager he asks you to dance," Sarah said, changing the subject.

Angie was silent. The thought of dancing with Lance Kincaid again made her quake inside. Good thing she wasn't going.

"I doubt Kincaid will stay in town once he realizes the full extent of what he has done. He half-killed our deputy marshal. No sane man would deliberately incur Del Ramo's and Johnny Winchester's wrath," Angie said. As they reached the sidewalk in front of *The Tea Time News* office, Angie stopped. Crisp white clouds momentarily covered the sun, reminding her how beautiful the desert looked with patches of sunlight and shadow. She had seen a stand of pricklepoppy she would love to have a picture of. "I just want to take one more picture. I haven't taken one shot of the desert," she remarked to Sarah.

But not even the desert could hold Angie's complete attention.

Her thoughts returned unexpectedly to the ill-fated lawman. Kincaid was still healing from the last bullet Johnny Winchester had put in him. Winchester didn't live in Durango, but he visited his cousin, Del Ramo, often enough to keep his memory alive in any man's mind who might consider crossing Ramo.

If Kincaid were as intelligent as he looked he would wire his superior and request soldiers who could ride into Durango fresh and not have half the town against them from the beginning.

If she saw Kincaid again, she would tell him about Ramo and Winchester. That settled, Angie vowed to put the lawman firmly out of her thoughts. Lance Kincaid was too smart a man to stay in Durango.

Ramo tethered his horse in front of the Baquero. Cort saw him, put down the cloth he had been wiping the bar with, and walked toward his office in the back.

Ramo dropped into the chair across from Cort's desk. "The ranger was wrong. The chink didn't die. I scared hell out of him, though. He probably wished he was dead for a minute."

"So, what happened?"

"Unless the old bastard was lying, Johnny and Rufe stopped on their way out of town to rob him. Then Rufe decided to rape the chinkilina. The old bastard went crazy, tried to kill 'em." Ramo stopped. "Reckon Johnny cut Rufe out."

Cort grunted. "Your cousin may be the fastest goddamned gun in the world, but he ain't got shit for brains."

Ramo grinned. He put his feet up on Cort's desk. "That ain't what you said to his face."

Cort snorted. Except for Kincaid, Johnny Winchester had killed every man who had ever had the nerve to stand up to him. Cort had wanted more information about that at the time, but Johnny had made it clear the subject was off limits. It didn't make sense, though. It had been in the papers. Johnny had sported a sling around his left arm for three weeks. Didn't seem to be any special shame about that. 'Course, Johnny was different from other gunmen Cort had known. Johnny claimed he didn't fight every man who wanted to fight him. Only the ones he felt would be a feather in his cap. He killed because he felt entitled to kill. *A man has to earn the right to stand up and die against Johnny Winchester.*

"So what do we do now?" Ramo growled.

"Go ahead just like the bastard never came into town," Cort said, "Why not?"

"Arrest Laramee Logan now, after what happened?" Ramo asked, his thin face pinched with worry.

Cort grinned. Ramo was the sort who preferred to do his dirty work on the spur of the moment. His waiting to come out into the open with an accusation against Logan had been the hangup from the beginning. Ramo was tough and mean, but he had no stomach for planning some future event and carrying it through. Planning just allowed Ramo's mind to imagine all sorts of ways he could be found out. But he'd do anything on the spur of the moment.

"If he resists arrest," Cort said patiently, "you'll just have to kill him. Knowing that bastard, Logan, he ain't going to allow you or anyone else to just ride out there and bring him in. He'll resist. You can count on it."

A light dawned, and Ramo smiled. "Somewhere between the ranch and here he's bound to resist. Then it don't matter whether I arrested the right man or not. He'll be dead..."

Sucking on a toothpick, Cort watched as Ramo finally realized that Logan didn't have to actually resist for Ramo to say he had. Sometimes Cort wondered why he surrounded himself with such dim minions.

A member of the city selectmen, chairman of two committees, prominent in the Catholic church, Cort was quick to put others into his debt, and just as quick to be certain that his benevolence did not go unrewarded. He worked at his saloon during the daytime and kept a busy social life at night.

"Just doing your duty," Cort grinned. "And we'll get everything we want."

We always have Johnny Winchester as our ace in the hole, Cort thought, standing up. Even if the bastard had stolen from them, he would come back, knowing they wouldn't dare confront him about the stolen goods.

Remembering that they didn't know where Johnny had gone, Cort bristled. They didn't need him anyway. Nothing would come up that Ramo couldn't handle.

"Hell. Just my word and Smalley's against a dead man's." Ramo grinned in self-satisfaction as he realized Cort was right. He was almost as good with a gun as his famous cousin. Logan was not someone he needed to fear. Logan was a cattleman—a man who used his hands in rough work—a man who had neither the time nor the energy to perfect his marksmanship or his draw. Logan was too busy trying to become the biggest damned cattle baron in Arizona. Too busy being a goddamned hoity-toity Logan. The thought that he would soon be out of their way brightened Ramo's spirits.

Cort laughed and punched Ramo in the ribs. "The sooner you

do it, the better. Oh, I forgot to mention that the ranger arrested your asshole deputy."

"What?"

"Smalley broke Hop Wo's legs. Kincaid arrested him. He's probably waiting for you at the jail."

Grimacing, Ramo headed out the door.

CHAPTER SEVEN

Unsheathing his gun, Lance walked back to where Smalley and his wounded friends struggled up into standing positions. Lance pointed his forty-five at them, then walked from one to the other and slipped their guns out of their holsters. "Get moving."

"What the hell?" Smalley demanded, blood oozing from his mouth where his tongue had been bitten through.

Lance waved the gun at him. "I said walk, not talk."

Smalley picked up his hat and jammed it onto his head. "You're gonna be thorry," he said, his tongue already swelling in his mouth.

"Already am," Lance growled, his own pain near breathtaking after so much exertion. He gestured impatiently with his gun.

The jail was empty except for its caged occupants. The keys were gone. Lance kicked chairs into the center of the room. "Sit." They sat. He laid his forty-five on the desk, pointed at Smalley, and then sat down in Ramo's chair and waited. Finally Del Ramo appeared at the door.

"Howdy," Lance said.

"Howdy, yourself," Ramo gritted, and walked around the desk where that morning he had looked at wanted posters and steeled himself to ride out to the Boxer brand to arrest Logan. His fear was that some sign of his intentions might be visible to the sharp-eyed ranger. "What's the meaning of this?"

"These men are under arrest."

Smalley let out a disgusted oath. "Ain't no law againth breaking a damned chinkth leg," he lisped.

Ramo looked from Kincaid to his deputy. Resentment against Kincaid for jeopardizing his and Cort's plans made him irritable and, at the same time, more cautious. "He's my deputy. He ain't going nowhere. You're just asking for trouble, pushing this. I can let him out on his own recognizance."

Lance shook his head. "The *judge* can let him out," he corrected him.

"Captain McNamara sent me to stop a race war. Any person engaging in hostilities against a person of another race is going to be arrested and held for trial."

"I ain't gonna lock my deputy in a cell!" Ramo exclaimed.

Lance pointed the gun at Ramo's forehead and cocked it. "How you gonna keep from it?"

Sweat beaded on Ramo's forehead. The look in the ranger's eyes—as if he would enjoy pulling the trigger—reminded Ramo of rumors that the territory was hiring maniacs to cope with the influx of opportunists who had turned to rustling, a very profitable—if high risk—business due to the high prices being paid for beef back east. McNamara's damned rangers had no mercy for law breakers. Some folks protested their high-handed tactics, but McNamara's war chest was being filled by cattlemen who wanted action not legality.

"Lock him up, or I shoot."

Ramo's lips tightened. A territorial ranger had more power than a city marshal. All the bastard would have to say was that poor old Ramo had obstructed a lawman in the course of his official duties. With the history of unresolved trouble in the town, the bastard ranger could probably make it stick. Cursing Johnny for leaving town just before he was needed and cursing his deputy for getting him into this spot, Ramo decided Smalley deserved to cool his heels in a cell. Scouring the ranger with a look he hoped would skin fur off a beaver, he stalked over and opened the cell door.

"Get your goddamned asses in here," he growled.

The school house, decorated with red bunting tacked up around the walls, brightly lit by extra lamps brought in for the purpose, and cleared of school desks, resounded with loud music, laughter, and the sounds of feet stamping against the wood floor. The rectangular room had five tall windows on each side. Under the open windows on the south, cookies, cakes, and pies filled the warm air with the rich, spicy smells of home baking.

A hog caller chanted the calls for a square dance. "Two ladies chain across the floor, chain those pretty girls back once more." Their faces glistening with perspiration, men hooped and hollered and clapped. Swinging their skirts, women skipped and danced through the calls.

Fighting homesickness, Lance leaned against the wall. He had meant to sleep but hadn't been able to. Loud music had drawn him here. Lance was rarely homesick, but the music reminded him of times when his father had invited half of Texas to their ranch to eat and dance and play games. People stayed for days, camping around the *casa grande* and eating meals cooked over huge outdoor pits by chefs imported from New York City for the occasion.

"Promenade that pretty little gal." The caller chanted in cadence to the music. Dancers in circles of eight skipped and clapped. Lance located Angie Logan dancing with the sandy-haired young man who had ridden that mean piece of horse flesh this afternoon. Sturdy, lithe, and lively, with a grin that no doubt influenced many a young woman to favor him, he appeared to be undamaged and having a good time. Angie wore a demure, maroon gown that emphasized her slenderness and the swell of her small breasts. Heads turned as Angie and her partner strolled and strutted to the calls.

Angie felt Kincaid's presence before she actually saw him. Her eyes swept the crowd until she saw Kincaid's bronzed face through the bobbing heads of the dancers. Kincaid nodded, and Angie's pulses quickened. She hadn't intended to come to the social. She had followed one stand of blooming desert flowers to the next, taking one picture after another, until almost dark, then she had rushed back to *The Tea Time News* to set type for the children's section. She would probably still be there, except Laramee stopped in and insisted she come to the dance. And she hadn't gone back to see Lily. That bothered Angie more than her unfinished work. She wanted to know that Lily was safe. Unfortunately when Angie started taking pictures of the desert around Durango, she lost track of time. Darkness and good sense precluded her going up to the Chinese section alone.

Laramee saw Sarah and let out an Indian yell. Ignoring him, Sarah sashayed past in another set. The next call was *allemande left.* Instead of executing it, Laramee spun his sister around and sent her flying toward Sarah's partner, who had no choice but to catch her. Laramee dragged Sarah out of her set and into his. Some yelled their displeasure; some laughed. Both sets stumbled for a few seconds and then picked up the rhythm again.

"Laramee Logan!" Sarah struggled to control the urge to grin at his antics.

"Sarah Elizabeth," he mimicked and executed the call to honor his partner and then his left-hand lady. He skipped past Sarah who fumed until they were reunited.

"You upset everybody!" she whispered, glaring at him.

"Anybody die?" he asked, grinning.

"You are insensitive, and selfish, Laramee!"

Laughing, Laramee ducked and sashayed around as she tried to swat him.

The set ended, and Laramee grabbed Sarah and hustled her toward the back door. Outside, he guided her into dark shadow, but Sarah barely noticed. The cool night air felt heavenly on her hot face. "You embarrassed me half to death," she whispered.

Ignoring her words, Laramee pulled her into his arms. His warm lips found hers, and she moaned. His strong hands outlined the flare of her hips, pressing her close to him, and his thigh wedged itself between her legs. She responded with urgency to the call of his lean, hard body. A hot, sweet pain lanced through her. Panting, she twisted away from him.

"Leave me alone, Laramee!"

He dragged in a deep breath. "I did. You been alone all week. Now I'm here," he growled, pulling her back into his arms.

"You're like a madman! Don't you ever think of anything else?"

"Why should I?"

"I can't spend my entire life kissing you…"

"You want to waste it, go ahead," he drawled. "Can only imagine one thing that would be more fun than kissing."

"Well, I'm not going to do that either," she said, furious with him.

"I gotta do something with this feeling," he growled.

"Do something useful."

"Like what?"

"I don't know. Something useful."

"How the hell am I going to do something useful at a dance?"

"You're so smart. Figure it out."

He lifted an arrogant eyebrow. "All right." He turned on his heel and stalked inside.

Curious, Sarah followed. Laramee sauntered over to a group of cowhands from another ranch. Flashes of mischief and rowdiness erupted as money passed to one man. Then Laramee strolled through the crowd to Lance Kincaid's side. Sarah had the wild urge to call Laramee off, but part of her was mesmerized with the possibilities.

• • •

"Howdy," Laramee drawled.

"Howdy."

"Stranger in town?"

Lance nodded. "Name's Kincaid. Lance Kincaid."

"Logan. Laramee Logan." He grinned. "Nothing personal in this, Kincaid, but I promised those men over there that I'd beat the tar out of you."

Lance chuckled; fire lanced outward from his left side. "What do you get if you do?"

"Hundred dollars."

"And if you don't?"

"I lose fifty."

"How hard're you willing to work for fifty greenbacks?"

"That's a month's wages," Laramee shrugged. "Work pretty hard for a few minutes anyway."

"You'll have to."

"Figured that's why they picked you."

"You could be wrong about that."

"What d'ya mean?"

"They could have picked me for some other reason."

"Like what?"

"Like maybe I'm an Arizona ranger, and I'll lock your ass in jail for a week for disturbing the peace."

Laramee's face was a picture of disgust. "Those shitheads are trying to shorten my stake rope."

Lance grinned. "You just get into town?"

"Yeah." Laramee looked as if he were trying to decide if he should try it anyway. Lance's side throbbed.

"You any relation to Angie Logan?"

Laramee's eyes narrowed. "My sister."

"Exceptional young woman."

Laramee laughed. "Every man in the territory agrees with you on that. She's saving herself for better things."

"Smart as she looks," Lance agreed.

"You don't sound like no cowpuncher."

"That a requirement?"

"Makes a man curious."

"About what?"

"About what kind of Arizona ranger sounds like a damned barrister."

"What do you do besides turn mean horses into shavetails?"

Lance countered.

"Ranching. Want some honest work?"

Lance grinned. "Don't want to work that hard."

"Smart." Laramee let his eyes flick over Lance. "So you're interested in my sister."

"Did I say that?"

"Don't have to. Every man with any juice atall is."

"She's safe with me."

Laramee squared his broad shoulders. "Wasn't her I was worried about, shortcake."

Laramee walked back to the group of men he'd left. He said a few words, and they roared with laughter. Then he found his sister and pulled her away from the people she was with.

"Laramee, what…?"

"I want you to meet someone."

They stopped in front of Lance. Angie smiled. "We've met."

The music started again. "Then shake a hoof with the man. Make him feel at home in Durango," Laramee said.

Relieved that he wasn't going to have to fight Logan, Lance held out his hand. "Would you like to dance?"

Angie shrugged. "Thank you." A small spot on his chin was raw and red where the razor had cut too close.

Lance had reason to regret asking her to dance. Angie was a lively, energetic partner. She smiled, clapped, swung her full skirts, and encouraged him to show off, which he did. Her dark eyes flashed with pure delight. When the set ended, Lance walked her to the punch bowl and tried to ignore the urge to limp.

Damp from exertion, her demure cotton gown molded itself to her reed-slender young body and reminded him that in Texas the young girls didn't wear corsets to dances. Angie's breasts pressed against the thin fabric, looking tender and unprotected.

Misreading the look in his eyes, she said softly, "You look thirsty."

Lance took the dipper from her. The contact jolted inside him. "May I?" Full and sweetly formed, her lips were open and soft. All he had to do was lean down and claim them. As if she had read his mind, she sucked her bottom lip into her mouth and covered it with her teeth. Lance cleared his throat.

She drank thirstily and set her cup down. "It's so hot in here," she said, fanning her face with her hand. "Could we step outside?"

Lance guided Angie through the noisy crowd. Outside, the chill night air felt crisp. The lively music faded. Couples hidden in dark places whispered and giggled.

Kincaid loomed tall and stalwart beside Angie. His throbbing nearness set off a sweet thrill of terror in her.

"Are you going to survive?"

"Smalley?" Lance asked. "He's nothing."

"Just a skunk who would as soon shoot you from ambush as look at you," she protested. "That *is* something."

"He won't be shooting anyone for a while," Lance said. She was right in her assessment of Smalley, but he was equally sure Ramo would wait for the district judge, hoping he would release Smalley with only a slap on the wrist. With Cadwallader that was a definite possibility, but it didn't matter. He had made his point. They would be careful not to instigate any trouble that could be traced back to themselves…

Light and flowery, her perfume filled his nostrils. Angie tossed her hair back with a slender hand. She had the sort of assurance that went with being admired too much. Knowing Virginia and Tennessee and how freely they lived, he would expect her to be composed by comparison, but she exhibited a flair for flawless, subtle coquetry that was unmatched in his experience.

"Don't underestimate him," she said softly. "I want you to survive so you can put a stop to our race war…"

"Did you fully recover from the fire?" Raspy and intimate, Kincaid's voice affected her breathing.

"I still cough a little…"

A sound behind him—furtive and hushed—caused the hair on Lance's neck to bristle. He stepped away from Angie and moved silently and quickly toward the sound. Footsteps broke into a run and pounded away. Lance knelt beside a bush and lit a match.

Angie stepped close. "What happened?"

"Don't know. Someone was hiding here."

Angie knelt down beside him. The blue flare of Kincaid's match illuminated a small burrowed-out place in the sand. A gleam of metal caught her eye. Angie brushed the sand aside and picked up a pearl-handled pocket knife. It felt warm.

"Do you recognize it?"

"I think so. It might be Atillo's. I think I've seen him whittling with it. If it is, there's no danger…he would never hurt anyone. He was only watching…"

Her shoulder brushed Kincaid's. In the glow from his match, her dark eyes filled his veins with ribbons of fire. Heat seared his fingers, and he dropped the match, cursing softly.

"Ohhh, your poor fingers." She touched his hand.

Her perfume smelled powdery and sensual. Her skin gleamed in the soft light from the windows and fairly cried out to be kissed. But, Lance thought, if he did, he would regret it. Yet Angie Logan, unkissed, left echoes of desire inside him.

A small turmoil started in Angie. Her lungs were strangely constricted, her legs weak, as if the excitement of the fire and Rufe Martin being killed had finally overwhelmed her. She felt like a fool kneeling in the bushes. She should back out of there…

Too late. His warm lips brushed her cheek lightly; his touch moved through her like a wave, rippling along the underside of her skin. His warmth and his pure masculine scent obliterated everything except awareness of him.

His lips nuzzled her cheek. Of its own accord, her mouth turned toward his. Smooth, heated lips sucked at her bottom lip and pulled it into his mouth. His teeth nipped gently at her chin and moved down to find the hollow of her throat.

Demanding more than just that gentle nipping and sucking, her mouth opened and groped for his. Warm hands slid down her back to press against her spine. His mouth claimed hers—devouring and torturing—and it wasn't enough.

She surged against him, grinding body and mouth into his, needing his fierceness, his hunger, and even the pain his urgent hands were inflicting. No gentleness now, no tenderness.

She barely heard her name called.

"Angie! Durn it, woman!"

Lance recognized Laramee Logan's voice from the depths of a haze. Letting go of Angie Logan was like ripping an arm off, but he forced himself to relinquish her lips.

"Noooo," she whispered, eyes closed. Her mouth groped for his to continue the kiss. Lance shuddered with the effort it took to capture her face in his hands and not kiss her.

"Your brother is looking for you," he breathed. Already bruised and swollen from his kisses, her mouth was too close, too sweet. Lance stifled a groan and pulled her to her feet.

"Angie!" Laramee yelled.

She hated the thought of facing Laramee. Her voice was unsteady, but she forced herself to say, "Over…here."

"What the heck are you doing?" Laramee demanded.

"What do you want?" Angie countered, praying that she did not look as thoroughly kissed as she felt.

"Want to be sure you're safe," he growled, moving to stand beside her. Hands on hips, his sharp eyes bored into Kincaid and then her. "This man treating you like a lady?"

Angie rolled her eyes in exasperation. "He is."

Laramee shook his head. "Don't look like it to me. Looks to me like he had you down on the ground kissing you."

Without waiting for either of them to answer, he punched Kincaid in the face. Lance took the blow on his jaw, blinked, and shook his head.

A yell of triumph cut the air. "He did it! I'll be dang blasted! He hit the ranger. Pay that boy his money!"

Laramee made a face toward his friends that said, *Told you I could do it.*

Lance rubbed his jaw and looked from Angie to Laramee. "Were you in on this?" he asked, turning back to Angie.

"I was not!"

"Good."

He turned and hit Laramee hard enough to fell a small steer. The young man fell backward and lay in the soft earth, rubbing his jaw. "Hey, no hard feelings. I had to win my bet."

Lance took Angie's arm, walked her back inside, and stopped in full view of the crowd drawn by the promise of excitement. "Thank you, Miss Logan. The dance was most enjoyable."

Lance turned on his heel, stalked across the dance floor, and walked out the front door.

Angie gritted her teeth. She didn't know whether to be angrier at Lance, Laramee, or herself. Damn! And she hadn't told him about Johnny Winchester.

She picked up her skirts, ran through the crowded room, and followed Lance Kincaid out into the darkness.

Laramee walked back into the schoolhouse. That blamed ranger had packed quite a wallop. Laramee would not soon forget that punch. Grinning ruefully, rubbing his chin, he strolled across the dance floor toward the front door.

Drift Rollins, a rider for the Circle C, turned to a man near Laramee. "You cain't save no woman who don't wanna be saved," he growled, shaking his head.

Laramee spun around, his eyes narrowed with fury. He had disliked Drift for years; he didn't think twice. Laramee grabbed Drift by the shirtfront and jerked him forward.

Pumped up by alcohol, Drift grinned and spoke loud enough for all to hear. "Looks to me like your sister's asking to be talked about. Cain't blame me for obliging her…"

Laramee hit him in the stomach, and, as he doubled over, in the face. Drift, who had just come in and had not yet surrendered his gun, staggered back, clawing for his revolver. Women screamed and scampered to get out of the line of fire.

"Don't," Laramee warned him. He was not wearing a gun, but his right hand vibrated at his side where his revolver should have been.

Drift clasped his gun and wavered between pulling it and backing down. He licked his lips. Laramee took a step toward Drift.

"You stay away from me," Drift yelled.

Sabbath Turk, arriving at the door of the schoolhouse, surveyed the tense situation quickly. Sabbath yelled a warning and tossed Laramee his gun.

"To hell with you, Logan!" Drift yelled, and brought his gun up. Logan's hand blurred outward and caught Turk's gun. Both men fired at once.

Sarah, walking from the back, screamed Laramee's name, covered her face, and collapsed. Bystanders rushed to her side.

The smoke slowly cleared. Drift doubled over, clutching his hand. Unscathed, Laramee stepped forward, picked up Drift's gun, and tossed it out a nearby window. "Get him to Doc Amberg," he yelled.

Laramee strode quickly to where Sarah lay, her face paled to near-white. Thick, dark lashes flickered. Slowly, glazed with terror only she could see, her eyes opened. She saw Laramee, cried out, and tried to scoot away.

Laramee scooped her into his arms and started for the door. Del Ramo blocked Laramee's path. People fell silent.

"Best come with me," Ramo said, his voice gruff.

"To hell with you," Laramee growled. "Get out of my way."

"You just shot a man…"

"It was self-defense. You saw that. Everybody saw it," Laramee gritted.

Ramo, who had been steeling himself for days to ride out and arrest Logan, blinked in confusion. The urge to arrest Logan was overpowering, but Logan was right. It had been self-defense. Confused, Ramo wavered.

Seeing his lack of conviction, Laramee started past him. Virgil Field, an ex-Boxer brand rider and a friend of Laramee's, reached out and touched Laramee's arm. "Best wait till the marshal questions folks who saw it."

"To hell with him," Laramee growled, and tried to shove past Virgil. Virgil ignored the stubborn, angry light in Laramee's eyes and pulled him aside. "I seen a shooting in Taos that was self-defense clear as day, but the marshal didn't question the witnesses right away, and some changed their stories," he cautioned.

Frustrated, Laramee realized Virgil was right, especially with a snake like Del Ramo. "All right, Ramo. Let's talk to the witnesses," he said, relinquishing Sarah to Virgil.

Laramee sighed. As much as he hated the thought of it, it couldn't hurt to deal with Ramo now. He would catch up with Angie and Kincaid as soon as he could. And then he would see Sarah…

CHAPTER EIGHT

Angie huddled in a doorway. Riders hurtled past, firing their guns into the air. Intuition had driven her this far, but her determination faltered. A sound beside her caused her heart to leap into her throat. She whirled around.

"Oh," she said, amazed that the sound came out in such a controlled manner.

"What are you doing out here?" Kincaid asked, stepping out of the shadows. His desire to stay away from her was an empty thing, easily overshadowed by her nearness.

Angie expelled a breath of relief. "I was looking for you. I wanted to apologize for my brother."

In the dim reflected light, shadows on his angular jaw hid more than they revealed. His lean, perilously masculine body throbbed with tension that seemed to warp the air between them.

"So you ran out here alone?" More gravel than silk, his tone was a warning. "I'll be lucky if I don't have to kill your brother tomorrow," he rasped.

"I'll take care of Laramee…" Her voice trailed off.

"Thanks," he growled.

"I came to ask if you would ride out to Lily's house with me."

"And do what?"

"Bring her home with me."

Grimacing, Lance shook his head. "You're starting your own benevolent society?"

Angie shrugged. "I just want to help this one person."

"I had an aunt like you. By the time she died she had twenty cats, six dogs, five painters, seven writers, and three sculptors. She started with one cat."

Enjoying the thought of herself becoming so wildly eccentric, Angie smiled. "I guess you're angry with me," she said.

"Maybe at your brother for interrupting. He's lucky I didn't kill him." Lance's raspy voice broke. He shifted position, and the pull of his warm hard body overwhelmed her good sense.

"Walk with me to the livery stable," she said.

"I'll walk you home."

"No, I have to go out there." Her feelings slightly injured by his refusal, she started to walk away.

Unable to help himself, Lance followed. At the livery stable she knocked on the door and called out, "Atillo, Atillo," in a soft, urgent voice. After a time she turned back to Lance.

"Well, I guess Atillo's not here…"

Lance hooked his thumbs in his belt. "Guess not."

"Would you ride out there with me?" she asked, her eyes watching him intently.

With her so close, the pain in his side diminished to a minor inconvenience. "I'll probably have to kill your brother if I do."

"I can handle Laramee."

"Sure. I noticed that," he said, grinning.

"I didn't have time then—"

"You might not again."

"He's behaved himself since I've been home. He caught me off guard—"

Lance laughed. "And me."

Angie's face flushed with heat. Had he been as lost to the world as she? "I didn't think lawmen ever lost track of what was going on."

"Law*men*. If there'd been three of us, two of them would have known exactly what was happening."

Angie laughed, a low sultry sound that was at odds with her clear speaking voice. "You have an interesting sense of humor, Mr. Kincaid."

"That's not humor, that's a fact."

Something in the timbre of Kincaid's voice jarred inside her. His presence made her giddy in an almost uncontrollable way.

"So will you accompany me?" she asked again.

"You going to protect me from your wild brother?"

"Yes."

"Well, I can't let you roam around town alone, can I?"

"I hope not. It is a little later than I'm accustomed to staying out alone. Maybe I'm beginning to understand my mother's admonitions against being outside after nightfall…"

"Why do these insights always seem to come to you fifteen

minutes too late?"

"Lucky, I guess."

"You saddle the horses," he said, moving to open the barn door, "and I'll ride out there with you."

"How's your side? It still bother you?"

"Naw. It's good as new," he lied. He found a lamp and lit it.

Once mounted and outside, Lance turned to Angie. "Where *is* your mother?" he asked, frowning.

"She's dead. My father too."

"Sorry. You sure you want to go through with this? I can go out there by myself," he said, knowing he was going to hate himself if she took the excuse he offered her.

"You need me. Lily will be afraid to go anywhere with a lone man."

"You suggesting a simple Chinese immigrant is smarter than you?"

Angie laughed, and the tone implied to Lance an effortless superiority. Her husky, sensual laughter showed clearer than words that she need not answer such a ridiculous sally.

They rode north on Rio Street. A crescent moon adorned the star-filled sky. Riding, even slowly, increased the chill of the air. Angie gave thanks for Kincaid's company. She would be terrified alone, but she was stubborn enough to know that she would have continued, terrified or not. She had been worrying about Lily for hours.

The Chinese quarter smelled of incense. Sweet and sinister, it floated on the air, making Angie wonder if perhaps she was wrong to interfere here. These people were so different.

A Chinese man staggered out of a dimly lit building. He took three steps, spun slowly around, and slumped onto the wooden porch. After a moment he began to snore.

Reining Pumpkin, Angie glanced sideways at Kincaid. "Is he all right?" she asked.

"If insensible is all right, he is."

"What's wrong with him?"

"Opium, probably," Kincaid murmured.

"Isn't it dangerous?"

"Poorhouses in China are filled with walking skeletons who can attest to its dangers. You've heard of the Opium Wars?"

"Vaguely."

"In 1840 the emperor of China tried to ban opium. He compelled the Canton opium merchants to give up their stockpiles. Twenty thousand chests of opium were destroyed. The British went to war against China to, quote, open China to trade, unquote. It was never mentioned in the treaties, but as soon as the war was won, the East India Company, backed by British interests, flooded China with newly legalized opium."

Anger roughened his voice. "The Chinese are temperate and superior in many ways. Oh, they'll drink a little *samshoo* and get a little red in the face, but nothing serious. Until the opium starts pouring in. Estimates are that fifty thousand chests of opium enter China each year. That's a lot of opium. Addiction naturally follows. Then corruption."

"Corruption? How does that follow?"

"Corruption at high levels leads to inept government, which leads to oppression, more taxation, brute-force collection procedures. People start leaving or they revolt. A friend—fellow I knew once said twenty-five million Chinese were killed in the Taiping Revolution. They're brave people, but even brave people can be starved for only so long before they leave. The penalty for emigrating from China is death by decapitation. 'Course, visiting in a foreign country is not considered emigrating unless they apply for citizenship."

"How awful!" They stopped north of the opium den. The sickly sweet odor nauseated Angie. "You mean these people are all fugitives from their own country?"

"Dreamers, fugitives, slaves, and prisoners."

"That seems contradictory—"

"They came here to get rich so they can go home and live prosperously. They are exploited from the moment they leave home. Many of them are shanghaied or killed before they leave their shores. If they make it this far, the Chinese in the homeland keep tabs on the them through their companies and tongs. The tongs protect them and exploit them. Depending upon what's happening at the moment."

"What are tongs?"

"Their churches, associations, cultural centers."

"How are they prisoners?"

"Most of them came here on money borrowed from one of the companies at home; they work for the company until the debt is paid."

He expelled an angry breath. "I read an agreement signed by a Chinese girl in San Francisco. She agreed to work for four years in exchange for six hundred dollars. All they had to do was feed her, and, for every ten days she was sick or unable to work, she had to serve thirty additional days. Since she was unable to work for one week every month, there was no way she could ever be free. When her mind got messed up and she couldn't work she was severely punished; she almost died."

Realizing he had been talking about a prostitute, Angie flushed at the question she had almost asked. "You know a great deal about the Chinese."

"Very little actually. I used to know a man who was half Chinese. He told me some stories…"

"I have a Chinese friend too."

"He wasn't my friend," Lance said grimly.

"Sorry."

Lance shrugged off the angry feeling the memory of Gilbert Lee had caused in him.

"I wonder what it would be like…being Chinese…" Angie mused.

"About like capping dynamite for a living."

His whiskey-tinged voice seeped into her mysteriously, shuddering through her midriff. His presence and controlled power pulled her like a tide.

"I forgot…I wanted to tell you that you will be in danger if you stay here," she said, her voice husky.

Lance smiled at her naïveté. When had he not been in danger?

Angie leaned forward and patted her horse's warm neck. "I mean from Marshal Ramo's cousin—Johnny Winchester."

"Winchester lives in Durango?" Lance asked, frowning.

"No. He visits Del Ramo. They're cousins." Pale starlight cast shadows across his handsome face.

"Does your jaw hurt where Laramee hit you?"

"Do you have more sympathy for injured men or healthy men?"

Angie laughed. "Just answer the question."

"It hurts like hell."

He was lying. Without thinking, she reached up and touched his cheek. The very air around his body seemed to conspire against her, crackling with tension, drawing her closer. Angie's horse stamped and moved closer to his. Her leg brushed his thigh. Kincaid leaned down. His face blurred out of focus. His lips brushed her mouth, moved to her cheek, then her eyes—not lighting anywhere—torturing her with the sense that he was going to kiss her.

Angie groaned deep in her throat—a small covert sound of desire. Her mouth opened, seeking his.

Responding, pulling her into his arms, his lips seared into hers, burning away thought and memory. Angie pressed against his sturdy chest.

"Is it better now?"

Her mouth was open against his cheek. Her warm breath tickled his ear and sent vibrations all the way down to his toes. "It still hurts over here."

She kissed the spot he pointed to. He pointed at another spot. "And here." She kissed that one, and he pointed at his mouth. "And here."

Angie kissed him softly. "Better now?"

"It's starting up again," he murmured.

Angie kissed his chin, and lips, cheeks, again. This time Kincaid took charge of the kiss. She was dizzy, barely able to think by the time he relinquished her lips.

Nunca tried to move away. Lance reined him, supporting himself and Angie. Dazed and breathless, she reminded him of a flower, open to the sun, open to him. Her sweet face glowed with the tender look of sleep.

"Let's go," he said, his voice thick.

A hundred yards from the Liang house, Lance reined his horse under a tree.

"What are we going to do?"

"Going to watch. See what's happening."

She waited patiently for several minutes. "Now what will we do?"

Lance grinned. "Are you cold?" he asked.

"A little." She shrugged to diminish its importance.

He took off his vest and put it over her shoulders. The warm, heavy leather had an intimate feel to it. Her loins quivered. "Won't you be cold?" she asked.

"Not a chance, Angel."

Angie blushed.

They watched for several minutes. Finally Lance kicked his horse into a slow walk, and Angie followed him across the road and into the shadowy yard. A strong smell of smoke and ash drifted from the burned barn. Angie was grateful they had spent the time watching. The shadows were less frightening now. Still, approaching the house gave her a strange chill.

Lance dismounted, walked up to the door, and knocked. Paper lanterns tied to the roof overhang rattled in the slight, cool breeze off the desert. Angie felt a moment of panic as she dismounted. This was insanity. What would she do with Lily, Toy, and Mei-ling once she got them home? Wouldn't the killer then come there if he wanted Lily?

"Lance!" she whispered.

"Yeah?"

"Why are you letting me do this?"

He grinned. "Finally came to? Because it'll be easier to keep track of the two of you if you're together. Don't worry. You're in no more danger with her there. I had already decided that Martin's killer might want you dead."

"Wasn't that just because I stumbled in there and made Rufe Martin angry?"

"You made Rufe angry enough to lock you in, but I don't think he's the one who started the fire. I think Rufe was dead when the fire started."

"You mean you think someone wants *me* dead? But why? I don't know anything except what I told you..."

"Hunches are hunches. I could be wrong."

"Why doesn't that reassure me?"

Lance knocked again on the door, and they waited in silence. People scurried around inside. The door opened.

A tall man was silhouetted in the doorway.

"Shades of Mrs. Lillian," Lance whispered.

Angie's heart leapt into her throat and pumped there. "What's wrong?"

Kincaid seemed to have forgotten her.

"Ahhh. Lance Kincaid." The voice that spoke was firm yet quiet and thoroughly accustomed to the English language.

"What are you doing here?" Lance asked, his voice all gravel now. It carried reluctant respect, obvious strain, and another emotion Angie could not identify. Bitterness?

"The Liangs are my foster parents."

"You know this man..." Angie said, faint with relief.

Lance stepped back to include Angie. "Gilbert James Lee, Angie Logan."

"How do you do," she said.

Inside, a light was lit. It filled the room, sending its yellow glow to touch Angie's face. Gil sucked in his breath.

Lance's hand on Angie's arm tightened. An awkward pause caused Angie to look from Gilbert Lee to Lance.

"Is my face dirty?"

Neither man spoke. Muscles in Kincaid's angular jaw tightened. The look in his eyes alternated between defensive and challenging.

Lee recovered first. "You resemble someone I knew a long time ago. She was very beautiful..." he murmured politely, dismissively. "In China, Miss Logan, a tree is known by its roots. Your mother is undoubtedly a woman of great beauty," he said and bowed deeply.

Lance choked back a comment. Gil's face, which would appear

artless and handsome to an innocent like Angie, was a refined mixture of Oriental and Caucasian, the aristocratic and the brutal. But hidden beneath his simple belted tunic and ankle length trousers was a ribbon of steel. Solidly planted, his slender, flat body contained tremendous strength. Though slighter than Lance, Gil's body was a more brutal weapon. A man would have to kill Gilbert Lee to stop him. Lance would negotiate. Gil would not. Lance was prone to be playful. He would fight if he had to, but he would rather not. Gil Lee was a block of cement when he chose to be, a flicker of light when necessary. His unblinking eyes smiled with deceptive gentleness.

Gil stepped aside. "Come inside, please."

With a firm hand on her waist, Lance guided Angie forward. Angie had never been inside the house. Her exchanges with Lily had always been at the pagoda by the stream. A lamp and several candles flickered. Imposing black-lacquered chairs sat against the walls. The wood floor was covered with straw mats. Woven screens had been rolled down to cover the windows. Hand-painted landscapes of ancient gnarled trees and graceful arched bridges over shimmering ponds lent the room a strange exotic beauty. On one wall, white felt banners hung from the ceiling, their double rows of oversized Chinese characters reaching to the floor. Potted chrysanthemums bloomed on either side of the door.

The spiky, sharp scent of the flowers and the sweet heavy odor of incense reminded Angie of the China seen on Delft porcelain, a China of palaces and bridges, of embroidered silk brocades.

"Honorable Father," Gil said, bowing to an elderly gentleman bruised on the forehead and left cheek. "It gives me great pleasure to introduce my friend, Lance Kincaid, and his companion, Angie Logan. Liang Third Uncle, my foster father. Kincaid and I attended the university together."

"Welcome to my humble home," Liang murmured, bowing deeply. "It gives me much pleasure to meet such esteemed friends of my adopted son."

As if he had stepped into the hallowed Shaolin temple, Lance felt a mantle of deferential regard fall over him. Gil Lee had been his kung-fu *sifu* for three years. Accepting Gil in that role had left Lance with permanent feelings of respect for Gil's leadership, wisdom, and skill. His speed, agility, and finesse were unequaled in Kincaid's experience. Nothing that had happened between them on a personal level could ever entirely efface their original relationship. Gil would always be *sifu* and he pupil.

Three women stepped into the room and were introduced as Toy,

Lily, and Mei-ling. Gil motioned them to sit. Lance held a chair for Angie and sat next to her.

With a start Angie realized Third Uncle was Lily's father, thought to have died in the fire. She wanted to point this out to Lance and to question Lily, but Third Uncle was speaking in his soft, cultured voice. Intimidated by the formality of the occasion, she waited. Toy scurried in on bound feet, carrying tiny cups and a pot of fragrant tea.

Her skin glowing in the candlelight, Lily bent forward and poured tea into the tiny cups. Her slender neck bowed like a graceful stem balancing a rose in a light wind. Her dainty hands caressed the delicate china teapot with perfect grace. Angie was enchanted. Gilbert Lee was also captivated.

Third Uncle and Mei-ling, a square-faced woman with a low forehead and prominent cheekbones, sat next to Gil. Mei-ling passed cups to the guests first, then to Third Uncle and Gil, and then to Lily and Toy. Third Uncle raised his cup to his lips. As if on a signal, they all sipped from the tiny cups.

Gil smiled. "My friend is a lawkeeper."

Angie sensed resistance in Kincaid. She slanted a sideways look at him, but his face was carefully controlled, uncommunicative. She remembered his words on the trail from town: *He is not my friend.* Was Gil Lee the one he had been talking about? This polite man with straight black brows and masked features?

Third Uncle smiled. The women tittered and giggled.

Gil bowed to Angie. "Forgive us our little joke, Miss Logan. We are Hakka. In China the soldiers who would be the equivalent of the lawkeepers are Manchu. Hakka are not allowed to intermarry with or even to gaze on the Manchu, who are fierce fighters. The Hakka are known in China as the guest people. We are the wanderers. Unlike the Miaos, who are the mountain people, and the Manchus, who are the soldiers, the Hakka are idealistic and adventurous. Hakka women do not bind their feet or wear corsets. They work side by side with their men. They look down on the foolishness of bound feet and prostitution for women."

Lily and Mei-ling whispered back and forth in Chinese, then Mei-ling spoke to Gil in Chinese, and the women laughed. Gil turned to Angie. "I have been rebuked for speaking so boldly to a virgin."

Angie blushed, and the women giggled and tittered. Angie glanced at Toy's bound feet. They were less than four inches long, stubbed so short they looked like they had been cut off at a sharp downward angle, almost even with her ankle. She wore tiny, elaborately decorated slippers.

Gil saw Angie's quick look and smiled. "Toy is of another tribe that values small feet. She is very proud of her "golden lilies." In the twelfth century the emperor's daughter, Lily, was born with club feet. From that day it was fashionable for each family to bind the feet of one daughter to honor the emperor's daughter. Later it became fashionable for all daughters, except among the Hakka and certain other tribes where strong, hardworking women are valued." Gil smiled at Toy. "When the Hakka men become wealthy, they can then afford the luxury of women who cannot work or walk great distances."

Angie looked at Lance. There was something unsettling about this window into another culture. Had Third Uncle taken Toy as his second wife or his concubine?

"What brings you here, my friend?" Gil asked.

Lance did not move perceptibly, but seemed to withdraw into either formality or stiffness. "Concern for the young woman. If I'd known you were here…"

"I appreciate your concern on her behalf. I arrived late this afternoon." Gil's voice was strangely gentle.

"We thought Lily's father died in the fire," Angie said, watching her friend's eyes, but Lily only lowered them demurely, allowing Gil to answer for her.

"As you can see," Gil said softly, indicating Liang with his hand, "except for bruises, Third Uncle is in excellent health. Fortunately he was not in the barn as Lily had assumed."

Lily's face glowed with joy. "I was mistaken," she said, taking her father's hand and kissing it.

"Mr. Liang, do you have any idea what Rufe Martin wanted from you?" Lance asked, watching the old man closely.

Third Uncle lowered his eyes. "Not with certainty. It appeared he wanted my daughter…"

He's lying. "Anything else?" Lance asked politely.

"Perhaps money, but we have so little…"

"Did you recognize the man with Martin?"

"I have never seen him before."

"Can you describe him?"

Third Uncle shook his head. "Tall, with fair hair like Miss Logan. I remember nothing else about him. I'm sorry."

Angie was relieved and at the same time perplexed. What had she heard in the barn? A scuffling sound…a groan…a heavy expulsion of breath. Then the unmistakable pain in Lily's scream when she woke and saw the burning barn.

The conversation had moved on. Angie was suddenly eager to leave. She wanted to ask Kincaid questions. It took longer than she would have liked, but finally they said their farewells and received the Liang family's polite bows.

Outside, Angie turned to Kincaid. "There really was someone in the barn," she said.

"I'll come back tomorrow and poke around the ashes."

"Is Mr. Lee capable of protecting them? Is it safe?"

Lance nodded. Gilbert James Lee was one of the deadliest fighters to come out of China. His polite facade masked an iron will and more competence than any one man had a right to, unless he had earned it the way Gil had. "Couldn't be any safer," he growled.

At the first sight of Gil, a pall had settled over Lance. Nothing had gone right for him since the first time he saw Angie Logan in Nogales. Between Angie Logan, Gil Lee, and Johnny Winchester…

They mounted and rode slowly back to Angie's house. The sounds of Saturday night in Durango had changed: Chinese gongs and drums close by, rinky-dink piano down the street, and the square-dance fiddler and hog caller in the distance. An occasional spurt of raucous male laughter interrupted the background sounds of barking dogs, whinnying horses, and chirping crickets.

The wind on her face chilled Angie. Neither she nor Lance spoke until they reached her house southeast of town.

They dismounted and walked slowly toward the front porch. She stepped up on the first step and turned to face him. "Thank you for going with me."

"You're welcome." Lance started to turn away.

"Would you like something to eat? I could fix you a bite. It wouldn't be anything fancy. I'd like to do something to repay you for taking me there…" Her heart swelled with each beat. "I have some chicken. I could heat it up for you."

Her eagerness to please him in some way lightened his mood. "I'd better go…I don't want your neighbors saying I let you spoon with me."

Caught off guard, Angie laughed.

"A man can't be too careful," he said.

"How about if I keep you out here on the porch? Think your reputation could stand that?"

Lance forgot about Gil Lee. "Maybe, for a few minutes anyway."

Lance leaned down and kissed her, and the sensation of his lips on hers filled her with joy and hunger. He gathered her into his arms and held her close for a long time. "Is your brother likely to come here looking for you?" His voice was a raspy whisper.

Dazed, Angie buried her face in his sturdy neck. His warm skin smelled clean and masculine; it filled her with euphoria.

"Is he?" he prodded.

"Yes, I guess so."

Lance kissed her cheek and then her eyelids. "He'll probably kill me."

"Not right away."

Lance snuffled into her ear. "I'm s'posed to be grateful for that, I take it."

"Laramee is a sweetheart," she murmured, kissing his cheek and running her fingertips through the short, crisp hairs at the nape of his neck. She loved the warm, hungry feel of his skin, his hair. She felt dizzy with pleasure.

"He's gonna drag me behind a horse all the way back to Phoenix," Kincaid whispered, holding her tight, rubbing his cheek against her hair. She had the softest, best-smelling hair he'd ever been close to.

Angie strained up to reach his mouth. She pressed tiny kisses around it, but she would not let him kiss her. "He wouldn't drag you that far. Laramee gets bored easy."

Lance nipped at her ear. "Good news. He's gonna drag me behind his horse only *halfway* to Phoenix. Don't this worry you none?"

"You worry more than any grown man I ever knew. You got on comfortable boots, don't you? A little walk back to Durango isn't going to hurt you."

Lance shook his head. "You ain't doing it right."

"What?" Angie asked, blinking.

"You ain't tawkin' right. You gotta tawk right else we cain't spoon."

Angie laughed. "What do I say?"

"A little ol' wawk back to D'rango ain't gonna hurt you none. Try it." Lance buried his nose in her hair. Angie nipped at his neck with her teeth. She repeated what he had said with difficulty. Lance laughed outright at the way her clear, concise voice tried to twist itself around *tawk*. He kissed her throat, and she lost her place in her recital.

"How come you sound like a cowboy when you spoon?"

"From kissing all those Texas girls. You gotta tawk right to kiss a little ol' Texas gal. They don't like furriners." He emphasized the long i's; *his* Texas drawl was perfect.

"I think I'm going to help Laramee drag you behind that horse."

Angie giggled and breathed in the smell of him. His heart beat hard against hers. The air felt silky and delicious on her arms. She wanted to feel his hands on her face. "Too bad you're such a sissy. I never could tolerate no sissy."

"I grow skin slower than most."

"Laramee does know how to raise a scab on occasion."

"Saves it for special occasions, does he? Like every third breath?" He nuzzled her ear with his lips. Waves of sensation moved out in every direction from his warm lips.

"My brother's no hothead."

"My brother ain't no hothaid," he corrected her.

"My brother ain't no hothaid. I'll have you know he's good-natured and sensitive."

Lance controlled the urge to burst into laughter. "'Bout the only fault the pore boy has, I reckon, is that he has a turrible liar for a sister."

Angie started to defend herself, but Lance lifted her chin and kissed her for a long, slow time. His lips seemed to reach down inside her and stir everything up. Her knees turned to rubber.

"'Course that'll probably be true about him being sensitive and all," he drawled against her cheek, "in about eighty years. I cain't wait that long."

"Touch my face," she said.

Lance put his hands on either side of her face, and she closed her eyes and sighed. His hands were radiant with heat. Sensations too delicious to believe coursed through her body.

"That ol' boy probably uses you for bait," he whispered, pressing warm kisses on her lips, her cheeks, her forehead, "so's he can practice up for live grizzly skinning."

Angie had never felt so good in her life. Even the air she breathed felt different, better. Her hearing was sharper, her sight keener. She burrowed her face against his hands in a frenzy of joy. Kincaid hugged her close.

"I think Laramee likes you," she whispered.

"My momma had liked me as well as him, she would a drowned me in a towsack."

He kissed her. "How come you tell such turrible lies when you spoon?" he whispered.

Angie giggled. Her mother had been a fourth-generation Philadelphian who had drilled proper elocution into her from the day she could coo. She'd learned to talk the way other people did from Laramee.

"From kissing all those Arizony boys. They won't let me kiss 'em at all unless I say the right things."

Lance chuckled and kissed her forehead. "I'm going to be going along now."

Angie pushed his hands aside and snuggled close against him. "Bye," she whispered.

He groaned and leaned back down to kiss her. "You've got to be the most treacherous girl…"

He kissed her again. She snuggled closer against him. Lance turned her and walked her forcibly to her door. "You git on in there, you hear me?"

"I swarn, I don't know why I put up with the likes of you, Lance Kincaid."

He kissed her again, and this time when he released her lips, she could barely stand. "Lock your door, and don't let anybody in, you hear me?"

Angie nodded. He lifted her chin. "Especially not me."

Laughing, Angie did as she was bid. From the window she watched him ride away. She lay in bed, hearing their voices in her head until she finally went to sleep.

CHAPTER NINE

Sunday morning, May 16, 1880

Sarah was up to her elbows in flour. A loud, insistent knocking sounded at her front door. She grabbed a towel off the table where she kneaded bread dough, ran the towel over her face, and looked at her hands. Dough was caked under her nails. Nothing short of a thorough washing would get them clean. She hurried to the door.

"Who is it?"

"Laramee. Open the door."

Sarah thought about telling him to go away, but she knew he wouldn't. "You open it. My hands are a mess."

She stepped back. The door opened, and he took a tentative step inside.

Clean-shaven and dressed in his Sunday best, his tawny good looks tugged at her heart. She regretted her vow. Except that no matter how clean and dear he might look, she knew better. This clear-eyed young Lochinvar had killed two men in gunfights. His actions last night at the dance had reminded her why she wasn't ever going to get involved with him again.

"Should I throw my hat in first?" he asked.

"You have an extra hat?"

"That bad, huh?" He was in trouble all right.

Sarah shrugged, gave him one look into her unfathomable emerald-green eyes, turned, and walked toward the kitchen.

"Aren't you going to invite me in?"

Sarah looked back at him with remote eyes. "You're in."

Undaunted, Laramee tossed his hat onto the sofa and followed her into the kitchen.

"Aren't you supposed to be at church?"

"I got so mad I couldn't concentrate. Lord don't want no man sitting in his church who can't concentrate," he said, shrugging.

"What'd you get mad about?"

"Reverend Collins told the congregation that them yella devils up there almost burned up my sister."

"You knew about that last night."

"That ain't what Anj told me. She didn't tell me they tried to burn her up."

"Well, they didn't. Rufe did." Sarah turned her back and plunged her hands back into her bread dough. Her slender shoulders looked rigid and untouchable. Her long dark hair was pulled back with a ribbon. He had come by the house much earlier, but Cort had said she was at mass.

"I didn't realize you were so mad," he said softly.

Sarah didn't answer. She lifted the chalky white wad of dough, slammed it back onto the table, and punched her small fist into it.

"Guess you wish that was me," he said lamely. Something had happened to him last night after Sarah left the dance. Frustration had been replaced by gnawing apprehension. He had followed her home and knocked on the door, but Cort had told him that she didn't want to see him. He hadn't slept until almost dawn. Nothing usually interfered with Laramee's sleep.

Sarah inclined her head and turned to face him. Neither of them spoke. She appraised his lithe rider's frame, lean and wiry and obdurately masculine, from the soft blond hair that fell forward when he wasn't wearing a hat, to his Sunday boots. She tried to ignore the gun he had strapped around his lean hips, but her eyes stopped there.

"Why wouldn't you see me?"

"I don't want to see you anymore," she said, turning away.

"Not ever?"

"I don't know…I don't want to talk about it," she said softly. "Why did you come here?"

"To talk to you." He took hold of her arms and gave her a shake to force her to look at him. "I want you to marry me…"

Confused, Sarah looked away to avoid the harsh light in his hazel eyes. "That's not necessary."

"Jesus!" he blurted out. "You are the damnedest woman! I propose marriage to you, and you talk nonsense."

She had known Laramee for twelve of her twenty-one years. For most of that time she had stood on the outside of a high fence and looked into a beautiful garden that was Angie's and his life. She had yearned for Laramee or what he represented so long that it had become habit.

When she was fourteen, Cort gave her a horse. He said it was hers only if she took care of it. Until then she had been just a kid to Laramee.

But one day after her fourteenth birthday, Laramee walked in the livery stable, leading his own horse. At eighteen he had seemed a young god to Sarah—tall and straight and lean-hipped with strong shoulders, curly blond hair, and fine hazel eyes. Sarah had been weak in the knees when he spoke to her. His soft "Hi, girl" was more intimate than anything anyone had ever said to her. At fourteen she had developed fully, and her curiosity about men was overwhelming.

Laramee had taught Sarah to ride, to care for her horse, all the things a man could teach a woman without bedding her. He had protected her, from himself and others.

Now he had proposed. She turned away. "When my mother was killed, I was at school. I didn't get to say good-bye to her. I didn't even get to *see* her until that night after my aunt had laid her out in the parlor. Friends came to pay their respects. I was sitting on the front porch looking at my shoes. They were dusty. My mother was lying in the parlor, dead, and I was thinking that tomorrow when I got up, my mother would make me wipe my shoes before wearing them to school. My mother was very careful about things like that. A good pair of shoes will last a long time if you're careful with them…"

Laramee sighed in frustration. "I proposed to you, Sarah. I want you to marry me."

"My mother was killed by a man who didn't even know her. She was just walking down the street. Two men she didn't know decided to shoot at each other. I'm grateful to you for honoring me with a proposal, Laramee. I had decided I wasn't good enough for you, that that's why you hadn't proposed. Now that you have, I can forgive you. We can be friends."

"I don't want to be your goddamned friend," Laramee said, taking her by the shoulders and forcing her to look at him. "I want you to be my wife."

Laramee wanted more than anything to slap some sense into Sarah's head. She belonged to him. He'd known it when she was just a kid all those years ago. He had been too damned busy with the ranch and taking care of Angie to see Sarah much, and somehow her need had passed. That was his mistake. But he considered it correctable.

Sarah was flesh and blood. She was soft and sweet and beautiful. Sometimes she was earthy and warm, but other times she seemed to live in a dream world. Now, apparently, she expected him to ignore their bond. Just go his separate way because she'd decided not to love him.

Sarah refused to look at Laramee. "Go away," she whispered. "I won't marry you."

Sarah bit her lip until the pain became too much for her. Something *was* wrong with her. She remembered a time last year when Laramee had ridden into town, stopped in the saloon for a drink, gotten into a fight with a stranger, and killed him. Later they found out that the man had been only hours ahead of the law. Laramee had been made out a hero by the town. They gave him a small reward and bought drinks to toast him.

Excited by his celebrity, Laramee had called on Sarah and told her about it. Sarah would never forget that day. She'd had to push him out of the house and slam the door in his face to keep him from seeing her vomit on the floor. She had been horrified because she knew he could hear her, crying and vomiting and crying, but she couldn't stop. He pounded on the door, but she wouldn't open it. He had finally gone to find a woman to come stay with her, but Sarah wouldn't let her in either. He had called on her twice that evening, but she instructed Cort to tell him that she was sick and couldn't be disturbed.

That night she'd dreamed she was lying in bed, probably sick or something. She couldn't get up. Bullets as large as small watermelons came tearing through the wall at her. They moved slowly, wobbling wildly as they came. She screamed and tried to get away from them, but her body wouldn't move. As each bullet hit, big bloody pieces of her flew off in all directions. She woke up screaming, her body covered with perspiration.

The next day she came down with a cold that turned into bronchitis. She recovered in two weeks, but she wouldn't see Laramee the next time he came to town. It was months before she let him call on her again. And then only because he wore her down.

Irritated, Laramee scowled at Sarah. He wished to hell she didn't appeal to him the way she did. She had been nothing but trouble to him lately. Five years ago when he was arrested for breaking up a saloon in a fight against three drunks, she had practically lived at the jail. Everyone in town commented on how Sarah had mooned around the jail, worrying and bringing him things. When he got out at six o'clock in the morning, she skipped school to be with him that day. Cort had raised hell about it, and she hadn't cared.

Sarah looked away from his piercing hazel eyes. Tears welled inside her. She had been miserable since the dance. The world had turned gray and hopeless the minute she made her decision. She could not live with Laramee or without him.

"I don't want to turn you down. I have to."

"Talk sense, girl."

"I can't marry you," she said, miserable.

"Sarah, you belong to me. You always have."

"I can't marry you, because—"

"Because what?"

"Because you'll die." She turned away from him.

"Everybody dies sooner or later."

"You'll die sooner."

"That makes a hell of a lot of sense, Sarah. Dammit, if I thought you were going to die right away, I'd be nice to you. You treat me like a cow turd."

Sarah turned away from him. Frustrated, Laramee pulled her into his arms and set his mouth over hers.

Sarah struggled against him, but she was trapped in his warm arms. His harsh mouth seared into her, reduced her to helpless trembling. She was powerless to resist even if she'd been given an opportunity to do so. The heat of his kiss cleansed her of all past emotion or remembrance.

Still kissing her, Laramee picked her up and carried her into her bedroom.

Naked, Laramee was different. Some of the hardness and the competence left him. She was glad about that. He seemed clumsy and dazed by her. He whispered words to her that seeped into her bones, warming them, warming her.

There was more fear than actual pain for her. Yet, she wanted it. She wanted this nakedness and the physical closeness with Laramee. It was a breathless, dazing, blinding experience. Part of her had wanted it all her life. He was a god to her. A handsome, capable god with broad yet almost timid hands. A man trying not to hurt her. Sarah tried not to cry out when he entered her, but she failed. And then he couldn't continue. And yet couldn't not continue. It was her turn to soothe him, to kiss him, to whisper words of encouragement to him.

Her arms lifted of their own volition, touched the short, crisp hair at the base of his neck. She was open to him now. Nothing mattered except the tender love she felt for him. She was capable of anything, as long as it pleased him, restored him.

Without her willing it, her body was caught up in the swell of their passion, swept along with his, though not to the same brink. She felt his urgency and the mindless nature of his fierce tension, but she did not fully share it.

Afterward, he lay beside her, panting softly, and she snuggled close to him and loved him, forgetting everything except that he had needed her.

A light film of pale hairs clustered in the center of his chest sparkled like candy floss. The sturdy symmetry of his lean hips and hard thighs mesmerized her.

"Set the date, Sarah. Pick one close," he said softly.

Part of her responded to his eagerness, but part of her remembered the terrifying crash of gunfire the night before. She shook her head. A husband was a man to grow old with, and Laramee would not grow old. He would die in a pool of blood in some dingy, dirty saloon, or his fine young face would be ground into some dusty boulevard. A hard knot of heavy pain moved inside her.

"I can't marry you."

Laramee sighed. How could she mean that? Part of him believed in his ability to take anything he wanted from her, but the look in her eyes, at once submissive, stubborn, and glazed with a residue of the mindless terror he had seen in her last night, told him she meant it. How could she love him and mean it?

As long as he'd known her, he'd had the feeling that part of her was sleeping, that if he could only wake her completely, she would belong to him. All of her. Not just the parts he could sometimes take from her or that she would yield. He rolled over to lie on top of her again.

With strong, warm hands on either side of her face, he forced her to look into his eyes. "I want you, Sarah. I love you. You're gonna marry me."

A tiny quiver of pride and fear pooled in her belly. Fear predominated. Sarah shivered. She had always been timid about forcing her wishes on other people. It was easier to seem to comply until the pressure of the moment passed, then she would do as she wished. She said nothing.

Fully restored now, sturdy and stubborn, Laramee shook his head, grinning at her. "You'll marry me, Sarah Elizabeth, because I'm not going away. I know what I want," he said, his bold hazel eyes confident and cocky again.

At this moment she did not have the courage to openly defy him, but she would escape somehow. She remembered the way he had looked at the dance, the automatic way his hand had reached for the gun that was not there.

Laramee sat up and looked at her. "Set the date."

"No."

Laramee expelled a breath of frustration. She was doing it again. Withdrawing from him. Furious, he pulled on his clothes, picked up his hat, and walked to the door.

Torn, Sarah grabbed her dressing gown and followed him.

"When will I see you again?" she asked, unable to stop herself.

"Why the hell would you want to see me again? You want to go wolfing, using me for bait?" he demanded, his voice tight with fury.

Sarah ached with loss. She was losing something. Something she had wanted so long, it had twisted her. "I might change my mind," she whispered.

"It might snow in hell too," he said grimly.

His sturdy hand reached for the doorknob, and a hard icy band clamped around Sarah's heart. "I'll hate you if you leave," she whispered.

Laramee adjusted his hat. "Think that'll make a difference in the way you treat me?" he growled.

Hates me enough, it might be a goddamned improvement.

CHAPTER TEN

Sunday, May 16, 1880

Gil walked in the middle of the road down the slight incline from the Liang house to the Chinese quarter. Barefoot children stopped playing to look at him. Their comments caused him to smile inside. His face, trained to his will, remained emotionless. They called him *chung may won hut yee*, the American-Chinese half-breed. A man stepped out of the wine shop, saw him, and called his friends out to laugh at the *won hut yee* with no pigtail, no honor. They called him *chop chung*, which caused Gil's face to grow hot. *Chop chung* had no literal equivalent in English, but the meaning was a crude reminder of his semi-illegitimacy.

Stung, unaccustomed to being laughed at by Chinese, Gil walked past the crowing men, chiding himself for his weakness. He had been insulated in Cambridge too long. He had grown soft.

No one stopped Gil as he walked through the dining room to Kincaid's table, but even among whites, heads turned.

Caught off guard, Lance eyed Gil dubiously. Gilbert Lee's body had lost none of its power. Even clothed as Lance was, Gil's body exuded indisputable strength. Even through a half-deserted dining room in a sleepy hotel Gil moved with the peculiar flatfooted walk of the warrior. The handsome smoothness of his Oriental features gave little away.

"May I sit down?"

Wary and distrustful, Lance nodded.

"Did you hear about the sermon?" Gil slipped into the chair opposite Kincaid.

"What sermon?"

Gil sat forward and tapped the white tablecloth. "The minister of the First Baptist Church peppered his congregation this morning. He's demanding that they run us 'yellow devils' from their midst. He claimed to be upset because Miss Logan was almost killed in the barn fire. He's calling us addicts, heathens, thiefs, and prostitutes."

Lance grimaced. "He didn't miss much, except maybe idol worship—"

"He mentioned that too."

Lance was in such a good mood after taking Angie Logan home last night that he could be civil even to Gil Lee. He leaned back and grinned. "Just what this town needs. A man of the cloth to spread oil on troubled waters and then light a match to it. How are the 'yellow devils' taking it?"

"The Liang family home burned during the riots in Nevada. They are terrified, but Third Uncle is a Taoist. He would turn the other cheek. Lily is more militant—she would give back slap for slap."

Lance grunted. "Spirited as she is beautiful..."

"Understatement. She could be a Manchu. Give her a sword..." He sighed with the memory of his fierce little foster cousin, and warmth filled his dark eyes. "If I'm not careful, I'll be leading the opposition forces." Gil frowned. Not *leading* them, he reminded himself, *perhaps beating them off.* He was as much an outcast among the Chinese of Durango as he had been among the whites of Cambridge. More so. In Cambridge he had been novel, but hardly disgraced.

Lance spread blunt bronzed fingers on the white tablecloth. Gil assessed him automatically, his mind noticing the changes in Kincaid. He seemed tougher now, less idealistic, and temporarily distracted.

"Where did you meet Miss Logan?" he asked softly.

"Nogales, Phoenix, then here. She and her camera seem to turn up everywhere," he said, his eyes challenging Gil to make something of it.

Gil shook his head. "She's very beautiful."

Kincaid nodded.

"You ever going to forgive me?" Gil asked quietly.

Rage rose up in Lance so unexpectedly that he almost could not contain it. The emotion felt like a grizzly lifting its paw, preparing to strike. "Don't give yourself so damned much credit," Lance gritted. "It's not a matter of forgiving. It's a matter of knowing who to trust and when to trust 'em. I've got better things to do than count and store grudges."

At any other time Gil might have reasoned with his old friend, but not today. Gil stood abruptly and walked away.

Lance reached for his coffee cup. His hand trembled. So much for making peace with Gil. He set the cup down and expelled a loud sigh. Gil was a murderer who deserved the guilt he carried. *I hope he stews in it. I hope the bastard croaks in it.*

A pain shot into Lance's side from the exertion of his "easy assignment." Damn McNamara anyway. He'd check on Nunca and take a nap.

• • •

Gil found Lily in the pagoda, kneeling before the family's ancestral sanctuary. In China the sanctuary would be equipped with bell, oil lamp, and soul tablets. But here, surrounded by boisterous, drunken men who thought Chinese ways hilarious, Third Uncle had buried the clothes of an ancient ancestor in a clothes grave to sanctify the pagoda.

Soul tablets were kept in the house for safety. Twenty-five generations of relatives had become soul tablets. According to Third Uncle, who showed unaccustomed bitterness in his telling, less than two dozen soul tablets remained. Each time the family fled their home a few more were lost.

Lily touched her head to the mat in obeisance. Gil watched from a respectful distance. She clenched her small fists on her knees and sat up. Tears streaked her cheeks.

A tiny flame of compassion rose within him. But then Gil thought of the Baptist minister's sermon and felt himself sinking into lethargy. He had the white man's tendency to moodiness.

His father, Lee Ah Wah, had been the third son of dispossessed peasants. Crippled in one of the peasant revolts, Ah Wah had wandered about selling his children and his wife to provide food and shelter. A white man bought Gil's mother and impregnated her. Ah Wah did not want the white man's bastard. The day Gil was born Ah Wah gave Gil, named Son of Autumn, to the monks at the Shaolin temple. He was raised a warrior. When Gil was ten, the white man died and set his mother free. She came for Gil and then went back to her husband, begging to be taken in. During the years his mother had lived with her white owner, she stole from his pantry and slipped food into the baskets of her other children, who appeared at the back door of the white man's house. Thankful for many years of gleanings from the white man's pantry and grateful for another woman and child to sell, Ah Wah agreed to take them back.

Ah Wah beat Gil for slight offenses. Accustomed to the stern fairness and the quiet of the temple, Gil chafed in misery. One night Gil ran away and walked back to the temple.

The monks let him stay until Ah Wah sent word that Third Uncle had bought Gil and his mother to be servants in the Liang family home. Shortly the Liang family moved to Chengtu. Gil lived in Chengtu until Third Uncle joined the staff of the embassy. Gil and his mother moved with the Liangs to Hong Kong. Third Uncle recognized Gil's intelligence and sent him to the English school. There he met Angell Burrill, a white instructor who became his friend and mentor and who eventually brought him to America with him. Burrill was a personal friend of Clayton James, vice-president of Harvard University. Burrill died and left Gil a paid scholarship to Harvard Law and a small cash inheritance, gone the second year. To pay his living expenses he worked nights teaching kung fu to rich young white students. Lance was one of his students, his most apt pupil, and the only one who seemed to understand that kung fu was more than just a way to fight.

At last Lily bowed and scooted backward. She stood up, saw Gil, and stopped. Her chin lifted, and she wiped at her eyes. Anger sparkled there.

"What transgression brings you here today?" Gil asked, struggling to keep his humor to himself.

"Nothing! I did nothing!"

Gil smiled.

"Almost nothing." She pouted. "I only told my Honorable Father the truth. That he was a fool to think the *fan quai* would protect him from white jackals."

"I am glad it was something so minor," Gil said, smiling in spite of his attempt not to. For a young Chinese girl trained from birth in obedience and respect for her elders, to call her father a fool was unthinkable disrespect.

"Dost thou agree with my honorable father?" she asked.

Thoroughly enchanted by Lily, Gil shook his head. "Your father lived through the Taiping Revolution. He has seen men revolt, fail, and die miserable deaths, all in vain. He uses the excuse that he hates hatred and loathes violence because he does not believe in rebellion, only in keeping quiet." Gil surprised himself; he had said too much. He spoke to the girl as if she instead of her father were his peer. Like so many Taoists, Third Uncle had arrived at his own distortion of the Tao, which is at heart an acceptance of life, of what is, of what cannot be spoken. True Taoism was a wedding with life rather than an attempt to control or to avoid life. Gil taught philosophy at Harvard. Religions were his forte, as were people's attempts to mangle religious doctrines to fit their own purposes.

"I will not know if I agree until I see what effect the sermon has. Nothing may come of it," he concluded, embarrassed.

"Nothing! Then thou art as blind as my honorable father," she said, anger brightening her dark eyes. "Three of my cousins rot in their temporary graves. They will send no money to their honorable mother in China. Someday a mail pouch will take her their bones. Unless tramp

Christians steal them to feed their dogs!"

"One cousin was killed by the devil worshipers in the City of Silver. No one cared that he had risked his life so the iron road could stretch from one ocean to another. They care only about their own desires. We will be refugees forever. Soul tablets of our ancestors will be scattered from one end of this continent to the other."

Gil sighed. Young and fierce, Lily did not venerate ancient ancestors so much as she resented the times her family had been forced to flee for their lives in the middle of the night and to leave most of their possessions behind.

To Chinese, veneration for the elderly was a worship as serious as Christianity. The names of sons were entered into the Family Book of Generations with great pride. Daughters were considered a liability. If they did not marry well, they had to be supported.

Gil wanted to comfort Lily, but words were meaningless to her. She was too close to the memories of the three young men who had died and still unsettled by the shock of believing Third Uncle had died in the burning barn.

Something about that misunderstanding bothered Gil, but he did not know what. "Walk with me," he said.

"I am not a courtesan. I will bring thee no comfort," she said scornfully.

"I wish none. I would like to give you comfort, if that is possible..."

Her gaze flicked over him, seeing his thick black glossy hair cut short in the Caucasian tradition, his handsome, half-Chinese, half-Caucasian features, his broad shoulders and slim hips. He was too tall for a Chinese, too Chinese for a Caucasian. "What wilt thou say to me? That only resolution and unrightness of spirit, virtues bequeathed to me by my ancient ancestors, can transform this ruin into resurgence?" she mocked.

"I would have you forget all that for a period of time, if you will," he said gently.

"Forget that the *fan quai* want to run us from yet another rat-infested place? Forget that the most generous ones begrudge us this small shack that would not have been good enough for our servants in China?"

"That is what I ask of you," he said, nodding.

Lily filled with outrage and anger. Gilbert James Lee was a dear friend of her honorable father. To deny his request would be the equivalent of being rude to her father. To Lily, schooled since birth to put filial duty above all else, this should have been unthinkable, but it was not. She lifted her chin and smiled mockingly.

"As thou doth wish," she said softly in an obvious caricature of a courtesan, perhaps Jade Precious, a beautiful singsong girl he had seen as he walked past the opium den.

Smiling, ignoring her jibe, Gil walked slowly beside her, being careful always to leave the most comfortable part of the path for her to walk.

His care was obvious to Lily, and she glanced sideways at him, wondering about this strange half Chinese who had the manners of a Confucian monk and friends in the white community. Born a peasant, he had been accepted as a member of the scholar-gentry, and yet he had the stance of a military officer. Her father looked up to him. Sturdy and lithe, he walked with the absolute poise of the warrior, feet firmly planted in case of attack, aware of his surroundings, secure, and self-contained. Son of Autumn was a man respected by other men, a man capable of defending himself. A man who chose his own destiny…

Her father had told her that Son of Autumn was an officer under Taohung, that he had saved Chengtu from the Niens, who were true guerrillas. Like locusts ferried by the wind, the Niens swept into provinces, using ambushcade and surprise raids to kill local officials and redistribute their hoards of grain.

Son of Autumn had visited China for two years during the Nien uprising and led troops in raids against the Niens. A true scholar, her father had not even tasted blood fighting his own peasants. He had been one of the few whose peasants did not rise up against him. As Third Uncle had only a daughter, he could not dedicate a son to a military career. Son of Autumn had dedicated himself in her father's name, saving face for him.

A thistle stung Lily's leg above the ankle, and she bent down angrily. "I hate this ugly land. I hate it. Even as I walk it reaches out to sting me," she hissed. A sob came up to embarrass her.

Gil bent down beside her. At sight of her tears, compassion flamed up in him. "You miss the honeysuckle arches of the Ram temple, the wisteria drooping over rocky ponds, the strolling young lovers talking earnestly of their futures…"

New tears welled in Lily's eyes. She looked quickly away.

"This land is different, but it is not ugly," he said gently. "Look," he said, lifting her up. He pointed to the chalk-white clouds floating in the azure blue sky, to the far-off mountains that rose so clearly and cleanly into the clouds that they looked like paintings propped against the horizon.

"To me it is ugly," she said stubbornly.

"All of it?" he asked softly.

"All of it," she proclaimed.

"The clouds are ugly?"

"Dragon breath cannot be ugly," she said stoutly, looking at him as if he lacked in understanding. "They are the same clouds that soar over China…"

"Then it is the sky that is ugly?"

"Sky cannot be ugly," she said.

"Then the distant mountains are ugly?"

"Mountains are not—" She stopped. A light flickered in her eyes, and a corresponding light moved in his eyes. A smile tugged at the corners of his lips.

"Thou hast tricked me," she said petulantly.

She turned her face away from him. Her hair, glossy and knotted into the smooth coiffure of the fashionable Chinese woman, heightened the impact of her beauty.

"You tricked yourself perhaps. I would not trick a woman as beautiful as you."

Flushing, Lily continued to look away. "Thou art very bold. Did thou learn such boldness from thy Christian family?"

Gil laughed. Angell Burrill had been Taoist. "All people of this continent are not Christians. There are many different religions here, just as there are in China."

Fury moved in her dark eyes. "I do not wish to hear about *fan quai* religions…not even from thee."

Gil held up his hands to ward off her angry remarks. "Torture would not pry details from me."

Unable to help herself, Lily laughed. "Thou art a true Hakka. Clannish, loyal, a ready fighter, strong, and, no doubt, a bad neighbor."

"The worst."

From the house, Third Uncle saw them together, Son of Autumn, tall and sturdy, and Lily, slender and graceful, and his heart was glad. Soon there would be a wedding announcement to make. It pleased him greatly.

Angie heard Kincaid's distinctive, low voice and stopped. Curious, she walked into the shade of the barn and pretended to fumble for something inside the brown paper bag she carried. She had shopped for food for Hop Wo's family. She had been on her way home to gather her purchases so she could take them to him. She needed to reassure herself that Hop Wo had gotten the medical help he needed for his broken legs. She turned and peered through the wide cracks in the wood. Kincaid and Atillo stood in the small corral behind the livery stable barn.

"That's a fine-looking horse you have there," Lance said, nodding at Atillo's chestnut pony.

"*Sí, señor*, she's beautiful, no?" Atillo's voice was full of pride. The chestnut pawed the dusty ground.

"She belong to you?"

"*Sí, Señorita* Angela gave her to me. I raised her from a colt. She's four years old next winter."

Angie had forgotten she gave Atillo that horse. When the chestnut was three months old, she had brought it into town to show it to Sarah, and Atillo had become attached to it. She hadn't realized it until she tried to take the pony back to the ranch. Eleven years old, Atillo's face had twisted with pain. Angie led the chestnut to the creek—trying to ignore the reflected pain in her chest—and stopped to let the colt drink. Atillo would get over it…

It wasn't even her horse. She looked back toward town. Atillo had followed them. She looked at his luminous brown eyes and decided that the person who needed the horse the most should have it; she gave the pony to Atillo and prepared to take her licking from Laramee. But he had surprised her. He only laughed and said, *Hell, every boy needs a colt. Reckon they don't get many young ones in there. His old man's as tight as the boards on a new barn.*

"She broke?" Lance asked.

"*Sí*, well, almost. She's not bit broke. But I can ride her with the *haquima*." Atillo held out a beautiful, softly gleaming silver bit. His eyes shone with pride.

"That's a mighty fine bit," Lance said.

"*Sí, señor*, it belonged to my grandfather. He was a fine *vaquero, muy caballero*, but he is too old to ride now."

"Does it fit the contours of her mouth?"

"*Sí*, it is perfect." Atillo's eyes clouded with perplexity. "I do not understand. I have done everything exactly as I hear it from my grandfather."

"I know the feeling well. Don Leonardo was the smartest man I ever knew about horses, and he had a saying: *El es asi.* That accounted for all the idiosyncrasies any horse ever had. *He is so.*"

Atillo frowned. "You mean maybe she is just not ready for the bit?"

Atillo squinted up at Lance, his face earnest.

"*Sí, amigo*, that is possible. Does she froth at the mouth when you ride her with the *haquima*?"

"No."

"Don Leonardo believed that a man should not bit a horse until the horse asks for the bit."

"*Ayie!*" Atillo cried. "But how does she do that?"

Lance paused. "Are you breaking her to be a cow pony?"

"*Sí*."

"Reining is important then. Better wait till she's four years old before bitting her. Tough mouths come from being bitted too soon. There's nothing worse than a tough-mouthed cow pony. Can get a man killed *pronto*."

"Did you raise Nunca from a pony?"

"No, he was four years old when I got him. The *vaquero* who sold him to me called him Nunca because he'd never been ridden, and they believed he couldn't be. He traded Nunca straight across for a seven-year-old burro I didn't want. He thought he got a bargain. I took Nunca into the mountains. It was summertime, and we stayed up there five months in a grassy *senaca* surrounded by steep cliffs. Just me and Nunca. By the end of that summer I was riding him. He never bucked."

As he talked, Lance edged around to the side of the corral. He leaned down and handed the silver bit to a small Chinese boy Angie had not noticed before. The boy was very thin, crouched on his haunches in the dirt, watching them with solemn eyes. His clothes were threadbare and tattered, and his feet were dirty. His cheeks were too thin, the skin stretched taut over his shaven crown.

"That's Tan Lin," Atillo said, squinting into the sun.

"My name's Kincaid. Lance Kincaid. Nice bit, huh?"

Small for his age, Tan Lin was probably seven or eight by now. He had been four or five when Angie left Durango. He looked from Atillo to Lance. Slowly Tan Lin held out his hand and touched the bit. Lance did not pull it away, so the boy took it in his hands and turned it over.

"Did you ever help with horse-breaking?" Atillo asked, shading his eyes to look up at Lance.

"*Sí*," Lance said, squatting between the two boys. "It was required."

"Bet you were good at it!" Atillo cried, his eyes glowing with worshipful light.

Lance laughed. "My father was very strict. To please him, I always tried to be good at those things a man is expected to do. What do you call her?"

"Savitar."

"What does that mean?"

"*Señorita* Angela helped me pick the name. It means golden god of motion."

Lance grinned, probably noting the incorrect gender, but he said nothing. Angie flushed. A male god's name for a female horse. Why hadn't she realized that before?

Atillo turned to the smaller boy. "Do Chinese ride horses?"

The boy looked back at him with unreadable black eyes.

"Do you ride?" Atillo demanded. "He doesn't talk."

Angie frowned. Tan Lin's mother had worked for the Ellington family before Angie left Durango. They were one of the few Chinese families Angie remembered. Hop Wo, the man injured by Neville Smalley in the fight yesterday, was Tan Lin's father.

Tan Lin's thinness nagged at Angie. She had an overwhelming impulse to feed him. Didn't his family take care of him? She rummaged in her grocery bag and located the out-of-season apples she had bought at great expense. She walked inside, past the stalls, and out into the sunlight.

"Atillo..." Lance squatted next to Tan Lin. Angie stopped in the middle of the high barn door opening, pretending to be surprised. "Oh, I hope I'm not intruding."

"Not at all," Lance said, standing up slowly. Angie wore a pale yellow organdy gown and deeper yellow bonnet, one of those wide-brimmed, lacy creations that filtered the light and looked feminine and provocative. In spite of the heat, she looked fresh and lovely.

Angie looked from Lance Kincaid's smiling face to Atillo and Tan Lin. "Good afternoon, gentlemen," she said, flushing.

Feeling an almost painful giddiness and excitement in the back of her head, Angie reached into her bag and drew out an apple. Hoping she was not too obvious, she offered one to Atillo. The handsome lad blushed.

"Here," she said. Under the spell of Kincaid's warmly smiling eyes, her voice had turned strangely husky and sensual.

"No, thank you, *Señorita* Angela," he whispered, backing away from the proffered apple.

"Whyever not?" she asked softly.

Suffering intensely from the pressure of the apple offered so sweetly, Atillo's face turned brick red.

Angie shook the apple. "Take it..." she insisted, unwilling to relent. If she did, how could she offer an apple to Tan Lin?

Shaking his head no, Atillo backed away.

Resting his elbows on the corral fence, Lance tasted bile in the back of his throat. In his head the image of Angie was replaced spontaneously with one of 'Cinda, holding out a champagne glass to him. The image was gone instantly, but the anger did not go with it. His impulse was to take the apple from Angie's hand and throw it as far as it would go. Rage rose up in him.

Angie flashed a glance at him, and he wanted to shake her, to change the expression in those smiling brown eyes.

"Take it," she whispered, determined to have her way, her tone cajoling, intense.

Overcome, Atillo sighed. He looked from Kincaid, who had gone quite still, to Angie, who smiled at him. The boy's hand wavered when he reached for the apple.

Relieved, Angie offered one to Tan Lin. Instead of taking it, Tan Lin looked solemnly back at her. She could not believe the trouble she was having giving an apple to this pitifully thin little boy. What had gotten into these children?

"Take it, please."

Tan Lin shook his head.

"May I give it to you?" she asked.

Resistance smoldered in Tan Lin's dark eyes. Why did everything have to be so difficult? Thinking fast, Angie said, "For giving my horse a few forkfuls of hay?"

Finally the younger boy nodded. He took the apple, put it into the pocket of his baggy pants, and started for the stable.

"Wait," Angie called. "Why don't you eat the apple first?"

The boy frowned at her.

"Please," she said. "Here's one for later…"

Tan Lin took the apple in his hand and looked at it, then licked it with the tip of his tongue.

Unable to wait, Angie said, "Eat it."

His dark eyes on Angie, Tan Lin bit into the apple. A smile showed in his eyes. He took another quick bite and chewed slowly, savoring the delicious flavor.

From the barn the sound of Chinese children became audible. Tan Lin turned and ran toward the barn.

"Where is he going?" Angie asked, frowning at Kincaid.

Remote and irritated, Lance shook his head.

Unsatisfied, Angie started after the boy. Lance followed her through the barn and into the alley.

Tan Lin was in the middle of a group of Chinese youngsters. The apples were making their way from mouth to mouth, the children chewing loudly, chattering like magpies.

"Drat!" Angie whispered. "I wanted *him* to eat those apples."

Lance took her by the arm and walked her back around the livery stable.

"Did I do something wrong?" she demanded, intimidated by the look in Kincaid's blue eyes, affected by the rough way his warm hand was holding her arm. She had hoped that he would at least give her an intimate, reassuring look, but his eyes were deliberately neutral.

"Chinese are clannish. They take care of one another when they can."

"I just didn't want the boy to go hungry. I couldn't bear that."

"Even if it's only a Chinese devil?" he asked.

"You heard about the sermon?"

Lance nodded.

"What do you think will happen?" she asked, wondering if this revelation accounted for his moodiness.

"Don't know."

"Guess," she urged.

"Someone will form an association to drive the yellow devils from Durango. They'll call it something like the Durango Protective and Anti-Coolie Association. They'll all be voters and upstanding citizens…"

"That's dreadful. I think you are maligning our citizens."

"I hope so," he said, his voice grim.

They were in the street now. Traffic was lighter today, but buggies and horsemen rattled and clattered past, billowing dust. She turned to face him. He took the bag of groceries from her. His anger faded like the image that sparked it.

"You left in a hurry last night. I wanted to ask you…"

"I left in a hurry!" Lance laughed, and the sound warmed every corner of Angie's body. "I risked my life to ride you home. You seen your brother today?"

"Laramee's probably gone back to the ranch."

"If you can get yourself an affidavit to that effect, I'll walk you home." Her empathic brown eyes sparkled with devilment. She squinted at the bright sunlight behind him.

"I'm used to young men who don't have time to walk a girl home, but I swarn Mr. Kincaid, I never yet met one who wanted a safe conduct."

"My momma didn't raise no fools, ma'am."

"She raise very many scaredy cats?"

"Jest me and my brothers. The girls came out fair to middlin'."

Angie giggled. She felt wonderful. The sky was bluer now, the clouds whiter.

"You about done with your shopping?"

"Why?"

"Thought maybe you'd like to make me that bite of food you mentioned last night. I'm plumb famished." Her fresh, powdery fragrance ignited a small pulse in his belly.

"You won't mind if I invite my brother, will you?"

"Instead of me?"

"In addition to you…"

"Sorry, ma'am, I ain't intending to eat dinner with no grizzly-skinner. Get my stomach all churned up, I might as well not eat."

"Walk to the creek with me."

"Ain't that the wrong way from dinner?"

"If you're starving, I have food in that bag."

Lance looked into the bag. "Reckon this'll do for me, but what are you going to do?"

Angie giggled. "Any man afraid of my brother won't keep me from getting anything I want. I been whipping him for years."

"Then why'd you let him scare me like that?"

"You complain more than any man I ever knew."

"Knowed. If'n you're gonna spoon with me, you gotta tawk right."

"Did you ever practice law, Kincaid?"

"About six months."

"You any good at it?"

"Showed some early promise, but I was too crooked to be any good at it over the long haul."

They ate by the creek. Angie expected him to eat a lot, but he barely touched his food. He lay on his back, and she leaned against her elbows facing him. He pillowed his head on his hands and looked entirely at ease. The temperature had to be near ninety-five degrees, but she was barely aware of the heat.

"Are you ever serious, Kincaid?"

"You've seen me serious."

"No, I haven't."

"Sure you have. Nogales."

"You didn't say anything at all."

"Threatened to shoot you, didn't I? If they'd given me my gun, we could have recuperated together."

"You might have killed me, though."

"You see where I plugged Winchester?"

"Yeah."

"A man can't shoot any straighter than that ain't a big threat to anyone but himself."

"Hisself," she teased. "Where did you grow up?"

"Everywhere."

"Specifically…"

"Well, rumor has it I was born in Texas. My dad has a ranch outside of Austin. A little place, about twenty thousand acres of mesquite and prickly pear, but the first place I remember is London, where he has a thousand acres or so. My daddy likes to own dirt. He owns English dirt, French dirt, New York City dirt, and Texas dirt. Last I heard he's trying to get control of water. Once he owns all the dirt and all the water, he'll probably get interested in air. Then we better look out."

"Haven't you ever wanted to own any dirt?"

"Just enough for one house and one barn. I don't know what I'd do with any more."

"…don't rightly know…" she corrected him.

"Why don't you stop picking on me before you scare me again? Lean down here and kiss me. We been spooning for nigh onto an hour, and you haven't once kissed me."

"I'm playing hard to get. Cousin Virginia wrote an article on it."

"I can't imagine Virginia advocating such a thing."

"She didn't. She was opposed to any form of coquetry, but she mentioned all the things women get who do practice it, so I just thought—"

"Hell, if there's something you want, just ask for it."

He sounded so wistful that Angie laughed. She leaned over him and kissed his warm mouth for a long time. Her head started to spin. She sat up to keep from falling.

"You call that puny thing a kiss?"

"You didn't like it?"

"I didn't hardly notice it, it was over so fast."

"You complain more than any man I ever—"

A gunshot interrupted her. Kincaid struggled to his feet, holding his side as he did, and grabbed his hat. "You wait here."

He walked quickly away, his limp diminishing as he warmed up.

Angie left the remnants of their picnic and ran after him. She was at a disadvantage. Her shoes didn't work as well as his low-heeled boots. "You stay here," he yelled over his shoulder.

"No, I'm coming with you."

CHAPTER ELEVEN

Kincaid stopped. "You might get shot."

"I might get several good shots," she agreed.

"I meant with a forty-five." Kincaid strode away in the direction of the gunshot. "Stay here, out of harm's way."

"I'm not a daisy, Kincaid. I'm not going to sit in a clay pot." Angie ran toward *The Tea Time News* to get her camera. Another gunshot and then another split the silence.

She unlocked the door and grabbed the Scenographe from beside the front door; she didn't have time to fool with the wagon. She locked the door and ran north toward the source of the gunfire.

She needn't have rushed. Kincaid sat on the sidewalk talking to a group of men. He couldn't have looked more relaxed. She stopped and tried to catch her breath while she waited impatiently for Kincaid to stop talking and notice her.

Finally Kincaid got up and strolled over to her side.

"What happened?" she asked, seeing his grin.

"Ramo's mad as a hatter. He lost ten dollars."

"How?"

"He arrested a fellow named Jake for the high crimes of littering, loitering, and cussing a marshal, and hauled him before the police court judge, who fined him twenty dollars. Jake figured the fine was too high, so he took out his gun and shot the judge."

The police court judge was empowered by the city selectmen to try minor offenses—petty larceny, petty thievery, and the like—to lighten the load on District Judge Leroy Cadwallader who got to Durango only about once every two weeks.

"Is he dead?"

"Yep. If you hurry, you can get a picture of him before they carry him away."

Angie shuddered. She did not want or need any more pictures of dead men. "That doesn't explain why Ramo lost ten dollars."

"The territory doesn't pay town marshals or police court judges a salary. So the police court judge splits fines with the marshal. All they get is what they can wring out of lawbreakers."

"What happened to Jake?"

"Ramo killed him. That's why he was mad. He aimed to wing him, but he died. He's about as bad a shot as I am. If I'd been marshal, I could a lost thirty-six dollars in Nogales."

"Why did that make Ramo mad? I should think he'd be ecstatic. He *loves* to kill people…"

"Dead men don't pay fines," he drawled.

Angie frowned. "I don't understand. You said you could have lost thirty-six dollars. You get paid by the body?"

"I said *if*. *If* we got paid by the men we bring in alive. Which we don't. The governor decided to pay rangers a flat salary. Guess he was hoping we'd be more honest that way."

"Does it work?"

"Most folks don't know how we get paid, so we fine 'em anyway and keep the fines."

"What are you going to do now?"

"I better strut around town a little while, make sure things settle down. I'd sure like to see you tonight, but I'm plumb tuckered out."

"Get your beauty rest, lawman. I'll see you tomorrow or the next day."

Lance walked down the street. He didn't realize he was grinning until he glanced at a street window to check the activity behind him. And there he was, grinning like crazy. Well, Angie Logan was some girl. She knew how to hold on kinda looselike. He grinned. He was even beginning to *tawk* like that when he spooned with her in his head.

Laramee left Sarah's house and walked north through town. Sarah's rejection of his marriage proposal hurt like hell.

Harry Sloan stepped out of the hotel where he had been enjoying late lunch. "Howdy, Shorty."

"Howdy yourself," Laramee said grimly. He didn't like Sloan. In school Sloan had towered over him. Laramee had grown six inches after he turned fifteen. Now Sloan, owner of *The Gazette*, was the same height as Laramee.

"I'd like to get your comments on the little set-to with the Chinese yesterday that almost cost your sister her life."

"You got more lip than a muley cow, you know that?" Laramee bit back his harsher comment.

Sloan ignored the insult. "How do you feel about Chinese endangering your sister's life?"

"You know, sonny, you're just about frying size. I'd be careful, I was you, that you don't get me mad. No one messes with my sister and gets away with it."

"Do you mean you might take the law into your own hands?" Sloan persisted.

Laramee tilted his head back and looked the reporter up and down. His eyes lingered on Sloan's soft middle, noting the way the flesh swelled over his belt. Sloan's freckled face was smooth and pale. Except for his belly, he still looked like the scrawny kid—a bookworm and teacher's pet—who had made life miserable for Laramee in school, but the softness was more pronounced now. Sloan looked puffy. Laramee grinned, feeling slightly better. "I mean what I said."

"Are you going to join the Durango Protective and Anti-Chinese Association?"

Laramee's eyebrows shot up. He grinned and rocked back and forth on his heels, enjoying himself now. "What the hell is the Anti-Chinese Protective Association?" he sneered, inflecting it just right so it sounded like a sissy organization, something Sloan would no doubt be associated with. Laramee enjoyed the way Sloan's smooth pink face reddened with heat.

"An association of respectable citizens who are banding together to run the Chinese out of Durango," Sloan said, ducking his head to write furiously on the pad he carried.

Laramee shook his head in disgust. "Sheeeit! Sounds like something a silly-assed bunch of old men thought of. Y'all gonna make quilts or sell cakes?" He shoved past Sloan, stomping his heels into the hollow-sounding sidewalk as he put distance between himself and the irritating reporter.

Angie left Kincaid and walked back to the office. She unlocked the door and put the Scenographe back in its place, then settled down to make up for the work she had forgotten to do yesterday. All the excitement and the pictures she had taken of the desert in bloom had distracted her. Angie worked steadily for three hours. A knock caused her to look up.

Harry Sloan banged on the window. Angie motioned him to come in. "I want to ask you what happened at that fire yesterday."

"I was on my way in from the ranch. I rode by the Liang house and caught Rufe Martin on top of Lily. I yelled at him, and he let her up. Then we heard something in the barn, and Lily screamed, and when Rufe noticed that I had heard it, he hit Lily and offered to leave with me. I asked about the two horses, the bay and the dun, and Rufe got real nervous. He tried to get me to leave, but I ran into the barn. Then Rufe or someone dropped the bar over the door and the windows and I couldn't get out. I looked out and saw Lily still lying where Martin had knocked her. Then I smelled kerosene and smoke. I tried to shoot the bar across the window, and that's the last thing I remember. Kincaid said he carried me outside, and I woke up."

"Why do you think the Chinese wanted to kill you?"

"The Chinese had nothing to do with my being locked in the barn. There were two horses, standing together. Rufe Martin and another man had come there together. Whoever rode off on that bay killed Rufe and tried to kill me."

"Maybe the Chinese want to be rid of both you and your brother?"

"That's not true! I have friends in the Chinese community. I'm certain I would know if there were any conspiracy."

Sloan thanked her for her information and left. Angie went back to work. Another knock caused her to sigh. She stepped outside the door this time, hoping she could shorten the visit by withdrawing when *she* was ready.

"I just heard about the fire," Ellen Smith said. Ellen was a stout woman with tired eyes and a starched apron over a faded gray gown.

Angie retold the story to Ellen. "I don't know what this town is coming to when a woman isn't even safe in broad daylight. Reverend Collins was right. It's time we got rid of them Chinese."

"It wasn't their fault," Angie said, amazed that Ellen hadn't heard anything she had said. "The Chinese were the ones being attacked. Those men rode to their house—"

"Well, you be careful, you hear?" Ellen interrupted. "Stay away from them chinks." Ellen walked quickly away.

Apparently Reverend Collins had spread the word so effectively, that nothing as simple as the truth mattered. Folks' minds were made up.

One person after another stopped to chat with Angie at *The Tea*

Time News. Besieged by friends and acquaintances wanting all the details, Angie gave up trying to work, locked up, and rode her bicycle home.

Lily passed a plate of dry-sugared, smoked fish to Gil. Her hand lingered beneath his. Gil glanced quickly at Third Uncle to see if this had alarmed him, but the old man seemed not to have noticed. Lily surprised Gil. During their walk earlier he had not sensed coquetry in Lily, only spirit and obstinance.

Thirty-eight years old and thoroughly aware of what was proper for him as a guest in Third Uncle's home, Gil refused to encourage the girl, who could be no more than seventeen. He took the bowl and averted his eyes.

A moment passed. "Wouldst thou sample the chicken gizzards?" Lily asked, her eyes engaging his boldly. Gil could see now why the child spent so much time making obeisance to her honorable ancestors.

After the elaborate meal ended, Third Uncle retired to the parlor to read. Mei-ling, Lily, and Toy busied themselves in the kitchen. Outside the window the sun neared the horizon. Durango still sweltered in the heat. Little relief from heat existed inside or outside the house. Gil picked up a book and started to follow his foster father. Lily lowered the serving tray she carried and brushed close to Gil, motioning him to bend down to hear her whispered words.

"Please. I need to speak with thee. Meet me tonight, in the pagoda…"

"When?"

"After my parents are asleep. *Please*."

Tan Lin watched his stepmother, and a feeling of guilt and misery swelled inside him. Earlier today he had given the apples to the children. He should have brought them home for his family. With shame he pushed the rice away.

His honorable stepmother, Du Pon Gai, ate slowly. His honorable grandfather, Li Ping, squatted on his chair and ate rice with his hand.

His honorable father lay on his sleeping mat, his face glistening with sweat from the heat and the fever that raged in him. In frustration Li Ping looked up from his empty bowl.

"You starve me, daughter. I am a man grown. I eat like a child," he said in Chinese, gesturing at Tan Lin's bowl, which had been filled exactly like his own.

Shame flooded into Gai. Her honorable father-in-law was right. There was not enough rice. She took her bowl and scooped her rice into his bowl. Li Ping pushed the bowl back at her, shaking his head.

"No. I want not your rice. I want my rice."

"There is no more rice. Only what is on the table," Gai said, bowing her head, unable to meet Li Ping's eyes.

Tan Lin shoved his bowl toward his grandfather. "Eat this, Honorable Grandfather. I am no longer hungry. See, I am full," he said, puffing out his belly.

Li Ping shook his head. A sad light burned in his eyes. He was sorry he had mentioned the thing of too little food. Hunger gnawed at his vitals. He pushed the bowl back in front of his grandson. Tan Lin was too thin, his belly already distended.

"Eat your rice," he roared. "Eat it or I will thrash you with bamboo."

Gai flinched away from the conflict. Bamboo did not grow in this desert, and Tan Lin knew it also. But her honorable father-in-law, who longed in his heart for China, pretended that all he had to do was walk outside and there would be rivers, wildly beautiful, bamboo groves dense with stiff, golden stems and flowery leaves, and sandstone streets wide enough for eight sedan chairs with eight carriers each to walk abreast. He had told her of these wonders many times.

Hop Wo groaned. Gai scooted off the rough wooden bench and hurried to his side. The sudden movement of standing up and rushing across the rough floor caused her head to spin with dizziness. They had not eaten today. She had saved the rice for the evening meal so that the night's rest would not be spoiled by hunger.

She lifted the small tin cup of water to his lips and trickled the warm water into his dry mouth. Hop Wo groaned. His forehead was hot with fever. Gai checked his leg. She had done everything she could. The herbalist, Kang Chou, had prepared clay in a wooden bowl, cut off the heads of three chickens, and let their blood flow over the clay. Then he carefully applied the clay to Hop Wo's broken legs and wrapped them with bandages and thin strips of bamboo and over this he spread the blood of another chicken. She had no doubt it would work. It always worked. Within a few months Hop Wo would be back at work.

Du Pon Gai, named after Dupont Street in San Francisco, fought back tears. It agonized her greatly to see her husband in pain. As a young man Hop Wo had fled China and gone to *Gum Shan*, the Golden

Mountain, called San Francisco by the white men. There Tan Lin's mother had died during childbirth. Gai had been destitute, working in a house of pleasure to feed her children, when she met Hop Wo, a laundry worker. He had been angry with her and had taken her forcefully out of the whorehouse. Until he took charge of them, home had been a corn crib in a livery stable. He had been a good father to her two children, grown now. Hop Wo bought them their first shoes. Together Hop Wo and Dun Pon Gai had worked hard, but for nothing. Lately Honorable Grandfather was always hungry.

Hop Wo groaned. Gai lifted his head and trickled the warm water into his mouth. He gagged, and, before she could find a bowl, he vomited on the bed and himself.

Gai wiped the vomit off his face with the rag she held. His eyes opened, begging for forgiveness. She closed his eyes with her lips, then pressed kisses against his forehead. Wordlessly she cleaned him. She held his forehead until he fell into sleep.

"Please don't cry, Honorable Stepmother," Tan Lin said softly in Chinese. He walked so noiselessly that she jumped.

"Go eat your dinner," she whispered.

"I am not hungry. I will walk to the store and get more rice."

Gai shuddered. She had spent the last of their money to have Hop Wo's legs set and to pay the week's rent.

"There is no money for rice."

Tan Lin's face struggled with the thought of no money. "Then I will ask him for credit. He has given us credit before."

"Hop Wo is sick, and I am no longer employed."

"But why, Honorable Mother? You are good worker."

Gai did not understand it herself. She had worked hard, much harder than anyone else, and could lift twice as many wet clothes as the white woman who had been retained. Her employer had talked about her stealing, but she had never taken anything except an occasional bar of soap. Her mind buzzed with the injustice of it. Without her own or Hop Wo's wages, there was no money for anything.

"You will find other work. There will always be work for a good laundress...please don't cry. I can work. There are no shoes for school anyway."

Tan Lin spoke the truth. Last year he had shared one pair of shoes with four other boys. Each day a different child had worn the shoes to school. Tan Lin went each Tuesday to the white school. This year he had outgrown the shoes. There had been no money for new ones.

The rule about shoes seemed wrong to Gai. In China the children could be educated without shoes. Here, no shoes, no education. She had learned hatred for this raw land. But there was no way to go to China—no money for passage and no way to earn any. Chinese were paid one half what white workers earned. There was barely enough to eat when they did work.

In many ways they had been lucky. They lived only four in one room. Their neighbors, so close on each side of them that they smelled their food and heard every word they said, lived eight and ten to a room. Her neighbors were Hakka. She, Hop Wo, and Li Ping were Miao, so she could not ask her neighbors for help. The Miao looked down on the Hakka, feeling themselves superior, so she could not ask without shaming her honorable father-in-law. Perhaps tomorrow she could go to the Ellingtons and get back her job as maid. The pay was even less than at the laundry, but they had a fine pantry. She could sneak food home for her family.

"I will buy food, Honorable Mother," Tan Lin whispered beside her cheek.

Gai covered her face with her hands. The boy would not stop talking to her. In exasperation she tried to hit him, but he only scampered out of her way.

"I will go to the store," Tan Lin said.

"*No.*" Furious, she swatted at him again, but he darted out the door. She called out to him to stop, but he ran fast.

Outside, Tan Lin slowed down to a walk.

Osborne's Grocery and General Mercantile smelled of stale food. Tan Lin nodded at the proprietor who stood behind the counter. He waited on a white woman. Tan Lin walked noiselessly to the rice bins and picked up a brown paper bag and filled it with the white grains. Enough rice to feed his family for a week, maybe longer. He swelled with pride that he had thought of this solution to their problem. His mother would be happy. He could see her pride as she set a heaping bowl of steaming rice before his honorable grandfather.

Heels clicked on the wood floor as the lady left the store.

"Let me weigh that for you," Osborne said, taking the bag from Tan Lin's hands.

"Anything else?" he asked, scratching with a pencil on a piece of butcher paper.

Tan Lin shook his head no.

"That'll be ten cents."

Tan Lin pointed to the credit book hanging on the wall behind the man.

A new member of the Durango Anti-Chinese Protective Association, Osborne shook his head. "Before, your papa and mama worked. No money, no food. I told her that once. I ain't gonna tell her again! You tell that sneaky little chink not to send her kid down here to beg. That don't go with me. Damned cunning little coolie…to send a kid…"

Tan Lin reached for the rice. Part of him had become attached to the rice and could not believe the man would take it away. Part of him knew better, knew pride, but heat flooded behind his eyes. Ashamed and afraid that he would cry in front of the man, Tan Lin drew back his hand and tried to pretend that the reaching had been a mistake. He was Miao.

He turned and walked into the pickle barrel. Embarrassed, smarting from a bump on the nose, he whirled and fled, as pressure pounded the inside of his chest. People on the sidewalk flashed by, mere blurs.

He ran until his legs ached, then stumbled and fell headlong into the dirt. Dizziness buzzed inside his skull. He didn't recognize the houses. He was lost. In shame and panic he had run the wrong direction.

Tan Lin had not cried in public for years. Now he lay in the dirt, fighting the hot tears that streamed down his cheeks. A black cloud formed inside him. His small fists pounded the hard-packed road.

At last the spasm passed, and he lifted his head. Exhausted, he pushed himself up into a sitting position. He looked in every direction, and his original terror left him. He knew the way home. He was not lost. Relieved, he sniffed and stood up.

He walked past houses that smelled of dinners cooking; his stomach growled. A curtain was pulled suspiciously aside; a blurred white face twisted in disapproval—a look he had seen many times before. He cringed inside. The dizziness buzzed louder. He felt sick. How could he go home and tell his mother that he had failed and been shamed into crying?

A chicken clucked, and Tan Lin stopped in his tracks. The chicken came toward him, alternately clucking and pecking at the hard ground, dipping its head down, then bobbing up and looking from side to side.

His mother could make a tasty dish with such a fat hen. She would be proud to place such a prize before his honorable grandfather. Li Ping would eat the hen with much relish. They would go to bed with full stomachs and sleep the whole night through. There would be enough food for a week. By then his honorable stepmother would find another job or perhaps he could earn money doing chores.

The chicken walked past him on brisk, jerky legs. Tan Lin reached out and grabbed it by the neck. It squawked and clawed him with its sharp spurs. Pain shot down his arms, and blood oozed from long slashes. Tan Lin caught one leg. The hen screeched and clucked. Feathers flew as it flopped wildly in his hands, but Tan Lin held fast. He ran toward home.

Ezra Wilkins heard the commotion and ran out of his house. "Here! You bring that pullet back here!" he shouted.

Tan Lin did not understand the words, but he knew the old man wanted the chicken. He looked over his shoulder and ran faster.

"You come back here! Filthy, chicken-stealing chink!" Ezra leapt off his porch and ran after the boy. Two blocks down the road he grabbed the boy by the scruff of his neck and shook him so hard he let go of the chicken. It landed upside down, squawked loud, and flapped away from them.

Ezra whacked the boy on his half-shaved head, stood him up, and marched him down the rutted road toward the jail.

Angie kept so busy with one thing and another that she didn't remember the bag of food she had bought for Hop Wo's family until she lay in bed almost ready to drift off. Drat! Well, she would try again tomorrow. Unfortunately there was no hope that the food she and Kincaid had abandoned when they heard gunshots would be there tomorrow. Dogs, desert creatures, children, horses, pigs, strays of all kinds, would do away with it long before morning.

Angie turned over and punched her pillow. Fortunately one basket of food was not going to inconvenience anyone too much. She would go back to the store in the morning. Hop Wo's family would need the food as much tomorrow or the next day as they would have today.

Lance could not sleep. He lay down thinking he would sleep instantly, as he usually did, but his mind kept oozing thoughts of Gilbert Lee. He felt sick with them. He resented Gil for coming back into his life and resurrecting old memories.

Since sleep evaded him, Lance walked to the window and looked out at the deserted road below. The sight of the Baquero reminded him of Angie. He heard her clear, perfectly concise voice trying to twist its way around a slow Texas drawl. *Wawk*. His smile started down low and climbed its way to his face. He pulled a straight-backed chair up to the window and sat down. The moon had set. *A little ol' wawk back to D'rango ain't gonna hurt you none.* Lance laughed outright. Such innocent fun…It'd been a long time since anything had been so uncomplicated.

Lance scowled. Maybe not so uncomplicated. Angie Logan was as sweet and beautiful as a woman could get, but she was still a woman, and women had certain expectations about what men had to do after they had kissed them in the moonlight. Though, he had to admit, he hadn't felt any hint of pressure or expectation. Angie Logan went about her business as determinedly and efficiently as any man he'd ever known.

How come you sound like a cowboy when you spoon?

From kissing all those Texas gals. You gotta tawk right to kiss a little ol' Texas gal. They don't like furriners. Angie had giggled. *I think I'm going to help Laramee drag you behind that horse.*

Angie Logan might be totally delightful, but she was still a woman. It couldn't hurt to keep track of that.

Near dawn Lance finally slept, and he dreamed.

He and Gil lived in a house with a woman he did not recognize. The woman had a little boy—two or three years old. A small boy. Slender and blond. He and Gil grew to love the boy. One day the boy slipped out of the house and drowned in the creek nearby. Gil accused him of allowing the boy to go to his death. He accused Gil. They fought bitterly, parted as enemies. Gil was sad for a few moments, then recovered. He himself was crushed by a sense of loss, of guilt, of hatred for Gil. Years later they met. Gil thanked him for taking the blame. He said, thank you for taking the brunt of that for me. I was guilty, but I could not have borne to admit it. It would have killed me.

Lance woke slowly, haltingly. Furious and sick, he struggled into a sitting position on the side of the bed. The dream slipped from his consciousness. He let it go. It had been an awful dream. He felt sick with its residue. He felt as if all his old grief had ambushed him. It took an extreme effort to go through his morning rituals and face the day ahead.

Monday morning, May 17, 1880

Del Ramo wrote out his telegram, gave it to the clerk, and counted out the necessary fee.

"How long will it take to get an answer," he asked, watching the careless way the clerk handled the wire.

"Depends. On whether or not the judge is in Tucson and whether or not he decides to answer..."

He'll answer, if he knows what's good for him. Judge Cadwallader was a practical man who had accepted more than one favor from Ramo and several from Cort Armstrong. Thanks to Cort's and his own access to inside information, a valuable piece of mining land in Tombstone carried his, Cort's, and Cadwallader's names. Cadwallader would answer.

The telegram was a request to release Smalley on his own recognizance. It also guaranteed that Smalley would be there to stand trial on the first of June—two weeks away—when Cadwallader stopped in Durango.

A positive reply would also be a signal to arrest Laramee Logan.

Ramo turned and prepared to leave the musty little telegraph office. "You get the answer to that, you bring it right over, you hear?" he demanded.

"Yes sir, Marshal."

Samantha Regier looked out the window of the carriage. She had never felt so blue in her entire life. The desert was barren. She hadn't slept last night, and she ached so desperately for Lance that she felt sick. The carriage swayed and rocked endlessly, and the dust was so thick that she could hardly breathe.

They stopped in a town the driver called Silver City. Samantha let Uncle Chantry help her down and lead her to the hotel. She barely looked at the raw little settlement. She was exhausted.

"Eat something, child," Uncle Chantry urged her.

"I'm too tired to eat."

"We won't stop again for four or five hours, and the next stop might not be this luxurious."

Samantha felt tears burning her eyes. She needed to be alone. Uncle Chantry and Mrs. Lillian ate, and the three of them walked back to the carriage Uncle Chantry had bought at the end of the railhead so they wouldn't have to share space with strangers. She was truly grateful for that now. She'd teased him about it at the time. Samantha spied a telegraph office. A thought came to her. She stopped.

"What's the matter, love?" Mrs. Lillian asked.

"I'm going back."

Uncle Chantry frowned. He looked so like Lance at that moment, Samantha's heart felt close to breaking. She blinked back tears. Mrs. Lillian patted Samantha's arm.

The driver, hired from Butterfield, yelled, "All aboard that's going aboard."

Chantry started to argue with her, but he knew a lost cause when he saw one. Samantha was a bright, determined young woman. She hadn't come to this decision lightly. She wasn't going to be swayed by anything he could say. He knew her too well to make that mistake. And this Wild West was not as outrageous as he'd thought. Men treated ladies with respect. She'd be protected all the way back to Phoenix, then Lance would take over. Maybe Lizzie would get her wish after all. Chantry glanced at Mrs. Lillian and expressed his approval. Samantha's eyes flooded with relief.

"You need any money, Samantha?"

"No, thank you, Uncle Chantry." She had carried a thousand dollars in big bills in an inside pocket of her chemise and hadn't spent any of it. Uncle Chantry paid for everything.

"If you need anything, you'll let us know."

Samantha swallowed. She was so grateful to him for all the things he didn't say that she couldn't speak. Tears blinded her as she stepped into his arms.

"Here now. Is that any way to stand a man up?"

"I love you," she murmured.

"*All aboard!*"

Chantry hugged her. Mrs. Lillian hugged her. Samantha waited on the sidewalk until the stagecoach rolled over a low hill and out of sight. She was insane. Would Lance be glad to see her? Would he let her stay—toss her out? The thought of retracing her trip without her uncle and Mrs. Lillian made tears flood her eyes. She blinked them back bravely and walked to the telegraph office.

Samantha wrote out a wire, then crumpled it and wrote another. Finally, surrounded by little wads of paper, she signaled the clerk that she was ready.

She reread her message again and reluctantly handed it over.

> MY DARLING LANCE CANNOT LEAVE YOU STOP IF I DO NOT HEAR IN TWO DAYS I AM COMING BACK STOP SAMANTHA STOP

At least he could not say she hadn't given him a chance to keep her from coming back. Satisfied, she walked to the hotel. That night she had her first good night's sleep since leaving Phoenix.

Del Ramo ripped open the sealed envelope and tossed it on the floor.

> TO SHERIFF RAMO STOP AUTHORITY GRANTED TO RELEASE SMALLEY AND FRIENDS ON OWN RECOGNIZANCE STOP JUDGE CADWALLADER STOP

Ramo shoved the telegram through the bars at Smalley and took the keys off the wall. He unlocked the cell; Smalley and his friends smiled and sauntered out.

Ramo took the telegram and tacked it up on the bulletin board behind his desk. "Guess that'll take some of the starch out of that cocky ranger," he growled.

"That don't, maybe us arresting the man responsible for the deaths of those three chinks'll do it," Smalley said, pinning on his badge. "Heard rangers don't like to be upstaged like that."

Ramo grinned. "Ain't that jest too bad."

Smalley patted his badge. "What d'ya want me to do first?"

"Might start by getting rid of that ranger."

Smalley grinned. "Shouldn't be too hard to do."

When Angie heard about Tan Lin's arrest, she visited him immediately and then gathered the basket of food she'd been planning for days and took it to Hop Wo's house. She spoke briefly with Du Pon Gai, but somehow giving the food, now that the damage had been done, did nothing to assuage her guilt.

She spent the day developing pictures, drying them, and pasting them to cardboard. As she saw what she had, her excitement grew. Tennessee and Virginia would be proud of her. She had some wonderful pictures. The content was unusual; the photography was excellent. She showed Sarah, and even though Sarah didn't have her knowledge of what to look for, she was equally impressed with the display.

Angie didn't see Kincaid all day. Sarah mentioned she'd seen him walk by a couple of times, but he looked as if folks were keeping him busy.

Kincaid avoided *The Tea Times News*. The dream stayed with him most of the day, like a pall hanging between him and the world, a grey veil between him and Angie—one he was strangely reluctant to disturb. He saw her from a distance, but he couldn't bring himself to walk over and say hello.

He managed to pass the day without talking to her. He ate dinner in the hotel, and the food seemed to ease his malaise. He drank cold lemonade and went up to his room. He felt a little tired, probably from the gunshot wound that was still healing on the inside. The doctor in Phoenix had said it would take months to heal down deep.

He went upstairs and laid down on his bed, but by eight o'clock he was tired of the room. A man could rest only so long. He grabbed his hat. He would walk over to the Baquero and see what kind of mischief was brewing.

The sky was a warm apricot color; sunset would ease the heat off a little. On the sidewalk he stopped and looked up and down the street. Just as he glanced south, Angie Logan stepped out of the newspaper office and looked up, directly into his eyes. There'd be no avoiding her. He nodded, started to walk across the street, but his feet didn't move. She walked toward him, and, strangely, a smile spread through him up to his face. Momentarily the pall lifted.

"How do," she said, lifting her chin and smiling the sardonic little smile that tickled something deep inside him.

"Howdy."

"You still strutting around trying to keep things under control?"

"You still trying to capture every square inch of Durango on those little papers?"

"No, I'm done for the night."

"Hear about the boy?"

"Tan Lin?" Angie grimaced. She felt partly responsible for the boy. If she'd remembered the basket of food…"Ramo is such a snake. He's not going to get away with that—arresting a skinny little boy. If our judge was alive, he'd fine him and let him go."

"Not much chance of that. The selectmen tried all day to appoint another judge. No one would take the job. Afraid of lead poisoning." Kincaid grinned. "Tan Lin'll be okay. Least he'll be well fed. Food's usually pretty good in jail. Lots of it anyway."

"I think it's an outrage."

"If you say so, Miss Logan. Sure don't want to get on your bad side. Only seen you a few times, and each time something bad happens to me."

"Me? I didn't cause you to get shot…"

"I've never been shot before," he drawled, extremely well satisfied with his logic.

"You can't blame that on me."

"Already did. It's a serious thing having your picture took. Probably got me flustered."

"You didn't look flustered."

"Probably so busy trying not to look flustered, I forgot to shoot my gun. You ever going to show me those pictures?"

"You want to see them?"

"Like to see if you're any good. See if I got shot for nothing."

Angie cast a sideways glance at his smiling profile. "If you really want to see them, we could walk back to the office. They're in my studio."

They laughed and talked all the way to the studio. He followed her up the stairs and walked from photograph to photograph in silence. Her heart pounding, she watched his face. Would he make a joke of this too?

"Well, what do you think?" she finally asked when she couldn't stand his silence any longer.

"You're good. You'll probably put an end to the legend of the Wild West with all this reality."

A rush of warmth filled her body. "The legend may not die, but at least I can clothe it in the truth."

"You've done that. I'm glad to see you haven't tried to make the Wild West into a work of art the way some have."

He was smart. A whole slew of photographers spent their time trying to create photographs that looked like paintings. They even added brush strokes.

"If I don't do anything else, I'd like to discredit that approach once and for all."

Kincaid stopped beside the pictures of him and Winchester. His teasing smile wavered. His eyes narrowed, and the lines on either side of his mouth deepened, arranged themselves into a look she had seen before he kissed her that first time.

"Well, what do you think?"

"What are you going to do with these?"

"Put them in a picture book of the Wild West."

"If I buy these, would that keep you from using them?"

"No. I would make copies. You're welcome to those if you want them."

"I don't especially want them, but I'd rather not be in your picture book."

"Why?"

"How'd you like pictures of you making a fool of yourself spread all over the country?"

"You certainly didn't make a fool of yourself."

"Well, I don't remember gettin' any awards for either quick or straight shootin'."

"No, but you handled yourself very well."

Kincaid's hand reached out and pulled her close. "You handle yourself pretty well too. Else you couldn't have gotten away with all the liberties you and your camera took with me."

He had forgotten to make a joke of it. His body throbbed, it had forgotten as well. The look in his narrowed eyes caused the pulse in her throat to race.

He tipped her chin up and lowered his head. "I've shot men for less..." His mouth was so close to hers she could feel the heat of it.

"But I'm not a man..."

"Probably the only thing that saved you."

His mouth touched hers—warm and soft and jolting to her system; she sighed and started to lift her arms, but he ended the kiss.

"There you go again, trying to compromise me." Lance especially enjoyed speaking this way to Angie, because there were probably not ten women in the world who would have allowed it without being scandalized.

He hustled her out of the building and back onto the sidewalk. Nunca stamped at sight of them.

Kincaid mounted and held out his arm for Angie to climb up behind him. His skin felt warm and damp.

"Better hold on tight," he said.

"Is this a trick to get me to hug you?"

"'Course it is," he said, his voice a raspy whisper. "If we'd stood there on the sidewalk, you'd of been too ladylike to run around back of me and put your arms around me with the whole town watching."

Angie put her arms around his waist.

He turned the horse southwest. "Where you are going? Home's thataway."

"I want to see something."

"What?"

"You'll see."

He stopped the chestnut in front of the school. "Did you go to school here?"

She nodded.

"I don't have eyes in the back of my head."

"How did you know I answered you then?"

"Felt the horse move."

"Yes, I did."

"How old were you?"

"From six to sixteen."

"You wore pigtails?"

"How did you know that?"

"Just a guess." He walked the horse over to the windows. The desks were back in place. History questions, covering the Napoleonic period, covered the blackboard. Windows were open. The smell of chalk brought back memories. "Were you a good student?"

"Of course. The teacher hated me. He wanted one of the boys to be smartest."

"Did you have a camera then?"

"No, I didn't have a camera until I went back east five years ago."

Ramo stood up from his desk. "Hey!"

Smalley put down the newspaper and scowled at him. "What?"

"There's Kincaid." Smalley stood up and walked to the window.

"It's getting dark," he said.

"Pretty soon it'll be dark enough so that if a man was to have an accident, nobody much would notice."

Smalley put on his hat, checked his revolver, and nodded at Ramo. "Think I'll go for a walk."

Ramo grinned. "Probably wouldn't need to shoot him. Just a blow or two in the right place might finish what Johnny started."

A light dawned in Smalley's eyes. "Be a shame if he was to ride into something, wouldn't it?"

"Just give him time to get rid of the girl."

Cort Armstrong saw the woman at the back of the room, peering through the beads that separated the saloon from the kitchen. Her face was attractive—for a chink. He left the rag he had been wiping the bar with and sauntered back to see what she wanted.

"Yeah?"

"Need to speak with you, prease," she said softly.

"So speak," he said, putting his hands on his hips. She was small and delicately made. Her skin was clear and her hair clean. She didn't smell dirty.

"Gai want work here," she said, her voice almost a whisper.

"Doing what?" he demanded.

"Upstairs, for turtle woman," she said.

Cort grunted. He knew enough Chinese to know that a turtle woman was a madam. "You ever done that before?"

"Yes. Gai *kam sam hock*, lived in San Francisco," she interpreted when she saw him scowl.

He had kept a China girl upstairs once. "You got any diseases?"

"No, prease."

"You don't talk like a chink. Where'd you learn such good English?"

"Gai born San Francisco, *kam sam hock*."

"Where you been working up till now?"

"Gai work laundry with husband, Hop Wo."

"Hop Wo, the boy from the laundry?"

"Yes."

"How's he doing?"

"Much pain. Not work long time. Family need money."

Guilt nibbled at Cort. He could have stopped Smalley; he hadn't expected the son of a bitch to break the pigtail's legs.

He cleared his throat. "You don't mind doing that kind of work?"

"Gai mind," she said.

"So, you're willing to work," he said, toying with an idea.

"Yes, prease."

Cort hesitated. She was a married woman. He couldn't put her to work upstairs, servicing the trail trash that came through the Baquero. "You do any housework?"

"Gai good *amah*. How much pay?"

"Ten dollars a week," he said. "You come to the house every day and clean things up, do the laundry, maybe cook a little."

Gai nodded. "When?"

"Whenever you can break away from nursing that man of yours," he growled, feeling like a fool for pampering a chink in this fashion. He hoped the goddamned Anti-Chinese association didn't get wind of this.

She bobbed her head. "Gai work hard. You see."

• • •

Gil unrolled his sleeping mat on the sand next to the pagoda, sat down noiselessly, and watched the sun slip beneath the horizon. Birds sang their nesting songs. Crickets chirped. South of the Liang house children ran and yelled. A dog barked. The water flowing in the shallow creek cooled the air, sweet from the blossoming plants on the desert.

Unaccustomed to living in close proximity with others, Gil had elected to sleep outside for privacy and peace of mind.

With a creak of rusty hinges, the kitchen door opened. Lily stepped down from the small back porch and walked quietly to his side.

Gil rose to his feet. "Would you like to sit?"

"Do you like the sunset?" she asked.

"Yes, it is the most beautiful time of day."

Lily sat on one side of the bamboo sleeping mat, Gil on the other. She did not know what to say. She had begged him yesterday to meet her, only to be thwarted by her parents. Mei-ling fought with Third Uncle and moved her sleeping mat into Lily's room. Her honorable mother, though outwardly complacent, had a temper that once aroused, rarely settled down without fireworks of some sort. It was a matter of no consequence, a simple domestic quarrel that amazed Lily. When Mei-ling discovered that her husband had gone to sleep with her still angry, she went in and woke him so they could fight again. Lily slept from exhaustion before they did. Today she had decided not to wait until they slept.

The sky had changed from apricot to bright purple.

Lily sat down beside Gil. Her heartbeat was unusually fast, disturbing her blood. He sat quietly, as if he were any ordinary person. Her mouth was as dry as uncooked grains of rice. *He is waiting for me to explain.*

"I would like to walk," she said shyly, defiantly, "Wilt thou walk with me?"

"A short distance only. For your safety…"

His voice, so controlled, so trained to restraint, could hide anything. It was at once quiet and forceful. *Arguing against him would do no good.* A chill ran down Lily's spine. A small pulse started in her throat. He stood as straight and as unhampered as an arrow in flight. She was so tired of seeing men like sea snails, their backs bent by whorls of laundry or wood. What a relief he was to her—so straight and free.

"Tell me about this place thou hast come from, this Cambridge."

Gil was taken aback. He had thought she would have some urgent question for him. A problem to solve.

"What did thou doest there?"

Gil told her about the university, his teaching duties, the town with its snobbish, intellectual air and its cliquishness. "Fortunately for me, half-Chinese professors of philosophy were fashionable," he ended, smiling.

Lily sighed. "Thou art lucky. I would think the Christians would not allow a Chinese in their universities."

"The East Coast of the United States is different from this frontier. Men are more learned. They are aware of different cultures and religions. My mentor's good friend was vice-president of Harvard. His bequest to Harvard included arrangements for my education and a teaching position after graduation."

"Thou wert lucky."

"Yes. I have been blessed in many ways."

"Except?"

"There was no Chinese community. And while Caucasians could learn from me and I from them, I was not free to mingle with their women except at strictly regulated social functions."

Lily was not surprised by this even though she had not thought of it before. "No women, not even singsong girls?"

"No, but I was fortunate. The Kincaid family adopted me and made me feel like a member of their clan. Later I accompanied Lance Kincaid to France and met a young woman there."

"Didst thou fall in love with her?"

"Yes."

"Chinese?"

"Yes."

"And she with thee?"

"Yes."

A darkness filled her. The languor of despair. She turned away from him.

"Thou art married, then?"

"No. She was not free to marry, for family reasons."

Lily's eyes widened. "She was married?"

"She was of noble family. Her family would not permit her to marry a half-breed."

Lily turned slightly away to hide her smile. The stars were bright again, twinkling with beautiful precision. She asked a hundred questions of Gilbert James Lee, and he answered them with humor and patience. She could have continued to ask them all night, so happy was she to listen to his soft voice and elegant accent. Did all men from the east-north United States of America speak so beautifully?

"We must go back now. Your father would be displeased if

he knew…"

Reluctantly she allowed him to lead her back to the house. Later she lay in her bed, spinning wonderful dreams of herself married to Gilbert James Lee, married to Son of Autumn, living in a real city with paved streets, green lawns, harbors with a thousand boats bobbing on waves, gently flowing rivers like the ones he had mentioned. She had thought that all of the North American continent was connected by rutted roads, lined by jerry-built wooden structures, populated by drunken white men and their broken, gaunt women and cunning, cruel, loud children. Gilbert James Lee had changed all that.

CHAPTER TWELVE

Monday evening, May 17, 1880

They rode in companionable silence. Angie felt happy to be alive. Going to the school had been a good idea. They had sat on the porch and talked about nonsense, but it felt wonderful. The color had disappeared from the sky, but the desert was in full bloom. Warm night smells of sweet blossoms filled the air. The light breeze on her face was a caress. Kincaid's hard belly was damp and warm under her hands. The pressure of his body against her was more meaningful than any touch she had ever felt. It was wonderful and frightening.

Kincaid kept Nunca to a comfortable walk. Angie loved the desert. She hadn't realized how much until she came home. She had a tendency to get so involved in her daily life that she often forgot life's special pleasures. They rode toward her house.

Nunca stopped, and Angie looked around her. "What?"

"I heard something."

She waited in silence; he listened. The sound came again. It sounded like a man yelling in Chinese. Lance kicked Nunca's sides, then reined him abruptly as if he had changed his mind. "You wait here."

"No. I'm going with you."

"I don't remember that being a question. I'd swear that was an order."

"It couldn't have been," she said firmly. "You would never order me around."

"That man sounds like they're scalping him. You can either hop off, or we'll sit here and listen to him scream."

"You can't do that," Angie protested.

"I can if you can."

Angie lifted off Kincaid's hat and hit Nunca with it as hard as she could. The unaccustomed slap startled the gelding; he leapt forward, the bit in his teeth. Angie kicked him hard to keep him moving. Kincaid let out a string of oaths.

"You should watch that mouth," she said, leaning forward to be sure he heard her over Nunca's pounding hooves. Her breasts pressed against his back, and the tingling reaction it created shot all the way to her toes.

Near a stand of saguaro cactus three men became visible in the dusk. One man wielded a whip. The other man had roped a Chinese man and held the rope taut so he couldn't get away. The Oriental bled from numerous long red gashes on his arms, as if he'd been dragged through cactus. Kincaid slowed Nunca about twenty feet from the three men. The Chinese cowered and tried to protect himself with his bleeding arms.

"Reckon this man's had about enough of your hospitality for this evening." Kincaid's voice had a decided Texas drawl to it.

"Says who?" the whip wielder asked, turning to glare at them.

"Says me and the Arizona Territory."

The one with the whip turned and grinned at the one holding the rope. "Talks pretty big for one man, don't he?"

"Likely find what he's looking for, he don't git on home where he belongs," the man holding the rope said.

A few feet away a masked man rode out from behind a giant pillarlike saguaro, cocked his rifle, and pointed it at Kincaid. One by one, masked men holding rifles stepped out from behind cactus stumps and mesquite bushes—six or more in all.

Lance's hand twitched for the feel of his gun. If he had been alone—but he wasn't. No sense worrying about that now.

"What's happening?" Angie asked softly, fear stabbing into her belly.

"Not sure. I think these boys are here to teach you to pay attention when a man asks you to get off his horse."

"Think they would accept my apology instead?"

"Be worth a try," he said, his tone dry.

The six riders stopped, forming a ring around Lance and Angie about five yards away. Their faces were covered by bandannas pulled up over their noses. The man with the rope opened his loop and let the Chinese go. He scampered to his feet and ran off toward town, picking cactus spines out of his arms as he ran.

"I guess you boys want something," Kincaid said quietly.

"Drop your gun, Kincaid."

Did that muffled voice belong to Neville Smalley? Angie leaned around to look at the speaker. In the near-dark it was hard to tell. Kincaid made no move to comply.

"Drop it, or we drop you."

Lance's instinct was to draw and fire, but with Angie behind him and six men shooting from different angles it was unthinkable. He wasn't willing to risk her life in that fashion. "You each had a mother, at one time anyway. You willing to shoot a young woman in the prime of her life? A woman who one day will bear babies and dandle 'em on her knee?" Kincaid asked, his raspy voice loud and gruff.

Surprised, the men looked at one another.

"You can't kill me and leave her alive, can you?" The men shifted uneasily in their saddles and glanced at one another.

"Hell," one of them grumbled. "I didn't sign on to shoot no woman."

"Me neither."

"You hush up that talk," one man protested. "We didn't come here to kill nobody." The speaker sounded like Smalley, but his voice was effectively muffled behind the bandanna. "We just want to visit with him a little."

"I ain't in no mood to visit. You try anything with me and I'll kill you first, then you, then you. And the rest of you are going to have to kill the girl. Which one of you is going to shoot her?"

The men looked at one another. It seemed unanimous. No one would admit to a willingness to shoot women.

"Come to think of it, you even look like a bunch of woman-killing skunks," Kincaid growled.

"Make him stop talking like that about us. We done never kilt no women," one man whined.

In the near darkness one shape looked like another. Even their voices blurred. Angie strained to find one detail that she could remember to identify these men by, and failed.

"You sure about that?" Kincaid demanded.

"Damned right we're sure."

"You ain't *never* killed a woman?"

The men shook their heads. "Never," they proclaimed in chorus.

"Good." Lance dug his heels into Nunca's sides. The startled gelding leapt forward, almost unseating Angie. She screamed and grabbed at Kincaid, who had aimed the horse at the man she had thought was Neville Smalley. The man's horse reared. As they flashed by him Kincaid stiff-armed him. Smacked in the face, the man cursed and fell off his plunging horse. Nunca lowered his head and pounded across the desert. Behind them, men yelled at one another.

"What the hell?"

"...kill that bastard..."

Angie hugged Kincaid and pressed her face against his warm, damp back, expecting bullets to come tearing into her. Her heart pounded painfully hard. Her nerves screamed at her, screamed at Nunca to run faster. At last they reached the road to her house. Angie looked back over her shoulder. Riders had recovered from their momentary disarray and pounded after them.

"Is there anyplace around here you can hide?"

"What about you?" Angie yelled.

"Answer me," he gritted.

"Yes. Under the porch. There's room to crawl around."

Lance stopped Nunca in front of her house, dismounted, and lifted Angie down, then slapped Nunca hard on the rear. A stand of honey mesquite in bloom shielded them from sight of their pursuers. Nunca ran down the road, and Kincaid dragged her toward the porch. "Get under there."

Angie knelt down and fumbled for the latch she had discovered earlier. "Here it is." She opened the narrow door.

"Get under there. And stay put this time." His voice was a low growl against her cheek.

"No! I'm going to stay with you."

"Those men are trying to kill me. They aren't going to let me hide behind your skirts again."

"You can't fight a half-dozen men—"

"Yes, I can, if I don't have to worry about you."

Angie squatted half under and half out from under the porch. She tugged on him. "They're coming."

They had argued so long that the riders were almost on top of them. Lance gave up trying to get Angie to obey him and scooted under the porch with her. He'd waited too long. Under the porch the aroma of onions was strong. The previous owners must have been Texans. Texans kept their onions under the porch. Lance pushed Angie to keep her moving. At the middle of the porch he let her stop, sure that he had cleared the last of the onion skins. Old dried onion skins crinkled louder than cellophane at the slightest touch.

Outside horses stopped. A man's voice said, "I think they got off the horse."

"They're around here somewhere. You men follow that horse just in case." Hooves pounded off down the road. Other horses walked slowly toward the house. "Which house is hers?"

"Gotta be this 'un. Fourth from the road."

"You boys go around thataway."

Horses walked to the porch. A saddle creaked, and a pair of boots tramped across the porch only inches over their heads. Angie's heart almost stopped. The porch was a little less than three feet above ground. She could hear everything clearly. Each creak of a saddle as one of the men changed position. The man knocked on her door. In her mind she imagined herself saying *Come in*. She scared herself so badly, her heart lurched.

"Go in and see if anyone's in there." The speaker sounded like Smalley.

The man on the porch rattled the doorknob. "Locked."

"You sure this is her place?"

"Sure as can be. Fourth house from the Tully road…"

"Keep it down. We don't want to disturb the neighbors unnecessarily." That *was* Smalley's voice. "Break that window. She owes you that 'cause they broke your nose."

Angie barely breathed. Any man blatant enough to ride out with five men to kill an innocent man would have another dozen who would testify they were all playing cards with them at the Baquero. They would not hesitate to kill both of them.

Thump! Angie flinched. *Thump. Thump.* The man above them stamped sand off his boots. Grains of sand drifted down on her. Kincaid's hand found hers. The sturdy feel of his skin soothed her.

A horse stamped the ground near them. A man coughed. Another one cursed.

"You hear something?" a man on the porch asked.

"Probably a cat. They's a lot of cats around here."

"How long we going to wait for them?"

"Hell, they won't come back here if they know what's good for 'em. We're wasting our time."

The one that sounded like Smalley uttered an oath. "I been thinking, dammit. Spread out. We'll hide behind that mesquite where they can't see us. They gotta come back here."

"Maybe they're inside."

"Break that window and see."

The man tapped her window, probably with his revolver, and the glass broke. He knocked the glass out and climbed inside. Angie could hear him walking from room to room.

Her blood raced with outrage and fear.

Lance knew how hard this was for Angie. It was her house the man was tramping through. Angie Logan squirmed under his hand. The men overhead were quiet, waiting for their friend to finish his inspection.

Lance wished he were outside. Up there in the dark alone, he would have had a chance against them; trapped here like a possum, lying next to Angie, he would only be endangering her life to trade shots with them.

"If they're in there, they're damned invisible."

Boots scraped as men tramped off the porch above them. The front door slammed.

From somewhere under the house a cat meowed.

"You hear that?"

Angie's heart constricted with pure fear. The cat would lead the men right to her and Lance.

Men were silent, waiting to hear the sound again. The silence stretched out. On the porch a hammer clicked as a gun was cocked.

Behind the house an owl moaned in the distance. It was a barn owl. Angie had heard it before.

"Hell, it was nothing but an owl."

The men laughed nervously.

"You stay around back, catch 'em if they come thataway. We'll be across the road a piece."

They listened to the men withdraw. Angie's heart slowed its beat. She could no longer hear the men. She imagined them sitting their horses behind the flowering honey mesquite and breathed a sigh of relief. She became aware of crickets for the first time. Had they just started their raspy sounds or had she just noticed them?

Lance moved to relieve a cramped muscle. Angie Logan breathed quietly beside him. Even in profile she looked relieved. Still scared, but relieved. Her hand in his was warm and small. Each beat of his heart spread tension into his body. This was a hell of a place for it, but her faint perfume and the firm pressure of her slim body bumping against him as they rode, hugging him hard after she almost fell off, had worked on him without his knowledge—like a snowball rolling unseen down a deserted mountainside. Once started, it grew in secret until it became unmanageable, until it roared down on unsuspecting towns and villages, destroying everything in its path. His body's reaction had started in Nogales the first time he saw Angie Logan, and it had picked up speed and energy each time he saw her or spent time with her. Like that snowball, at each step of the way, his reaction to Angie was stronger, more unmanageable. Instead of having a tiny avalanche to deal with, he had a monstrous one that thundered down the mountainside at full speed. Now, after only a few minutes lying beside her, his body ached for her as if they had been spooning for hours. He wanted her with such urgency at this moment that if he could, he would get up and leave. Should get up and leave.

"Does your mama know you live like this?" she asked, her voice a low whisper.

"Lord, no, she'd split a corset stay."

Angie smiled. She could almost feel Kincaid's grin. She clapped her hand over her mouth to keep from laughing aloud. "Corset stays are whalebone."

"My mama can split whalebone."

Angie grinned over at him. "I'll bet you gave those Texas girls a fit."

Lance shook his head. "I done never. I've always been nice to girls. Girls have always been mean to me. But I've always been nice to girls." He pronounced *nice* with a long, long *i* that caused her to smile. His husky voice dropped so naturally into the innocence of dialect that she felt warmed and comforted, almost forgot the danger outside. "I sure Lord don't b'lieve a word o' that."

"Swear to God, it's true. They do turrible things."

"Like what?"

"Come over and want to clean my house, turrible stuff like that."

"That seems fairly tolerable to me."

"That's only 'cause you ain't never had no girls coming into your house wantin' to clean it. Making turmoil. Crowding your bachelor ways. Moving your chairs around so's you walk into 'em in the dark."

Angie turned onto her side facing him. She ran a finger over his warm cheek.

"Turrible mean to me," he whispered.

Angie kissed his cheek. "What do you want a poor woman to do?"

"Want 'em to hold on kinda loose-like."

Angie stroked his chin, throat, and chest, her fingers barely touching his magnetic skin. "That loose enough?"

Her fingertips moving over him sent flames leaping through him. "That might be a tad too loose," he said, pulling her close. He found her mouth in the dark, didn't even mind that he had to kiss her forehead, eyes, and cheeks to get there.

Angie sighed. His heart beat hard against her breast. His mouth burned hot on hers. He kissed her as if he intended to do it forever.

Slowly, reluctantly, but firmly, Lance ended the kiss and rolled over onto his back. He wanted Angie Logan with a fierceness and need that were near unbearable. His body was on fire. He didn't dare touch her again.

They lay in silence for a long time.

"Did I do something wrong?" she whispered.

Lance smiled into the dark. "Don't reckon God made anything as insecure as a woman."

"I'm not insecure. I'm curious," she said.

"Sure glad to hear that." Lance closed his eyes. The grin on his face almost burst into a chuckle that would have been audible for at least a hundred yards.

"Then why did you stop kissing me?"

Lance thought about his answer. Any other girl in the world and he would tell her a lie, but with Angie…

"Reckon I'm feeling as harassed as a stump-tailed bull at the height of fly season."

Angie peered through the darkness at his face. In spite of his teasing tone he throbbed with intensity. She felt the throb of him as clearly as if she actually touched him. It seeped into her and made her crazy. She was on fire.

"We're crazy," she whispered. Kincaid didn't speak.

She wanted him more than she wanted life itself. The sensation in her loins was so rich and hungry for whatever it was he would do to her that she reached over and put her hand on his heart. Its beating penetrated her whole body. She found his mouth with hers and felt the shudder that moved through him like a wave.

"Angie," he groaned. His mouth ravished hers. Ground into hers with hunger and urgency.

It was so hot and close under the porch, it was almost a relief to feel her gown fall open.

"You're beautiful, Angel."

Kincaid's broad chest was smooth and hairless, adding to the sense of his nakedness. His body—so lean and powerfully built—gleamed with sweat sheen and caused the already smothering beat of her heart to accelerate.

"Sure about this?" he rasped against her cheek.

Instead of trying to pull away, she pressed close to him, surrendering to the alchemy between them. It was too strong, too elemental. Her body—trembling and flaming with the need he had awakened in her—took over. Her one last thought before he took her was that she knew now what it was he had planted in that first glance after he'd been shot in Nogales, what he had watered and nurtured when he teased her with his silly talk and his soft kisses.

It was desire. And it had grown in her slowly and inexorably without her knowing, without her learning to control its power. Now desire—unmanageable and undeniable—coiled tensely in her belly and released her slender arching body up to his.

Angie stirred. She couldn't tell how much time had passed. Kincaid stroked her hair. Crickets dominated the night sounds again. It was done. He had taken her, claimed her completely. That knowledge, combined with the exhilaration of so much danger all around, sent a heavy thrill coursing through her body. She had accepted this exultant, masterful man into her body. Peace filled her every pore, as if something mysterious and vital were finally back in its proper place.

It was quiet outside now. The men must have gone. Then she remembered what they had said about waiting across the road in the stand of honey mesquite. The smell of onions wafted over to her. How close was the nearest man? Could he hear a whisper in the stillness?

Lance sighed in perfect contentment. His hand stroked Angie's belly. Her soft damp skin felt as smooth as warm butter. The feel of her lulled him into a dream state.

Angie lay on her back in the dirt next to Kincaid. Her cheek tingled. Dampness came off on her hand. Had she cried?

"What are you thinking about?" she asked softly.

Kincaid slanted a look at her. "Why is it when a woman wants to tell you what she's thinking she asks what you're thinking about? What were *you* thinking about?"

She was thinking how different he was from James. James had made several attempts to make love to her, but he had never made it seem indispensable the way Lance had. With Lance there had been no question of it, only if it could happen soon enough to save her life. She reached over and pinched him on the chest. "You know too much. I was thinking that I'm glad that's over with," Angie said.

"Thank you, Miss Logan," he said with wry humor.

"No! It was wonderful," Angie protested. "I'm just glad that now we can relax."

"You read your cousin's newspaper, don't you?"

His hand caressed her breast, lingered there. Angie's blood stirred, became languorous again.

Lance leaned over Angie, and kissed her cheek, and then her throat, where a tiny pulse pumped against his lips. It was his last choice, but his first choice would entail making love to her again.

"What are we going to do?" she asked.

"Sleep."

"What if one of us snores?" she asked.

"Good point. So we'll stay awake." Lance ran his fingers through his hair.

"What will we do tomorrow?"

"They have to leave sometime. When they do, I'll find Nunca and slip into the hotel. You stay here."

"Why?"

"This little town may be the hind end of creation, but I don't want folks saying that anyone who tries can compromise me."

Kincaid's dry humor was just the right touch. She felt wonderful. She'd been afraid he would do or say something disgusting to spoil their lovemaking or to hurt her feelings. She rested her head against his sturdy chest. She felt such peace. Eyes closed, sighing, she lifted her mouth to be kissed.

"Greedy little thing, aren't you?" Against his better judgment, Lance kissed her cheeks, eyes, throat, and mouth, lingering there for a long time. She was so tender and soft, so tender and open to him. A flame of compassion and tenderness kindled in his loins. He was within seconds of having to make love to her again. And he didn't have the strength. He took her face in his hands and stopped himself. "Go to sleep. I'll watch to be sure you don't do anything loud enough to give us away. Are you cold?"

Angie floated in warm lethargy. "I may never be cold again."

"Sleep well," he said. She slept almost before he finished speaking.

The sun rose hot.

Lily walked from her sleeping mat into the kitchen. Toy sat at the small table. She smiled and greeted her in Chinese. "Good morning, beautiful Lily. Did you hear about Tan Lin? He was arrested yesterday by the lawkeeper."

Lily found her father in the parlor, just rising from his meditation. Without greeting him she demanded to know what was going to be done about Tan Lin.

Third Uncle sighed and wondered what he had done to deserve

such an unworthy daughter. "The elders met yesterday as soon as it was learned. They agreed to wait for the white man's trial."

"Our honorable elders are sheep," she sneered.

"Enough. Do not push me to punish you so early in the day," he warned wearily.

Furious, Lily stormed out of the house and went in search of Gilbert James Lee. She found him sitting beside the creek, staring at the stream that slipped over the shallow, gravelly watercourse. His motionless body was coiled into one of the most advanced meditation postures.

She stopped beside him. Slowly he relaxed into the lotus posture.

"A small boy has been arrested by *fan quai*. My honorable father says that we must wait for the judge. Dost thou agree with that?"

Gil inhaled the fine sweet smell of sage mingled with sweet desert blossoms. The coolness of the water lifted his spirits. "I do not know. I am not truly patient, but at the same time I do not advocate violence if it can be avoided by the simple act of a trial."

"Tan Lin will not receive justice at the white man's trial!" Lily hissed.

Looking up into her face, Gil had the feeling that the violence and belligerence of hundreds of generations of warriors had been distilled into this one woman's spirit. He was both excited and repelled by her fierceness. Her spirit excited him; his memories of the reality of war repelled him. The part of him that had risen within like a tiger—ready to break out and kill the men who could terrify and torment a small, helpless boy—would not be denied. He had been meditating on the self-indulgence of his attachment to the boy.

"If he does not receive justice befitting his tender years and the insignificance of his crime, I promise you that I will personally seek a solution."

"Thou wilt lead the opposition forces when the Chinese rise up against the white man's injustice?"

Gil shook his head. Lily had not noticed. His being a half-breed meant little to her but everything to the Chinese. If there had been peace between the whites and the Chinese, his acceptance in either camp would have been an easy thing. Since there was war, he was accepted in neither camp.

"Thou wouldst refuse?" Lily knelt beside Gil.

"I am a half-breed. No one would follow me."

"They would be fortunate to have thee on their side."

Gil wore the traditional Chinese costume. She touched the silk sleeve of his tunic and felt the warmth of his arm beneath. Her heart leapt into a faster rhythm. His eyes told her that he would not pursue her. She reached out and touched his cheek. His skin was smooth and warm. His eyes were dark and filled still with pain for the boy.

Gil remained silent. Lily took his silence for agreement. "Thou art beautiful," she whispered. "And strong."

"I am neither." *Just a man prepared to die in spite of fear.*

As if she had heard his thoughts, quick tears glazed her eyes. She knelt beside him and kissed his cheek. Diffuse, heavy heat flooded his body.

Rising effortlessly, Gil lifted Lily with him. He stepped back, as if to move away from her. Lily stepped forward, lifting her mouth to meet his in a kiss that she hoped would please him. Eighteen years old next fall, she had not yet been kissed by a man. It was something she had only dreamed about.

He was insane to allow this to happen. True, they were sheltered by the desert itself—mesquite and cholla and an occasional saguaro between them and Chung Tu's house across the way—but being found out was not what stopped Gil. He owed his life to Third Uncle. His life and his mother's. He could not betray him in this fashion. Third Uncle was conservative. In China men did not meet and court women. Maiden Chinese girls did not kiss a man until after their marriage, but Lily's warm lips did not know this. They clung to his with fiery hunger. His hands, usually so reliable and capable, refused to defend him against this silky assault. They hung at his sides like drawstrings. Paralyzed from within, helpless to stop what was happening, Gil fed on the delicate sweetness of her mouth—like a melon, hot from the sun, irresistible. Slowly he pulled her into his arms.

Angie woke up to the sound of birds chirping in the trees. Her first thought was of the Chinese man who had been injured by the men who tried to kill Kincaid. She wanted to find the Chinese, take his picture, and talk to him. She would use the big Hale camera. So the pictures would be a decent size. She would take pictures of Tan Lin too. She was so excited that at first she didn't realize she wasn't in her own bed. Then her eyes focused on the one-by-fours overhead. She glanced quickly around her. She was under the porch. Alone. Sunshine peeked through the cracks in the weathered wood, and she was naked.

"Kincaid?"

Lord. As best she could under the low porch and in the dirt, Angie dressed herself, straightened her hair, and looked around her. A pile of onions sent out their sweet, dry, pungent aroma. She crawled over them and looked out a crack. Her neighbor lifted a wet shirt to hang it on the line behind her house. A fire burned under her wash pot. It must be Wednesday. Etta always washed on Wednesdays. Angie grabbed up a couple of onions and pushed on the boards nearby. One swung outward, and she crawled outside and stood up. Etta turned.

"Morning," Angie said.

"My, don't you look a sight. Canning?"

Angie held up the onions as if they explained her appearance. "Why, yes," she said. The woman turned back to her wash and Angie fled into her house.

Cort left his horse at the hitching post and stomped up onto the sidewalk in front of the Baquero. He was hot and frustrated from a fruitless ride out to Laramee Logan's ranch. Damn Ramo! If this didn't satisfy the bastard, nothing would.

"Get Marshal Ramo for me."

One of the boys on the sidewalk caught the dime Cort flipped at them and ran toward the jail.

Cort stalked past the bar to a table against the back wall. In a couple of minutes Del Ramo stopped at the door of the saloon, surveyed the interior, and sauntered in. He kicked the chair next to Cort, caught it before it could fall all the way back, and then twirled it around so he could sit backward on it, his hands draped on the backrest.

"What's up?" Ramo asked.

"Wanted to let you know that I made Logan an offer."

"And?"

"He refused it," Cort said, feeling like a fool. He must be getting soft. First Du Pon Gai, and now this…

"He's crazy," Ramo spat.

"He promised his old man he'd keep the ranch intact."

"Treats that goddamned piece of land like an ugly virgin," Ramo snorted. "You tell him you just want that strip where the chinks live?"

Nodding, Cort asked, "You want something to drink?"

"It's hotter'n hell already. I'll have beer."

Cort gestured to the bartender, who carried a beer over. Ramo sipped it and sighed.

"Jesus, that's good! So what the hell do we do now?"

"You mean after your goddamned deputy let Kincaid get away?"

"You jest had to say it, didn't you?" Ramo asked bitterly.

"Why, no, actually. I thought you and him planned it that way. That Kincaid would ride away looking like a damned hero for rescuing that chink, and six of our best friends would look like a laughingstock, at least among themselves. We're damned lucky they didn't show their faces." Cort spat into a nearby spittoon to show his contempt for Smalley's efforts. "Kincaid couldn't be any safer if he had your protection."

Ramo slammed his beer mug down on the table. Beer swoshed up and splattered out. Cort shook his head. "Nice."

"You think it's so damned easy to get that bastard, why don't you try it?"

"Don't reckon I could do any worse than your asshole deputy's done."

Ramo expelled an angry breath. "I'll kill that damned ranger if it's the last thing I do."

"You don't have to actually kill him. Just open up a bleeder. Johnny already half-killed him. All you gotta do is just give him a good poke in the right place."

Ramo appeared to consider Cort's words, and slowly the angry look on his pinched face smoothed out. "I guess so. Just kinda hit 'im right, and I reckon he would bleed till his gills turned white, wouldn't he?"

Cort grinned. "Wouldn't even be anything anybody could blame you for. Even if they knew it was you. A man walks around half dead, ain't nobody's fault but his if he gets himself hurt, is it?"

Ramo grinned. "Hell no. Wouldn't be my fault, would it?"

"Pick your time so's you don't call unnecessary attention to yourself, a lawman and all."

Ramo swigged his beer. "Hell, he won't even see me. That's the mistake Smalley made. Letting the son of a bitch see him. The ranger won't know what hit 'em. Till it's too late."

"Take your time, but you better do it before he throws a bone into our works. You still got that knife?"

Ramo nodded.

"Why don't you ride out and make sure who it belongs to..."

"Like I just found out it was his?" Ramo asked, frowning.

Cort could see Ramo getting tensed up. "You got the goddamned judge in your pocket. It's your word against Logan's. Who's Cadwallader going to believe?"

"Yeah," Ramo said, a grin spreading across his features as he remembered how promptly Cadwallader had answered his wire.

Another dark thought interrupted. Ramo frowned again. "But what if—"

Cort cut him off before he could get attached to his worries. "If he resists, you don't have any choice, do you? A man resisting an officer of the law…a killer like that…nothing else you can do but defend yourself. He won't know what hit him. Besides, it'll make the governor happy to hear you've arrested the man that killed those damned chinks he's so concerned about."

In the Tuesday *Gazette*, no mention was made of the two horses. The headline read: CIVIL WAR IN CHINESE QUARTER, and in smaller print below the headline: STRIFE TAKES LIFE OF RUFE MARTIN AND ENDANGERS DURANGO WOMAN.

Furious, Angie read the story. "Harry Sloan made that whole thing up!" she said, slamming the paper onto Sarah's desk.

Sarah read from the newspaper and shook her head. "Civil war… Chinese tong punish the Chinese for not paying their debentures. Listen to this quote from Ed Millicent: 'We shouldn't allow these people in the country. We just fought one war to outlaw slavery. Now we have the Chinese bringing their slavery and their opium into our city. It ain't right.'"

"I don't understand how a white man trying to rape a Chinese woman could be called civil war!" Angie gritted.

"The way those three murders were called tong retributions. No one is willing to believe that white men could have caused the problem," Sarah said.

Angie picked up the paper and turned to page two. "Listen to this. 'Citizens met at the Baquero Saloon and Pleasure Palace to discuss formation of the Durango Protective and Anti-Chinese Association.' That was almost the exact name Lance predicted…" she said in an aside to Sarah. "'Action to be pursued includes refusing to hire Chinese. Members will call on local employers. Charter members include upstanding citizens from all walks of community life: Cort Armstrong, Neville Smalley, Del Ramo, Harry Sloan, Ed Millicent…' It goes on and on. Oh, listen to this. 'Laramee Logan, local rancher, declined to join, stating that he preferred more direct action to rid the community of the yellow menace.'"

Sarah's mouth tightened. She could see Laramee, furious with her, being stopped by the officious Sloan and uttering those angry words. "He was in a dreadful mood when he left my house yesterday."

Angie heard the guilt between the lines. "Laramee will be fine. He talks like that, but he doesn't do anything about it. He would never hurt anyone who wasn't trying to hurt him."

Looking thoroughly miserable, Sarah shrugged. "The man who killed my mother wasn't trying to hurt her…I was in school when she died. No one remembered to come get me…or they didn't want to upset me. I didn't know for an hour that she was dead."

Angie had heard Sarah's story about her mother's death so many times that it barely registered anymore. "Can you believe Harry Sloan would print blatant lies?" Angie demanded, patting Sarah absently, expelling an angry breath. "Compare that with the stories we're writing."

Angie picked up a piece of copy she had placed on Sarah's desk Friday, which seemed weeks ago now after so many things had happened. "'Canned fruits and meats now available in stores'…and this one," she said, picking up another article written in her own script. "'Australian frozen meat on sale in London, can Durango be far behind?' Now, these are stories of vital concern!"

Sarah nodded absently, but her action lacked commitment. The man who shot her mother hadn't even known her. Her mother was only accidentally dead. Accidentally buried. Did that mean that she herself was only accidentally an orphan?

Angie sighed. Sarah had withdrawn again. Perhaps her listlessness had something to do with Laramee. It usually did, but Angie was afraid to ask about it. If Sarah confided in her, she would feel obligated to confide in Sarah about Kincaid, and she wasn't ready to do that yet. There would be time later. Thank goodness she didn't believe in anything as infantile as love at first sight…

"I'm going to give Harry Sloan a piece of my mind," Angie said. She walked to the hat rack and put on her hat. "Are you coming with me?"

"Me?"

"I wish you would. You do have an arrangement with Sloan so the two of you can buy paper in large quantities. You can order the paper we need."

With a reluctant Sarah at her side, Angie walked into the office of the Durango *Gazette* and stopped at the desk. The place looked worse than *The Tea Time News*. The surface of Harry's desk had disappeared under a mound of paper almost a foot high. Everything in sight looked dusty or grimy.

From the back of the room Harry Sloan waved and yelled. "Be right there!"

Angie tapped her dusty black slipper on the dirty floor. Sloan came forward, wiping his ink-stained hands on his apron. "Well! How do?"

Sloan was a little too soft for Angie's taste, though an attractive young man, with good, if somewhat freckled, pinkish features. Sloan wiped the perspiration off his face with his sleeve and stopped in front of them.

"You know very well how I am. I am furious," Angie said, glaring at him.

"But…why?" he asked, his eyes glancing lightly over Angie to linger on Sarah's face.

"I told you exactly what happened at that fire," Angie said, "and you made up some cock-and-bull story about a civil war! How do you figure that a white man trying to…to…force himself on a Chinese girl is civil war?" She held up the newspaper and tapped the headline—a full six columns wide that fairly shouted—CIVIL WAR IN CHINESE SECTION.

Harry's face flushed with heat. "If you take that fire out of context, you get one story; if you put it in context, as I did, you get a completely different story."

"Oh!" Sarah said, rolling her eyes.

Angie waved the newspaper in his face. "We are not talking about a matter of context. These are blatant lies."

Sloan shook his head stubbornly. "The Chinese traditionally execute one another for small transgressions. The companies or the tongs keep them in line that way. If they don't pay their debentures, if they refuse to do anything they are told, the companies punish them. Everyone knows that! Only last year, when those two chinks fought over the girl, they didn't kill each other—they killed her. The Chinese are barbaric! They aren't like us. They drink their tea, smoke their opium, eat their rice and their salted fish, and steal our chickens. They don't attend our churches."

"Or swill booze with our drunks. That's really it, isn't it? They don't play cards and drink rotgut!"

"You sure look pretty when you're all fired up that away, Miss Sarah," he said, looking at Sarah as if she were the one talking.

"This is a waste of time," Angie said, backing toward the door.

"Wait, Angie, we still have to finish our other business," Sarah said, panicking.

"You finish it. I'm not wasting any more time here."

Anxious because Angie had left angry, Sarah gave Sloan her order and turned to go.

"You sure look pretty," he said softly. "I'm no gunfighter. Sure wish I was."

Sarah frowned. "What does that have to do with anything?"

"If I was the sort of man comfortable killing other men, shooting 'em, that sort of thing, I'd ask you to walk out with me. But since I'm not, I better not get Laramee riled up."

An image of her mother lying in the parlor, surrounded by strangers and neighbors chattering like evil black ravens, pretending to mourn, saying how awful it was in those gloating, sanctimonious voices, swept over Sarah. The shocked faces, superficially grieving but showing covertly that the only thing that really mattered was that Mary Armstrong was dead and they weren't. *I was standing this close to her. Another foot…If I'd just walked a little slower…*

Nausea overwhelmed Sarah. "I'm not walking out with Laramee anymore…"

"You're not? Since when?" he demanded, remembering he had seen them dancing together on Saturday night. This was only Tuesday.

"Since yesterday."

"Well, that being the case, any chance you would have dinner with me?"

Laramee would be furious with her if she did, and she didn't even especially like Sloan. She certainly did not like his ethics. Yet she found herself shrugging. "Where?"

"If you want to go home first, I'll pick you up there."

"I'm working late tonight."

"How about if I meet you at the hotel dining room at six-thirty?" he asked.

Harry Sloan watched Sarah leave. He couldn't imagine what he had said to get that reaction from Sarah, but he thanked whatever gods were watching over him for his sudden good fortune.

Angie walked back to the office in a rage. She grabbed a piece of paper, wrote down everything she was mad about, and then read it again. She rewrote it to take the temper out and strengthen her logic, then pulled a plate of lead type over and began to set the story. She would print a flier to tell folks what really happened at that barn.

Sarah walked in and sat down. Angie glanced up. Sarah looked shaky.

"You okay?"

"I don't know."

"Did you order the paper?"

"Yes."

Angie put down the capital B and sighed. "You think it would be okay if I used the press to print a rebuttal to Harry Sloan's story? I'll pay for the paper and the ink and anything else I use."

Sarah blinked. Cort would have a hissy fit. But as it was, folks didn't know anything except the lies Sloan told them. "I'll run the press for you."

"No, you won't. When Cort flies apart, I want you to be able to say you had nothing to do with it."

Angie finished setting the type, adjusted the printing press to accommodate a nine-by-twelve flier, and printed a hundred copies. She stacked them to dry and then washed her hands. "I'm going to take some pictures of the man who was beaten by those bullies last night."

At the Chinese quarter Angie found any number of willing subjects, but not the man she wanted. Perhaps he was one of the miners. When the shift changed at four, she'd catch him.

She took a picture of a Chinese woman hanging clothes on the line. Her shy smile peeked over the flimsy rag and her dirty toes dug into the sand, counterpoint to the line of dark and light clothes. In the background, apartments crowded together in one block, their back doors sagging open to let in a breath of air.

"You been here all day?"

Angie wiped her wispy hairs out of her eyes. Kincaid's raspy voice could turn up just about anywhere. She turned to greet him.

"Afternoon."

"Get some good pictures?"

Angie's grin reflected so much excitement that Lance's toes curled. Her skirts were dirty halfway up to her waist. Sand burs and beggars lice, those pesky, prickly weeds, had embedded themselves in the fabric of her skirt. She must have been at this for hours.

"These people are wonderful. They're sincere and shy. They remind me of fawns."

"Gonna eat a bite?"

"What time is it?" Chinese family life had astounded Angie and kept her enthralled. That anyone could live in such close, primitive conditions amazed her. Families of eight or ten occupied a single room—living, cooking, eating, sleeping, and carrying on a small business or laundry.

They showed no signs of objecting to, or even noticing, how cramped they were.

In her cousins' weekly, it had been printed that whatever the white men scorned to do, the Chinese took up. Mild-mannered, artful, and insinuating, they were the gap fillers, doing what no one else would do for the price offered, adapting themselves to the white man's needs and slipping away unprotestingly to other tasks when the white man wanted their jobs. Until today Angie had not known exactly what that had meant. Today she had seen men, women, and children scrabbling to make a dime anyway they could.

"'Bout three o'clock, going on."

"It couldn't be that late. I've been here only a few minutes."

"Take a little break from that and let's get a bite to eat."

Angie had been so busy she hadn't felt hungry, but suddenly she did feel like she might eat something. "You wearing that red shirt for a target?" she asked, squinting up into his face.

"Thought I might as well."

"As my brother would say, you're the blamedest man I ever did see."

"What you talking about, girl?"

"How many crimes did you solve today?"

"This'll be my first." He took her arm.

"Wait. We can't leave my camera here."

"Maybe I can sell it for you."

Lance pulled the camera wagon, and she walked beside him to the general store. Kincaid bought a window and told the man to hold on to it for him. Angie wondered when he had measured the window sash. She glanced up at him and closed her mouth. He had probably eyeballed it whenever he sneaked away from her.

Kincaid bought enough apples, cheese, bread, butter, sliced beef, pickled eggs, and tea cakes for six people. They carried it out to the creek and sat down in the shade of a big cholla cactus. Angie ate as if she were starving. Kincaid laughed at her. "Good thing I found you. You might have starved to death."

"I'm just eating this to please you. You spent enough money on it."

Lance lay back on the sand and smiled. "Don't you ever run out of those plates you take pictures on?"

"No, silly. I reuse them."

"What's it going to take to stop you, then?"

"I'll never stop. I love taking pictures. I love the people. I love the desert. I love everything about it."

She looked at the water slipping over the pebbles. The cooler air near the water smelled good to her. "How come you're doing this instead of being an attorney? Rangering?"

"I got time off for good behavior."

Angie grinned. "I thought you'd say you failed at it or something."

"Well, I suppose I was so bad at it that I could have failed if I'd taken the time to, but I didn't wait around that long."

"What'd you do, just ride off one day?"

"I didn't know I was going to, but then one day I did just that. I packed some of my things and bought a ticket on a ship headed for San Francisco."

"I bet your folks were upset. What are they like?"

"I don't know." He picked up a handful of sand and let the grains slip through his fingers. "I guess like anybody's folks. My father makes a lot of money and wonders where he went wrong raising me. My mother gives a lot of parties and wonders what she ever did to deserve three sons who won't settle down and make grandbabies."

"Are your brothers like you?"

"They're the same sex."

Angie giggled.

"But I guess the resemblance stops there."

"Where *did* they go wrong raising you?"

"Tawk about wishful thinking," he said, affecting his spoonin' dialect. "I'm gonna spend a lot less time worrying about my younguns. There's only so much a parent can do that affects the outcome. Younguns find their own way, even when parents don't want them to. If my folks did anything wrong, it was in failing to recognize my natural talent for causing my own trouble."

Angie leaned back on her hands. She felt satisfied. And she had never tasted such good food. She would have to ask Kincaid how he had learned to pick such wonderful combinations of odd things.

"What are you thinking about?" he asked.

"Oh, nothing."

Lance sat up and pulled her into his arms. "You look mighty pretty with your hair all messed up like that." He burrowed his face into the crook of her neck. He liked the way she smelled, all warm and soft. Her skin intoxicated him.

"Someone will see us," she murmured.

"You trying to tell me you care?" He had never met a more relaxed, natural girl in his life. In the east he had known girls so twisted by the demands of society and by their own weird thoughts that a man couldn't hold their hand without worrying that their papa was going to come after him with a .22. That was the norm. Angie Logan was something special.

"Just testing to see how easy you are to discourage."

He kissed her neck. She turned her face and found his mouth. He kissed her so long she got dizzy and had to stop him.

"I have work to do."

"Do it tomorrow."

"I have different work for tomorrow."

"It'll keep."

"So will you."

Lance grimaced. "Don't feel like it."

Angie felt breathless. She pulled away. He had a way of making her heart beat strangely. "Look at this mess." Food containers and half-eaten items scattered all around them.

"There's enough left for another meal. Have dinner with me," he urged.

"I don't know. I've used so much of the day I don't know if I'll finish in time for dinner."

Lance walked her back to *The Tea Time News*. Jasper, the blacksmith, waited at the door for her. Kincaid waved and left her at the door.

The sun was sinking toward the horizon. Seven o'clock. Laramee's hands were cuffed together in front of him. With a look of barely controlled rage on his face, he rode between Ramo and Smalley and was followed at a distance by six of the Boxer brand's most loyal riders.

Laramee could not believe he had allowed Ramo to arrest him. Nothing could account for it. Except he hadn't thought they were serious. By the time he realized they were, Ramo had him covered with that goddamned shotgun.

He'd had the blamedest feeling that Ramo would have welcomed resistance and answered it with deadly force. He hoped he was wrong about that. He was almost positive he was wrong about that. Ramo had no reason to want to kill him. They weren't crazy about each other, and Ramo was a snake, but he was only a grass snake. Six of Laramee's best men followed him into town because they didn't trust Ramo either.

As the two groups proceeded through the town, people stepped out onto porches and sidewalks to watch them pass. Friends of Laramee's yelled, trying to find out what was going on; he tipped his hat at them, too furious to speak.

In front of the hotel Sarah Armstrong and Harry Sloan left their table by the window and stood beside the doorway as Laramee passed. Sarah bit her knuckle, disbelief turning to anguish on her face.

More hurt than furious, Laramee refused to meet her gaze. At least now he knew why she had refused to marry him.

Angie opened her door. Sarah burst into tears at the sight of her. "Sarah! What in heaven's name…"

"They arrested Laramee," she finally managed to say. "Ramo and Smalley! For the murders of the Chinese brothers…"

"That is ludicrous," Angie protested, pulling her friend into the sparsely furnished parlor.

"Surely, no one really believes that—"

"Harry ran over to the jail and asked a bunch of questions. Ramo had Laramee's knife. When Laramee admitted it was his, they arrested him."

"I'll get Kincaid. He'll do something."

The four Chinese carriers of the luxurious sedan chair stopped in the Liang front yard. The head carrier pulled himself up to his full height and faced the Liang house. "Chung Tu has arrived," he shouted in announcement.

Inside, Liang frowned. Chung Tu was not welcome in his home. Chung Tu had eaten Christianity for personal gain. Nothing could be more distasteful.

Liang pulled the shade aside and looked out the window. The magnificence of Tu's sedan chair certified to Third Uncle that Tu's betrayal of his heritage had been financially most beneficial. Luxuriously padded inside, the fine mahogany chair was carved and inlaid with jade. Few Chinese in the territories could afford a sedan chair, much less one of such excellence, with four carriers.

A peasant in China, Chung Tu now lived better than the scholar-gentry had lived in their homeland. Liang regretted the event that had cost his three young nephews their lives, but his guilt in that one thing was as nothing compared to the guilt that should accrue to Chung Tu from many things. Head of the local tong, Tu controlled both the flow of opium and all manner of illegal activities. He was both protector and oppressor of the Chinese in Durango. In trouble or in need, Chinese traditionally went to the local tong head, whose power among the Chinese was far greater than any local dignitary among the whites. Tu alone decided the fates of his countrymen.

When it suited Tu, he could be beneficent. Once, when a woman complained to him that her husband had mistreated her, Tu had the man whipped. When Tu's order for execution orphaned the Kong boy, Tu arranged a pension and placed the child with a good family.

When he chose, Tu became cruel, vengeful. Once, when reformists tried to overthrow Tu and take control of the tong for the benefit of all, Tu's henchmen foiled the coup and executed the reformists. He ordered them cut in half at the waist and incinerated so their bones could not be sent home to their families. No worse end could be imagined by a Chinese.

White men rarely knew what transpired within the Chinese quarter. Most were unable even to distinguish one Chinese from another. No one dared complain to the white authorities lest they also die. The deaths of the three brothers last month could have been hidden as well if Jade Precious, girlfriend to one of the dead men, had not become hysterical and sent for the town marshal.

Tu stepped out of the sedan. Short and slender as a boy, he straightened his black top hat and adjusted his gold and green silk robes. Tu walked slowly toward the house, flicking ashes from his long cigar onto the grass. Third Uncle looked around his small house with trepidation. Chung Tu had been inside the house last year, before they made the improvements. Would Tu notice the newly lacquered floor or other signs of prosperity? Tu knew everything that went on in the town among Chinese and whites. Had he come there to demand a share?

With great reluctance Liang stepped through the open door and out onto the porch to greet his visitor.

"Welcome to my humble home," he said solemnly.

Chung Tu bowed from the waist. The glasses perched on his button nose slipped down and almost fell off. "Thank you for your sincere welcome, friend," he said, pushing his spectacles back into place.

"Come in," Third Uncle said, bowing.

"Ahhh. Thank you, thank you. Your chrysanthemums are most impressive," Tu said, bowing to the flowers that traditionally adorned the entry way of the sitting room of a patriarch. Liang led Tu into the parlor of the small house and motioned for Tu to be seated.

As the men chatted, Lily listened from the other room. She flushed with embarrassment that her father was so conditioned to politeness that he would tolerate a piece of dung like Tu.

"You wish something from me?" Third Uncle asked, intimidated, but deliberately not offering Tu any refreshment after his trip.

Tu nodded, pretending not to notice the slight. They spoke of other matters, and then Tu smiled. "I have come to offer for your daughter, Lily, for my son, Chih-peh."

Liang hid his surprise. "That is both a great honor to my family and most unfortunate. Lily is already promised," he said, not quite lying. He had seen the happy smiles on the faces of Son of Autumn and Lily. An offer on her behalf was imminent.

"I have not seen or heard any announcement that would indicate your daughter has been spoken for," Tu protested. "I can give much in the way of dowry to welcome your daughter into my family."

Pleased that he could foil Tu in this matter, Liang remained completely still. "I am sure that you can, but as I say, it is already settled."

After Tu left, Lily ran into the parlor and threw herself into her father's arms. "Thank thee, thank thee, thank thee. I will obey thee forevermore. I will love thee forevermore. Thou art most wonderful!"

Liang staggered under the onslaught. Lily pressed him in her embrace; her slim arms hugged him hard. "Here, here," he protested. "What is this? Had I known your obedience was so easily secured, I would have saved myself many years of your disobedience."

Father Bergman closed the door of the rectory and stepped outside. The sound of chattering Chinese caused him to look up. Tu's sedan chair approached.

Chung Tu was Father John Bergman's first successful convert to Catholicism in Durango. To Father Bergman and his superior, Bishop Sullivan, Tu was partial proof that Father Bergman had managed to introduce Christianity into heathen life. Because Father Bergman did not understand what had moved Tu to make the conversion, he handled Tu with great care, lest he inadvertently undo whatever he had done.

As Tu stepped down from his chair, Father Bergman invited him into the chancellery behind the church. The office was sparsely furnished, with only a desk, an enormous Bible, four large leather armchairs, and an antique globe poised in an ornate stand.

"Won't you sit down?" he said, motioning to the chair next to him. "You look troubled, my son."

"You are very perceptive, Father," Tu said, taking the chair he had indicated. "I have made an offer for a young girl for my son, and even though the girl is not promised to another, the girl's father has refused my offer."

Father Bergman frowned. He did not see any way he could assist Tu in this personal matter.

Tu noted the priest's expression. Bergman's smooth, boyish face half covered by slate-gray, shoulder-length whiskers, barely concealed his distaste. "I have given more in donations than most, have I not?" he asked softly.

"That is correct," Father Bergman said, hiding his distaste for the subject of donations. Speaking of it smacked of blackmail. Bergman hated financial matters.

Tu took a small purse—fat and heavy with coin—from his pocket and laid it discreetly on Father Bergman's desk. "I ask nothing for myself, but my son, who has been a dutiful child and has grown into a thoughtful Christian, wishes to take this heathen girl and convert her to Christianity. We would like your help in this."

Perplexed and vexed by the crassness of Tu's approach, Father Bergman shook his head, frowning. "But how can I be of service in this matter?"

"Chinese cannot testify in your courts. You could testify on my son's and my behalf. Ask the court to grant my son's offer for the woman, Lily."

"On what basis?"

"I am not familiar with your Christian courts. Perhaps for so much silver you can discover a basis that would be effective." Tu watched closely to see if more silver was needed. It was important to him that Chih-peh marry Lily. Lily was the only member of the scholar gentry in Durango. Chih-peh had been born a peasant as he had, but Chih-peh would marry an aristocrat. With Tu's money and the Liang family's prestige, Chih-peh would father a dynasty of rich, respectable Chungs.

Father Bergman scowled and chewed on the insides of his thin lips. Tu picked up the fat purse and dropped it into the priest's hand. The purse was worth a great deal. Father Bergman expelled a long breath. The money meant nothing to him; the young woman's immortal soul meant everything. If he could bring her from the darkness of idol worship, if he could save her from her family's pagan ways...God wanted every soul—

no matter from whence it came. The girl's conversion might influence others. Then Bishop Sullivan would know that Father Bergman was truly effective. He thought Tu a fluke, that no others would follow. If he could save the girl…

"Yes," Father Bergman said softly, "perhaps I could think of a way to help both your son and the young woman."

CHAPTER THIRTEEN

Tuesday evening, May 18, 1880

Angie and Sarah walked to town as fast as they could. Angie spotted Kincaid leaving the jail and waved at him. He walked to meet them. A knot of Boxer brand riders sat on the porch in front of the jail.

"Is he okay?"

"Your brother's fine," he said, noting the fear in her wide, dark eyes. "But it won't hurt to leave a couple of men on guard to see he stays that way."

"You think Ramo—"

"You'd know him better than I do, but I wouldn't trust him any farther than I could toss him."

Angie hurried into the jail to see Laramee. Sarah sighed. "I knew he would die…"

"He's not dead, ma'am. Just arrested."

"I know, but he will be."

Lance couldn't figure Sarah. He gave up trying. "I'll hold down the sidewalk if you want to see him."

"He doesn't want to see me."

Kincaid nodded. He had seen Sarah with her young man at dinner. Apparently Logan had as well.

"Are you all right?" Angie asked.

"My jaws ache from being so blamed mad," he said. "I'm about as happy as a jaybird in a blueberry pie."

"I'll wire Austin first thing tomorrow morning and arrange for a good attorney."

"Why Austin?"

"Because that's the closest place I know of one that's any good. I wouldn't trust Ellington as far as I could toss him. He could get a priest jailed for doing a good deed."

Lance had two days ago mentioned the name of Nicholas Shadow, an attorney he knew and trusted.

"I didn't kill those bastards!" Laramee growled.

"I know you didn't kill them, but we need a good attorney to save you."

"With a leaky-mouth like Kincaid around? Nah. He'll just tal 'em to death."

Laramee watched Angie's eyes for any sign that would tell him what was going on in that quarter.

He had wondered about it ever since Angie left the dance Saturday night. Laramee had gone directly to her house, but she wasn't there. He figured if she went to Kincaid's room at the hotel he'd have heard about it before now. Laramee hadn't asked her about it because he knew she would tell him the truth. Angie was as likely to speak bluntly as he was. She'd do pretty much whatever she damn well pleased. Laramee both feared and respected her independence.

He'd meant it when he'd told Kincaid at the dance about not being concerned about Angie. On the other hand, if Sarah were his sister, he would raise holy hell if she left with a smooth-talking lawdog like Kincaid. Sarah was like a sleepwalker—anyone could take advantage of her.

Angie asked other questions, but Laramee had no information she didn't already know. She gave up and hugged him good-bye. "I'll be close by. I won't let anything happen to you. I promise."

Kincaid lounged on the sidewalk in front of the store next door to the jail, his long legs stretched in front of him. He stood up as she walked out. Ramo walked toward the jail from the Baquero. Angie stopped beside Sabbath Turk, who stood guard.

"Anything going on here, Sabbath?"

"No, ma'am."

"I want you to keep a guard on this jail twenty-four hours a day, is that understood?" she said loudly enough for Ramo to hear her.

"Yes, ma'am."

"You are not to trust anyone, Sabbath, least of all Marshal Ramo or anyone he befriends, is that plain?"

Ramo's lips tightened into a lipless slit. He affected a defiant, sneering smile and pretended not to be concerned with her opinion.

Angie stalked across the road, Lance beside her. "Sure glad you didn't upset him," Lance said, slanting a look at her.

"If I had a gun, I'd shoot him."

Angie Logan wore a yellow gown that brought out the golden highlights in her hair and the peachy flush of her skin. In anger, her lovely face was rich and glowing. Her lips opened, revealing the wet, translucent gleam of white teeth. His blood leapt into a faster rhythm.

"I'll go poke around and see what I find."

Angie stopped at the door of *The Tea Time News*. She expelled an angry breath. Kincaid gazed off at the north end of town. He was probably waiting for her to cool down.

"I appreciate your looking into it."

Kincaid nodded and headed north.

Angie went inside. Sarah had waited at the office for her. She looked up. "How's Laramee?"

"Angry."

Sarah shook her head. "Did he say anything about me?"

Nothing Sarah would want to hear. "No."

"Well, if it helps, I feel terrible. If I had known, I would have poisoned Harry Sloan's soup." Harry Sloan, Cort, Ramo, Smalley, and Johnny Winchester were a clique. When one did anything, it was normal to assume they were all in on it.

"Ah! Good. Dissension between the new couple? Please don't expect me to be sorry…"

"Ohhh! *Et tu, Brute?* My best friend in the world?" Sarah cried.

"Well, you had dinner with him—"

"One time!"

"One very important time!" Angie reminded her. "Laramee is being arrested for a crime he didn't commit, and you're off having dinner with the enemy."

"I said I was sorry," Sarah said, tears forming in her eyes.

"I'm sorry, Sarah. I'm crazy with fear for Laramee. That snake Ramo—" Angie pulled Sarah out of her chair and hugged her.

"It's okay. I forgive you." Sarah's eyes turned bleak. "Laramee hates me now."

"He's confused. If you want him to love you, he'll love you. No man can stop loving a woman instantly, even if he would like to."

• • •

Angie stepped out of *The Tea Time News* office looking dejected and scared. A pulse of compassion started back near Lance's spine. He walked over and took her arm. "I'll walk you home."

A man stepped out of the hotel and ran across the street. Panting, he stopped in front of Angie.

"What are you doing here?" she asked, surprised to see Virgil Field, an ex-Boxer brand rider, a wiry, balding man with kindly eyes, panting from the run.

"I'm working at the hotel. Got tired of sleeping on the ground. Thought, what the heck. I been just about everything else. A barber, a sailor, a buffalo hunter, bartender, and cowpuncher. One more job to add to my list...I'll keep an eye on Laramee for you too. Another set of eyeballs can't hurt none, can it?"

"No, it can't hurt. Thanks, Virgil."

Virgil frowned. "There's anything I can do, you let me know, you hear?"

"Thanks, Virgil. I'll count you as a friend."

Angie watched him walk back across the dusty road. She blinked. "You could—" she stopped.

"What?" Lance asked, searching her face.

"...make Ramo let him go."

"I can't."

"Of course you can," she said, frowning. "You're a ranger, aren't you?"

"A ranger, not a judge. There's a difference."

"What does that mean? That he has to stay in jail for something he didn't do?" Angie demanded, her anger rising. Usually as softly colored as a ripening peach, her cheeks had flushed with bright spots of coral. Her emphatic brown eyes blazed with reproach.

"Look, I would like nothing better than to stomp in there, set your brother free, and scatter Ramo and Smalley all over the block, but it doesn't work like that. If Ramo arrests someone, I'm not the one to second-guess him. The judge does that."

Tears welled in Angie's expressive, dark eyes. She turned away. "Thanks," she said softly, not meaning it.

Pity for her plight was more powerful in him than sexual desire. "Look," Lance said quietly. "I'm sorry I can't change things right this minute."

Angie turned back. "You probably think it'll be good to teach Laramee a lesson. I know how you feel about Laramee. I just thought you would set your personal feelings aside."

"I don't even do everything they pay me for, and I'm dang sure not getting paid to teach people lessons. If your brother is innocent—" the horrified look on her face brought his hand up to still her angry comment—"and I'm sure he is, Nick Shadow can be sure that comes out at the trial. There's not a blame thing I can do right this minute," he said gently.

Lance took her arm. "Your brother is going to be fine. I won't let Ramo hang him, but I can't march in there and take him out of jail. I have to let the judge handle it for now."

His voice was low and earnest. Angie blinked. She was doing it again, fighting for Laramee like dogs fight for scraps. But she couldn't seem to stop herself.

"I'll find someone else to help him," she said grimly.

Lance followed her down the sidewalk at a leisurely pace, waiting for her to tire herself out a little. She reached the edge of town and started off down the road to her house; he lengthened his strides to catch her. In her anger, Angie had forgotten all about her bicycle. Beyond the range of sharp eyes, he took her arm and slowed her to a walk. "Look, it's not going to help your brother to fight with me, and it might hurt my feelings. You wouldn't want to do that, would you?"

"I might."

"Sure glad you don't get upset at the drop of a hat," he said.

"My brother raised me. He did without things so I could go to school in the East. He took care of me after our folks were killed. I'm not going to let him sit in that damned jail for a crime he didn't commit. I'm going home to get my gun and get him out."

"Well, that's just great. I'm trying to help your brother and you're going to cash in your six-shooter for his life and make my job that much harder."

"You're not doing piddly!" She jerked her arm out of his fingers and stalked away from him. Lance followed.

"Probably never will. If you try a jailbreak, I'll be just dumb enough to help you, and then I'll spend the rest of my life running from the law. Laramee and I'll probably hang side by side."

"Would you do that?"

Lance expelled a heavy breath. Her dark eyes stirred things in him that would be better left alone. "Probably would. I never did have good sense."

Angie searched Kincaid's face. He wasn't teasing. His clear blue eyes showed more feeling than she had ever seen there before.

More pleased than she would admit, she turned and walked more slowly. "So, you're not interested in starting your life of crime here in Durango?"

"Not particularly."

"I just can't let them hurt him, Kincaid. You have brothers and sisters. You know how I feel."

"Yeah. But we have to use our heads."

"And do what?"

"Find out what Ramo thinks he has on Laramee for starters."

"Can you do that?"

"Don't know, but that's where I'll start."

Angie sighed. He had talked her out of her anger—at him anyway. Her fury still burned for Ramo and Smalley, but she was no longer ready to kill Kincaid for leaving Laramee in that cell. Laramee was right. Kincaid *was* quite a talker. In the East conversation ranked as an art, and men good at it were well-rewarded—elected to high office and eulogized in newspapers and magazines. The East had inherited Europe's high regard for the spoken and written word. In the West a flair for conversation stirred suspicion. Men might talk a little or a lot, but smart ones practiced being as noncommittal as possible. A man knowing too much about your business could get your throat cut. Kincaid had the easterner's facility for conversing and the westerner's habit of using it to hide more than he told. But today he'd been straight with her, and she appreciated it.

"So what should I do?" she asked finally.

"Go make your brother a pitcher of lemonade, and I'll walk you back with it."

"I wanted it to be something wonderful."

"He'll think it is. It's hot as hell in that jail. All you can do now is make him comfortable while we wait for Cadwallader and Nick Shadow."

Sarah let herself in, sniffed, and stopped. The house smelled wonderful. "Cort?"

A short Chinese woman poked her head around the bedroom door. "Is Du Pon Gai," she said in a soft voice.

"What are you doing here?"

"Mister let Gai earn money while husband sick."

"Mister? Oh, Cort. You're Hop Wo's wife?"

"Yes, prease. Hop Wo wife."

"What's your name?"

"Du Pon Gai."

"All that? Mine's Sarah. Do you have everything you need? To clean…"

"Yes, prease. Strong arm. Rag. You can call Gai."

Sarah smiled. "Would you like some lye soap?"

"Yes, prease. Thank you."

A beef stew bubbled on the stove. "Did you make this?"

"Yes, prease. Hope it okay."

"It smells wonderful."

Gai had set the table for two. "Cort won't be home until much later. Would you join me?"

Du Pon Gai looked puzzled. "No, prease. Du Pon Gai go home now. Okay?"

"That's fine. How is your husband?"

"Much pain. Long time heal."

Sarah went to her closet and pulled out a pair of crutches she had used when she had sprained her ankle at fifteen.

"Later, when he's up and around, maybe these will come in handy. I don't need them. How much do I owe you for today?"

"Mister say ten dollar a week."

Sarah went into her room, rummaged in her drawer, and came out with two dollars.

"Tankee, tankee," Gai said, backing out the door, bowing, the crutches bumping the doorjamb.

Cort came home, and they ate Gai's tasty stew in silence. His gruffness warned Sarah not to say one word. After dinner he settled down with the paper and never once commented on the fact that the house smelled of lemon oil. Sarah wanted to ask him about the contradiction of joining the association at the same time he hired Hop Wo's wife to work for them, but fear of jeopardizing Gai's job stopped her. A heavy knock on the door startled her. She looked at Cort.

"You get it," Cort said, not looking up from his paper. He didn't usually stay home in the evening, but tonight he had no committee meeting and no intention of visiting any of his lady friends.

Sarah opened the door, recognized Harry Sloan, and stepped back, assuming he had come to see her father. "It's for you," she said to Cort.

"No, no, Sarah. I came to see you," Sloan said quickly, looking embarrassed. "Would you just give me a few minutes of your time?

Please?" His usually pink face was pale and earnest, completely different from the cool, reckless look of Laramee's sunbrowned image.

Sarah's mouth tightened. "You are not a friend—you printed..." Intimidated by Cort's presence behind her, she floundered into silence. Cort hated it when she went against him.

"Please, just come outside for a second. Let me explain, please?"

Recognizing Sloan's voice, Cort stood up and walked to the door. "Well! Harry! What brings you all the way out here?" Cort asked, extending his big hand. Bluff and hearty, he dwarfed Sarah, who hated the obvious way he showed that he was impressed by Sloan.

Sarah went back to her chair and the doily she was crocheting. The two men talked for a few minutes, then lowered their voices so that Sarah couldn't hear them.

"Sarah!" Cort called.

"Yes?"

"What d'ya mean, girl? Being rude to a publisher of Mr. Sloan's caliber?" Cort asked, winking at Harry.

Harry grinned foolishly. Sarah's mouth tightened into a slit. "He knows why."

"That's just business, Sarah," Harry said, his voice soft and wheedling.

"That's the trouble with women, ain't it?" Cort asked. "Always getting emotionally involved in their business. Mr. Sloan came all this way to apologize to you, Sarah, now, you get over here and let him do it."

Intimidated by Cort's tone, Sarah stood up and walked to the door.

Cort shook hands with Sloan and went into the kitchen leaving the couple alone.

"Won't you step outside, Miss Sarah? It's cooling off now. Going to be a real nice night. See, a quarter moon coming up..."

Sarah followed Sloan out onto the porch. Windows of houses up and down the block glowed with yellow lamplight. The air felt cool on her face.

He fished into his pocket and pulled out a small box. "This is for you. I felt bad that you were mad at me."

He shoved the small black box at her. Sarah shook her head. "No, I couldn't..."

"See?" Harry asked, opening the box. A small gold locket on a gold chain gleamed against the black velvet.

"Ohhhh!" Sarah gasped. An irresistible feeling of desire swept over her. When Angie was thirteen, her father had bought her a gold locket and chain like that. She wore it to school every day. Sarah had yearned for a locket like that from Cort, but Sarah was too terrified of her father to suggest it. To Sarah the locket had meant that Angie was special to her father, that he loved her. Sarah had been special to her mother. Since losing her, she had longed to be special to Cort; she never had been. All her life she had waited for her father to love her, for any man to love her. Laramee had seemed to, but he was too wild to live long enough for it to count.

"I can't accept your present, Harry," she whispered.

"It'd look real pretty against your skin," he said, holding the locket up and squinting at her. "Be a shame not to even look at it…"

Sarah felt as if she were going to cry.

"Here, let me put in on you so you can see how pretty you look," he said, turning her.

The tiny gold heart felt so special around her neck. Sarah picked up one of the lamps and walked to the mirror in her bedroom. The gold gleamed against her warm skin as if it belonged there. A heavy ache rose up in her throat.

Why couldn't Laramee have been the one to give her a locket? Or Cort? Her head ached slightly. She couldn't bear the thought of him taking the necklace away from her—it was hers.

"Can I come see?" Harry called out.

Startled, Sarah picked up the light and walked back into the parlor.

Harry's eyes were smug and admiring; he smiled as if he had known she couldn't give it up once it was around her neck. "Looks like it was made for you," he said.

"Please take it off."

A mock-serious look of consternation came into his eyes. "With a catch like that, once you put it on, it doesn't come off," he said, spreading his slender, smooth hands.

"You're teasing me now," Sarah said, surprised, beginning to smile in spite of herself.

"Think so? Try to take it off."

Sarah couldn't work the delicate, tiny clasp.

"See! Told you."

"There must be a way…"

"Sarah, please keep it," he said. "I feel bad about us being on opposing sides of any issue. Besides, I got permission from Cort before I gave it to you. We don't have to be enemies, do we? If you take it, I'll feel like we're still friends, even if we feel different about some things. Men can be friends and differ," he said, implying to Sarah that she was somehow inferior if she couldn't do the same. She hesitated, wondering how Angie would decide.

From the kitchen Cort called out. "Oh, hell, take it! It's only a trinket, for God's sake. We ain't talking about the Taj Mahal."

That night when Sarah went to bed, she stood for a long time in front of the mirror, watching the way the light caught the locket and threw it back at her reflection, loving that tiny locket more than she had ever loved any other possession in her life.

Lily opened the front door only a crack and peered through. "Yes?" she asked in English.

"I am here to see Mr. Liang," Father Bergman said, nodding at the beautiful young woman who must be the subject of his call.

Lily turned to her father, who sat in his chair, reading the Book of Tao. Her father nodded to her without looking up.

"Come in please," Lily said, stepping back, bowing.

Tall and thin, Father Bergman resisted the urge to stoop. The house was built like any other in Durango. It was only the satin wall hangings and the black lacquered floors that caused his eye to misjudge the ceilings and think them too low.

Liang did not stand, as was customary when receiving a guest. He held the priest in even lower esteem than Tu. "Sit, please," he offered, hiding the misgivings that the priest's black robe caused in him. He motioned to a chair in the place of honor beside himself.

Father Bergman sat down heavily. He did not like the smell of foreign incense, thinking it connected in some fashion to heathen rites.

"A matter of some importance brings me here," Bergman announced uncomfortably. While he wanted to please Tu almost as much as he wanted another Christian convert among the Chinese, he had been unwilling to bring suit at court regarding Lily. This visit was a compromise. If it did not work, he would give up. He did not truly like parishioner Chung Tu, thinking him somehow still impure in spite of his conversion. Perhaps paganism could not truly be banished once it had taken root.

"I came to discuss the matter of your daughter, Lily."

Fear leapt alive within Liang; he bowed. Lily was the light of his life, though he would never let her suspect it for fear his devotion would cause her to place an unrealistic value upon herself. It was not good for a

Chinese woman to have too much power. Also, it was not good to let the gods know one cared too much about a child, lest the gods take it away.

"Did not the three brothers who were killed work for you at the time?" Father Bergman asked.

The question felt like a rock dropped from a great height. Confused by the word *killed*, Liang's bowels trembled with anxiety, but he forced himself to meet the priest's impolite stare.

"It was most unfortunate."

"Yes, yes," Father Bergman agreed, sorry that he had digressed. "Most unfortunate. Tu tells me that he made an offer for Lily, and that you refused him…"

"That is correct. Lily is promised to another."

"Someone who can match the eminence of Chung Tu's family?" Father Bergman pressed.

Beginning to smother under the priest's questioning, Liang considered his reply carefully. Son of Autumn had little wealth. But he did have education, which the Liang clan valued more highly than wealth. And he was a long-time friend of the family. He had dedicated himself to military service in the Liang clan's name and had saved the family from disgrace. It would take very little to match the hollow eminence of Chung Tu's family. Tu was an opium dealer and a whoremonger. He had gained his wealth by stealing life from others.

Liang wiped sweat off his forehead with a tiny handkerchief. "Someone whose qualifications exceed the eminence of Tu's family," he said carefully.

Father Bergman saw Liang's discomfort and smiled. He enjoyed this struggle for control. It pleased him that he could make this cagey old pagan uncomfortable. More Catholic homes *should* be established in this utter pagan darkness. It would glorify God if Bergman could bring the light of the savior to this family as he had to Tu's family. He smiled. "And have the vows been publicly posted?"

"They have not, but they are as certain as if they had been," Liang replied firmly.

"Tu assures me that there can be no certainty without the posting of the banns." This was pure speculation, but Liang paled, and Bergman tingled with triumph.

"We are in a new country. This is no longer China. There is not always time for rituals."

I might not understand exactly what is going on here, but I recognize fear when I see it. This old goat has violated some law. "That is true," Bergman said smoothly. "And at the same time, the Catholic Church has its traditions and rituals, and from what Tu tells me, you have violated both." Bergman waited. It pleased him to see the light mist of perspiration appear on his opponent's forehead. Solemn and earnest on the surface, Liang's eyes failed to meet Father Bergman's determined gaze. They faltered and veered away. Liang's chin moved closer to his chest.

"Is there some law then that my daughter must marry the first one who offers for her?" Liang asked, his breath catching in his throat.

"It is not law," Father Bergman said, choosing his words carefully. It would please him greatly to convert the beautiful Lily. Others would surely follow one such as her. "It is the Church's wish," he concluded, taking the liberty of speaking for the Church.

Liang felt the priest's words like a death knoll inside him. In China no one dared go to law against a priest or one of the converts to the Catholic Church. Priests, like diplomats, claimed immunity. Both the Church and the converts could do anything they pleased and escape the due process of ordinary laws. Since the Opium Wars, Chinese had been prostrate at the feet of the English and their church. In the law courts English Catholics and their church had advantage over others. In China Christians were so powerful that people said, *An egg does not stand up against a stone.*

"Your house appears more prosperous than those of your neighbors," Bergman mused. "Tell me, what is your business?"

Liang felt light-headed. Such rudeness coupled with so many covert threats overwhelmed him. "We are in the business of making paper spills," he said softly, praying to the Tao of the ancient kings that his voice did not tremble and betray him.

"Pray tell, what is a paper spill?"

"It is a roll of thin rice paper that burns admirably and for a long time. It has a wonderful fragrance and is cheaper than incense."

"And where do you do this?" Bergman inquired.

"We did it in the barn, until it was burned down," he lied.

"And what do you do now? Since your work site has been destroyed?"

Liang felt suffocated. The priest probed into the most sensitive areas. Soon everything would lay exposed before him. Then nothing could save them. The whole family would be doomed. He had no recourse.

Liang saw in his mind's eye the great happiness of Lily and Son of Autumn when they were together. But, compared to the reality of politics, that happy picture was as nothing. In China the Catholic priests formed militia bands of their own and demanded and obtained the best lands in the cities for their churches, evicting the inhabitants and paying no compensation. When priests moved through the streets in their sedan chairs, everyone on the street where they passed, on pain of being beaten with heavy bamboo rods, had to stop work, stand up, and unroll their headbands in obeisance to the Catholic bishop.

The saying in Szechuan when Liang was a boy had been: *Become a Christian sheep, and the judge will do obeisance to your dung.*

In China no magistrate would dare protect him and his family against the Catholic bishop. *Even the Dragon Throne quakes when a foreigner shouts.* This country was worse than China in that regard. Tu rode the foreign wind to power.

With bitterness like gall in his mouth, Liang bowed to Father Bergman. "It shall be as you wish."

Father Bergman blinked. He had expected more of a tussle from this old scoundrel.

Unbidden, a slender Chinese girl with ludicrously tiny, ornate shoes on her stunted feet scurried into the room and placed a teapot and two cups before Liang. She knelt down and poured, offering first to the guest, with a deep bow, and then to her patriarch.

Father Bergman lifted his cup. "Is it appropriate in your culture to drink a toast to the engaged couple?"

Liang lifted his cup, his eyes hooded as if against a strong wind.

Lily ran from the house, tears streaming down her cheeks. She found Son of Autumn inside the family ancestral sanctuary, kneeling. Nearby, gurgling softly, the creek slipped over its gravelly bed. When Lily entered, Son of Autumn bowed low and then turned to face her.

"There is more trouble?" he asked, seeing the look on her lovely face.

Lily closed her eyes. She was ashamed of the tears that flowed so freely from her eyes—suddenly unsure of herself. Perhaps her father had spoken to Son of Autumn, and he had said to honor Tu's request.

"My honorable father has betrothed me to Chih-peh, Chung Tu's son," she said softly, watching Gil's eyes for any sign that the many hours they had spent together in the last week had meant nothing to him.

Gil paled. "When did this happen?"

"Moments ago." Lily turned away, filled with relief that her beloved did not appear to have known ahead of her. "I will not marry him. He hath eaten Christianity. He is a swine."

Gil sighed. "I know that is your wish, Lily, as it is my wish also, but you have been raised a virtuous woman."

That Son of Autumn could say such an empty, sanctimonious thing to her in light of the seriousness of this problem caused a flurry of rage. Turning, Lily kicked out at anything her small feet could reach.

Gil waited in silence. Furious, Lily faced him, her black eyes sparkling. "There *is* no virtue! *Where* is the virtue in allowing myself to be bartered like some...some...*slave*? There are no rewards! Thy *virtue* means nothing! Only to live a life of diligence and frugality and self-sacrifice! I am as *nothing!* I make wonderful, succulent pickles! Therefore I am a prized possession! To be given away by a cowardly old man! To be owned by a *jackal* who would eat carrion! I am *nothing!*"

Her face blazed with the fury that whirled in her. "A priest from the Catholic Church can sip tea with my honorable father, and it is decided! I am turned out!"

The weight of her entire culture rested on her slender shoulders. Lily saw herself pulled from her family like a twig from a branch and tossed on a raging river. She would drown in the unrelenting river, suffocated by the muddy, swirling water, crashed against the rocks to die unnoticed. She sobbed wildly and tore at her hair. Her lovely jade-encrusted comb fell to the floor. Seeing it and the alarm on Gil's face, she stepped on the curved comb, breaking it in half.

Gil wanted desperately to touch her, but he dared not. He knew her torment, because it was his as well. However, once Liang promised Lily to Tu's son, nothing could stop the marriage. Failure to honor his sacred commitment would be sacrilege—equivalent to dishonoring sacred ancestors. Gil's heart bled, for he and Lily were of the same spirit—his more refined by time and experience and by his position in their culture, hers fiercer and more passionate. Adjustment would be harder for her.

Now he had no choice except to help her bear what must be borne. He knelt and picked up the broken comb. "I will always be your friend," he said softly.

"Get thee...away from me!" she screamed, sobbing. "Thou art as bad as he! Next thou wilt tell me that if I satisfy my honorable father's insane commitment, I will be eulogized in a commemorative essay on my gravestone! I want no eulogies! I strangle in moral rectitude! I suffocate with filial devotion! Moralisms are phrases for calligraphers to inscribe on lacquered boards. It is not possible to live within such confines!"

Gil bowed his head. Lily could struggle against her birthright and her culture, but she could not prevail. Family councils routinely decided careers of the sons, alliances to be contracted through marriages, and the buying and selling of land. Continuity was an invisible, relentless thread that bound the family together no matter what an individual might wish. Lily would marry Tu's son and bear Tu's grandchildren. Eventually she would be reconciled to her fate.

Gil ached to touch Lily, to caress the soft curve of her slender back, but he dared not indulge himself. She was engaged. Nothing he could say would deny the truth of her passionate words. Nothing would alleviate her grief or his own.

A small crowd of Chinese stood around the jail, talking in low voices. Seeing their somber, truculent faces, Sarah guessed that Chinese, once aroused, would be fierce fighters. Their usual conciliatory smiles were not visible today.

Before she could change her mind and flee, Sarah stepped forward, and a path opened for her. Laramee might not want to see her.

Marshal Ramo was seated at his desk, reading Wanted posters. He looked up. A familiar sneer twisted his thin face.

"Guess you're here to see Logan."

Sarah nodded.

Ramo gestured at the cells in the back half of the room. Fifteen men jammed the cells. Since the death of the police court judge, all offenders waited for the district judge to come.

"Be my guest..." Without waiting for her to respond, he returned his attention to the posters.

Laramee stretched out on his bunk, in his own private cell since he was wanted for murder.

Sight of his lean, hard-muscled body made her heart beat faster. Sarah hated that about herself. No matter how prone to sudden death Laramee might be, all she had to do was see him—the angle of his jaw, the certain slant of his back as he sat a horse, the cut of his thighs—and her heart flip-flopped in her chest. She hated herself when she wasn't with him because she was filled with a terrible longing. She hated herself when she was with him because she had given in to it.

Sarah stopped beside the cell door. "Laramee..."

He swung into a sitting position. His eyes raked over her. The demure gown she wore could not completely conceal the voluptuous softness of her shapely body. Just looking at her, his hands tingled with the memory of her soft firm flesh.

Sudden rage rose up in him. "Surprised you had time to stop by."

"Don't be mean to me, Laramee."

"Lord's truth," he said, refusing to look at her. "I said to myself as I rode by the hotel. 'Don't think I'll be seeing much of old what's-her-name.'"

"You did not," Sarah said, angry in spite of her resolve. She was sorry she had come. She wouldn't have, except the compulsion to explain herself to Laramee overwhelmed her.

Laramee had obviously thought they had struck some sort of bargain by his making love to her. And perhaps she had thought so, too, but once asleep, she had had the nightmare again. Monstrous bullets had torn through her bedroom wall. They moved slowly, but no matter how frantically she tried, she couldn't get out of their way, and neither could Laramee. He had appeared in her dream for the first time last night. One second she had been alone in her bedroom, screaming, and the next he had been beside her on the bed, kissing her. She had screamed at him and tried to show him the bullets, but he hadn't cared about them. The bullets moved in slow motion as they came toward them. She screamed at Laramee to save himself, to save her, but he only laughed and buried his face between her breasts. She felt hot and damp between her legs, and when he touched her there, she could almost forget the bullets coming so slowly and inexorably toward them. But her mother watched from above, and when Sarah stopped screaming, her mother tugged at them to see the bullets, to get out of their way. The first bullet hit Laramee, and he exploded. The next one hit her, and she woke up, screaming.

Laramee chuckled. "Taken up card-reading, have you?"

Sarah bit her bottom lip. "Are you all right?" she asked softly. "Did they hurt you…?"

"Hurt my feelings that I let a couple of sidewinders sneak up on me like that."

"Have you seen Kincaid?"

"He stopped by to pay his respects. He wasn't in on this deal. Leastways, I don't think he was."

"He'll straighten this out."

"Ohhh," Laramee said, nodding sagely. "You have a new hero now, do you? *Good old Kincaid will straighten this out*," he mimicked. "Just snap his blamed fingers and pop everything into its proper place, will he? I don't want that son of a bitch within a mile of me!"

Sarah shook her head in exasperation. "That's a rotten thing to say about a man who's trying to save your life!"

Ramo set aside the posters, stretched, and walked outside. On the sidewalk Ramo yelled at the Chinese to get the hell on home, where they belonged. Indecipherable honks and snorts of Chinese words filled the air.

"I don't want that bastard saving anything of mine! I didn't kill those chinks, and everyone knows it! Ramo and Smalley cooked up this mess of cow patties for their own reasons."

"Please keep your voice down," she pleaded, glancing at the other cells, where men pretended not to be listening to them. "I came here to help you."

"I don't need your sympathy," Laramee said, his voice low and taut with emotion. "You just go back to your blamed sweetheart and don't worry about me, okay?"

"He's not my sweetheart. We just ate dinner…"

"That's how it starts, ain't it?" Laramee sneered, moving closer to the bars.

Furious, Sarah pressed herself against the bars. She reached out and tried to hit him. Her green eyes blazed. Her voice was a low, furious whisper. "You…you've been trying to seduce me for years!"

He was amazed that she fought with him. She'd never fought back at anyone in her life. What had gotten into Sarah?

"If I'd *tried*, shortcake, it would have happened years ago," he whispered, his face close to hers. "I took care of you! Because I wanted to marry you." Furious, he started to turn away from her.

Sarah hit him in the side as hard as she could. Laramee grabbed her wrist; she tried to hit him with her other hand. He captured it and pulled her tight against the bars. They glared at each other, barely breathing.

Sarah wavered first. Slowly she stepped back from the cell; he let her go.

"Don't be mad at me," she pleaded.

"You make me so blamed mad," he growled.

The sound of cloth on cloth reminded Sarah that they were not alone. Sarah blinked as if she had stepped into strong light after darkness. Five men crowded into each of the other cells. A small boy huddled in the far corner of the cell next to Laramee's, his face covered.

Frustrated, Laramee looked at the boy. "He don't like being locked up any better than I do, I reckon."

Sighing, hoping to distract herself from Laramee's influence, Sarah walked to the boy's cell. "What's wrong?" she asked softly. The boy peered at her from between his spread fingers.

"Are you all right?" she repeated.

"He don't talk, leastways not to anyone here."

"Did we scare you?" she asked softly. "Come here."

Tan Lin shook his head.

"I have something for you," she said. "Some cookies."

Sarah reached into the deep pocket of her calling costume and took out a small bag of cookies she had brought for Laramee. "You can share them with him," she said, gesturing at Laramee. "Have you met him?" Sarah knelt and put the cookies on the floor inside the boy's cell.

Tan Lin shook his head.

"What's your name?" she asked.

The boy let his fingers slide down to reveal a square, earnest Oriental face. His head was shaved to the crown, his hair braided into one pigtail that hung down his back.

"He don't speak English," Laramee repeated.

Sarah walked back to Laramee's cell. The suffering of children incapacitated her. Her mind could not cope with the thought of a child, frightened and alone, in a jail cell.

Laramee waited a moment. "There is one thing he needs," he said softly, "a quart jar."

"Then I'll bring him one," Sarah said. "Is it okay if I come see you?"

Laramee shook his head, his green eyes bright and hard in his handsome face. "Don't want you making your new sweetheart mad on my account."

"He's not my sweetheart."

Laramee sighed. "Well, blame it. How could you do such a thing? You know how I feel about that windsucker."

Sarah bent her head, shamed to the core. "I know. Angie and I went over there only to tell him how mad we were about that story. I got confused."

"Don't take much to confuse you," he said crossly. "Why don't you just say you'll marry me, and then you won't have so many decisions to worry about?"

When she was with Laramee, she wanted whatever he wanted. But later…"Just be *nice* to me."

Laramee repressed a furious curse, then relaxed slightly. "So what kind of cookies did you bring me?"

Relieved, Sarah dug another small bag out of her pocket and held them out to him. Laramee took one, tasted it, and grinned. "Guess I'll have to be. Being mean to a good cook like you while I'm locked up would be like burning down my own house to get rid of the rats."

CHAPTER FOURTEEN

Wednesday night, May 19, 1880

"Thou art alone?"

Lily's soft voice startled him. Coiling forward, Gil stood up. She was dressed in the silver silk sheath he had admired at dinner and, if possible, looked even more lovely.

"Yes."

"May I join thee?"

The sun had set. Gil had watched it and been moved by it. Now birds settled down for the night. Barn swallows sang in the distance. The red desert reflected the fiery sunset.

Gil bowed.

Lily turned away. He was so *formal.* So determined to remind her that she was betrothed to another. Rage flushed into her and quickly changed into helplessness. She had been miserable ever since her tantrum in the pagoda.

"Walk with me," she whispered.

Gil sighed. Her eyes dared him to refuse. The rules forbade him to be alone with the betrothed of another. It mattered not. Gil nodded.

They walked north, away from the town, along the bank of the creek. Trees and bushes clotted the waterway. Gil watched the path. Lily watched him. They walked until no houses were within sight, and Lily stopped.

"You have avoided me," she whispered, looking past him at the deep red of the sky. Her fierce winged eyebrows accentuated the seduction in her eyes. In profile her partially opened mouth seemed to beckon to him.

Gil nodded.

"Because you do not want to see me?"

"Because it is best for you…and for me—"

"I thought you cared for me…"

"I do."

Boldly Lily looked into his eyes.

Gil shook his head. Lily had been four years old when he left China the second time. Even now she was only a child. He must protect her. "This will only make it harder for you…"

"I care not!" she breathed.

"…for both of us…"

"No! I will choose for myself," she cried.

"We must go back," he said.

Lily despaired. Each time she had to fight the battle over again. Each time she parted from him, he gained strength to resist her. Now his face was masked and without expression. His unblinking eyes reflected only determination. His eyebrows formed a straight line. Nothing ruffled the handsome smoothness of his features. To move him a man would have to kill him.

But a woman…Lily stepped close to him and slipped her arms around his waist. He was like a rock, except for the slight vibration that gave him away. Lily tightened her arms around him and pressed her cheek to his chest. Deep and powerful, his heart beat like a drum.

Lily pressed her lips against his chest.

"You must not—"

"I must!"

In spite of his resolve, Gil was swamped by his need for her. "This is madness," he cried, trying to remove her arms from around him. Hands that could kill with a single blow were ineffectual against arms as delicate as bird's wings.

"If we should be caught…"

In China, if a woman commited adultery, she might be punished by the other villagers. Here, in this godforsaken town, with the villagers homesick and oppressed, they would tear her apart. When times were good, transgressions could be dealt with lightly. When times were bad, transgressions were dealt with severely, brutally. His own aunt had been torn apart by dogs while the villagers who set the dogs on her screamed insults and the man she had commited adultery with watched from a distance. For a man it was accepted. For a woman…

Sweat popped out on Gil's forehead. Taking her arms, he turned Lily forcefully and walked her back to the house. Before she could completely unman him, he whispered good night and left her by the door, a slender stalk of silver beneath the moon, tears like snail tracks on her cheeks.

• • •

Laramee watched the moon filling his window, then closed his eyes. Was that what woke him? The moon shining on him? Sighing, he turned over. It would be morning soon. Then noon, then sunset, then night again. He had not known how fortunate he was before. With the possibility of hanging for crimes he did not commit, jail chafed intolerably. Sarah letting that damned Harry Sloan buy her dinner chafed too. He hated Sloan. How could Sarah pick the one man in town he hated? At times like this he wished he were a bull instead of a man. A bull didn't get particularly attached to one blamed cow. The bull took care of his own business, the cow took care of hers, and they were a damned sight happier than most people he knew.

Sounds of Tan Lin moving in his cell caused Laramee to sit up and peer through the darkness. Tan Lin stood on the bunk and lifted the quart jar through the window to someone outside. Laramee punched his mattress into a more accommodating lumpiness. It was only the boy, giving away his food again.

Gil opened his eyes. A sound nearby alerted him that someone moved in the stiff grass near his sleeping mat. Stars flickered overhead. The quarter moon hung bright in the night sky. In the house a hundred feet away, Third Uncle and Mei-ling snored quietly. A dog howled in the distance. A slender silhouette blotted out a portion of the sky, and Gil sighed.

Lily knelt on the ground beside his sleeping mat.

"What are you doing here?"

"Thou art awake?"

"Yes."

"Wilt thou hold me?"

Despair filled Gil. He sat up. "You are engaged. It would be sacrilege."

"Please?" she asked him. The tears in her voice tore at his heart. Earlier tonight he had been stronger. Now, after hours of lying awake, thinking about her tear-streaked face, he was too weakened to remember anything except her pain. Sighing, he held out his arms to her. Sobbing quietly, Lily slipped into them. Soft and sweet and warm, like a wraith dissolving, she melted into him irresistibly. His heart beat with increased vigor.

"You cannot stay here," he cautioned her.

"It matters not. A moment in thy arms is as the world to me." Her slender, cool fingers slipped around his waist and under his sleeping tunic. He stifled the groan that tore at his throat. This verged on the unbearable, and yet he could not send her away again.

"Let thy Lily lie with thee? Please?"

Gil shook his head. "I can hold you in my arms as a friend. There is no way I can justify lying with you. As it is, if we are discovered, your father would be very angry. He would have every right to kill me."

"My honorable father kills no one," Lily whispered. "If we should be found out, I will tell him the truth, that I begged you."

"No, if we are found out, my love, you must allow me to take the blame. I am old enough to know better. I will allow you to stay only if you promise you will let me protect you from any punishment forthcoming."

Delirious with happiness, Lily promised. She would do what she wanted if they were caught. Nothing mattered to her except being with the man she loved. "Hold me, Son of Autumn!" she said, ecstatic. "Please hold me!"

Overcome with need, Gil pulled her to him. Pressing her warm slim body against his own, she snuggled closer to him. He sighed and willed himself to resist her. They listened to the night sounds from the desert and the town. Crickets made their rasping sounds. Mating cats howled in the distance. Faint singsong music from the opium den drifted on the chill wind. A horse whinnied.

"I love thee. I belong only to thee," Lily said softly, her breath like a feather against his throat. "I knew the first day when I saw thee, standing before my father's door…"

Unable to withhold the words of love, Gil closed his eyes. "What I feel for you, little one, goes deeper than love. You are a part of me that has been missing all my life, that only now has returned. Even though you will marry another, I will not lose you. You will live forever in my heart. The universe is richer because you have come into my life."

Lily's breath caught in her throat. "Make love to me."

A heavy pulse beat against Gil's temple. "No. I cannot." She was a child. She had no idea what it meant for a man to make love to a woman. To her they were only words. To him—this perilous child-woman had the power to destroy him…

"You are unable…physically?"

"I am unable morally."

"Because I am of no value?"

"Because you are of incomparable value." He stroked the curve of her cheek, feeling her tears through every layer of his being. Third Uncle deserved far more than betrayal.

"If that is true, then how can I be damaged by an act of love?"

"Your body belongs to your future husband."

"The way my life belongs to my father now and my husband later?"

Gil flushed with shame. He had been led into the trap of truth from which there was no extrication.

Her hand slipped down to his buttocks. Firmly, closing his eyes against the rush of desire, he moved her hand up and put it around his neck. She squirmed closer to him; her warm, hard little breasts burned into his chest. This was both agony and ecstasy. Vibrantly, painfully alive, his body soaked up the feel of her.

"You must behave yourself," he ordered her, but his words held no authority.

"I will," she lied, and waited for a full minute before her hand strayed again.

"I have something for you," Gil said, disengaging himself from her clinging arms. He reached under his pillow, felt around until he found what he looked for and handed it to her.

"What is it?"

"Unwrap it."

"Will I like it?"

Gil chuckled. "Only you know that, little warrior."

Lily removed the tissue paper and held it up, trying to focus the dim reflected moonlight on it. "Oh! It is a mirror. Thy Lily wilt treasure this as long as she lives." In the moonlight the mirror and its jade frame sparkled faintly. A mirror was one of the eight precious objects. It symbolized the soul. That he would give her this. "Ohhh! It is beautiful!"

Gil did not expect so much. Like a small storm she turned back into his arms, pressed kisses on his face, and tumbled him back onto the mattress. "Thank thee! Thank thee. Thank thee…" Her lips found his and filled him with dizzying, sweet fire.

He had distracted her, but it was not working as he had hoped. Her passionate kisses robbed him of the will to resist. Soon nothing could save her…

Liang stood by the window and looked out at the two figures huddled on Son of Autumn's sleeping mat. He faked a soft snoring sound and slowly walked back to his own sleeping mat. If the whoremaster's son, Chih-peh, should be cheated in his wedding bed, that would be a grievous shame, would it not?

Enjoying the thoughts that danced in his head, he lay down and turned onto his side.

• • •

Thursday, May 20, 1880

"You got mail for Kincaid-san?"

"Likely strike something if'n I look close enough." Woody turned around and checked the slots behind him. "Yep, here 'tis." He handed Yoshio two envelopes.

A letter from Kincaid's mama-san and a telegram from Missy Samanta. Yoshio tucked them into his trouser pocket. Kincaid-san sure glad to have Missy Samanta on her way home. Yoshio lucky to survive that.

Yoshio drove the wagon back to Kincaid-san's house and began to unload the supplies he had purchased in town. As he walked into the house, a buggy stopped out front. Missy Samanta stepped out of the buggy, looked around, and Yoshio's heart leapt and began to pound. Yoshio had spoken too soon. Probably would not survive Missy Samanta at all.

Yoshio opened the door. "Good day, Missy Samanta."

"Is Lance here?"

"No, Missy Samanta. Kincaid-san gone work."

"Do you know where he is?"

"So solly. Yoshio not know. Come in prease."

Samantha shook her head. "No. I'll stay at the hotel. If he comes, tell him I'm waiting for him." She turned back to the buggy and driver she had rented from the livery stable. Lance had to come back sometime.

Del Ramo stopped in front of Cort Armstrong.

"You seen this?" In his hand he waved a yellow paper.

Cort glanced at the sheet, which resembled Sarah's little rag. "This Thursday already?"

"Yep, but this is extra. No charge for this one. Neville got it from someone who got it from Charlie over at the tobacco shop."

Puzzled, Cort took the flier and read slowly. As his eyes moved down the page, rage came up in him like a bear rising from a winter's sleep.

> On Saturday afternoon, Deputy Marshal Neville Smalley bullied Hop Wo, a Chinese laundry worker delivering towels to the Baquero Saloon and Pleasure Palace. Smalley ended by breaking both Hop Wo's legs. Observed in this dreadful deed by Arizona ranger, Lance Kincaid, the deputy marshal was

> arrested and delivered to the jail to await his trial.
>
> Also on Saturday afternoon an eight-year-old Chinese boy named Tan Lin was arrested by Marshal Ramo for *trying* to steal a chicken from Ezra Wilkins. Tan Lin was incarcerated and is being held for trial.
>
> Has corruption taken such firm hold in Durango that no one dares question the marshal? And how is it that *The Gazette*, instead of printing a news story about Smalley breaking Hop Wo's legs, ran an editorial blaming the incident on the governor?
>
> On Monday afternoon Ramo and Smalley accused local rancher, Laramee Logan, of murder. The accusation was based on the evidence of a knife, admittedly owned by Logan, which they assert was the murder weapon found at the scene of the murder of three Chinese brothers a month ago. Logan stated that he had lost the knife weeks before the killings. Without further investigation, ignoring Logan's explanation, Ramo arrested him.
>
> If this knife were the murder weapon, why didn't Ramo bring his evidence forward sooner? Why did he wait almost a month? What purpose of Ramo's is being served by this latest arrest?

Crumbling the flier in his hand, Cort bellowed at the piano player to get behind the bar. He stalked out of the Baquero, ignoring nods of passersby. A half block up the street he threw open the door of *The Gazette* and slapped the flier on Harry Sloan's desk.

"Did you print this?"

Sloan's lips tightened. "Do I look stupid enough to print that kind of shit about myself?" He shook his head, his face tight with anger. "You're the tenth fool to ask me that."

Without another word Cort turned and stormed out the door, slamming it so hard, the glass window broke. Without looking back he angled across the street, dodging buggies and riders. He stopped in front of *The Tea Time News* and eyed the sign, the window with the fancy writing, and the colorful awning he had bought to satisfy his daughter's eye for harmony.

Sarah stuck her head out the door. The look on her father's face caused her heart to stop. He carried the flier. She wished she were more like Angie, whose face could conceal anything she wanted it to, but she wasn't.

"What are you doing?" she asked, knowing it was wrong the second the words left her mouth.

"I'm deciding where to start dismantling this place. You think I should rip that awning down first or would you prefer I knocked out that window?"

Sarah swallowed hard. All the years she had lived with him he had terrified her; periodically he flew into rages that temporarily destroyed all the order in their lives. He had always provided a home for her, so it wasn't as bad as it could have been, but his temper terrified her.

Fear constricted her breathing. "Are you serious?"

"Does a card mechanic lose more than he wins? You damn well betcha I'm serious," he said, his arrogantly handsome face contorted by fury. He handed her the crumpled flier. "You remember our agreement?"

Hands trembling, Sarah scanned the flier and stalled for time. She feared him so much, she would say anything to cool his rage, and she resented him bitterly for this. Cort lived his life by impulse; Sarah hated that about him.

"I had nothing to do with this," she lied, forcing herself to look him in the eye.

Cort made a fist and brought it up. If she were anyone except his daughter, he would knock her across the room for a lie like that. It amazed him that he didn't anyway. It was damned foolishness to allow her to stand there and lie to him.

Her hands trembled so badly she finally hid them behind her back. In spite of her fear, she had printed a flier detrimental to his interests and lied to him about it. His face burned, but strangely, he could not bring himself to do more.

His own mother had remarried when he was eight years old. His stepfather had been so tight he had made life miserable for Cort and his mother. Edgar Bloome had counted every bite of food Cort put into his mouth and had nagged about every expenditure. Finally, at fourteen, frustrated beyond endurance, Cort broke every window in the house, stole the household money, and ran away, satisfied that losing a little money and having to replace all that glass would be punishment enough for his stingy stepfather.

"Then you better get control of your assistant, because somebody is using your press to print lies!"

"I don't know who did this." Trying to hide her shaking fingers, Sarah handed the flier back to Cort.

Cort grunted. Sarah's eyes glittered with terror; her voice shook. She lied through her teeth, and he knew it. But suddenly he had an image of himself, sweating like crazy, defying his stepfather about some piddly-assed nothing that didn't mean a damned thing except to his stepfather. Cort tasted iron. He shouldn't let Sarah get away with this, but he was not going to play Edgar Bloome to his own terrified daughter—no matter what.

Turning, Cort stalked away from Sarah. At the last minute, even though he knew she had lied, he turned and shouted at her. "If I find out you're lying to me, I'm going to keep my promise about this newspaper of yours. You hear me?"

"Yes, sir," Sarah said, swallowing.

"You better not forget it!"

Cort stormed away. Sarah walked slowly into the shop and collapsed onto her chair, still shaking from her father's wrath.

By noon it appeared that everyone in Durango had heard about the flier. Harry Sloan, livid, came by *The Tea Time News* and told Sarah that she would have to find some other way to order her paper.

Angie comforted Sarah, worked on the children's section, and watched out the window for Kincaid. This week the children's section would feature little Amy Jefferson who had gotten the highest grade on the weekly spelling test. But her thoughts drifted to Kincaid; he had become a necessary part of her life. If a day went by when she didn't see him, she felt cheated.

People certainly kept the good-natured lawman busy. If he wasn't chasing horse thieves and bootleggers, he was dealing with card sharks and drunks making trouble outside the town limits where Ramo didn't have to bother with them.

Angie kept Lance busy too. He had fixed her broken window. And he was helping her eat the watermelons that had come ripe all at once. *Sure wouldn't want them to go bad on you. Least I can do*, he'd said, taking another big bite of the melon.

Angie smiled. She had enough pictures for two western picture books, but she was trapped here until Laramee's trial. Besides, Sarah needed her.

What about Kincaid? a small voice inside her asked. Her smile faded. She would worry about the future when it came.

CHAPTER FIFTEEN

Friday, May 21, 1880

Ramo opened the telegram with a frown, read it, smiled, then passed it to Smalley.

"It's about time," Smalley said, pleased.

Ramo grinned. "Judge won't be here till next Saturday. Damn, I was hoping we'd be rid of our guests soon."

"Too bad. You think he'll"—Smalley stopped, lowered his voice, looked around suspiciously—"be…" Logan was watching them. Smalley felt it.

Ramo knew Smalley wondered if Cadwallader would be sympathetic to their need to get rid of Logan. Ramo grinned. "Are chinks yella?"

Smalley relaxed.

Ramo jammed his hat on his head.

"Where you going?"

"To tell Cort. Get him off my back."

Strangers stopped speaking when Angie walked past them. To some she was enemy and to some friend. Gruff cattlemen who had only nodded to her in the past stopped her to ask about Laramee and to speak their support of his cause.

In the afternoon Sarah came into the shop from an errand and put her bonnet on the hat rack. "There is a definite chill outside," she said, glancing at Angie, who scowled at a tray of type and searched for an end slug.

"A noticeable chill," Angie agreed, looking up. "I hope I haven't ruined your business."

"I thought you were going to photograph the Benson heir apparent," Sarah said, glancing at the clock.

The Bensons had not come in. "Mayhap Mrs. Benson doesn't want me to photograph her son," Angie replied, shrugging.

"Well, it's her loss."

"Thanks, friend."

"We seem to be acquiring a great number of people who don't want us to do things for them," Sarah said.

"I hope they don't find out how pleased I feel with myself." She glanced at Sarah. "Have you recovered from Cort's tantrum?"

Sarah shrugged. "He didn't say anything last night."

"I've been thinking about this a lot. I was wondering if you'd sell me the paper."

"Just because he's cranky with me?"

"No. Because Durango needs two newspapers. Two points of view. I worked with my cousins on their paper during summers. I know almost every aspect of the publishing business. Not in great depth, but I can learn. You could stay on with me."

"I don't know. I thought you were going back east as soon as your picture book was finished."

"I might not," she said, thinking of Kincaid. "Are you afraid of Cort's reaction?"

"I guess."

"What could he do to you?"

"Boot me out of the house for starters."

"Then you could move in with me. It would be perfect."

"Or kill me."

"He won't kill you," Angie protested. "He has a temper, but he wouldn't kill you."

"I never sold anything he bought for me either."

"Well, there's no rush. Think on it. See how you feel later. I have some money my father set aside for me."

A delicate yellow wildflower had bloomed beside Angie's porch. Her spirits buoyantly high, she bent down to smell it. Laramee had looked at her with new respect. He had been impressed with the flier, and he had known instantly that she wrote it. That pleased Angie tremendously. The flier had been circulated two days ago, and Laramee still looked at her as if she were running for president of the United States—ahead of the opposition.

Angie sponged herself off and changed into a pretty gown that wouldn't look too obvious if Kincaid should stop by.

A knock sounded on her front door. Her heart leapt with joy. It was him.

Atillo waited on the front porch.

"Well, hi," Angie said, smiling, surprised to see him.

"*Señorita* Sarah said you look for me—"

Frowning, Angie started to deny it, then remembered the pocket knife she had found under the bush during the dance. She had forgotten about the knife in all the excitement.

"Wait here," she said. She found the knife on her dresser and walked back to the door. A skinny red puppy had wandered into the yard and lured Atillo off the porch and out into the yard. Atillo played with the pup beside the red-tipped coachwhip bush at the side of the house.

"Is this yours?" she asked, showing him the pearl-handled pocket knife.

Relinquishing the pup, Atillo stood up. His liquid brown eyes widened. "*Sí, señorita*, but where did you find it?"

"Under a bush near the school." She paused. "What were you doing there?"

Atillo shrugged. "My father makes me go," he said.

Angie shook her head, "No, I don't mean to *school*. What were you doing there the night of the dance?"

He opened his mouth to deny it. She'd know that look anywhere. Angie reached out and touched his lips. "Don't lie to me, Atillo. I am your friend. I will tell no one. I promise you that."

Atillo flushed. He looked in terrible agony. "I cannot, *señorita*."

"Atillo! I am your friend!"

Sighing, Atillo bowed his head. "I was watching you," he mumbled.

"Me? But why?"

Atillo looked up at her, his eyes filled with an agony of embarrassment. "You are very beautiful," he whispered. "I'm sorry."

Relieved, Angie smiled. "Well, no harm was done," she said gently. "And now you have your knife back."

The red-faced boy left. Angie walked back toward the house. Kincaid sat his horse beside the porch. When had he ridden up? A flush of warmth and happiness started down near her spine, traveled slowly upward, and curved her lips into a smile.

"You're looking rested," she said.

Lance scowled. Atillo couldn't be more than fourteen or fifteen years old.

"What's wrong?" Angie asked.

Long, curling lashes, enough to drive any woman mad with envy, lowered, shielding him. His skin glowed ruddy and smooth. Just looking at it made her want to touch him.

"Don't you have enough to keep you busy without picking on him?"

"What?"

"Atillo. Don't have to have every man in the county chasing after you, do you? Thought I'd be enough," he said, trying to pull it off as a joke and failing.

"What do you mean?"

"He's a boy. Boys don't fare too well against older women." His voice was thicker than usual. It seemed to search for the dialect and miss.

"Older women…me?" she scoffed.

"You *are* older than fifteen, aren't you? I'd sure hate to think I robbed the cradle that bad."

"Atillo is my *friend*."

Something hardened in his eyes, then disappeared as quickly as it had come, but she understood his nickname now.

"The boy spies on you. He's in love with you. I gonna have to lock you up to keep you from doing damage?"

"You're teasing with me—no, you're not."

"Just don't want you trampling all over a little boy's feelings, that's all." Kincaid flushed with embarrassment.

Angie shrugged. "It's okay if I skin him and hang him over the mantelpiece, though, isn't it?"

Kincaid grimaced. "Maybe. Depends on how you do it."

The moment passed. Angie led him into the house and fixed him a bite to eat.

"You want a ride into town?" he asked.

"Depends on how much it costs," she said, smiling, giving him an opportunity to demand a kiss.

"It's free."

A weight formed in her chest. He wasn't going to stay, and he wasn't going to kiss her before he left. "Oh. Well, I guess I can't pass up an opportunity like that. On second thought, I don't really need a ride. I'll ride my bicycle in, then you won't have to worry about me." Her heart ached. She felt light-headed, almost sick.

She wheeled the bicycle out of the spare bedroom. "You want to try it?"

He grimaced. "Nope."

"Why not?"

"Don't trust any machine built by a man who thinks a human body comes to a little point at the tail end."

Angie looked at the seat. It *was* small. "I'll race you to town," she said, suddenly filled with coldness and eager to be away from him. He had arranged it so he could leave by offering her a ride into town. Then she had arranged so he didn't have to give her one. Why was she going into town? Just to get out of an embarrassing situation? What was wrong? Usually by now she would be in his arms.

Kincaid stopped at the door. She started to wheel the bicycle past him. She looked up into his eyes. He looked as uncomfortable as she felt. "Are you okay?" she asked.

"Yeah."

"You don't sound it."

"I'm okay."

Angie rode into town and coated some plates for the next day's picture taking. When she finished, she walked around her studio and gazed at the proof of her hard work. Usually seeing how good the prints were would fill her with excitement, but tonight she felt nothing.

Maybe whatever was bothering Kincaid would pass.

Lance rode alongside Angie until she reached town, and then, unwilling to face his hotel room so early, he turned Nunca and rode south into the desert. The evening promised to stay hot. He rode slowly. That was another mistake he had made. Riding too hard. His side still ached when he exerted himself. Seeing Angie and the boy had triggered old feelings that tightened the muscles of his stomach so hard he thought he would be sick. Angie Logan did not need a man who could be made sick by the mere sight of her with a boy. A man who wasn't made of any sterner stuff than that had no business even talking to such a woman.

He dismounted and hunkered down beside a cactus. Feeling dizzy and sick, he stayed there until the sound of a big blackbird cawing overhead roused him out of his weakness.

Lance expelled a breath of frustration and stood up. His side ached damnably. He should rest more and stay away from Angie Logan. Nothing in the world was worth having these feelings again. Too bad he didn't remember that until after he saw her.

He mounted Nunca and turned him back toward town. It was good to finally make a decision about Angie. A painful decision, but one that would be easier in the long run.

The sun had set, and the evening sky had turned from pink to purple. Full dark would fall before he got back into town. Good. He would go to bed.

He knew from experience that anything could be gotten through with determination. Anything.

He rode into a stand of ocotillo. In Texas they'd called it flamingsword for the bright red blossoms that tipped each long, thorny stem. In the near dark the flowers looked black. Nunca whinnied and pulled back. "Matter, boy?"

Lance glanced around him. His reflexes were off, otherwise he never would have ridden into such a stand in the first place. Not in the dark. The hair on the back of his neck prickled. Lance patted Nunca. Behind Lance the sound of air *whooshing* over a moving surface alerted him to the source of the danger he had sensed. Too late. Whatever it was connected with the back of his skull. Bright lights exploded in his head.

Del Ramo dropped the two-by-four and eased his revolver out of its holster. The ranger had dropped like a sack of potatoes, but Ramo wasn't taking any chances. The chestnut whinnied and nuzzled at the ranger, but the bastard didn't move. Ramo transferred the gun to his left hand and picked up the two-by-four again. He would cold-cock that horse a few times so he wouldn't run back into town and draw attention to the fact that the ranger was afoot somewhere. Unfortunately the horse reared up, turned, and galloped around a stand of saguaro.

Damn. He should have used a bullet, but he wanted this to look like an accident. Ramo turned back to Kincaid's slumped form. Using the two-by-four like a prod, Ramo turned the ranger over, pulled his shirt out of his pants, and struck a match. The reddish scar tissue was on the left side. Ramo turned Kincaid onto his right side, stood up, and kicked hard into the ranger's left side. Even passed out like he was, Kincaid grunted and doubled over.

That should play hell with his healing up inside. But just to be sure, Ramo kicked Kincaid again, then leaned down and struck another match. Blood and pus poured out of the ranger's side. Jesus. The bastard smelled dead already. Ramo gagged and turned away. Revolted, he stepped back from the smell, mounted his horse, and rode away, shaking his head.

Away from that mess, Ramo called and whistled for the gelding, but couldn't find him. He carried the two-by-four about a mile and then tossed it away. He wouldn't find that damned horse in the dark.

• • •

Ramo swaggered into the Baquero. Cort broke away from some men he'd been visiting with and joined Ramo at a table.

"Well?"

"Nothing to it. The bastard didn't even see me."

Cort grinned.

Ramo leaned back and dragged in a heavy breath. "The sun'll finish him off tomorrow. If he lasts that long," he said, remembering the smell that had almost gagged him. No man who smelled like that could live long.

Angie unlocked her front door and wheeled her bicycle into the bedroom. She lit a lamp and set about fixing herself some supper. She wasn't hungry, but she would eat something and go to bed. A horse whinnied close by. Angie walked to the front window and looked out. Kincaid's chestnut stood next to the porch. His reins trailed in the sand.

Angie stepped outside and held out her hand. "Good boy, Nunca. Where's Kincaid?"

Nunca whinnied again, stamped, and walked away. "Wait," she yelled, and ran after him. She caught his reins and stopped him. His coat was lathered. Wherever he had gone, he had come back very fast and alone. That chilled her. A man alone on the desert.

"Easy, boy." She caught the pommel and pulled herself into the saddle. The big horse seemed to know where he wanted to go, so she gave him his head.

About three miles outside of town Angie pulled the big gelding to a halt. She had come too far. She looked back at the town. No lights twinkled in the distance.

Nunca ignored the tug of her hand and walked toward a stand of coachwhip that towered up fifteen feet or more into the air. She disliked the thorny ocotillo. It could rip a gown quicker than a man could spit. She tried to steer Nunca away from the treacherous stems, but he whinnied and quickened his gait.

Angie wished she had brought a lantern. She must be crazy to be out here stumbling around in the dark. Nunca stopped and stamped his front hoof. A dark shape on the ground caused Angie to cry out.

• • •

Angie paced in Doc Amberg's parlor. She should be too exhausted to move, but her body fairly vibrated with nervous energy. She had wrestled a half-conscious, weak-kneed, bleeding, foul-smelling Kincaid onto Nunca's back. It took all her strength to hold him in the saddle as she sneaked him into town. Once she reached the doctor's house and saw the oozing wound in Kincaid's side, she'd lost all hope.

Doc Amberg had been in there too long. He should have come out by now. But Kincaid must still be alive; the doc wouldn't waste time with a dead man.

At last the door to Doc Amberg's examining room opened, and he stepped out.

Angie held her ground. Part of her wanted to rush forward and demand a prognosis, but another part was too afraid to ask.

Doc looked into her eyes, his own were tired and red-rimmed.

"He's going to take some nursing. I drained the rest of that abscess, sewed up a couple of torn veins, and mopped up a little. He's got a badly bruised kidney. May lose it."

Angie struggled to stay upright. Her knees felt like rubber. He would live. "Was he shot?"

"At some point I'm sure he was. Looked like he got hit with something sharp. Maybe some boot surgery. Tore hell out of his new scar tissue and that kidney. But whatever happened might have saved his life—if he lives, that is."

"What do you mean?"

"Had an abscess. Reckon that's why he hasn't been too chipper. Shudder to think what that would have done if it had busted loose inside instead of pouring out like it done."

Angie closed her eyes. Thank goodness. "I'll look after him. I guess I can get Ida May to stay with him when I can't be there." Ida May had been her mother's closest friend. She was a widow who might be glad for the company.

Doc nodded. "Sort of thought you could."

Under cover of darkness Sabbath Turk and Virgil Field moved Kincaid in a flatbed wagon to Angie's house.

Angie impressed upon Doc Amberg, Sabbath, and Virgil that

Laramee's life as well as the ranger's might depend on their silence. Absolutely no one must know the ranger had lived. As weak as he was, the fourth attempt on Kincaid's life would no doubt be fatal. Especially with no one except herself and Ida May there to prevent it. In the interests of secrecy, she didn't dare order men to stand guard at her house.

The wagon ride to her house seemed interminable. Kincaid opened his eyes once but appeared not to recognize her. The wagon finally stopped. They lifted him down, and, trapped between unconsciousness and intense pain, Kincaid tossed fitfully and almost caused them to drop him.

"Damn!"

"Be careful."

Angie ran ahead to lower the window shades. Sabbath and Virgil put Kincaid on the bed in Angie's spare room. Angie asked Sabbath to pick up Ida May and her things and then to take Nunca out to the ranch before anyone saw the big horse and suspected that Kincaid had survived. Angie cooked the poultice Dr. Amberg had given her and took it in to lay it on Kincaid's badly injured side.

Unconscious, Kincaid ground his teeth against the pain. Searching her memory for her cousin's instructions, Angie knelt at the head of the bed, put her hands on the pulse points at his temples, and waited. At first the pulses were so weak he felt dead. After a few moments his blood seemed to return, as if called back by her hands. Slowly his pulses grew stronger, more stable, more normal.

Kincaid seemed to relax a little.

Since that had seemed to work, Angie decided to try other things she remembered from the summers she had spent with her cousins. In her checkered past Virginia had been a healer—a proponent of ancient Ayurvedic medicine and Chinese acupuncture. Using their combined wisdoms, she had been able to effect cures in a number of people by balancing and repolarizing the energy currents in the body, allowing the body to heal itself. Virginia had written a book on the subject that had gained quite a following among exponents of natural healing. Virginia stressed that she healed no one. She merely removed blockages that kept people from healing themselves. She taught Angie the method, which consisted of holding the reflex points in feet, hands, head, throat, groin, shoulders, and knees. According to Virginia, simply holding the pulse points caused the body to redistribute energy into the limbs and alleviate shock.

Fascinated by what appeared to be a small success, Angie moved to the foot of the bed. Kincaid's feet felt like ice blocks. Pulse points in his ankles were as muted as the ones in his temples had been. It took a long time of patient holding before his pulses responded. Slowly, ever so slowly, they became stronger. Warmth returned to his feet.

Angie moved up to his middle. It seemed all the formerly pulsating life in him now flowed into his wound like a whirlpool. With her left hand, not touching, just hovering over the wound, she could not remember what to do with her right hand. Amazed that she, a neophyte, could detect the imbalance so readily, she tried to remember what to do about it. The pulses were strong near the wound, weak at the extremities. According to Virginia's book, that was the imbalance that needed to be adjusted. But how?

Then she remembered what Virginia had told her that night they worked on Tennessee after her accident. *Your right hand goes wherever the pulses are weakest. Just block out your own thoughts and let her body guide you.*

Angie held her right hand over his forehead, throat, and shoulders. Slowly his breathing relaxed. Hands and feet stayed warm. A visible pulse appeared in his throat. Her own shoulders and back felt strained, permanently cramped. Kincaid slipped into a deep sleep. She collapsed into a chair beside his bed.

Angie woke suddenly. The room was cool. The lamp on the bureau flickered as if about to go out. Kincaid tossed on the bed, his jaws gritted together. Semi-conscious, he moved in protest against the pain that was apparently becoming more unbearable by the moment. Angie touched his damp forehead. He sighed.

"You are extremely easy to spoil, Ranger Kincaid," she whispered to his unconscious body. "Wait."

From the other room she got a pillow, tossed it on the floor at the head of the bed, and wiggled around until she found a comfortable kneeling position.

Angie held his temples until his breathing evened out and he fell into a deep sleep. Then she moved down to his feet and held them until she was so cramped up that she felt frozen in place. Finally, groaning, she staggered to the chair and slept again.

Just before dawn, when Angie's strength was at its weakest, Kincaid's fever soared. Angie changed the poultice and woke Ida May, who had agreed to sleep nights and take care of Kincaid days. They worked together, and it took all of their combined skill and determination to keep Kincaid from dying. Ida May boiled the odoriferous poultices, and Angie forced Kang Chou's vile-smelling tea between Kincaid's lips. Angie taught Virginia's techniques to Ida May, and then forced herself to dress and go to town so she would not become conspicuous by her absence.

Groggy from lack of sleep, but forcing herself to appear bright and jovial, Angie stopped at the jail to be sure Ramo saw her. At the *The Tea Time News* office she told Sarah what had happened, and Sarah substituted for Angie while she slept in the darkroom. At lunchtime Angie rushed home to relieve Ida May.

Angie had been home only a few minutes when Sarah brought her a telegram from Nick Shadow. She opened it with shaking hands. Shadow was supposed to be in Durango by now. Angie read the telegram and passed it to Sarah.

Sarah paled. Nick Shadow's wife was critically ill. He would not be coming as planned.

"I'll wire the two men he suggested, and see if either one of them can come." Fear caused Angie's voice to break.

Sarah and Angie rushed into town to the telegraph office. Angie sent wires to the two replacements Nick Shadow had suggested, offered any fee they charged if they would come immediately, then went to visit Laramee.

When Angie arrived, Laramee was sprawled on his bunk. When he saw his sister he stood and walked to the bars. Angie's heart went out to him.

"How are you?"

Laramee was silent. The jail was more crowded than yesterday. Twelve men filled each of the two cells next to Laramee's.

"You need anything? I can bring it next time I come." Angie hesitated over burdening Laramee with the bad news. He had his own problems coping with jail.

Laramee glanced at Tan Lin. Today Tan Lin had barely eaten. At each meal he had scraped most of his food into the quart jar Sarah had brought him.

"You could get Doc Amberg to come take a look at this kid," Laramee snapped. "I think he's dying."

Angie's nerves screamed in protest at the thought of anything else to worry about, but she couldn't ignore Tan Lin. Alarmed, she found Dr. Amberg and insisted that he come with her to the jail. Grumbling, the old man wrapped his cheese and crackers in a handkerchief and rose wearily to his feet. "Let me get my bag, Miss Angie. I swear, you're becoming nearly as bossy as your ma."

Angie and Laramee watched while Doc Amberg examined the boy and asked questions Tan Lin didn't answer. Doc lifted Tan Lin's arm and probed his swollen belly. Finally closing his bag, the irritable doctor stepped close to Angie. Ramo watched over the top of his newspaper.

"Malnutrition, mostly. The boy needs to be home with his ma," Doc Amberg said, loud enough for Ramo to hear.

"Is there anything we can do?" Angie asked.

"Talk him into eating some of his food."

"Is he going to be okay?"

The doctor shrugged. "Ten years ago or so I seen a case like this. A ten-year-old girl. Her mama tossed her out of the house, and she just stopped eating. Couldn't pry a spoon into that girl's mouth with a crowbar. Died two weeks later."

Chung Tu waited patiently in the back room of the Baquero Saloon and Pleasure Palace. At last the bead curtains parted and Cort Armstrong appeared, a look of irritation on his coarse white face. Cort walked past Tu, seated himself at his desk, and then fixed his eyes on his visitor.

"What do you want?" Armstrong's voice rang with unaccustomed coldness. Apparently the man wished to forget their past amicable dealings. Ignoring the Caucasian's desire to distance himself, adjusting the spectacles that drooped on his nose, Tu passed a fragrant cigar to Cort and let his hand come to rest on the black silk top hat perched on his lap. "It is what I can do for you."

Cort fingered the cigar, dragged in a deep breath, and sat back in his chair. He wasn't sure he could continue to do business with Tu since the Durango Protective and Anti-Chinese Association had drawn the lines, but if no one knew…

"What do you have in mind?" Cort demanded.

"There is a favor I would ask," Tu murmured.

Cort stuck the cigar into his mouth and bit the tip off. On principle, Cort resisted doing business with any man who wore apricot silk skirts in public. But Tu was useful in ways that other men were not. And Cort was in a good mood, or he would be if this little chink wasn't here. Del Ramo had gotten rid of the ranger. Cort could afford to be generous. At least half his problems were solved. The others would be solved on Sunday, when Cadwallader hanged Logan. "What's the favor?"

"My son is going to be married in the Catholic Church. It is my wish that this be a pleasant experience for my family. I ask your protection for the wedding party."

Cort grinned. "That's a pretty tall order. What kind of information you have?"

Tu's hooded eyes gave the impression that he had far more power than he allowed anyone to guess. A rumor that Tu had put some chinks to death for double-crossing him—something about cutting them in half—had made the rounds, but Cort didn't believe it.

"How do I know I want this information you've got?"

Tu shrugged. "I hear that at one time you were interested in silver."

Cort's eyebrows lowered in consternation.

Tu smiled. "A young servant in the Liang household came to me to exchange silver for U.S. dollars…"

Cort stifled a curse. Those goddamned chinks were trying their level best to ruin his plans.

"How much silver?" Cort demanded.

"Two hundred dollars."

"Nuggets?"

"Nuggets."

"So?" Cort leaned back and put his heels on his desk. "That's nothing to me."

"As surprising information, perhaps not. But as a secret, between you and me?"

The pigtail had a point. If Tu mouthed it around that the Liangs were turning up with silver, soon word would be all over town. If that happened, it would be only a matter of time before the wrong people figured out everything. Cort reached forward, struck a match, and held it out to Tu.

Cort lit Tu's and then his own cigar and leaned back. "When is this wedding?"

"June first."

"I'll do what I can."

Tu smiled. "You are most powerful man in Durango. Your word gives Tu much hope for amiability of son's wedding."

Tu stood, and, bowing again, backed out of the room.

Outside, Tu climbed into his sedan chair and instructed his carriers to take him home. There was one more small matter to be pondered. He rested his head against the upholstered seatback. The matter of Gilbert Lee. Lee was an impediment. A young girl could become dazzled by a man like Lee. She could be induced to make a mistake. An idea formed in Tu's mind. He would do away with Lee. It was too bad about Liang, who appeared to be fond of the *chop chung*.

• • •

Kincaid's life seemed to hang by a thread that started to unravel before dawn. Angie had covered the windows of the spare bedroom with two thicknesses of blankets so no one from outside could see in. She feared for Ida May, herself, and Lance if Ramo should suspect the lawman was alive.

Angie prayed and did what she could, but Kincaid continued to toss fitfully with pain and fever. Angie changed the poultices, held his temples until her muscles cramped into knots, and dozed when he dozed.

The sun came up, and almost like magic Kincaid dropped into a deeper, more restful sleep. Angie fell wearily into bed and slept until the sound of neighbor children walking past woke her. Angie struggled out of bed, sponged off in the washbowl, and changed her clothes. She found Ida May spooning liquid into Kincaid's mouth. Angie would have liked to stay at home to rest, but she had to show her face in town, or Ramo and Smalley would be suspicious. And she had promised Laramee she would call on Du Pon Gai. Filled with fear and exhaustion, Angie staggered into the kitchen and packed a basket.

Angie reached town before nine o'clock that morning. She opened the office, pulled her wagon with the Hale camera out the door, across the busy street, and into the jail. Ramo shook his head in disgust, but he remained quiet. She took pictures of Laramee, Tan Lin and the men crowded into one of the cells, and then one of Ramo. Even he couldn't resist posing for her. Laramee looked so sleepy that after a brief conversation, she bid him good-bye and started to leave.

Angie stopped beside Ramo's desk. "Have you seen the ranger?"

Ramo shook his head. "Nope."

"I wonder what could have happened to him?"

"Probably joined up with his company. Didn't take him long to figure out we don't need him around here."

"I suppose," Angie agreed. She turned to leave.

"What you gonna do with them pictures?"

"I'm going to write Tan Lin's story. I'm going to show the world a picture of the marshal who killed an eight-year-old boy." She ignored Ramo's sputtering denials and pulled her wagon out the door. *That should give him something to worry about besides Kincaid.*

Apparently people in town had grown accustomed to her eccentricity. No one pointed or commented as she dragged the wagon across the street to *The Tea Time News*.

She left the wagon inside and wheeled her bicycle out the door. The basket hung from her handlebars. Sarah was out for the moment, probably attending some social event or other. Sarah had no doubt told Angie where, but she always forgot. She would see Sarah when she came back from her visit to Du Pon Gai.

The pharmacy sandwiched between two other buildings smelled of numerous unpleasant aromas.

Lily held the doorknob with a trembling hand, inhaled slowly, and prayed that she not faint before she completed the task that brought her here. The door opened easily but only a crack. Kang Chou, the old man, half blinded by cataracts, peered through the crack at her. He looked older than time.

"What do you wish?" he demanded in Chinese.

Lily froze, unable to reply.

"What do you wish?" he repeated.

Her mind and voice almost failed her. "I need…poison…for rats," she said softly, her voice breaking.

"You have money?"

The man was of incredible rudeness for a Chinese. Lily could barely breathe. Fear gripped her. "Yes, yes."

"Come in." The old man opened the door wide. Shelves covered every wall. Herbs and medicines in dusty bottles lined every shelf. A thousand varieties of remedies were stored in jars and bottles. The Arizona desert provided bugs, birds, snakes, shellfish, turtles, deer, flies, teeth, horns, bones, whiskers, claws, horned toads, scorpions, centipedes, and worms. Dried, peeled, crushed, and distilled, they waited only to be mixed and used.

Almost smothered by the heavy smells, Lily followed him inside, keeping a careful distance between him and herself. In large towns there might be four or five Chinese medicine shops, each with four or five men employed in cutting, mixing, and putting up prescriptions. From early morning to late at night they would be busy decocting and drying their remedies. In Durango the pharmacist was also the doctor.

"What do you want the poison for?" Kang Chou demanded.

"R-rats," Lily stuttered.

"There is cheaper rat poison at the white man's store."

Shuddering, Lily looked down, unable to meet his eyes. "I have been told that the white man's rat poison causes great pain when taken internally."

The old man laughed, the sound shrill and frightening to Lily. "That is as it should be," he cackled. "What import is this to you? How a rat dies?" He picked up a dried rat from one of the jars and shook it at her. "In my house when we find a rat, we pretend it is the white man and we cut off first its front legs, then its hind legs, and then its head. You have heard what the *fan quai* plans for Tan Lin? He will never get out of the white man's prison alive. Nothing is too bad for *fan quai* or a rat."

Lily's stomach churned with fear. "I have no hatred for the white man or for rats. I wish to be rid of them, but I do not wish for them to suffer."

The old man snickered. He had nothing but contempt for Third Uncle. Such false concern reeked of her father's timidity. "He who would coddle a rat wastes his compassion."

"I have money," Lily said, filled with desperation. "Dost thou want it or not?"

Cackling, Kang Chou moved to one of the jars. He shook out a dark-colored powder. "How big these rats be?"

Almost overcome at having to answer so many questions, Lily blanched. Her heart felt as if it would burst, pumping so much blood so quickly. "They are…big."

"As dogs?"

Lying did not come naturally to Lily. She felt surely Kang Chou would see her hesitation and know her secret. "Small dogs."

Kang Chou took a small brown paper sack and shook some of the powder into it. He weighed it, shook some out, then held it out to her. "Five dollars," he said, his rheumy eyes as glazed as dirty pond water.

"This poison…it is of a kind that will cause the least pain…to the rats?"

The old man nodded, his cloudy eyes boring into her. "This poison is fit for a king. There will be no pain in the taking of it or in the dying."

Eager to leave, Lily took the bill out of her tunic, passed it to the old man, took the bag out of his hand, and stepped outside quickly. He called after her in Chinese, imploring her to give his regards to her father, but Lily did not respond.

"Lily, wait!"

Lily lifted her skirts and readied herself for anything. It was only Logan Angie, pushing her riding machine.

Courtesy demanded that Lily stop to chat with her new friend, but she could not. Lily shielded her face with the demure positioning of her fan, bowed deeply, and turned toward her sedan chair, which waited in the street.

Charmed by Lily's solemn, quaint manners, her elegant, red and gold tunic, her sleek, exotically knotted hair, Angie almost allowed Lily to leave before she remembered.

"Wait, please," Angie said, and walked quickly to Lily's side.

Lily wanted only to take her package home and hide it, but her upbringing was too ingrained to resist.

"Lily, no one from Tan Lin's family has come to visit him. Do you know why?"

"No." Emotion raged in Lily. Her mind spun with her own frustrated desires, but she bit back the most honest reply. Bitterness about the powerlessness of women and children burned in her. It took all her strength to silence her tongue.

Tan Lin's plight was similar to her own. Her mind filled with darkness. Like herself, Tan Lin was yet another sacrifice. *If the boy must die, perhaps now would be a blessing. Once he is an adult, and truly understands how good life can be, it will only be harder for him.*

Lily bowed her head. "Chinese are very strict. They demand a great deal of their children and of themselves."

Hearing the pain in Lily's soft voice, Angie touched her arm. "I don't understand."

Bitterness flared in Lily. "Thou dost understand all that is understandable."

Angie felt Lily's pain keenly. "I am ashamed. My people are cruel to Tan Lin. They have warm hearts, but they have closed them." She walked Lily to her sedan chair.

On the sidewalk three Chinese—chanting as they ran, their burdens swaying from bamboo poles—trotted past. Seeing them, Angie realized how difficult it was to comprehend the vast differences in their two cultures. She could only peer across a chasm and make vague guesses at life on the other side.

"I hear you're going to be married," Angie said, repeating the rumor she had heard that morning from Sarah, who had probably heard it from Cort. Saloons were worse than tea parties for gossip.

Lily's face lost its color and elasticity. "Yes," she said softly.

"I wish you much happiness."

"Thou art very kind," Lily said stiffly, tapping on the chair with her fan to signal her carriers. As the chair moved forward, Lily sat back. *Rotten wood cannot be carved nor walls of dirt be plastered.* The phrase buzzed persistently through her head and made her dizzy.

Angie watched Lily's chair move quickly away from her. She felt sick with embarrassment. Only after the words were out of her mouth had she remembered the shy looks that had passed between Gilbert James Lee and Lily. *Big mouth! You have a mouth like a catfish.*

Doors of the tiny apartments, little more than rooms, gaped open to take advantage of any breeze that might blow through. A dog ran by, pursued by noisy Chinese children, laughing and chattering in their indecipherable language. From one of the buildings farther down the street, the brazen beating and drumming of celestial music filled the hot afternoon.

A frequent visitor to this section of town, Angie walked to Du Pon Gai's door and tapped lightly with her knuckle. Sounds inside ceased, the door opened wide, and a sweat-shiny, round female face peered out.

Angie handed Du Pon Gai the basket of food. "How is Hop Wo?"

"Hop Wo better. Tankee." Too polite to look inside the basket, Du Pon Gai bowed and waited.

Momentary panic seized Angie. Past Gai's short athletic blue-clad form, four beds crowded the far wall, two below, two overhead. Hop Wo lay on the bottom mattress, his face glistening with sweat sheen. Eyes closed, he looked more dead than alive.

The old grandfather squatted on a chair and looked at Angie with murky brown eyes. She glanced away quickly, as if she had invaded the old man's privacy. The inside of the house spoke of such grinding poverty that she abandoned her original intent. How could she ask these people not to share Tan Lin's meals? Then perhaps they would not eat at all.

"I came because of your son, Tan Lin. He is very frightened. He needs you to visit him."

Gai's face, smooth and unlined, lacked the delicacy of Lily's lovely face. Gai's darker color and sturdier features were not ugly, only less sensitive, less sheltered from the elements. "No go jail. Tan Lin steal *fan quai* chicken. Gai not go. He grow up now."

Angie had assumed Gai didn't go because Hop Wo was sick or because she worked at Sarah's. "But he is only a child. We all *want* children to be obedient and well-behaved, but Tan Lin is being punished far more strenuously than another would be in his place. He is frightened in the white man's jail. He needs his mother."

"Tan Lin shame family."

"Your son loves you. He needs you."

Angie looked into Gai's unchanged face and saw the futility of her mission, but she refused to give up. "If you withdraw your love to punish him, he will die. Tan Lin made a mistake, stealing the chicken, but he is only eight years old. No child should die for one mistake. They are punishing Tan Lin far more than he deserves. If you also punish him, he will die. Your son needs you. So he can survive the injustice that is being forced upon him."

"Tan Lin *nine* years old. Time learn be man. He soft. Because you speak for him, I pray to Tao. Tankee."

Frustrated, Angie sighed. "Thank you for listening"—the door closed—"to my mad ramblings," she said, filled with helpless anger.

Damn. Angie could almost hear Laramee's words in her head. *You did everything you can. Nothing short of a thirty-thirty is going to get her to go to that jail.*

Angie hurried to the jail.

Asleep, Tan Lin turned over in his bunk.

"I can't believe his mother won't even visit him. I did everything except threaten to take her at gunpoint," Angie murmured.

Laramee turned and looked at the boy, who appeared in sleep as if he had been flung onto the bunk by a careless hand. "Jail is rough on me, and I'm old enough to know what's going on," Laramee said. Actually it was unbearable to Laramee too. He was eager for the trial. No matter which way it went.

"She's not going to budge," Angie said grimly.

"Guess that shoots their theory to hell," he said.

Angie frowned. "What theory?"

"That's he's a trained thief."

Angie walked slowly back to *The Tea Time News*. Her double life was wearing on her. Sarah was out. Angie put out a sign that she was in the darkroom and dragged herself upstairs. She sat down at the table where she usually mounted pictures.

She didn't remember falling asleep. A loud noise caused her to jump. She stood up guiltily, as if she had been caught doing something she shouldn't be doing.

A man's voice yelled again. "Come on. They're fightin'."

Angie ran to the window in time to see Atillo run past on the sidewalk. She called out to him, and he stopped.

"What's happening?"

"There's a fight up there," he yelled, his face flushed with excitement. He pointed toward the Chinese quarter.

Angie ran downstairs and grabbed her Scenographe. She rolled her bicycle out and pedaled as fast as she could. Charlie Miller, standing in front of the cigar store, filled her in on all the details. A white miner took a sheet of a Chinese miner's newspaper and tried to wipe up spilled coffee with it. The Chinese owner of the newspaper and all the Chinese within sight went crazy. Apparently to them Chinese word characters were sacred. Chinese read them and burned them in a sacred kiln. Three white men had been injured.

To mock them and to retaliate, a group of white men stormed into the winehouse and took a Chinese newspaper away from one of the patrons there. They tore the paper into shreds and scattered it all over the road in front of the copper mine. Word spread, and Chinese spilled out of the mine like marbles out of a toppled bucket. Work did not resume at the mine until the Chinese had picked up every scrap. John Copley showed up and threatened to dock whites and Chinese alike a half day's wages if they all did not instantly return to work.

Economics won over anger. Men grumbled, but they trudged back into the mine. Exhausted, Angie dragged her wagon back to the office. Sarah met her halfway there, and the two of them visited Laramee, then locked up. Angie rushed home to see how Kincaid had fared.

The aromas of beef stew, corn bread, and coffee greeted Angie from the front porch. The house itself smelled of furniture polish and ammonia.

Ida May looked up from the pot she stirred on the stove. "You look tired, child."

"You must be invincible," Angie said, shaking her head at the older woman.

"Couldn't have been any easier. Mr. Kincaid slept most of the day, and so did I. I cut this stew early this morning. It done cooked itself."

"Stew's like that. How's our patient?"

"Barely moved. I had to force him to take water and broth, but he taken it. Believe you me," she said, pride and stubbornness evident on her strong face, "that young man knows who's boss in this house."

Angie smiled. "I'm sure he does." Ida May's tyranny might be thinly disguised under a cheerful veneer, but it could not be long hidden.

"He appears to have rounded the corner. I boiled another prescription of that chink medicine. I swarn I jest cain't believe Dr. Amberg would give a body a poultice from that dreadful Chinaman, but it do appear to be drawing the poison out. You have time to look in on him while I set the table."

Smelling of alcohol and ammonia, the room fairly steamed. The blanket still covered the window, and a lamp burned on the bureau. Ida May must have given Kincaid an alcohol rub.

Rising and falling with his rhythmic breathing, Kincaid's broad, naturally bronze chest glowed with the sheen of perspiration. The sheet had crept down to his waist. Blood veins corded his muscular arms. A clean bandage looked white as a daisy against his dark skin. Angie lifted the corner of the poultice and peeked in. The angry redness was more localized.

Kincaid's eyes were closed. His forehead was warm, but no warmer than her own. At her touch his eyes opened; they appeared lucid and clear for the first time in days.

"How do you feel?"

"Like a very large man beat hell out of me. You didn't happen to see him, did you?" His voice was thick and raspy from disuse.

Relief made Angie giddy. She didn't realize until that moment that all day long she had been in agony worrying about Kincaid. "So you're feeling better?"

"I understand I can thank you for that."

"Your body did the work, but you're welcome."

"If I'd known you were a medicine woman, I'd have been more respectful."

Angie left Kincaid, ate some of Ida May's stew, dipped a cup of the broth for Kincaid, and walked quietly back into his room. Asleep, he fascinated her. His ruddy complexion, though unnaturally pale now, seemed too flawless for a man. Only beard stubble marred the perfection. Long black thickly curling lashes lifted to reveal clear blue eyes regarding her thoughtfully.

"I thought you were asleep."

Lance shook his head. He had been thinking about her. He had wanted never to see her again. The thought of recuperating in her house promised nothing but pure torment.

"You look mighty good, ranger," she teased. "Are you sure you're sick?"

"I'm sure." Pain, even diminished as it was by such expert nursing, was a wearying thing. "It hurts like hell. I'm just brave."

Angie laughed. "And humble. Oh, Dr. Amberg found a small piece of that bullet. You had an abscess. He thinks you should heal rather quickly now."

This morning when Angie stopped in to ask Dr. Amberg to sneak out after dark and check Kincaid because he peed blood, the doctor had said he hadn't expected the lawman to survive that first night. Angie was glad she hadn't known that at the time. *Keep pushing the liquids through him. Maybe he can grow that blood back faster than he can pee it out.*

"Hope he's right. Feel like I'm overdue for an easy one."

Angie lifted the cup of broth. "You have to drink some of this. Can you lift your head?"

"Always been able to before."

"You hadn't been operated on before, though, had you?"

"Not for a month or so, but I've been lifting my head every fifteen minutes since your friend woke up. I wouldn't want to get on her bad side."

"That's extremely wise."

Angie put her hand behind Lance's head and lifted it so he could drink out of the cup. He took several swallows voluntarily and then a couple she forced on him. She let him relax back onto the pillow.

"Well done, Kincaid."

"You ever been in the army?"

"No."

"Could have fooled me."

"Where's your family?"

"Why?"

"So I can write them and let them know of your condition."

"No." He shook his head. If his father found out he had been injured again, there was no telling what measures he would take to get Lance out of Arizona and into some occupation he deemed safe. The uncertainty would be an unnecessary hardship on his mother. "I don't bother them when I'm healthy. I can't see worrying them when I'm not," he said, his tone grim.

"Are you fond of your family?"

"I love them, but there's nothing they can do now except get upset."

"My experience with families is that they like to know when

something happens to someone they love. They live in South Hadley?"

"No." Lance stopped himself before he could tell her they were probably in New York or Austin. He did not want her sending any telegrams.

"Do you have a big family?"

"Two brothers and three, I mean two, sisters."

Angie smiled. "I've never met anyone before who didn't know how many sisters he had."

Lance flushed. "My folks raised a friend's daughter. I always thought of her as my sister."

"As you should." She stood up. "Rest."

That night Lance had the nightmare again about the little boy who drowned. Lance woke in the middle of the night, filled with grief and hopelessness. His heart pounded. Nausea knotted his stomach and filled his throat.

The lamp wick had been turned down low so that it barely lighted the room. He looked around for something to throw up in. Gagging, he forgot and tried to get out of bed. Pain cut through him like a hot saber. A wave of dizziness almost caused him to black out. Sight of the blanket over the window reminded him that he was in Angie's house. Angie. Lance closed his eyes. A picture of Angie Logan shimmered in his mind's eye and got all mixed up with the sickness in him. The feelings worsened. The dream had something to do with Angie. He shuddered involuntarily, but he forced himself to lie still. He didn't want her to touch him.

On Wednesday a Chinese man died at the opium den. Comments in the white part of town were harsh, ranging from hostile to jubilant. Some said they all should die and save the town a lot of trouble.

The family of the dead man set out a feast for the Chinese gods—roast pig, salted fish, tiny Chinese cakes, warm wine, heaping bowls of rice—all placed on a wooden bier in the street, each dish precisely placed, and the bier itself festively decorated. Drunken white men stole the roasted pig. Chinese tried to take it back; a fight with sticks and clubs ensued.

Angie grabbed the Scenographe and ran north on Rio Street. She stopped across the road from the confrontation.

The crowd shifted, and Angie saw Gil Lee, surrounded by four husky Orientals. Angie frowned at Charlie Miller, who only grimaced and raised his hands as if he didn't know how the original fight had stopped and this one had started. The four men circled cautiously. Chinese cheering the combatants and shouting in dialect gathered around.

White men poured out of saloons and ran to watch.

Angie ran to the sidewalk and climbed onto a window ledge to see better. She knew almost nothing about fighting or fighters, but Gilbert Lee, though surrounded by four burly Chinese, appeared not the least disadvantaged. Gil wasted not a single motion. He barely seemed to move, but his attackers flew outward as if picked up and thrown out by a tornado. Angie balanced the Scenographe, meant to stand on its walking-stick tripod, and took pictures as fast as she could change plates. The ultimate fighting machine, Gil felled one after the other of his opponents—men who usually carried Chung Tu's sedan chair. The Chinese became more quiet. When the last men fell, the crowd surged forward to surround Gil. Men slapped him on the back and shouted approval.

Others, who had not come out before, opened their doors and gathered around Gil. Angie couldn't understand what they said, but it appeared that Gil Lee was their new hero.

Angie rushed home to tell Kincaid of Gil's victory. He listened in silence. "Thanks." His raspy voice grew distant. He didn't look at her.

"Well, I guess I'll sit outside awhile. I wish we could uncover the window so it wouldn't be so hot in here."

"I'm okay."

Though his fever had broken, perspiration still glistened on his face, chest, and arms. At a loss for words, Angie finally wandered out of his room and onto the porch. She took her patient water at bedtime, but he was either asleep or pretending to be asleep. Angie went to bed at nine o'clock but was plagued by a vague restlessness.

She didn't understand Kincaid. He had kissed her to his heart's content, and her own, and he had done a satisfactory amount of talking. Unfortunately he didn't say anything. In comparison, Laramee said little, but it all had meaning. Lance talked far more and said far less. Usually that would have been fine with Angie. In the long run, talking didn't make a plugged nickel's worth of difference, but she enjoyed a man who talked over one who didn't. She knew both types of men, and she knew that both married and both didn't. Kincaid would or would not fall in love with her, and what he did or said ahead of time hardly affected the outcome.

Kincaid had been careful of her reputation. If they hadn't been trapped under the house that one time, he'd probably never have touched her.

Angie was honest enough with herself to admit that she had expected Lance to fall instantly in love with her, even though she knew in her heart she would not make any man a good wife. By publicly accepted standards she was too self-centered and self-contained to be suitable for much. Her hope was that she would make one odd man an odd wife.

She catalogued her liabilities. She didn't want children. She didn't particularly like most adults. She didn't like housework. She didn't like anything that interfered with her doing what she wanted to do. That didn't leave much to recommend her.

Angie got out of bed and walked to the window. The moon was almost full. Kincaid was probably doing her a favor. She didn't need a full-time man to make thoroughly miserable with her eccentricity. She should take her lead from Tennessee. Tennessee had married, and she said she would never make that mistake again. Frank Trumbull had thought he married himself a combination cook, housekeeper, sex slave, mother, laundress, and hostess. In reality what he got was a woman who liked to write until three o'clock in the morning, sleep until noon, and sit in stylish coffeehouses arguing with her unconventional friends until dinner, which she wanted to be cooked and waiting for her when she got home. Poor Frank had almost died of apoplexy trying to get Tennessee to conform to what he had thought were minimum standards for a wife.

Angie couldn't marry. She wanted to compete on an equal basis with photographers like Charles Manville, Mathew Brady, Alexander Gardner, and Julia Cameron. She had nothing to recommend her to Kincaid or any man. And she certainly did not want to be tied down. Then why did she feel this emptiness? This disappointment?

CHAPTER SIXTEEN

Friday morning, May 28, 1880

Gil walked to *The Tea Time News*. Sarah invited him in and then ran upstairs. Angie descended the stairs tentatively, as though wakened from a deep sleep.

"Have you seen Lance Kincaid?"

Angie glanced at the door. "Come upstairs, Gil."

She explained the events of week before on the desert and then took Gil to see Lance. She knew Ida May wouldn't allow anyone in to see the lawman, especially not a Chinese.

At the sight of Gil, Lance waved a hand at the chair beside his bed. "You look like hell."

Gil started to pretend Lance meant his rough clothes, but he changed his mind. In spite of their current estrangement and the wary, distrustful look on Kincaid's face, they had been friends too long for subterfuge between them.

"Lily is to marry Chung Tu's son next week," Gil said quietly, sinking down beside Lance.

Angie bid Gil good-bye, and pretended she did not notice the way Kincaid's eyes avoided any real contact with hers. She walked to her bicycle, which she had leaned against the porch.

Lance waited to speak until Angie was out the front door. "How did this marriage come about?"

Gil told him about the priest's visit to Third Uncle and the old man's fear of the clergy.

"Why the hell can't the Church stay out of people's lives?" Lance demanded.

"You know little of your Christian religion," Gil chided him. "All lives belong to God. The Church interprets that to mean that all lives belong to the Church. The people are here to serve the Church, not vice versa. But enough of my bitterness. What happened to you?"

Lance told him briefly, then brought up the matter that had been most bothersome to Angie. "Tan Lin is sick. His mother won't visit him, and he isn't eating enough to keep a bedbug alive. The doc thinks he's dying. Maybe you could talk to him. Angie tried, but he doesn't speak English."

Gil closed his eyes. He had wondered about the purpose of his life. Now it all became clear to him. He had been born to come to this small frontier town and sacrifice himself to rescue a child. He would kill Ramo and Smalley, get the boy to freedom, and then die in some fashion—hopefully not too painfully. He hated pain.

That would solve two problems—Tan Lin's and Lily's. With him gone, his fine, militant Lily would have no reason not to do her duty and marry Tu's son. She would raise fine, filial children with fierce, winged eyebrows, and she would forget him in time. With his immortal soul stored in a soul tablet, perhaps he could forget her.

"I will do what I can for the boy."

"How's Lily bearing up under this?"

Gil looked away, his dark eyes shielded by lowered lids. "She would have me kill Tu and his son."

"And you?"

"I love her. I cannot have her. She will adjust."

"That's bullshit. Why should the two of you sacrifice yourselves to please a couple of dried-up buffalo chips who have no business making arrangements for other people to keep?"

"It is the Chinese way. One person is but one thread in China's giant tapestry. It does not matter that we live and die on other soil. We are Chinese. Not to recognize that..."

Gil's voice faltered. Pain echoed inside Lance. Anxious lest the pain get out of control caused him to speak more gruffly than he would have liked. "So you intend to go along with this."

Gil sighed. "I scream more than most, but I also will adjust. And how do you fare with the beautiful Angela Logan?"

Lance didn't answer. "Are you in love with her?" Gil asked, surprising himself with the question, inexcusable under the circumstances. He flushed with shame. He would pick the offending question out of the air if he could and swallow it though it strangled him.

Lance shook his head. He had made a mistake talking to Gil as a friend. Gil was not his friend. He had been given proof of that almost six years ago. "Hell, I don't fall in love. I love all women. And none," he drawled, grinning.

Gil sank more heavily into the chair. Kincaid gave him answers to make Gil sorry he had asked. He deserved no better. But he puzzled over Kincaid's choice of words. *I don't fall in love.* That was not his memory of Lance Kincaid. Gil remembered a young man very much in love. One summer day Lance spent the morning decorating Lucinda's small apartment with hundreds of flowers. When she came home, flowers peeked out of crevices, adorned the wrought iron fence, lay along the sidewalk, stuck out of the keyhole, and filled vases in every room. A chain of flowers guarded the front door like a good-luck omen to keep out evil spirits.

Gil did not know Angie Logan, but he had seen certain things in her face. He had deduced other things based on her desire to protect and befriend Lily and her family, her concern for Tan Lin, and her writing of the flier that had caused such a stir in the town.

"Maybe I should have asked how's Lucinda?" Gil asked, giving vent to frustration and again unable to stop the words that came out of his offending mouth.

Anger, instantaneous and fiery, blazed in Kincaid's eyes. His voice was raspy, rage-filled. "Last I heard, she was still dead," he said angrily.

Gil stood up. "Just as I am over Lily because her father decided she would marry Tu's son. Perhaps I am lucky. I have no choice. If you want to forfeit what you could have with Angie because you are still furious that Lucinda died, that is your business. But don't malign our ways. We at least have logical reasons for our customs. The elders arrange marriages for the young people. Ninety-five percent of the time they work beautifully."

Gil's usually unreadable eyes stabbed into Lance. Gil's husky voice shook. "You arrange your own affairs, and not once have they worked out to your satisfaction."

Lance had the insane impulse to tell Gil the truth about his feelings for 'Cinda. He did not love her. 'Cinda meant nothing to him. Less than nothing. The thought of her disgusted him.

He wanted Gil to know, but his need shamed him. Gil was not his friend. Gil indulged himself by feeling superior and sorry for others. To hell with Gil.

Gil looked into Kincaid's eyes, saw the hatred and fury there, stood up, and walked out of the room and out of the house without another word.

• • •

Saturday, May 29, 1880

The stagecoach stopped in front of the Butterfield office at three-ten in the afternoon. As the orange dust cloud settled, a tall man dressed in a black frock coat and matching trousers picked up his briefcase and stepped out. He glanced up and down the street and headed for the Orlando Hotel.

Marshal Del Ramo looked out the jail window, put on his hat, and called out to Smalley. "You keep an eye on things here. I'm gonna see Cadwallader."

Smooth-shaven and gaunt, with a face that could have been handsome if it were not so painfully skeletal, Judge Cadwallader stopped when he saw Ramo walking toward him. Ramo edged into the shade of the high, false-fronted hotel building.

"Glad to see you, Leroy."

"Tell me about this Logan fellow."

Talking quietly, they walked into the hotel.

At *The Tea Time News*, Angie heard within minutes that Judge Cadwallader had arrived in town. Instead of the relief she expected, fear rippled through her. Too many times in the past it had been hard to tell the difference between criminal and judge. Crooked officials were a plague in most frontier towns. Now that her brother's life hung in the balance, Angie truly understood the bitterness she had sensed in others.

Terrified, Angie and Sarah rushed to the jail. They found Laramee sprawled on his bunk, tossing cards into his Stetson. In the next cell Tan Lin huddled in a corner and stared at the opposite wall.

Unable to help herself, Sarah stopped in front of Laramee's cell, hungry for sight of his lean, lanky body. She had missed him. A lump came up in her throat and ached there.

To give them a moment alone, Angie stopped by Tan Lin's cell. "Tan Lin," Angie whispered, ignoring his cellmates and Neville Smalley, who watched her as if she were about to start a jailbreak. The boy did not respond.

"Tan Lin," Angie said more insistently.

Laramee stood up and walked to the bars. His gaze raked over Sarah, from her tense face to her lush, demurely clothed young body. She was vague and irritating, but something in him still hungered for her.

"He thinks they're gonna cut off his head."

Sarah's eyes filled with pain and anger. "Oh, no!" Shuddering, she crossed herself.

Laramee's heart leapt into a hard, fast rhythm. He reached out and touched Sarah's arm; she jerked as if she'd been burned. Exasperated, Laramee hit the cell door with the side of his fist. The loud noise caused Sarah to cry out.

"What the hell did you come here for?" he growled.

"To be sure…you're…safe." She sobbed.

"So you don't have to worry about me? Or have a goddamned guilty conscience?" His eyes caught the gleam of gold at her throat.

"What's this?" he demanded, reaching out to touch the gold locket. "Your boyfriend give that to you?"

Shame and fear mingled in Sarah and robbed her of the ability to think.

"Get the hell out of here," Laramee growled, reading the truth in her eyes. "I ain't so bad off I need another man's woman hanging around pitying me."

"I ain't nobody's woman," Sarah cried. She backed away, turned, and ran out of the jail.

"Laramee! Why do you treat her that way?"

"Why the hell not?"

"She loves you."

"Oh sure! That's why she's walking out with that turd hound, Sloan. 'Cause she's so goddamned crazy about me. I wouldn't give a hatful of beggar's lice for that bastard's life when I get out of here."

"Sarah's confused."

"You're blamed right about that."

"Don't be mean to her. What are you two fighting about this time?"

"She won't marry me." He turned away, his face tense with the effort not to show how much that hurt.

"Well, I shouldn't wonder. The way you treat her." The look of pain and misery on Laramee's face softened Angie. "I'll talk to her."

"Won't do a damn bit of good."

Angie opened her mouth to reply. Ramo flung the door open and walked inside. Seeing Angie, he nodded at her. "Well, guess you heard the judge is in town," he said, taking off his hat. He tossed it at the hat rack. It sailed up, connected, and spun a moment before it settled onto the top hook.

Angie took a step toward Ramo. "Tomorrow?"

Ramo nodded. Sunday mattered very little to a judge with a busy circuit. "Nine o'clock. Smalley's, then the chink's, and then your brother's. The judge figures that'll take the longest. He's going to set up a court here this evening to take care of the rest of these men."

A cheer went up from the other cells.

Angie's heart constricted with fear. Until today and the judge's arrival she had sustained herself with the certainty that when Laramee was tried, he would be found innocent and set free. Now, looking into Del Ramo's smug eyes, she no longer believed Laramee would get justice at the court's hands. Angie looked at Tan Lin huddled in the corner, confused and sick. The child had assumed from the start they would cut his head off. Perhaps he had been in touch with reality all along.

Gil tried to sit in meditation, but his mind refused. Tan Lin waited for him at the jail. Lily waited for him to kill Tu and his son. His body waited for nightfall so Lily could torture him with her naked body.

Gil's head pounded with unaccustomed pain. It was time to act. He was not used to inactivity. He would move against the white men. Either he would succeed or fail, and it mattered not.

The house was empty. Grateful for that, Sarah threw herself across her bed, crying hard. Laramee was right. Something dreadful plagued her. She couldn't do anything right. Other people instinctively knew the right things to do. She never did. She loved Laramee. Part of her longed for him. But even that was not simple or straightforward. When Laramee came near her, he terrified her.

Now he knew about the necklace. Shame and self-hatred boiled up in her. Sarah stood up, walked into the kitchen, and pulled out the top drawer of the oak cupboard. A long knife gleamed among the eating utensils. Her heart pounding, Sarah took the butcher knife out of the drawer. Suddenly weak in the knees, she sat down at the kitchen table. It occurred to her that she should write Angie a note—Angie was her best friend in the whole world—but she hadn't the strength for it.

• • •

Angie rode home, greeted Ida May, and walked into Lance's bedroom. She saw him, and two feelings arose unbidden inside her at the same time. The tension that had started the minute she left him the last time relaxed, and all her fears for her brother surfaced full force. She sank down into the chair and looked at him.

Lance felt like hell. Angie Logan's eloquent dark eyes dominated her pale face. Intense pain darkened her eyes. Something purely primitive and relentless rose up in him like a jungle cat stepping out of the shadows to take on anything or everything that hurt her. It was a feeling he could not control. He felt her pain like a fist in his stomach.

"You been like this long?" he asked.

"Ever since Cadwallader refused to delay Laramee's trial. I begged him. I am so ashamed. I wired both men Nicholas Shadow suggested, and neither one of them would come."

"Cadwallader give you any reason why not?"

Angie trembled with anger. "He said it wasn't necessary. He appointed Ellington to represent Laramee. Ellington agreed. The man is incompetent," she said, her voice trembling with rage.

"Your brother'll be fine."

"No, he wo—" Angie's usually clear voice quavered and broke. A tear spilled over and ran down her cheek. She wiped it with an angry fist.

Her pain triggered his pain and his need to soothe her. Lance struggled into a sitting position and pulled her into his arms. She cried as if it were natural to her. Blessed with warmth and spontaneity, she was one of those rare women who could, apparently at will, either show what she felt or conceal her emotions with perfect composure. She cried hard and for a long time. Lance wiped rattails of wet hair from her forehead. Her flushed, damp face, so passionate and vulnerable, called forth his need to protect her.

"You've done all you can for your brother."

"It wasn't good enough."

"You did all anyone could do. Nick promised to come. He's a man of his word. How could you know ahead of time that his wife would get sick? Ellington might be just fine."

"No, he won't. They'll hang Laramee."

She dissolved into fresh tears. Lance held her until she cried herself out.

Dazed by her own turbulent emotions, Angie opened her eyes and sighed with exhaustion. His right hand supported her back; his left stroked her hair and face.

Angie sniffed. "I didn't mean to—"

"Hush," he whispered. He wished he had something solid and hopeful to say to her, but he had poked around the creek and the Chinese section and asked questions of everyone who might be able to give any information. He had come up with nothing more than he'd had before he started. No one would admit to knowing anything about anything. Too much time had passed. Laramee's only hope rested with Cadwallader. If he had nothing to gain either way…But if he had…Perhaps Logan would be lucky. What could Cadwallader gain by convicting Logan of a crime he didn't commit? He wished to hell Ruth Shadow hadn't fallen ill.

Lance held Angie close. His body felt at peace.

"Lance…"

"Um-hmm?"

Lance stroked her back, oblivious to everything except the feel of her.

"Did I do something to make you angry?"

Lance started to deny it. An image from his dream, an image of the boy who had drowned, flashed in memory. A rush of emotion—part pain, part grief, part rage—filled him. He remembered in time that he did not want to love *any* woman. Ever again. He did not want to give up his freedom or his peace of mind. They had been too hard to get back. Tender thoughts for Angie congealed within him. He drew back from her. "You'd better get some rest. We have to get up early tomorrow."

"You are angry."

"I'm not angry," he said, hearing the testiness he was unable to keep out of his voice.

"Well, you're acting like you're angry."

"How do I have to act to convince you I'm not angry."

"Never mind." She turned abruptly and moved away from him. Fighting the urge to cry again, she tried to stand up but his hand caught her wrist.

"You said I should go to bed. So let me *go*."

Lance expelled an angry breath. The tone of her voice triggered an old memory. He'd fought with 'Cinda once, and she'd used that exact tone. They made up later, but apparently he hadn't forgotten. Lance didn't know what to say. He should have let Angie walk away. He couldn't seem to do anything right. He would rather cut off his arm than cause her more pain tonight, and that was exactly what he was doing.

Angie recoiled from the confusion and anger in Kincaid's eyes. He let her wrist drop. His hand balled into a fist and dropped to his side.

A question came into her head, and once it was there, it had to be asked. It was the only thing that seemed to explain his actions lately. "Are you engaged to Samantha?"

The question seemed to shimmer in the air between them.

Lance scowled. The look in Angie's eyes cut him like a razor. Her lovely thick-lashed brown eyes, so eloquent and emphatic in spite of the tears she had cried, flashed once, and then her gaze settled on some distant object. What could he say? *I'm not engaged to Samantha, and I'm not about to be engaged to you. Or. I'm engaged to Samantha, and I'm going to marry her so I don't have to worry about making the same mistake twice. Or, I can't love anyone. Don't love me. Don't need me. There's something wrong with me. My heart doesn't work like it's supposed to. It's like a broken tool.* It was too late. Pain flashed in Angie's eyes. Nothing he could say would take away the pain he had already caused her. Just as nothing would cancel the damage he'd done her because of his damned weakness and irresponsibility, his damned lust.

Angie looked away. "I'm sorry. I hope you will believe me when I say I didn't mean to infringe on Samantha's territory. Now, if you will excuse me…"

She turned and walked out of his room.

Woodenly Lance lay back on his bed. He no longer had to worry about Angie Logan falling in love with him.

He'd done the right thing. It was better to end it now. Better yet if he had ended it before he made love to her. Every time he got involved with a woman his life spiraled out of control. The harder he tried to untangle himself, the more damage he did.

But for Angie's sake it made sense to end it now. He didn't want fresh abuses of Angie Logan on his conscience when he rode out of Durango after the trial. It was settled, then. So why did he feel sick?

Lance closed his eyes. He would be fine. Angie would be fine. But for the moment his gut ached.

CHAPTER SEVENTEEN

Saturday night, May 29, 1880

Angie turned. North of her a man yelled; men spilled out of the Baquero.

"What the hell?" one of the men shouted.

Coming from the north, like a swarm of fireflies, torches seemed to float on the early night air.

Say nothing, no matter what they say to you. Do nothing, no matter what the provocation, Gil had warned them. *We are unarmed. We are peaceful. We only show our support for Tan Lin.*

Under Gil's direction, copying the Nein people of China, the Chinese of Durango had made straw torches, dipped them in lard, lit them, and marched en masse toward the jail. Where it had been thoroughly effective when done by the Neins, who numbered in the millions, with fewer than a hundred small Chinese men, many of them trembling with fear, it was a pathetic show. Gil put these thoughts aside. The Hakka people were brave, but they had been taught in a thousand ways to fear the wrath of *fan quai.*

They marched behind him, a ragged parade of torchbearers, silent and thankfully inscrutable to the people who stepped out of stores and businesses to line the roadway.

The procession moved south down Rio Street slowly. Men from the Baquero stepped out on the sidewalk and watched, silent at first. One man shouted a crude comment and others followed suit. Someone picked up a rock and hurled it.

The rock struck Gil. He refused even to acknowledge the blow and walked as if nothing had happened. Other missiles followed, striking or missing. Few could tell. The Chinese drew closer together, making a more clotted procession. Walking next to him, refusing to acknowledge the tormentors, Third Uncle gazed straight ahead.

Men ran alongside the Chinese, taunting them, hurling anything they could find. Some watched in disapproving silence. One man, a lone voice in the darkness, yelled, "Leave them alone! Let them walk!" Another voice shouted back, "Chink lover! Goddamned coolie lover!" But the throwing stopped.

Gil breathed more freely. He had planned this as a sign to Tan Lin that he would be protected. But once they were on the road, he realized how foolish a gesture this could turn into if the white men turned ugly and violent. It was always dangerous to provoke the wildness that lurked beneath the surface of *fan quai*.

Angie quickly crossed the street and watched from the darkened doorway of *The Tea Time News*. She wanted pictures of this, but as yet no camera she had, perhaps no camera anywhere, would capture anything on plates at night. After leaving Kincaid, she had been too stricken and miserable to sleep, too restless with fear for Laramee to lie quietly in bed, too terrified to breathe when she thought of tomorrow and the trial. She had decided to walk to Sarah's. Maybe between the two of them they could figure out some way to help Laramee tomorrow. And this might be the ideal time to approach Sarah about Laramee. Surely his trial tomorrow would soften her heart if anything would. If she couldn't do anything about her situation, she could at least try to help Sarah and Laramee.

The procession of torchbearers spoke to her heart. Pride for their bravery in the face of hundreds of belligerent, possibly drunken hecklers rose like a torch in her own darkness.

The Chinese stopped in front of the jail. Ramo reached there at the same time. He had been summoned by a boy sent by Smalley. Silence descended on the waiting crowd. "What the hell are you doing here?" Ramo panted, his gruff voice filled with authority and determination.

Gil stepped forward. His low voice was clear, ringing. "We have come to show support for the boy, Tan Lin."

"There ain't nothing you can do for him tonight. He stands trial tomorrow, and that's that," Ramo yelled. "Now, get your yella asses back home where they belong."

Gil shook his head. "The boy's mother wants to be with her son this night. We are here to let the boy feel our presence. We will stay with him through the night."

Previously hidden in the middle of the marchers, Du Pon Gai

stepped away from the clot of Chinese. Taking her arm, Gil walked her to the window of her son's cell. She called out to him in Chinese. He answered her, his voice sounding thin and childish.

A hush fell over the hecklers.

Embarrassed at the thought of the boy and his mother, Cort Armstrong turned and walked back inside. "I'm buying. Anybody want a cold beer?" The men followed Cort inside.

Ramo saw this out of the corner of his eye and shook his head in disgust. Sometimes he didn't know whose side Cort was on. "She can stay, but you better not make any trouble, or I'll put your yella asses in jail, you hear me?"

Gil nodded. "We understand and accept your terms."

"Jesus!" Ramo turned to go inside.

Flushed with gratitude at Gil for bringing Tan Lin's mother, Angie stepped into the street, made her way through the torch-carrying Chinese, and touched Gil's arm.

"What did Gai say to Tan Lin?"

A slow smile warmed Gil's face. "She threatened to beat him with a bamboo rod if he did not begin immediately to take care of himself."

Angie grinned. "I should have known it would be something maternal."

Gil nodded. "Love words disguised. As ice holds all that we need ever know of winter..."

"Thank you, Gilbert James Lee. You are a good man."

Angie turned and hurried away toward Sarah's house.

"Sarah."

"Yeah?"

"What are you doing sitting out here in the dark?" Angie asked and sat down on the front porch beside her friend. She'd gone there mostly to worry about Laramee and the trial and Nick Shadow not coming, but now that she had arrived, she didn't feel like reopening all that again.

Sarah pushed the butcher knife under her gown. She'd finally decided to do it out here, to spare the house. Cort would be mad as hell if she bloodied up the place. He liked things neat and orderly.

"You all right?" Angie asked, peering through the darkness.

"Yeah."

"You don't seem so pert. You know, Sarah, I've been thinking. You and Laramee have been leading up to this for a long time, haven't you?"

"Yeah."

"I think you should do it."

Sarah's heart almost stopped. "You do?"

"Yes, I do. You've been putting it off long enough. You know it's gonna happen sooner or later. What are you waiting for?"

Sarah reached under her skirt and touched the cold blade of the knife. "I figured you'd be the one person in the world who'd try to stop me."

"What? Me? Laramee's a grown man. He can take care of himself."

Sarah stirred, looked up at her friend. "Did you ever want to?"

Angie didn't know what she wanted in that regard. If Kincaid had asked her to marry him tonight instead of telling her he was going to marry Samantha, she probably would have accepted, but she had never actively wanted to be married. "I'm not sure. I want some of the benefits, like not having to worry about certain things, but I don't think I could buy the whole kit and kaboodle."

"But you want me to," Sarah said accusingly.

"You're different, Sarah. I'm too selfish. Men don't like me, anyway."

"Kincaid does."

"Kincaid is engaged to Samantha Regier."

"That rat."

"Did Laramee ever make love to you?"

"Yes."

"You remember your mother very well?"

"Yes."

"Did she ever tell you about men and making love?"

"No. I was too young."

"Mine did. She warned me that I must never, ever, under any circumstances allow a man to make love to me before he married me."

"Did Kincaid make love to you?"

"Yes."

"If your mother told you that…"

"She told me all kinds of things, but she never mentioned that when the time came, and a man *tried* to make love to me, I wouldn't have any desire to stop him."

Sarah giggled. "I wonder why they didn't tell us the important things?"

"Do you love Laramee?"

"I don't know. I think so."

"Why don't you marry him?"

"He scares me."

"Laramee loves you so much, he's crazy with it."

"Then why do you want me to kill myself?"

"Would you talk sense? I don't want you to kill yourself, I want you to marry my brother."

"Marry your brother?" Sarah sighed. "I thought you wanted me to kill myself."

"Why on earth would I want that?"

"I don't know. You said I should."

"I did? When?"

"When you first started talking to me."

Angie shook her head. This was getting more and more confusing.

Sarah sighed. "Well, it doesn't matter. I can't face folks when they find out..."

"What are you talking about?"

"About that necklace."

"Throw the blamed thing away!"

Sarah started to cry. Angie pulled Sarah into her arms.

"Who's going to tell? Now, what's wrong?"

"But I love it," Sarah sobbed. "I've always wanted a necklace like that..."

"It's not worth dying for!" Angie shook Sarah hard. "Nothing is worth that," she whispered, holding her friend tight. "Tell me something, Sarah Armstrong. Do you care for Harry Sloan?"

"No."

"Then throw it away. That is an order. I'll buy you one ten times better."

"That's not the real problem," Sarah burst into new tears.

"What is, then?"

"I don't know...how...to act," she sobbed quietly. "I always do stupid things! *You* wouldn't have taken it..."

"That's not true about your doing stupid things. You have wonderful, warm instincts, Sarah. You have a heart as big as Durango, as big as the desert. If I had to think of a fault for you, it would be that you don't trust yourself. You don't trust your goodness and your instincts. You keep trying to do what you think you should be doing."

"My instinct a few minutes ago was to kill myself..."

"Hogwash. You decided to kill yourself because you thought you *had* to. Your *instinct* was *not* to kill yourself. Thank God you trusted it. Frankly, I don't see how it could be so bad marrying Laramee. He loves you. He'd do about anything for you. Any woman who'd do something as silly as think about killing herself should be willing to get married. It can't be any worse."

Angie kissed Sarah's cheek. "I'll make us some tea. We aren't going to be able to sleep anyway."

Sarah shuddered. Angie was so smart. Having a brother gave Angie an advantage in worldly wisdom that Sarah lacked. She'd wanted a brother all her life.

A brother, but not one like Laramee. Laramee would be tried tomorrow. He was innocent, but they would try him and hang him anyway. He would die a horrible death, and she would suffer from his loss the rest of her life. He ceased to exist for her except as a problem she was about to have because of him.

An almost full moon dominated a clear star-filled sky. A coyote yipped in the distance, and a dog howled a reply. Crickets made their steady, insistent, raspy sounds. Sarah's nerves screamed. She regretted ever getting involved with Laramee Logan.

Angie returned with tea, and they worried over Laramee for an hour, alternately talking and sipping their tea.

With childish passion Angie wanted to kill Ramo and the judge. It was the sort of solution that came easily to mind, was fun to talk about, but as useful as hoping Ramo and the judge would both die of natural causes before dawn. Somehow they had to stop the trial before they could convict him.

Angie got up to reheat their tea from the softly rumbling pot. A small brown paper bag sat on the table beside the stove. Angie picked the bag up and carried it to Sarah.

Sarah looked at her, puzzled.

"It reminded me of the medicine Lily bought…"

"So?"

"Maybe I could get something for Judge Cadwallader…"

Sarah shook her head. "We don't want to cure him, we want to kill him."

Angie nodded. "Precisely."

Kang Chou shuffled from his living quarters in the back and opened the door. He was surprised to find the slender blond Caucasian on his doorstep so early in the morning. The clock read six-thirty. Bowing, he bid her enter.

"Good morning," he said, his words loud and explosive.

Angie glanced nervously around the small room. It reeked of mingled herbs, a soft, smothering smell. "I need a special mixture that will incapacitate a man—"

"In what way?"

"So that he cannot work."

Kang Chou nodded, his face unreadable. "What kind work you wish prevent?"

Angie swallowed. How much could she trust to his discretion? Had Kang Chou been one of the men who marched on the jail last night?

Taking a chance, she said, "The man is a judge. I would like to prevent him from sitting on the bench, from deciding cases…"

Muddy black eyes did not flicker. He scanned the jars of herbs and nodded again. "How this be given?"

"In coffee. Is that possible?"

Smiling, Chou's eyes receded into the surrounding leathery flesh. "With herbs, everything is possible." He moved a stepstool across the room and climbed it to reach a top shelf. He took down a jar of dried, crumbled leaves and carried it to a table. He shook some of the leaves into a brown paper sack. "When boil coffee, add to coffee grounds."

"How long will it take to work?"

"Everyone different. If drinks lot or little…if large man, slow digestion, it take hours; small man, different metabolism." He shrugged. "Chou not know."

"Give me all of it."

"That cost lot of money."

"I don't care."

Sarah pushed the back door open and stepped inside. At seven o'clock in the morning the hotel kitchen smelled of rancid grease, bacon, and coffee.

Steam rose from a pot where eggs boiled. Ben, wiping his hands on a dirty apron, swore at young Clive, who had just spilled milk over a wide area of the floor. Ben glanced up, saw Sarah, and walked away from the mess, waving his hands in disgust.

"Clumsy polecat," he groused. "Won't last a week in here."

"Hi, Ben."

"Hey, sweetheart. How's your old man treating you? You keeping Cort in line?" Until Ben took this job at the hotel, he had worked for Cort. Sarah liked and trusted Ben. He had been like a favorite uncle to her.

"I need a favor, Ben."

Charlie Miller, Durango's city clerk, served as court clerk. He cleared his throat and stood up. "Any person caught throwing turnips, cigar stumps, beets, or old quids of tobacco at this court will be immediately arraigned before this bar of justice. Trot out the wicked and the unfortunate, and let the cotillion begin. The court will now hear the case against Neville Smalley, deputy marshal. Is there a witness to testify against Smalley?"

Ramo stepped forward. "No."

Cadwallader raised his gavel. "Case dis—"

Lance Kincaid stepped into the doorway. "Yes."

All eyes turned to Kincaid. Angie glanced quickly at Ramo. His mouth dropped open. Cort stood up and glared at Ramo, who caught himself in time to close his mouth.

Kincaid walked up to the judge's makeshift bench, a door atop two sawhorses, and raised his right hand. Charlie Miller swore him in. Cadwallader asked the questions and Lance answered them. Lance had been right about the trial of Neville Smalley. Judge Cadwallader barely listened to Kincaid's testimony before slamming his gavel on the wooden table and finding Smalley *not guilty of aggravated assault against Hop Wo.*

Murmurs of satisfaction and dissent rumbled through the makeshift courtroom set up in the lobby of the Orlando Hotel. Angie burned with outrage, but she was more concerned with how Kincaid would hold up in his weakened condition and how long the coffee would take to work.

For his part, Kincaid appeared to be putting on a show for the people of Durango. He walked and moved as if every step or gesture had sinister meaning. He emanated power and authority. When he wasn't testifying, he stood against the wall, his arms crossed over his chest, his scowl obviously calculated to threaten, his eyes as cold as a Texas blue norther.

Angie watched the crowd and Kincaid. To her discerning eye, Lance looked pale. To others he probably appeared intense, as if he had to restrain himself to keep from bursting into some act of violence. Slung low and tied fast, the gun on his lean hip glistened with oily menace.

Ramo and Smalley looked ashen, properly intimidated. *Hombre de verdad* had risen from the grave. No one would guess he had been near death nine days before. Only Doc Amberg, Ida May, and Angie knew the effort his charade must be costing him.

Judge Cadwallader took another sip of his coffee, kept constantly hot by a young man from the kitchen. Each time the judge took a sip, the young man refilled the cup. Cadwallader smiled. About time he got the respect he deserved.

A pot had been set out, courtesy of the hotel, on a table moved into the lobby for that purpose. When he wasn't serving the judge, the young man hovered near the pot, keeping it full.

Miller stood up and yelled for silence. "The court will now hear the case against Tan Lin," he said, gesturing for Ramo to lead the boy up to the table reserved for defendants.

Dressed in a clean tunic and knee-length baggy pants, Tan Lin bowed from the waist and took his seat at the table. He was so small that his shoulders barely reached the tabletop. He climbed up on the chair and scooted back. His toenails were dirty and ragged, and his bare feet stuck straight out in front of him.

CHAPTER EIGHTEEN

Sunday morning, May 30, 1880

Angie twisted her mother's pearl ring. Why wasn't the concoction she had paid so dearly for working? Judge Cadwallader sipped at his coffee. His gaze darted around the courtroom. Nervous, Angie glanced from Sarah, seated next to her, to Lance, an imposing figure against the side wall.

Ezra Wilkins tramped up and took the oath. He told the judge in his own words what had happened the afternoon his chicken was almost stolen. He turned and gave Tan Lin a hard look. "That chicken ran off and died, and it was three days afore I found her, stinking to high heaven. And that's the boy that done it," he said, pointing a crooked, hairy trembling finger at Tan Lin.

The judge looked around the courtroom. "Anyone here who disputes the truth of Ezra Wilkins's statement to the court?"

Gilbert Lee stepped forward. "I would like to make a statement on the boy's behalf, Your Honor."

Judge Cadwallader sat forward in his chair and peered at Gil, who was not wearing the expected pigtail, and was dressed in the traditional western white shirt, black vest, frock coat, and black trousers. "Is this man Chinese?" he asked, ignoring Gil.

Ellington, Laramee's attorney, stood up and cleared his throat. "Appears to be, at least partially."

"I would be happy to answer that question if it were directed to me," Gil said, his tone amiable.

"Get that chink out of my courtroom. You know chinks cain't testify in court," Cadwallader sputtered.

A hum started among the crowd packed into the lobby of the hotel. Ramo and Smalley started forward.

Angie leaned close to Sarah. "Why doesn't he drink the coffee? We should have used poison," she hissed.

"Your Honor," Gil said. "I do not wish to testify. I am Tan Lin's attorney. I wish to make a statement on his behalf."

Judge Cadwallader rapped his gavel hard. "No chinks allowed to testify in this courtroom!" he yelled. "Get this coolie out of my court!"

Drink the coffee, Angie prayed. *Just drink the coffee!*

"Your Honor, I wish to make a statement on Tan Lin's behalf. He is entitled to be heard," Gil insisted.

"He will get a hearing," Cadwallader shouted, rapping his gavel for punctuation. "Get that chink out of my court!"

Lance thought about interceding on Gil's behalf but decided against it. He was a lawman, sworn to uphold the law, and Cadwallader could exclude Gil if he wanted to. Lance had to conserve his energy if he was going to save Laramee Logan.

Ramo and Smalley grabbed Gil by the arms. Furious but controlled, Gil allowed himself to be led outside, where a crowd of Chinese waited, their voices raised in angry protest.

Inside, Judge Cadwallader took a sip of his coffee and rapped his gavel. "The prisoner will rise for sentencing."

The clerk stood up from his small makeshift desk and walked the short distance to where Tan Lin sat. He took the boy by the arm and helped him off the chair.

"Tan Lin," the judge started, then stopped. "Does this kid speak English?"

Ramo stepped forward. "Yes, Your Honor."

"That's a bald-faced lie," Angie whispered, barely able to sit still. She wouldn't have kept quiet, except whether Tan Lin did or did not speak English would not change the outcome.

Cadwallader nodded, then eyed the boy. A stern frown wrinkled his skeletal face. "You heard the charge against you. You stole Mr. Wilkins's chicken, and it died as a result of your manhandling it. You got anything to say on your own behalf?"

Tan Lin stood stock-still.

"I have been asked to spare you because of your young age," Cadwallader said, looking at the horde of Chinese clustered around the windows. "And I might have done that, but I don't like people trying to intimidate me. Don't like it one little bit. I'm talking about your people who marched through the town last night with torches trying to scare folks with their foreign ways. You put this in your pipe and smoke it, all you China boys who think your ways are so special," he said, glaring out the windows at the Chinese who peered in. "Judge Leroy Cadwallader cannot be intimidated by the likes of a scraggly bunch of coolies."

He turned back to the boy, took a sip of his coffee, and cleared his throat. "Tan Lin, the Territory of Arizona sentences you to five years in Yuma Prison." Cadwallader rapped the gavel and nodded at Ramo. "Take him away."

Outside, Gil interpreted for his people. When he finished, the Chinese went crazy, gesturing and yelling. They almost charged the courtroom, but Gil yelled them down and led them away.

The courtroom buzzed with folks agreeing or disagreeing with the sentence. The crowd seemed equally divided.

"Silence!" Charlie Miller yelled.

"Silence!" Cadwallader echoed, banging his gavel on the desk. "Next case!" The hum slowly subsided.

Ramo and Smalley strode in with Laramee. Cadwallader motioned to Clive, the young man from the kitchen. Clive walked to the judge's side. Cadwallader whispered to him and handed him his coffee cup. Clive walked away toward the kitchen with it. He shot Sarah a quick look.

Sarah stood up and walked toward the toilet. Out of sight of the courtroom, she ran toward the kitchen. Back by the stove, Clive walked up to Ben. "Got another compliment on your coffee, Ben. Must be better than usual. The judge says it tastes like shit," he said, pouring a fresh cup from the pot on the stove.

"You thank the judge for me," Ben growled, winking at Sarah.

Relieved, Sarah rushed back to her seat and whispered the news to Angie. A moment went by. "Why doesn't he get sick?" Sarah whispered.

"Either he is stronger than he looks or Kang Chou sold me a bill of goods," Angie said grimly.

Laramee took his place at the table, the jury was selected, and the judge called Ramo's witnesses—one after the other. He worked slowly and meticulously, establishing ownership of the knife, fixing the knife as the death weapon by questioning Ramo and Smalley, and establishing motive for Laramee to have killed them. It was the first time Angie had heard that the three brothers had bought lumber and stacked it on Boxer land, preparing to build a house. It was also the first time she learned that Laramee had called on the three brothers and warned them not to start another house on his land.

Laramee's attorney acted as if he'd been hired to defend Jack the Ripper. His questions added more to the testimony against Laramee than to his defense.

At twelve o'clock the judge called for the noon recess, and Angie gave up. She could tell from the faces in the courtroom that they had lost. It was all over but the actual hearing of the sentence. She was too scared to eat. She sat in the hotel dining room with Sarah, heartsick about Tan Lin, fearful for Laramee, and too dispirited to talk.

Charlie Miller walked over to their table to tell them it was time to start again. Angie searched out Kincaid and walked over to stand in front of him. "If they try to hang him, will you do something?"

Lance nodded slowly. Her tortured eyes caused his stomach to tighten. He was only one man. "I'll do what I can."

She didn't know what that meant exactly. Would he do all that was possible? Or all that his conscience would allow him to do? Or all that superhuman effort would accomplish? It didn't matter. His voice—so husky and earnest—reassured her when nothing else could have.

"Thank you." He didn't love her, but he did care for her. She saw it in his eyes.

People scrambled back toward their seats. Finally, Judge Cadwallader walked in and sat down. His face was pale, but it was probably no paler than usual. Angie exchanged worried looks with Sarah.

Laramee's attorney made his closing argument. He asked for a dismissal, claiming there were no laws on the books in Arizona that specifically forbade the killing of Chinese. He quoted instances in both Texas and California where men had not been convicted of murder in the deaths of Chinese because there were no laws forbidding it.

A murmur of both outrage and glee rose up in the watching crowd. Angie glared from Sarah's incredulous face to Lance Kincaid. Lance knew what she wanted and regretted that he hadn't spent a few years practicing criminal law so he could answer her. He had specialized in corporate law, which was entirely different. He did know enough to realize that Ellington was a worthless bumbler, not fit to practice law. Angie had been wise to worry when Nick wired her he couldn't make it.

Angie stood up. "I'm not going to let this man speak for my brother. He is incompetent to practice tiddlywinks, much less law." Her clear voice rang like a bell.

Every head in the room swung around and looked at her. The judge rapped his gavel. Charlie grimaced, stood up, and started to walk across the room. Angie sat down reluctantly.

Sarah took Angie's hand. "Good for you."

"You want to continue?" the judge asked.

Ellington nodded. He droned on and on. Angie had never had any particular feelings about Ellington before. Now she hated him with intense passion. If she'd had a gun, she would have shot him between the shoulder blades.

The judge interrupted Ellington. "Are you about through with that tirade you're on, Mr. Ellington?"

"No, Your Honor," he said, as if proud of that fact.

"How much longer?"

"Ten, fifteen minutes, Your Honor."

"Then I'm going to call a recess for fifteen minutes to let you catch your breath." He rapped the gavel, stood up, and hurried from the room.

For the first time, Angie felt grateful to the pompous dullard appointed as their attorney. Angie looked at Sarah. A small demonic gleam in Sarah's eye struck a cord in Angie. Angie felt hysteria rising in Sarah and in herself. It would take very little to set it off. She sensed the same hysteria in the courtroom. It gave a close, violent stench to the air.

Laramee turned and looked at them. He grinned at Angie but became serious again as he looked at Sarah.

Sarah understood instantly that Laramee knew he'd already been convicted. Pain and fear mingled in her unbearably. Tears pooled in her eyes. Laramee turned away abruptly.

People were up, milling around, impatient for the trial to continue. Ramo and Smalley stood beside the door talking with Cort Armstrong. Twenty minutes passed. Finally Marshal Ramo went down the hallway, following the path taken by Judge Cadwallader. Ramo came back in five minutes and spoke to Cort, then went back down the hall. Angie and Sarah exchanged hopeful glances. The crowd hushed. Down the hall a line had formed at the water closet.

Angie walked over to Jacob Ellington. "Go find out what's happening."

"How?" he asked, frowning.

"Walk over to Ramo, open your mouth, and ask a question."

Irritated at her tone, but intimidated by the look Laramee Logan gave him, Ellington walked toward Ramo. When he got halfway there, Judge Cadwallader stepped into the doorway. The excited babble of the crowd increased. The clerk yelled, "All rise!"

Angie exchanged a disappointed glance with Sarah and walked back to her chair. Their last hope had died. The judge would turn the case over to the jury. Another trial in Durango where a man had been convicted of murder a few years ago surfaced in Angie's memory. Within minutes of the verdict, the bloodthirsty crowd took the man outside and hanged him. Fear almost swamped Angie. She bowed her head and prayed for the strength to help Laramee, and, if that failed, the strength to help herself and Sarah bear whatever happened.

Angie found Sarah's hand and gripped it.

Jacob Ellington ended his closing remarks. An expectant hush fell over the room. Cadwallader opened his mouth. The fear that had started to grow in her when she got Nicholas Shadow's telegram brought Angie to her feet. She stepped into the area reserved for the defendant and his attorney.

"What is this?" the judge demanded, looking from Ramo to Charlie.

"My name is Angela Brianna Logan, Your Honor, and I have a few words to say about what has gone on here today. This ninny, Jacob Ellington, was appointed by you after you refused to give me a delay to find an attorney. Mr. Ellington couldn't defend Jesus Christ against charges of blasphemy! There is something crooked going on here, and I am not going to take this lying down!"

"Get this woman out of my courtroom!"

Ramo and Smalley started toward Angie. Kincaid stepped forward, gun already in hand. "Let her speak."

Ramo stopped. Kincaid looked at him like all he wanted was an excuse to blow six kinds of holes in him. Ordinarily Ramo wasn't that scared of gunplay, but Kincaid was reputed to be a crack shot. And Ramo had not adjusted to seeing Kincaid alive. Ramo sat down.

"Thank you, Mr. Kincaid," Angie said stiffly. "My brother has been framed. He no more killed those brothers than I did, and I was in South Hadley when they died. You people know Laramee. You've grown up with him. If he's mad at you, he tells you so, but he doesn't sneak into your house in the middle of the night and stab you!"

Angie warmed up to her subject, and the judge's face turned from white to red. His eyes bugged out. He stood up and rapped his gavel.

"You sit down! Sit down right this minute," Angie yelled. Cadwallader dropped his gavel, turned, and ran from the room.

Howling, talking, and gesturing excitedly, the crowd went wild. No one understood exactly what had happened.

CHAPTER NINETEEN

Sunday afternoon, May 30, 1880

Angie drove Lance to her house in silence. She stopped the team, and they sat there for a moment, both looking at the porch.

"What'd you do? Put something in his coffee?" Lance glanced over at Angie. Her face was pale, her eyes big and dejected.

Angie put her head in her hands. What would happen if she admitted it to Kincaid? Her relief that Cadwallader had finally succumbed to their coffee had died a quick death. Laramee would be tried again, and next time Cadwallader might be harder on him because he suspected she'd had something to do with his getting sick.

"Me?"

Warned by the mock innocence of her expression, Lance shook his head. "Reckon I'd better not know."

Angie was too agitated to sit still. She stood up and climbed down. "So what happens now?" she asked, her voice strained. "Will there be another trial?"

Lance climbed down with difficulty. "Either when he recovers or next time he makes the circuit." Her hand had clenched into a tight little fist. The tawny skin on the back of her hand looked smooth as butter. Lance wanted to pry her fist open and press a kiss against her palm. He had been miserable ever since he let her believe he was engaged to Samantha. He didn't know why he did it, and he didn't know why he couldn't undo it. Part of him yearned for Angie Logan. Another part of him started to smother when he thought about her. The only thing he truly understood was that when he saw her or touched her, he wanted her. Standing so close to her, he felt feverish, swollen with need. Wanting her made him angry and impatient with himself and his lust. Sick of himself. Sick of his indecision and his yearning for a woman he didn't want to be involved with.

"What's wrong?" she asked, her smooth tawny brow momentarily wrinkled.

Out of the corner of his eye he noticed that her garden had died. The vines had yellowed and withered. "Think I'd better lie down."

Angie took his arm and helped him up the steps. Lance wanted to resist. The way she held his arm, as if he were some sort of invalid, not quite a man, infuriated him.

Angie jerked his left arm, and he grunted with the pain, but she didn't care. Lance Kincaid couldn't wait to get away from her. Sudden anger burned in her. Ignoring the resistance she felt in him for her help, she walked him to the bedroom, led him to the bed, pushed him down, and turned abruptly. "Bye."

Lance glanced at her stiff back. That clipped little *bye* jarred him. "In a hurry to be rid of me?"

"I thought you had to rest."

"Not this minute."

But she was right. He should be resting. His body felt like lead. But somehow he needed to talk to her. He said the first thing that came into his head. "Looks like your garden died of sunstroke."

Angie grimaced. Laramee had warned her. "The melons didn't. Neither did the goobers."

"You call those little bitty gourds watermelons? Why, in Texas we'd call them little runty things gourds."

"You didn't complain so loud when you ate that last one," she reminded him.

"That's a rank lie. I remember complainin' about it being so little. I cain't imagine a Texas boy not noticin' a thing like that. In Texas our watermelons are big as ponies."

Angie smiled, and Lance felt his reward all the way down to his toes. "What are you going to do?"

"Now?" she asked, frowning at the wall.

"The rest of the day."

"I don't know."

Angie searched his face. Did he think that because she was what magazines referred to as a *modern woman* she would be as available to him now as she had been before? Anger seethed in her. He could go to hell. He could rot there for all she cared. She hated him suddenly. "I have things to do," she said, struggling to control the tremor in her voice.

"You always have things to do. Take a day off. You're too upset to do any good." He paused. She didn't respond. She looked cool and distant. Lance sighed. "A lot can happen before he's tried again."

"I know. Ramo will come after you again."

Lance sighed. "I know."

"Well, what are you going to do about it?"

"I'll decide that when he comes."

Angie walked out of the room. Both Ramo's plans had fallen apart in the same day. She now had two things to worry about. Ramo and his men might try to kill Laramee—they certainly would try to kill Kincaid.

Gil found Lily beside the creek, which was narrowed now to a thin trickle. Her yellow silk sheath pulled up around her knees so it would not get wet, Lily knelt at the water's edge and washed a small puppy. The dog squirmed wildly under her hands.

Lily's smooth black hair formed a fashionable knot at her neck. She looked up, and her eyes, black and shining, went from playful to angry at the sight of him.

Lily stood up, and the small, yipping puppy flipped itself over and ran away.

"What happens now?" she asked, wiping her hands together.

"We watch the jail, and when they try to move him to the prison at Yuma, we take him from them."

"Many will die," she said.

"Perhaps."

"The Chinese were born to die? Thou wilt go out to be slaughtered," she said, contempt flaring in her dark eyes.

"I do not go to die, I go to save Tan Lin," he said.

Lily stopped the words she had been about to speak. She imagined him at the head of a fierce, purposeful army of men. A thrill started in her throat and moved through her, and her breath quickened. As did her anger.

At night, like a wounded creature, she slipped into Gil's bed, so filled with need she was incoherent. Today she hated him and his easy acceptance of her coming marriage.

"Cattle do not kill their tenders," she sneered, enjoying the pain in his eyes as she twisted the knife. He deserved to suffer. He had done nothing to stop her engagement to Tu's son. "I don't belong here! I've never truly belonged. The plan of my life is unrolling; I struggle with it; I fight against it. But it is unstoppable." Her eyes filled with the horror of her helplessness. "Thou art cattle to let it happen…cattle!" she sobbed.

Mindless of the danger of being seen with her, Gil took her by the shoulders and guided her into the pagoda. "I am not cattle," he told her harshly, turning her, pulling her into his arms.

Contempt flared in Lily's eyes. "Go tell thy heroism to the joy girls at Tu's winehouse. Have your bowl of warm wine, and let Jade Precious comfort thee," she said, jerking to free herself from his steely embrace.

"What would you have me do? Kill Tu's son? A young man who is no more at fault than you are?"

"Thou couldst take me from here," she gritted.

"And shame your father?"

Tears pooled in her eyes and slipped over; they made shiny tracks on the lovely curve of her cheeks. Gil felt her pain like a cold blade against his heart. He had known the exact second her eyes would waver and look downward.

Her pale cheeks and demurely lowered eyelids caused tenderness to sweep through him. Her slender stemlike neck demanded to be kissed. A tiny, hardened nipple swelled against the light silk of her robe. Desire for this slender, graceful, arrogant girl flamed and burned away conscience. In truth, they had done everything together that they could do without penetration. If she were still virginal, it was by sheer technicality. He knew the taste and feel of every inch of her firm young body, every opening. His nights were feverish hells of semi-satisfaction and unending passion. He greeted each morning with exhaustion.

Groaning, Gil lifted her chin and kissed her, pouring his pain and heartbreak into his kiss.

Lily surged upward and pressed her slim young body hard against him. Her mouth opened under his heated assault; half crazed from wanting her, Gil picked Lily up and carried her into the deserted house.

He stopped inside the front door. Four trunks filled Third Uncle's sitting room. One trunk lay open. It looked like a jeweler's case, filled with jade, pearl, and gold ornaments—earrings, hair brooches, fans, bracelets. Beneath, a red and gold satin wedding gown reflected back the sunlight. On the table a red box lay open, and the bride's diadem of small pearls and emeralds caught the light and gleamed richly.

Gil stood Lily gently on the floor beside him. He tried to move away from her, but she went crazy. She doubled her fist and hit him in the face. The one blow called forth a hundred more. She pounded him and screamed and cried. Gil made no move to defend himself from her. He accepted her blows in silence, in gratitude. She hit him until she dropped exhausted to the floor.

Gil gathered her into his arms and held her while she sobbed brokenly. Her arms lifted to cling to him, and they were incredibly strong, or he was incredibly weak.

He gazed at the four chests of gifts that had come from the bridegroom's family and shook his head. "I cannot," he whispered.

"Please," she begged. "Please…it is all I wilt ever have of thee."

"No." Knowing the strictness of their culture and the harsh penalty that would await her if she went to her husband's bed without her virginity, he shook his head and moved away from her. He had been temporarily insane. Thanks be to Tao that he had seen the wedding chests.

Lily pulled away from him, and his blood withdrew from his body. He knew now what death felt like.

"Thou hast reminded me that the full extent of my value is in the fact that I have received no man's seed."

Gil closed his eyes. Never in his life had he expected or even imagined that he could be tortured with such exquisite skill. "Gold is plentiful in the world. You are rare and precious without measure."

Softened by his words, Lily stepped close to him. "A kiss will not damage the goods promised to Chung Tu's son."

"No more kisses," he whispered. "We only torture ourselves."

"I care not!" Lily cried. "If thou lovest me, thou wilt kiss me."

Gil took comfort in the fact that later, when she reconciled herself to being married, she would be grateful to him for his sacrifice. He pulled her close and kissed her with the restrained tenderness of love. He meant only a short kiss, but with Lily, only what she wanted happened. She surged wildly against him, like a small storm, burrowing into his very pores, giving her sweet lips until his body burned and his head buzzed with dizziness. Aflame with need, he relinquished her lips and forced her away from him.

"No," he whispered, panting.

Wild with pain, Lily threw herself against him. She clasped her hands behind his neck, hugged him hard, and tried to forget the small packet of poison that waited in her jewelry case.

Cort walked out of the hotel with Ramo. Once they were away from the crowd, Cort hissed an angry breath. "I thought you killed that bastard."

"I thought I had. I kicked the shit out of him."

"I'm tired of messing around with that son of a bitch. Send your little friend after Winchester."

"You mean Tip?"

"The one who always knows where to find him," Cort said.

"It was your idea to hit him where he was already shot, to just let him die," Ramo reminded Cort.

"Just do what I asked."

Immediately after she left Lance at her house, Angie sent for one of the Boxer brand riders to guard the ranger. On the surface she was polite and unconcerned toward Kincaid, but her body waited for sight of him with relentless anticipation.

She saw him several times on Monday. And each time he flashed her a look of recognition, and her heart lurched. She tried not to think about him, but the tension between them was constant. No matter how far she wandered, Angie felt the tug of his warm body, as if they were connected by an invisible quivering thread.

Angie visited Laramee in jail, roamed the town with her rolling camera wagon, and then stayed in her studio printing photographs of the family members of cattlemen who had decided to support her or of settlers passing through Durango for parts west. She worked steadily, and her cache of photographs would soon grow beyond what was needed for two picture books.

She got a letter from Cousin Tennessee asking when the picture book would be finished, when they could expect her. She put it aside unanswered. She wouldn't know the answer to that until Laramee was either freed or…Angie could not complete that thought. Freed.

Sarah visited Laramee whenever she could. Apparently Angie had convinced Laramee that Harry Sloan meant nothing to Sarah. Sarah decided to go to the jail at least once a day, sometimes two or three times. Occasionally, when she felt like braving the remarks of the other prisoners, she kissed Laramee through the bars.

Laramee wanted Sarah even more than before, but it was easier for him. He would rather suffer and see her and hold her in his arms than have her stay away. He was careful not to demand that she set the wedding date.

Tan Lin ate his food now. Assured of his stepmother's love, he thrived in spite of the threat of imprisonment that hung over his head.

With dread Lily watched the date of her wedding approach. Her parents had required her to spend time every morning with Suyun. Chung

Tu's sister was in charge of the marriage arrangements. Each afternoon for the past week two women of Suyun's choosing had come to instruct Lily in her duties as wife and daughter-in-law. Sleepy and distracted, Lily endured their daytime instruction while mentally rehearsing new ways to torment Gil at night. Gil had ordered her to stay away from him, but she ignored his commands. She slipped into his arms while he slept, and, once he had touched her, it was too late—his sleeping body was easier to control than his waking mind.

Since Judge Cadwallader had rushed off to Phoenix without waiting to complete Laramee's trial, tension and hostility continued to simmer beneath the surface of every interchange between Chinese and whites. Beneath the routine of daily activity Durango rumbled like a volcano ready to explode.

Chinese watched the jail for any attempt on the part of Marshal Ramo to move Tan Lin.

Lance avoided Angie Logan by pretending to be asleep. Finally he could not stand it any longer. He had lain awake half the night thinking about Angie. He had decided to tell her he wasn't engaged to Sam. He would have some explaining to do, but he'd been wrong to let that lie stand. He'd paid enough for it. He should own the damned thing—lock, stock, and barrel—by now. He had forgotten everything except the need to see Angie's big eyes and feel her butter-soft skin.

Mid-afternoon Lance heard her outside, talking the neighbor children into posing for her. With less difficulty than the day before, he stood up and walked outside. She faced away from him.

"Howdy, ma'am."

Angie didn't bother to uncover her head. She would recognize that husky tenor anytime, anywhere. "Howdy, yourself."

"Working hard, I see."

"What are you doing out here?"

"Got a complaint that there was a rowdy out here pestering children. Thought I'd walk out and arrest him. Right glad to see it's only you. Probably won't get hurt too bad after all."

"Arrest me for what?" she asked, uncovering her head. Sweat trickled down her neck; her face was probably shiny and flushed. She purely resented him showing up when she couldn't look any worse.

"Reckon if the criminal had a been dangerous enough, I could of thought of some charge."

Angie didn't know whether to laugh or cry. Sight of him caused some hungry, lonesome thing inside her to wake up and demand attention. The intense light in his cornflower-blue eyes did not quite match his casual tone. She looked away, then back. His right hand, tanned from long exposure to the sun, rested on the porch support. His manly wrist and the muscular bulge next to his little finger mesmerized her. So calm and purposeful. A man's hand was so different from a woman's. Her own hand had started to tremble. She would like to take a picture of his strong brick-brown hand, its roundness and muscular strength, the crisp black hairs on his sturdy forearm. Her throat constricted. "Well, as you can see, I'm no threat to children."

"Not too sure about that," he said, grinning.

"What do you think I could do?"

"Incite them to riot maybe."

"Three children? Ha!"

Lance shrugged. "I should probably take you in and jail you for your own good. You're gonna take sunstroke out here. Shrivel up like your old garden. You realize how hot it is?"

Angie shook her head. How could she not know how hot it was? She was about to die from the heat, but she would not give him the satisfaction. "Run along, Kincaid. Heat doesn't bother me when I'm doing something I enjoy. I'm a watermelon, not a turnip."

"You need some help getting that stuff in the house?"

"No, thank you. I got it out here. I can get it back."

Lance walked back inside. Angie Logan didn't expect anything from him. Where the hell had he ever gotten the idea she did? Was that why he'd let her think he was engaged to Sam? To protect him from Angie's supposed expectations? If so, he had withdrawn without reason. He had flattered himself. If he hadn't been so damned foolish, he could have continued to see her as long as he stayed in Durango. She didn't intend to stay in Arizona.

She really *was* the young cosmopolitan he had thought her at first meeting—more than a match for either Virginia or Tennessee, personal friends to 'Cinda and companions in her modern, eclectic life-style. When he was at Harvard, Lance had gotten to know them through 'Cinda. Angie's cousins practiced free love and pursued a personal freedom virtually unparalleled in the history of western women. Angie Logan did not need or want him. She had enjoyed him for a time, the way he had enjoyed her, but she did not need him.

Heat suffused his face. He had suffered intensely last night, and it had weakened him to the point where he had no pride. To the point where he had hunted Angie down and thrown himself at her the way he had thrown himself at 'Cinda. Shame rose up, black and nauseating.

Sabbath Turk stood up as Lance walked back in. "You need any help?"

Lance started to say no, but he remembered he was almost out of money. He had wanted to give Angie money to help with the cost of taking care of him, but his pocket had been empty. He'd used the last of his money to pay for his hotel room. Virgil had gathered up his things from the hotel and brought them out.

"Would you send a wire for me?"

Sabbath nodded. "When someone comes to relieve me. Miss Angie don't want us leaving you alone."

Lance wrote out his message:

> YOSHIO SEND FIFTY DOLLARS STOP BE HOME IN TWO WEEKS STOP KINCAID.

Sabbath put the message into his pocket. Lance lay down on his bed. That would be enough money to last until after Logan's trial.

By late Monday afternoon word came that the district judge would be coming back to Durango the following Friday. Ramo went looking for Cort Armstrong at the Baquero. He found Cort upstairs, sitting alone at a table, nursing a beer. Five men around another table played poker. A couple of Cort's girls flitted around and vied for their attention.

Ramo sat down heavily.

"What the hell's wrong now?" Cort demanded, tired of having to nurse this bastard along as if he were three years old. He wished to hell Johnny would get here. What was keeping the bastard?

"The judge is coming on the fourth, and it won't be Cadwallader. The bastard retired."

"So?"

Ramo felt a surge of hatred for Cort. "So everything falls apart, that's what's so!" he hissed.

"Where the hell were you during that trial? We didn't need Cadwallader. If everybody hadn't got the shits, we would have hung Logan that day."

"I don't know why I even bother talkin' to you."

"Damned sure won't find out from me," Cort answered.

"What do I tell folks?"

"Tell 'em Cadwallader's coming. Why not?" Cort's laughter was loud and booming. "Get 'em scared enough, they might do something stupid."

When Angie heard that Judge Cadwallader was coming back to Durango on the fourth, fear nearly paralyzed her. Sarah closed the office early for the day, and the friends boldly exited *The Tea Time News* determined to put on a brave front for Laramee in spite of their apprehension.

After they left the jail, Sarah walked to the mercantile store and Angie rode her bicycle home. Kincaid sat on the front porch in plain sight of any sniper who might want to take a shot at him.

His narrowed blue eyes swept down her body and caused a strange tightness in her chest. "Did you hear about the judge?" she asked.

Angie Logan's dark eyes mirrored her fears. She looked vulnerable in a way she hadn't since the trial. He should not stay with her now. He knew better than to risk so much exposure.

"Cadwallader coming back?"

"Yes."

The sky rumbled with dark-gray silver-edged clouds. An unusual, welcome wind had risen up. The air smelled of rain. It was still hot, but not unbearably so.

To the north, Sacaton Mountain sat gray and pockmarked with trees and bushes, its peak lost in misty clouds.

Angie looked at the mountain but spoke to Lance. "Are you in love with Samantha?" The question fell between them, surprising Angie as much as Kincaid.

He glanced at her, a slanting, wary look that made her redden with embarrassment.

"I don't think it's possible for men and women to discuss love intelligently," he said.

"Why not?"

"Because we're not talking about the same thing."

"How do you know that?"

"Love's different for a man."

"In what way?"

"When a woman falls in love, she gives herself to a man without reservation. A man receives her gift with gratitude."

Angie picked up a rock and sent it skipping across a stretch of desert. A hot wind sucked at her skin, drying it.

She faced him. "Hogwash."

Lance laughed. "You been home too long. What a woman feels and calls love is not the same thing that a man feels and calls love. If you put the two images together, you don't have a mirror image. You have a nut and a bolt. The one fits into the other. God made us different so love could happen."

"So, you *have* been in love."

Angie Logan, with her emphatic brown eyes and her firm little breasts pressing against her absurd, demure gown—trying in vain to cover such buttery richness—reminded him of a dark-eyed buttercup. She was nothing more than a perfect accident of nature. It would be catastrophic for him if he insisted on looking at her and remembered the way her skin felt under his stroking hands.

"I've been loved and cherished by a woman—I was grateful."

Angie began to enjoy herself. "How thoughtful of you."

"Well, durn," he drawled, dropping partially into his teasing dialect. "It purely irritates you that I want to be understood with some precision, don't it, ma'am?"

"It amuses me. Nothing more."

A dark fringe of lashes hid her eyes. She pushed her hair back with a quick, feminine gesture that could not help but be charming.

Lance felt good suddenly. Better than he had felt in weeks. His body glowed with vitality. His mind felt more alert; it buzzed with things he wanted to say to her. She was the only woman he had ever known he could really talk to. Angie Logan accepted the most outrageous statements, things no man anywhere could say to a woman without being misunderstood or hanged, and she understood them. She not only understood them. Her flashing brown eyes, filled with sardonic amusement, told him she also enjoyed his offerings.

"Making love is different for men than for women," he continued. Even that statement did not shock Angie. Men did not mention anything to do with sex in front of women. Not having babies, not kissing. The word *bed* could not be uttered in front of a young unmarried woman. Women were trained from birth to be shocked at anything to do with anatomy, yet Angie Logan looked straight into his eyes, and her smile deepened. At that moment it was as if they had never been estranged at all. It was wonderful, yet frightening, to realize that if they talked together for any length of time, it was almost impossible for him not to be seduced into a feeling of comfort.

Angie lifted her skirt to swish it playfully. "Yes, making love is different for men and women...*that* is obvious."

"It's different in less obvious ways."

"How?"

"For a man sex may have nothing to do with love." This pronouncement should have caused her tawny face to flush with scarlet heat, but she only flashed him that sardonic smile again.

"Nothing? Come now, Mr. Kincaid."

He laughed, infected with her. "If a man is in particular physical need, and a woman agrees to help him, his gratitude could make him love her."

"How self-serving."

"Isn't that what love is all about?"

"I hope not."

"You're not being honest with yourself," he said.

Angie faced him and scowled. "How so?"

"What do *you* think love is?" he countered.

"Love is...love is putting the needs of another person before your own."

"That's what I said. For a woman, that *is* love. For a man, love is his gratitude that she is willing to do that."

"I think I've been tricked."

Lance laughed. "Into what?"

"Into...I don't know," she admitted. Angie felt a small warning inside. Kincaid's whiskey-tinged voice had dropped into irresistible huskiness.

"Then it can't be too serious, can it?"

His eyes narrowed against the sun. Filled with that singular look of resolute masculinity, the wary light in them warmed some secret storehouse of tremulousness in her. She was like a blind woman futilely groping toward something she sensed in him that probably wasn't even there. She dreamed it and then yearned for it. Suddenly she hated him. He was so self-possessed. *Touch me at your risk*, he dared.

Angie stood up and walked away. Kincaid followed her, and even that irritated her. She burned to march away angrily, but even more than that, she burned for him.

Distant thunder rumbled, charging the air with electricity and excitement. Angie glanced at the roiling sky. "You should be in bed."

Yes. I should be in bed with you, he reflected, though remaining silent.

His eyes must have given him away, for Angie flushed deeply. "Why did you stop being grateful to the young woman who loved you?"

"I didn't stop being grateful. She stopped loving me." He had tried for lightness, and he had *almost* pulled it off.

Angie turned away. "I'm sorry."

They walked in silence for a while. Angie glanced back occasionally. Sabbath Turk followed at a respectful distance. Gray clouds moved overhead, changing constantly. Angie glanced at them, then at Kincaid's clean profile. "How long ago did the lady love you?"

"Six years."

"You were only a child. You should try falling in love now that you're almost grown."

"Almost?"

"Almost."

Angie stopped near a granite boulder. Kincaid sat down. The house, once a low profile against the horizon behind them, had disappeared. Angie felt disoriented. As if she were lost.

"And you haven't been loved since then?"

Kincaid laughed. His laughter seeped inside her and moved against secret surfaces.

"My record's not that perfect. I've been offered love, but I haven't returned it."

"What about Samantha?"

Caught, Lance shrugged. "She's different."

"In what way?"

"What about you?" he countered. "Have you been in love?"

"Have I been willing to give myself without reservation as you said? Joyfully? No, I guess I haven't—that would entail complete trust in the man chosen to receive that doubtful gift, wouldn't it?" Angie gazed across the desert. Her view limited only by the desert itself, its vegetation looming around her. They had walked into a dense thicket of seepwillow and mesquite.

The wind had come up. It whipped her hair around her shoulders. Grateful for the distraction, Angie captured her hair and divided it into three fat ropes. Kincaid smoldered beside her, watching. His narrowed, brooding eyes caused her heart to quicken its beat. She braided her hair into one thick braid and tossed it behind her head. Her hands barely trembled. She was proud of herself.

"Maybe I'm too cautious," she said, slanting a sideways look at his manly profile.

"Ever been tempted?"

"Are you looking for a compliment? What do you want me to say? Have *you* ever wanted to receive this doubtful gift of a woman's life, laid into your reluctant hands?"

Lance leaned down and picked up a rock. He sent it sailing into the heavy air. "I've been scared a few times."

"Given any of them serious consideration?"

Lance kicked a tin can, sent it skipping into a cactus. "Not until recently."

"Samantha?"

"You."

Unable to meet the piercing light in his eyes, Angie turned away. She wanted to ask if he had been engaged to Samantha at birth, but she wouldn't. "Why are you telling me this?"

Lance ran his hand through his hair and shrugged. "I don't know." That was a lie. He had told her because some treacherous part of him had betrayed him. He had missed her so much, he had become crazed by his body's continual hunger to touch her skin, to feel her mouth opening under his, to taste her warm, sweet flesh.

"Perhaps you want me to help you with your physical problem?" she asked, tensing in spite of her attempt to act the young cosmopolitan.

"I want you," he said deliberately.

"This is extremely disillusioning, Kincaid. I thought that men and women fell in love, married, and then made love. We met, made love, and are talking about making more *love*, but neither of us is willing to fall *in love*. Me for lack of trust, and you for what? Lack of interest? Lack of?…"

Angie spoke her mind as if she had not received the training instilled in young women of her class. Or as if she had rejected it at birth, refused to be infected by hypocrisy and subterfuge.

"Lack of trust," he answered gruffly. Her honesty called forth his own, bypassing his natural reticence about exposing himself to someone who could destroy him.

"If a woman gives herself completely, what is there not to trust?"

"She can take herself back."

"I see. You're looking for a woman you can trust not to rescind her doubtful gift?"

"That's what all men look for."

"Is that the only criteria?"

"Of course not. Use your head. The other criteria have to be in place before you worry about that one."

"True. Perhaps I'm objecting because your analysis isn't very romantic."

"Love is too serious to be treated romantically."

"What does that mean?"

He cocked a skeptical eye at her. "Are you so young you've never been hurt in love?"

"I guess so."

"You've loved *someone*."

"Yes."

"Ever lost anyone you loved?"

Her voice grew lower—and more strained. "Yes."

"Were you angry at that person for dying? For leaving you?"

A quicksilver rippling of guilt and shame crossed her face. Angie presented him with her adorable profile, sighed, then bowed her head. "Yes." Her honesty kindled a flame in his loins. He wanted to retract his question, but before he could, another one spilled from his lips.

"You feel betrayed for bothering to love him?" he asked, certain she was thinking of her father.

Her bottom lip trembled momentarily. Angie's earnest, elegantly lashed brown eyes looked frantically skyward, fighting back the urge to cry. "Yes, I felt betrayed."

"Did you rush out and try to find someone to fill that place?"

Outraged, Angie faced him. "*No.*"

Angie searched his face. Kincaid didn't meet her gaze. Instead, he scanned the horizon made ragged by scrub mesquite. His eyes were bleak. "That's the lesson." Little more than a whisper, his voice sounded rough.

Angie swallowed. "A parent is different. That is a special loss."

"They're all special losses. We're sheltered more from losing a parent than from losing a sweetheart."

Angie squinted up at him, her dark eyes searching his.

"That's not true."

Her emphatic brown eyes dared him to prove his point. Lance warmed to the challenge. She stirred him intellectually the way only Gil Lee ever had. Perhaps that was why he knew better than to get involved with her. Gil Lee had betrayed him too. "Think about it. Your father is so close you don't know anything about him. You love him almost symbolically. Like a buffer between yourself and your own death. As long as he's in his place, you don't have to worry about dying." Lance brushed silky strands of hair out of her eyes, off her forehead, but the wind whipped them back. "If you lost someone your own age, someone you'd spent years getting to know, someone you'd given yourself to completely—"

"What are you telling me, Kincaid?" Her silky voice had turned husky. The diffuse sunlight filtered through dense clouds made her tawny skin look pale, her eyes more intense.

A heavy pulsing of lust made it difficult for him to speak. "Nothing. And that I want you."

He had done it again. Said something that his mind hadn't acknowledged until the words came out of his mouth. She lifted her face and looked at him through narrowed eyes. The curve of her neck, the tiny pulse that beat in the hollow of her throat, quickened the pulsing in him.

"What is that worth exactly?" she asked. Lance had surprised her again. Against the cloudy sky his eyes looked more silver-gray than blue. Firing twin dimples in the deep grooves on either side of his mouth, a muscle tightened and relaxed in his wide jaw. Sabbath Turk had stopped some distance away so as not to intrude on their privacy. His back was turned to them.

"Only you can decide that."

Lance Kincaid was the only man Angie had ever known who had the ability to leave her feverish without even moving an eyelash. He was too close to her. Or too far away. Her throat constricted and made her light-headed. "And if I can't handle it on that basis, I must say no thank you," she said, reaching up to touch his cheek, unable to help herself.

"I guess so," he said. His finger stroked the tender, butter-smooth flesh of her inner arm. She sucked in a breath. The feel of her warm, vibrant arm surprised him, making his heart pound.

"Could that ever change?"

"Change is the only thing we can count on, isn't it?"

"If I hadn't tricked you into walking with me, you'd never have said any of this, would you?"

"I don't know." Lance withdrew into himself. *Did I say something? And even if I did, I don't know what it's worth. I'll leave Durango as soon as Tan Lin's and Logan's fates are sealed. Angie saved my life. She showed me a part of herself. She was honest and warm and caring. I owe her more than I can ever repay. So I guess I owed her, at the very least, some honesty. Maybe I wouldn't have been able to leave without speaking my mind to Angie. But I've left women before. Words exchanged in the heat of lust have little meaning in the long run. But I said them to her in the light of day. I spoke the truth.*

Angie turned away from him, and the knowledge that she could walk away made his body feel angry and deprived.

Lance stood up and moved to stand behind her; his hands touched her shoulders. "You want romance? You want to hear how much I want you? How many nights I've lain awake thinking about you? Wanting you?" *He had done it again. The exact opposite of what he wanted to do.*

An exultant flush started in her middle, burned there for a moment, and then spread upward, blinding her to reason. Lance Kincaid would marry Samantha Regier, but not today. Nothing mattered except that he wanted her, perhaps as much as she wanted him. Angie turned into his arms, slipped her arms around him, pulled him against her, and exulted in the feel of his warm, damp skin under his shirt, the vibration that shuddered through his lean body.

"Yes. I want to hear all of it. How much you've suffered. How long. How deeply."

Lance laughed. "No dice." His words tried to turn into a groan as the pain from his laughter stabbed into him.

Angie grimaced. He shouldn't be out walking. He should be in bed. Only a week and a half had passed since she found him on the desert, dying. And he was still engaged to Samantha. Of course, engagements could be broken. People were allowed to change their minds. But Kincaid had not indicated a willingness to abandon Samantha, only to have Angie as well. She had heard of women who lived their entire lives on the outskirts of some man's real life. That might not be such a dreadful thing for a woman like Angie. She wasn't willing to give all her time to a man. Angie shook her head.

"I would be crazy to make love with you again, Kincaid."

"I know that," he answered, his husky voice tight with need.

Unable to stop herself, Angie went up on tiptoe and touched his lips with her own. "I'd have to be insane to help you with your problem," she murmured against his lips. His breath came faster now. Closing her eyes, Angie brushed his lips lightly and savored the heat and attraction they held for her.

Slowly, as she kissed him, he unbraided her hair. When it whipped around them, he tangled his hand in it and deepened the kiss, then moved down to kiss her neck where a tiny pulse hammered against her throat. "You'd have to be insane," he whispered, his hot breath sending a warm shiver down her body.

Angie barely remembered what they were talking about. "I'd have to be worse than demented."

Half-crazed himself, Lance kissed her breast through her gown; his teeth nipped at her hard little nipple. "Yeah."

Angie shuddered. She was insane. Hopeless. "Make love to me," she whispered against his cheek.

Lance groaned. Angie had changed sides. He had depended on her ability to reject him. Now he wanted her so bad he hurt, and there was no way to stop it, except to stop, but his hands would not let go of her. "I have no heart for love or marriage. Only this." His urgent hands bit into the soft flesh over her hip bones.

"I don't care," she whispered against his mouth.

Kincaid leaned against a waist high rock and pulled her between his thighs. His mouth—so open and hungry—devastated Angie. She fed there like a woman who lost all reason. She must be insane, to give herself again to a man who admitted he didn't love her, wouldn't marry her. *I have no heart*...But it didn't matter. Her body wanted his, desperately...

With trembling hands Angie helped Lance lift her skirts and unbutton his pants. In a fever of wanting she guided him into her, groaned deep in her throat, tightened her legs around his hips, and prayed that if Sabbath Turk glanced around at them all he would see was her gown billowed out behind her.

She clung to Lance and allowed him to immerse her in the wild feverishness of their hunger, their own special madness. Beneath his shirt, above the bandage tight around his lean waist his skin was damp and slick and hot under her clutching hands. His probing tongue tasted of salt. His heady scent, as indescribable as the smell of the ocean, dazed her. Grinding her hips against him, she wanted to devour him, to become part of him, to burn up in the bright incandescence of this moment. And she wanted it to last forever, but Lance groaned and stiffened. Her body convulsed around him.

Panting, he buried his face against her throat, and Angie inhaled the smell of their lovemaking. A glorious flush tingled through her. She wanted to stay in his arms forever, but even as she tested the thought, she felt him withdrawing—physically and emotionally.

Angie felt the shift in Kincaid the way she had sensed other catastrophes—reluctantly. His eyes were still closed, but he had armored himself in some way. Shakily Angie pulled away and righted herself. He let her.

Kincaid's eyes did not meet hers. The evening sky glowed bright. Lit from beneath, fiery orange clouds resembled a bed of hot coals. Black and screeching against the fiery sky, a bird soared high overhead.

"We better get back," he said.

Angie trembled with feelings too intense for words. His warm hand steadied her, but, unwilling to have him read her distress, she turned away and walked toward the house.

Sabbath Turk appeared to have seen nothing out of the ordinary. Lance followed her back in silence. Near the house he stopped her. "I want to thank you for saving my life, Angie, for taking me in." He stopped, glanced away. "I appreciate all you've done."

Angie frowned. The sun was gone now, so she didn't have to squint against it, but she did. "You're leaving."

"If I can borrow your man to take me to the hotel."

Angie's mind protested a dozen reasons why it was too soon. "Of course," she said.

Ida May had dinner ready on the stove. Kincaid begged off. He wasn't hungry. Ida May chatted about things Angie would never remember. Angie and Sabbath ate in silence. Then Sabbath rode into town and borrowed a buggy, and he and Kincaid departed.

June first dawned bright and clear. Birds sang, and their songs, coming in her window, woke Lily. She opened her eyes and realized she had fallen asleep waiting for Gil. Apparently he had not come home last night. Her wedding day had arrived. A thrill of terror and dread tingled in her stomach. She turned over in bed and hid her face, attempting to shield herself from what lay ahead.

Her door opened. Mei-ling and Toy stuck their heads in. "There is much to do this day, Lily. Thou must rise."

Her mother's words caused a sharp ache of melancholy in her. Son of Autumn had stayed away last night, and she was afraid he would stay away today as well. Lily sat up, and the simple act took all her energy. She had grown more listless and more filled with darkness as each day dawned.

Mei-ling walked into the room, smiling a false smile, pretending that Lily was a joyful bride. "Come, Lily. Many young girls have cried a *kang* of tears on their wedding morn, only to find bliss. *Kuan-yin* works her miracles and keeps her own counsel. It is not for thee to question."

Lily's strength to withstand the inevitable had fled days ago. She bowed her head, and her long black hair swung forward in a glossy black fall, shielding her from her mother's gaze. The packet from Kang Chou—hidden among her jewels—illuminated a secret spot of terror inside her. The tiny thread of fear in her bowels had grown as the wedding day neared. Now it encompassed her whole body. Before she had felt arrogant and strong. Now she felt as fragile and unprotected as a butterfly's wing.

"Yes, Honorable Mother," she said softly. Lily moved into her mother's arms and buried her face against Mei-ling's shoulder. "I love thee."

Shocked and touched by her daughter's unaccustomed compliance, Mei-ling left Lily and sought out her husband.

"Thy beloved daughter is unwell," she said. Liang read the Chinese newspaper that had come in the mail packet from San Francisco.

"Unwell? In what way?"

"I know not, only that she is more obedient than usual."

"Marriage adds maturity and stability even to the most flighty of young girls. Lily will do well," he said, forgetting for the moment that he had despised the thought of her forthcoming marriage as much as she.

Lily watched for Son of Autumn and dressed herself in the hated robes of red and gold satin brocade sent by her bridegroom. She sat fully dressed in her wedding gown, all feelings suspended, and waited with every fiber of her being. Mei-ling twisted Lily's hair into the artful dragon ensemble to accommodate the jeweled diadem.

Instead of real shoes, her feet were covered by dainty flower shoes, handwoven by herself and Mei-ling under the watchful eye of Suyun. Six carts piled high with her dowry waited to be presented to her husband's family after the wedding. Twelve sets of everything, from nightgowns to towels to bedlinens, rested in fragrant pine chests. All was in readiness. It had taken a great deal of work to reach this point, and not once had Lily shown her anger or spoken a harsh word to anyone except Gil.

Noting Lily's docility yet again, a feather of foreboding brushed the surface of Mei-ling's mind. She took Toy aside. "Our Lily is unwell," she said, a frown creasing her short brow.

"It is only the reluctance of the bride. She will be fine," Toy said, remembering her own bitter tears when she had been forced to say yes to the man who had bought her from the slave master in San Francisco. Acquiescing was part of the ritual when a slave changed hands. For young girls, the wedding ceremony was part of their ritual of passage from one family to another.

As Liang's concubine, Toy had been treated with much greater solicitude and respect than ever before. She trusted that all would be well with Lily. Toy had seen Tu's son, Chih-peh, and he was neither as short nor as ugly as his father. It was unfortunate that Chih-peh had eaten Christianity and that Lily preferred Son of Autumn, but Lily would adjust.

Shortly before the time to leave for the church, Lily saw Son of Autumn kneeling before the altar in the gazebo. Relieved, she picked up a packet from the small table in her bedroom and ran out of the house, causing her mother to cry out in consternation against the damage she might do to the dainty flower slippers.

Gil heard her steps in the stiff, yellowed grass and turned. Armored by a night's meditation in which he prayed without pause for the strength to endure this day, Gil's face gave little away.

To Lily he appeared pale and drawn. Joy swelled in her. Without waiting for him to speak, she stepped close to him and touched his arm.

"Do not make it harder on yourself," he said, his voice low and strained.

"It matters not how hard. I would say good-bye to thee if I must do so with my robes in flames."

Gil closed his eyes, his grief so fierce inside him that he would not allow her to see it.

"I love thee, Son of Autumn. My woman-heart aches for thee. Please do not forget thy Lily. Our souls belong together. Thy Lily is the reflection of thy soul, the mirror of thy heart. Without thee, there can be no Lily. Somewhere, sometime, on earth or in heaven, I shall belong to thee again."

She strained up on tiptoe, pressed her cold, trembling lips to his, and slipped a letter into his hands. "Read this tonight after thy Lily is gone and not before, promise me," she said, her eyes pleading with him.

Lips tight, Gil nodded. She pulled his head down and kissed him until her lips grew warm on his, and his body ached with wanting more. When she had reduced him by her torturing kiss to a pitiful, needy beggar, she turned and fled back into the house.

At one-thirty Suyun led Lily from the house and helped her into the elaborately decorated sedan chair upholstered inside with red cloth, outside by hundreds of tiny fragrant flowers. In the extreme heat, weighed down by her wedding robes, heavy ornate headdress, diadem, and silk veil, Lily sagged in one corner of the closed sedan chair. Four carriers, instead of the usual two, lifted the chair to carry her to the church for the Catholic wedding ceremony. Later they would stand ready to carry her to the Chinese service with its many intricate rituals and exchanges at the bridegroom's house.

To Mei-ling's watchful eye, only Lily's small, flower-covered feet showed beneath the red curtains that shielded the bride from the eyes of curious onlookers.

Mei-ling's chair followed immediately after Lily's. Third Uncle's sedan chair followed Mei-ling's; he dreaded the ordeal of the wedding procession and the drunken tormentors he knew would follow them.

The colorful, flower-decked sedan chairs made their way south down Rio Street lined on both sides by Chinese who cheered and waved small red flags. Firecrackers exploded with regularity and added to the air of festivity. Bobbing and weaving in the hot breeze, Chinese kites flew overhead.

From the roof of the Baquero, Cort Armstrong congratulated himself on the success of his horse race west of town. *Maybe I'm missing a bet. With this kind of noggin power, I should run for mayor, not just city selectman. There won't be one damned incident between whites and chinks today. There damned well better not be one rumor leaked about the appearance of silver among the Chinese living on Logan land. Or some slant-eyed heads will roll.*

Angie pulled her wagon into position near the Catholic Church. Invited guests, all Chinese, waited under the oak tree in groups of two or three. As she stopped the wagon, men and women who knew her bowed politely in her direction.

Angie bowed at each of them and turned back to her equipment. She checked her plate box. Lily had not been pleased that Angie wanted pictures of the wedding. Angie had had to promise not to show them to Gil or to Lily's family. Angie understood the condition, in the light of Lily's feelings for Gil, and felt lucky to be here. Her heart went out to Lily. It was too easy to imagine herself being forced into marriage with a man not of her own choosing. But an event as colorful and as unique as a Chinese wedding on the western frontier could not be allowed to pass into oblivion without a few photographs for posterity.

Poor Lily. Perhaps it would be easier for her after Gil left. Lily had said Gil would leave for San Francisco immediately after the wedding.

Perhaps he had already left. He was not in sight.

A line of festively decorated sedan chairs stopped in front of the church, the only stone structure in Durango except for the bank. A woman who must be Suyun—Lily had called her the bird woman and this woman looked like a bird—stepped forward to assist the bride from her sedan chair.

A wiry carrier stepped between Angie and Lily's chair. Angie quickly pulled the wagon forward, looked through the lens, and slipped her hand over the smooth mahogany of the camera box until she found the button to trip the shutter. Angie could see everything—the flower-covered sedan chair, the red silk curtain, the smooth, tightly twisted strands of Suyun's shiny black hair, and the back of her elaborately embroidered blue tunic. Beneath the curtain, Lily's dainty flower shoes matched the sedan chair in brightness and beauty. A sliver of her slim, white ankles showed from beneath the red satin sheath.

Suyun pulled back the curtain, Angie snapped a shot, and Suyun uttered a hoarse cry and stepped back. Inside the chair, her chin on her chest, Lily slumped into one corner. Had she fainted from the heat? Angie could certainly understand it if she had. It was over a hundred degrees in the shade, and Lily wore more clothes than anyone—a veil, a heavy crown of jewels—and she sat fully enclosed so that even a breeze did not stir inside the small chair.

People crowded forward. The carriers sat the chair down, and Lily's limp body sagged forward and almost fell out. Suyun caught Lily, leaned forward, and sniffed the air inside the sedan chair. Angie watched in puzzlement.

Chung Tu, resplendent in red and blue satin brocade robes and shiny black top hat, stepped from the church and approached the small group.

"What is this?" he demanded.

Suyun stepped away from the bride's sedan chair. "She has taken poison," she cried, her voice shrill, angry. "I smelled it."

Chung Tu turned on Third Uncle. "You will be sorry for this! No one defies Chung Tu and insults the honor of his family! No one scorns Chung Tu's son!"

Gil ran across the road from where he had watched the wedding procession, elbowed his way through the crowd around the bride's sedan chair, scooped Lily up into his arms, and carried her back toward the Liang house. Too stunned to remember her camera, too stunned even to cry, Angie followed from a distance. Mei-ling ran behind Gil and sobbed like a woman whose heart had broken.

At the house, Gil placed Lily on her sleeping mat and knelt beside her, his own face pale and strained. Limp and white, Lily looked more dead than alive. Toy wiped Lily's face and fanned her. Liang sat down beside his daughter and did not move. Unseeing, he stared out the window.

"Is there anything I can do?" Angie asked.

Gil turned and looked at her as if too confused to comprehend the meaning of her words. Angie repeated her question.

"No. There may be nothing anyone can do."

Devastated, Angie walked back to the deserted church and claimed her abandoned camera wagon.

CHAPTER TWENTY

Tuesday, June 1, 1880

At three-fifteen the Butterfield stage pulled into Durango. Sneezing at the cloud of red dust that billowed around her, Samantha Regier stepped out of the coach and looked up and down the main street. This small scab on the desert was just big enough so she would have to go to three hotels before she found the one where Lance stayed. She had the money he had requested. Yoshio had tried to dissuade her, but once she knew exactly where he was and that he would be there another two weeks, there was no hope of Yoshio's keeping her in Phoenix.

She would find Lance, but first she would take a bath to wash away this dust and sweat and grit. *Please God, let them have water*, she prayed.

Gil searched Lily's room until he found a small brown paper sack hidden in her jewelry case. Kang Chou had insisted that he could not remember what he had sold Lily. *Perhaps if I see it or smell it...*Kang Chou had said, lifting his hands in resignation.

Gil smelled the musty decoction. He took the bag to Third Uncle and asked if he recognized the contents. Then to Toy. They had never seen it before.

His heart pounding, he rushed out the front door and ran as fast as he could toward the building that housed Kang Chou's pharmacy.

Angie put down the picture she had been gluing to cardboard and glanced up to rest her eyes. She walked to the window. Traffic moved continually on the street. Dust filled her nostrils. Thinking about Lily, she gazed at the weary line of buggies, her eyes unfocused, unseeing. With Kincaid gone, Ida May had gone back to her own house. The silence had been deafening. At least here she could keep an eye on the jail and watch for word of Lily.

"Angie, are you up there?" Sarah called up the stairs.

Angie started. Her eyes focused, and, unexpectedly, she saw a bay horse standing in front of the Baquero. The brand on its flank was unreadable.

She frowned. Where had she seen that horse before?

Then it came to her. That was the bay horse that had been standing in Lily's yard the day the barn burned…

"I'm up here."

Sarah ran up the stairs and stopped. "Did you hear? Lily took poison. They think she's dying."

"I was there. I took her picture before I realized…"

"Oh, you poor thing—"

"I have to find Kincaid," Angie said, dismissing Sarah's attempt to comfort her. "He needs to know that the man who killed Rufe Martin is back in town."

"What?"

Angie shouted an explanation over her shoulder, ran downstairs, and grabbed her bicycle. There was no telling where Kincaid would be. As she pushed her bicycle onto the sidewalk, Lance Kincaid stepped out of the hotel. Angie dropped the bicycle and walked to meet him.

He must have read it on her face. "Something wrong?"

"Lily took poison."

"She dead?"

"Not yet."

His first impulse was to ride up there and offer his help, but he knew what Gil had to be feeling. After 'Cinda was murdered he had avoided everyone, resenting the vague, embarrassed looks of concern, the need to be civil. Gil would not be fit company for anyone, least of all Lance. Angie's face lost its battle for composure. As if embarrassed by the tears that spilled down her cheeks, she tried to cover her face with her trembling hand. Lance sighed heavily.

A hot, suffocating pain constricted his heart. All his old pain was suddenly alive again. Angie walked away and stepped around the door of *The Tea Time News*. He followed her. She huddled against the entry wall, her eyes scrunched shut and her lips pressed tight together as she fought back tears.

Uncomfortable, Lance shifted his weight and then, unable to help himself, he reached out and touched her shoulder. "This looks like something that needs to be shared."

He turned her and pulled her into his arms. "Breathe," he said softly. Her mouth opened, and air rushed in and bubbled out in a loud sob. Angie took another breath, and, like a dam breaking, other sobs followed. She tried to stifle them, but they were too much for her.

Lance stroked her hair and held her trembling body tight. "If this is going to go on awhile, I think I'd better be the one leaning against the wall."

Angie laughed, a small hysterical sound. "You're worthless, Kincaid," she gulped. "Completely worthless."

He turned with her so he could lean against the wall. "I never claimed I was worth anything." He kissed her hair, and his warm, smoky voice had a smile in it. "You assumed that."

A surprised laugh escaped, only to turn back into sobs. Her arms clutched him tightly, and she gave up and cried with a depth that only a woman who felt deep pain could muster. Lance held her, partly for himself and partly for her, and strangely, even though he couldn't cry, he was strengthened and cleansed by her tears. The heavy ache around his heart subsided slowly.

Lance lost track of time. Finally Angie sniffed, gave one of those pitiful, ragged little sighs, and wiped her face with a shaky hand. "I need a handkerchief," she whispered, her nose plugged, her eyes red.

"You've certainly earned it," he whispered back.

"Are you making fun of me?" she asked softly, understanding his teasing remark, but needing to talk to him, to hear his voice.

"Not me. I have nothing but admiration for the way you handled that."

"Well, you'd better not poke fun at me, Kincaid. I'm very fierce when I'm not crying."

"I know." She moved out of his arms and rummaged for a handkerchief. "Mine's a mess, but you're welcome to it."

Angie took his handkerchief and blew her nose. "I'll wash it for you." She glanced around. "Where's Sabbath?"

"I sent him back to the ranch."

"Oh, no."

"I can take care of myself now. I don't need a bodyguard." In truth he probably did need one, but he wasn't willing to let the town know.

"You going to be okay?" he asked before she could pursue the other question.

"No." Her tears looked like they would start again. "Remember the bay horse I told you about at the barn fire?"

Lance nodded.

Angie swallowed. Another reason for her tears. She had watched until the bay's rider came out of the saloon. "It's back in town. Johnny Winchester is riding it."

Lance eased his ivory-handled .45 out of his holster and slipped a bullet into the empty chamber under the hammer. Eyes narrowed against the sun, he glanced at the Baquero. Angie's memory of the gunfight between Lance and Winchester filled her with fear for Kincaid. "You're in no condition to do that, to go after him."

Lance twirled the cylinder and eased the revolver back into the holster tied low on his thigh. "No choice."

Lance started at the Baquero, where Angie had seen the bay, and stopped at every saloon in town. Lance left word at each stop that he wanted Johnny Winchester. Word spread through town like wildfire, but Winchester didn't show himself. Where was he?

An unfamiliar sound caused Gil to stop shoveling and straighten up to listen. The night before, the earth had caved in near the barn, and Third Uncle had become upset about it. Gil had volunteered to fill the cave-in, and, with Lily dying inside, he was too upset to sit still. Manual labor suited him.

Gil listened again but heard nothing. He stabbed the shovel into dirt and enjoyed the feel and weight of it before he tossed it away. Gil filled the wheelbarrow and rolled it around the house toward the barn. Third Uncle had asked him to use the dirt and sand from a high spot, thereby leveling the ground a little more. Third Uncle was accustomed to the wonderful landscaped yards of his home in China. Even though a real garden was out of the question, he still longed to recreate that lush loveliness here in the desert.

The sound came again. Gil listened intently, then put down the shovel, wiped his forehead, and walked around the side of the house. A tall man leaned against the wall. Gil recognized the man and the danger he represented. A tingle started at the back of Gil's neck. He backed up, sorry he carried no gun.

"What do you want?" Gil asked.

"Just wanted to stop by and introduce myself. Name's Johnny Winchester. I came for the rest of my silver." Looking frightened, Toy stood on the other side of Winchester, who pulled his gun and pointed it at Gil's chest. Toy gave a small cry and covered her mouth.

Gil knew the man but not the name. The name had to be new, assumed. Winchester had shot Lance Kincaid. He was the marshal's cousin and the man who…

"Where is it?" Winchester waved his gun impatiently.

"What?" Gil stood at the corner of the house. If he threw himself behind the house, he could escape momentarily, but Winchester had full access to Toy, the Liangs, and Lily.

Winchester took Toy by the arm, put his gun barrel against Toy's throat, and led her down the steps. "Silver. Get it. If you try anything, she dies. You got that?"

Gil shook his head. "I know nothing of silver."

Winchester's pale gray eyes reflected no emotion, only a strange, cold intelligence that was more unsettling to Gil than a wild animal's rage or thoughtless cruelty would have been. Where Ramo was tentative and sly, this man was blatantly aware of all the ramifications of his actions and patently unconcerned with them. To Winchester, Toy's life had no value, less than none. He could blow her brains out, wipe the blood off his hands, and walk away unaffected. Ramo might sweat about it a little.

"If there ain't any silver, then I guess I'll just have to get my reward some other way. Maybe given a little persuasion, you'll remember where some is."

Gil started forward.

"Don't move!" Winchester cocked the .45 at Toy's throat.

"Turn around, or she dies." Slowly Gil turned. The sound of cloth against cloth as Winchester's arm rose behind Gil signaled Winchester's intent, but Gil could do nothing without jeopardizing Toy's life. Pain exploded in Gil's head. As he folded forward, Toy screamed.

"What's going to happen?" Sarah asked.

"I don't know. Johnny shot Lance once. I suppose he thinks he can do it again," Angie said.

"Well," Sarah sighed, "we're too upset to work anymore. Why don't we call it a day?"

Angie did not want to see Lance Kincaid shoot it out with Johnny Winchester. Yet part of her was so terrified, she was sure she wouldn't be able to stop herself. She would have to watch.

Winchester was fast with a gun, and Del Ramo was a crook. His stint as marshal hadn't affected him in any discernible way. Ramo would have no qualms about shooting Kincaid in the back. That thought chilled her blood. Ramo was such a snake. He would do any crooked thing he could.

"What are you going to do?"

"I'm going to see Gil. Maybe he can help Lance."

Angie ran to the livery stable. She would get Gil. He could protect Lance's rear. He could keep an eye on Ramo and Smalley. Gil would not let Lance die.

"Mr. Kincaid!"

Lance had stopped in the tobacco shop to rest. He turned toward that thin, piping voice. "Yeah?"

"There's a lady looking for you."

"Where?" It had to be Angie.

"At the Orlando. She gave me a quarter to find you. She wants to see you right away," the kid panted.

Slowly, weaker than he cared to admit, Lance walked to the hotel. He stepped into the cooler interior and stopped.

At sight of his familiar outline in the doorway, Samantha stood up. She had been waiting for weeks to see Lance again. Impatiently. Now suddenly she was terrified. What if he sent her away?

Lance scowled, and her heart almost stopped. Was he furious with her? Already?

Ignoring her fears, she rushed forward into his arms. The most he could do would be to scold her, and he looked too startled for anything that simple. His handsome face sent joy sweeping through Samantha.

Lance expelled a heavy breath. "Sam?" Dressed in an elegant traveling gown and bonnet, Sam looked thinner than he had remembered.

"Are you furious with me?" Samantha asked, leaning back in his arms to search his face. "You look pale."

She couldn't have picked a worse time. But Sam was family, the little pest he loved and protected—most of the time. "Your timing could have been a little better. What happened to your grand tour of Europe?"

"I've seen Europe, all I want of it."

Samantha drew in a ragged breath. "I sent a telegram to give you a chance to stop me from coming back—" She stopped. "You didn't get it, did you?"

• • •

Lance stopped at the door of *The Tea Time News*. He tried the knob and found it locked. Damn! He walked next door.

"Do you know where Miss Logan is?"

"Not for sure. Saw her and Sarah leave some time ago."

"Which direction?"

"Miss Logan went to the livery stable. Maybe going out to the ranch. I don't know."

"Much obliged."

Atillo was nowhere to be found. Gingerly Lance saddled Nunca himself. Sabbath had brought the chestnut in after the trial. He was fat and glad to see Lance. Pumpkin stamped in his stall. Angie had obviously walked or taken her bicycle. She couldn't get too far. Sam had promised to wait for him at the hotel. He wanted to find Angie and tell her Sam was here before she found out for herself. He needed to find Angie. Some core of urgency drove him.

Angie stopped to rest. The Chinese quarter simmered under the blistering sun. Smells of food cooking filled the still air.

Under the tree scarred by the fire, Johnny Winchester's bay horse nipped at spiky yellow grass. Her heart rose up and pumped against her throat. Fear for Gil, Lily, and the Liang family overwhelmed Angie.

Angie turned her bicycle. She would get help.

"Where you think you're going, little lady?"

Startled, Angie turned. A tall blond man with an insincere smile faced her. Pointing a gun at her, he stepped closer, caught her handlebars, and motioned with his gun. "Get in there."

Her bicycle fell over. With a rough hand on her arm, Winchester propelled Angie across the lawn and into the house. She stumbled on the baseboard, caught herself, and stopped in the middle of the parlor. Gil sat tied to a chair. His head slumped forward; blood dripped down the side of his face.

Her gown pulled down around her waist to bare small dark-tipped breasts, Toy stood in the corner. Tears glistened on her cheeks. Third Uncle and Mei-ling huddled on the floor. Unmoving, unblinking, making no effort to cover herself, Toy appeared in shock.

Johnny smiled his mirthless smile at Angie again. He was handsome in a classic way. There was nothing disgusting about his face, nothing to warn of danger in his appearance until she looked into his eyes, then Angie's skin crawled.

"Remember me?" he asked, watching her closely.

Angie nodded. "Johnny Winchester."

Winchester laughed, pleased by his notoriety. He looked at her now and realized that she was the one—he hadn't really looked at her in Nogales—the photographer. She was also the one who had scared the hell out of him in the chink's barn, running in there just as he climbed down the mine shaft after that damned little chink. He'd lifted the lid on the corn crib, seen her through the slit, and thought he was seeing a damned ghost. Lucinda would have enjoyed that.

"You're kinda hard to kill, aren't you? Did those pictures come out?" His laughter grated her nerves like chalk on a blackboard. Angie decided to ignore Winchester. "Is Gil dead?" she asked of Liang.

Liang's no was nearly inaudible.

Angie appealed to Winchester. "You don't have to kill anyone… what do you want?"

"Silver!" Liang said. "He wants silver!"

Johnny grinned. Del had finally done him a favor with his damned show of trying to make himself look innocent because he was the damned marshal. Because of Del's squeamishness, Johnny had decided he'd pick up the silver first, gun down the crippled ranger, and then ride out of town. Just made sense to get the silver first. Del would have to form a posse and take off after him, but Del would stop before he got too close.

"If you have silver, give it to him!" Angie whispered, looking from Toy to Gil's slumped body. Lily lay in the next room, either dead or dying. How could they worry about their silver tea service or whatever silver they had at a time like this? "What could be worth this?"

"We have no silver," Liang said.

"They have no silver," she repeated.

Ignoring her words, Winchester looked at Angie as if he could not tear his eyes away from her. "I find you fascinating, Miss Logan."

"How do you know my name?"

Winchester laughed. "I know all about you."

Angie frowned. "What do you want?"

"I want you," Winchester said softly.

Angie was surprised to hear her own voice sounding calm and matter-of-fact. "Then send them away. Let them go. You don't perform in front of crowds, do you?"

Winchester looked at her with disgust. "Am I supposed to admire your spunk?"

"Let them go."

"For what?"

"For…whatever you want from me."

"I'll take whatever I want from you, picture lady. You've nothing to bargain with…" He lifted a pale, arched eyebrow. "Tell me, Miss Logan, you like strangers making love to you?"

"What do you want?" she whispered.

"Take off the blouse."

Angie glanced at Toy then at Gil. Winchester pointed the gun at Gil and cocked it. "Do as you're told, or he dies."

Her heart pounding, Angie reached up and unfastened one of the buttons on her blouse. Nothing stirred in Winchester's pale gray eyes.

Angie's fingers trembled on the small buttons. Winchester was going to kill them all anyway. She should stand up to him. She didn't want him to touch her. She should make him kill her before he could…

Johnny slipped his gun back into his holster. "Take it off," he grated.

The fact that he was no longer holding his gun gave her hope. A plan formed in her mind. The last button on her pale yellow blouse opened to her trembling fingers.

"Take it off!"

Shaking inside, Angie shrugged the blouse off her shoulders. The cloth slid past her hips and fell to the floor.

"Now the rest."

Angie tried to push the chemise up over her head, but her hands would not obey the signal.

"You're like her," Winchester said, his voice thick, vibrant. His eyes remained dead—a direct contrast to the excitement in his voice. A chill paralyzed Angie.

"You like it this way too, don't you?"

Without taking his eyes off her, Winchester reached out and pushed the chemise down, exposing one round breast.

Blood rushed into Angie's head. She moaned, and Winchester pulled her close. His hands touched her breasts. Angie ignored the jolt of revulsion and lifted her mouth to his. Eyes closed, head back, Angie concentrated all her energies on kissing him, on not pulling away. Slowly her hand located the butt of his revolver. Faint with fear, she lifted it free of his holster.

• • •

Rage flushed into Lance like a tide. Winchester's words and the look on Angie Logan's face as he touched her plump little round breasts and pulled her into his arms sent his body into a state of alarm. Hatred for both of them flushed through him. The urge to send bullets slamming into their bodies was more powerful than the will to live.

"Enough! Don't move!" a familiar, whiskey-tinged voice cut the air. Angie clutched the gun and tried to get free of Winchester. How had Kincaid gotten into the house? With his feet planted wide apart, he stood at the back door of the parlor, his gun pointed at Winchester, his face twisted with hate.

Next to her Winchester clawed for his gun, slapped an empty holster, and spun her around to use her as a shield. His hand clamped around her wrist and twisted savagely, trying to force the gun from her hand.

"You little bitch!" he growled.

"Let her go!" Kincaid yelled.

Angie went limp in Winchester's grip. He cursed and adjusted his hold on her; she struggled free of him and threw herself at the wall, still clutching Winchester's gun.

"Move, and you die!" Kincaid shouted, his gun aimed at Winchester's chest.

Winchester straightened and faced Kincaid.

"You going to shoot an unarmed man?" Winchester taunted. "Think your reputation can handle it?"

Kincaid shook his head. "I'll watch you hang."

"Can't hang me. I didn't take anything out of this house. They can't do anything to me."

"Wrong," Lance said. "You killed Rufe Martin." Without taking his eyes off Winchester, Lance directed his words at Liang. "This man came here with Martin, didn't he, Liang?"

Liang nodded.

Winchester laughed. "Taking the easy way, Kincaid? What's the matter? You scared? You should be. You know damned good and well you can't beat me to the draw."

"Save your breath."

Johnny laughed. "Let's finish what we started in Nogales."

Lance shook his head. "I wanna see you take that short drop, Winchester."

Johnny shook his head. "Like hell. I'll walk out of here a free man."

• • •

Gil blinked and opened his eyes. With consciousness came pain. His head throbbed with a dull ache. In a daze he listened to Winchester and Lance. They were leaving something out, something important. Gil straightened in the chair.

"Johnny," he said softly. Lance and Winchester looked at him. "Tell him where you were in 'seventy-four. Tell him about the apartment you rented on the west side of Cambridge. Tell him—"

"Go to hell!" Winchester snarled.

Kincaid looked from Gil to Winchester, his piercing gaze darting from man to man, commanding their answers. Angie felt the pulsing of Kincaid's fiery, volcanic core all the way through her body.

"You remember back in 'seventy-five when I tried to tell you certain things?" Gil asked Lance.

As ominously contained as a stick of dynamite, Lance nodded.

"I told you that Lucinda went to that apartment of her own free will. She wasn't kidnapped. She wasn't forced"—Gil turned to Winchester—"was she—what do you call yourself now? Winchester?" he sneered. "Did you have to kidnap Lucinda? Did you have to force her in any way?"

Lance's mouth tightened. The gun in his hand wavered, as if he would turn it on Gil. Gil ignored the threat. He knew what he had to do. Nothing could stop him now.

"Hell, no," Winchester answered easily, grinning at Kincaid's furious countenance. "She was crazy about me. She wanted me, not you!"

"You're a goddamn liar! She stayed with me!"

"Money! You had all the goddamned money in the world. You think she was going to walk away from that?"

Lance's finger tightened on the trigger. "And it doesn't matter, Winchester. You killed 'Cinda," he snarled, his lips drawing back. "That's all I need to know!"

"I didn't kill her. When I left she was alive."

Gil shook his head. "He lies."

"Shut your goddamned mouth! I've had all I'm gonna take from you, you slit-eyed yellow bastard!" Winchester's hand flashed down to his boot and came up with a knife. His hand moved so fast, Angie could barely comprehend what happened. Lance ducked, and the knife hissed over his head. Winchester slapped his other boot, and another knife appeared in his hand. He yelled and leapt at Gil. Toy and Angie screamed.

Gil tipped the chair over to avoid Winchester's knife. He took

Winchester and the chair with him. Lance couldn't shoot for fear of hitting Gil. He sheathed his gun and leapt forward. He hit Winchester in the side, and took him to the floor. Once he had his hands on the man, his body knew instinctively what to do.

"Stop him. He's gone mad!"

From a black haze Lance heard someone screaming. What had happened? He was on the floor atop Winchester's sprawled body. Winchester's face looked like raw meat. His own right hand was poised for a palm-heel strike into Winchester's nose, a blow that would kill instantly. Lance stopped. Winchester was a dead man, and he knew it. Gil must have been the one who yelled. Still tied to the toppled chair, Gil's eyes had filled with the look of a man who had seen too much violence. A sudden wave of nausea washed over Lance. No more killing. He had killed enough for 'Cinda. Roughly he turned Winchester over.

"Get me a rope!" he barked.

Angie stumbled once and turned to Liang. "A rope?"

Liang did not respond. Angie rushed to Gil's side and untied the ropes that bound him to the chair. Gil came slowly to his feet. Angie gave the rope to Kincaid and staggered back to lean weakly against the wall.

Gil's eyes commanded Angie to keep away from him. Was it not over then? Angie picked up her blouse and slipped into it.

Kincaid tied Winchester securely, then stood and faced Gil like a man on the verge of a second act of violence. Sighing, Gil motioned Lance to follow him outside. Grimly Lance obeyed. They stopped under the singed tree.

"I don't want to hear your goddamned excuses."

Gil stood his ground. "This time you will listen. I let you shut the truth out once. I won't again."

Lance put his open hand on Gil's chest and shoved him backward. "I'm not going to listen to your lies! It was your fault. You damned well knew she was going there, else you couldn't have known the rest. You let her go and get killed. Do you think I will ever forgive you for that?" He stepped back.

Still restraining himself, but quietly and thoroughly enraged, Gil moved forward. In kung fu, when instructing pupils, he called it "to enter Kincaid's door." In effect it was a maneuver to make Kincaid vulnerable to attack, to remove the distance that protected him, to gain control of both Kincaid and the choices available to him.

Lance crouched and backed up. Even in his heightened state of arousal, he had no hope of killing Gil, because no self-respecting *sifu* ever taught his student as much as he himself knew about his art, until he was ready to die. Lance didn't care. He had to try. He wanted to tear the bastard's head off. He wanted to feel his hands rip into Gil's body. He wanted to tear hunks out of Gil and hear the bastard scream.

Moving from rage to cold calculation, Lance crouched in the bent-knee stance that lowered his center of gravity and provided stability. In the past Gil had been most effective in the stance of the tiger. Lance did not wait for Gil to adopt a stance or to strike. Lance executed his own lunging strike.

With practiced savagery Gil deflected it, grabbed Kincaid's arm at the wrist and elbow, and closed the distance between them. With his foot behind Kincaid's leading leg, Gil fired a palm strike. Lance blocked it.

Furious, Gil pushed Kincaid's arm up and took him to the ground. With Lance pinned, it should have been over, but he had reckoned without full account for Kincaid's strength and determination. Lance broke his hold and came to his feet. Gil reciprocated with a hard strike to Kincaid's face. They fought silently, furiously.

Screaming, Angie and Toy ran out the door.

Lance and Gil looked like jungle cats, circling, looking for an opening.

"Stop it!" Angie screamed. "Stop it." She ran between them. Lance backed away from her as if she were contaminated.

Reluctantly Gil backed away.

"What is the matter with you?" Angie screamed. Lance pushed Angie away.

"Get back inside!" he shouted.

"You should know better!" Angie cried, turning to Gil. "He's half dead!" She said to Gil, "You were just beaten half to death. What is wrong with you two?"

She turned to Lance accusingly. "This man is your friend."

All of Kincaid's intensity pooled in his smoldering blue eyes. Panting, he shook his head. "No, he's not. He never was," he sneered.

"He *is* your friend," Angie screamed. "He loves you. He wants to help you."

Lance glanced from Angie's pleading, horrified face to Gil's determined countenance. They could not finish what they had to do in front of women. He stepped back and relaxed. "You're too well-protected now," he growled.

Lance stalked into the house, pulled Winchester to his feet, and propelled him out the door. He stumbled, and Lance prodded him toward the waiting horse. Holding one end of the rope tied around

Winchester's hand, Lance mounted. Kincaid turned the gelding and kicked him into a canter toward town. Cursing, half-falling, Winchester staggered along behind.

Angie sagged against the tree. Toy sobbed in fear. Gil spoke Chinese to Toy and patted her shoulder. Liang and Mei-ling slowly walked outside. Angie pushed herself away from the tree and ran for her bicycle. She had to stop, reason with Lance before he hurt himself or Gil.

Lance took Winchester to the hotel, rented another room, prodded Winchester up the stairs and into the room, and tied him hand and foot to the bed. He would not trust Winchester to his cousin's tender care. Still furious, Lance went to find Samantha and tell her that they would be leaving on the next stage.

Sam met him in the lobby. She had just come from the general store. "Are you okay?" she demanded. A bruise darkened his jaw. He looked furious. "What's wrong?"

"Nothing."

Samantha started to protest, but before she could, Angie Logan raced through the door of the hotel, saw them, and stopped dead in her tracks. Samantha's face reflected her own shock and surprise. Lance turned slowly, saw Angie, and his jaw tightened. Angie nodded at Samantha, noted the familiar way Kincaid's hand rested on her waist, and withdrew from the hotel without a word.

Lance looked from Angie's departing back to Samantha's troubled blue eyes. Like a woman looking for a hidden wound, Sam watched Lance's face for any sign that he loved Angie Logan.

Sam started to speak, stopped, and waited, her eyes filled with the question she tried to avoid—and the dreaded answer that would send her soul spiraling to its doom.

"I'm going to Phoenix when the stage comes through." The stage ran every other day. He had seen it today, so it would be back day after tomorrow. "Are you going with me?"

His voice was gruff. Samantha didn't understand any of it, but she nodded, flushed with gratitude. She wanted to be wherever Lance was. Always.

• • •

The next morning Jack Millicent found Atillo lying senseless inside the livery stable. Jack ran for Dr. Amberg, who pronounced Atillo drunk on opium.

Doc purely hated to do it. But he couldn't see lying. He made his pronouncement and stood back and watched. Rage and turmoil vied for supremacy. He suspected there was a certain deliciousness about such pure, self-righteous anger. Outraged women scoffed, shook their heads, rolled their eyes, and said how awful it was that those heathens infected good Christian children with their vile habits. Amberg probably enjoyed that the most: women calling Atillo a good Christian. It ranked as one of the nicest things they'd ever called him.

Men said they had taken enough from *those damned coolies*. They were not going to sit idly by while *crazy celestials* from the Flowery Kingdom spread their evil vices to white children. Men left their jobs and hung around the saloons and talked themselves into a fighting mood. By late afternoon a mob had formed in front of the Baquero. Men waved clubs and guns and shouted that it was high time they did something.

Doc Amberg made up a fresh set of bandages. This conflict looked like it could rival the Civil War if something didn't happen to stop it soon.

Angie had worked in the darkroom all morning. She hadn't slept the night before. Kincaid hadn't followed her, and she had been too startled by seeing Samantha to insist on talking to him. Her stomach felt as if she had swallowed a cold rock. It wouldn't dissolve no matter how feverishly she worked or how hard she tried to ignore it.

Loud noises down on the street peaked her curiosity. She peered out the window. An angry crowd on the street filled her with instant fear for Laramee's life; she rushed down the stairs. Sarah walked in the door.

"What's going on?"

"Where've you been?" Sarah panted. "The townsmen are going to march into the Chinese quarter. They're going to burn it."

So great was his pain, Liang felt crushed beneath it. He sat in his and Mei-ling's bedroom between Lily's sleeping form and Mei-ling's weeping one.

Panting, Toy ran in the house from outside. She had run a great distance on her tiny feet. "Son of Autumn," she cried. "Come quickly."

"Go away," Liang said softly. "Do not bother him."

"*Fan quai* are coming to burn our house!" she cried.

In Toy's room Gil lay on Toy's sleeping mat, stared at the ceiling, and willed himself not to give way to the pain that racked his body. In its treachery the ceiling wavered before his eyes, became a screen for images of Lily's gamin, sideways smile, her stubborn little eyebrows, her lovely head held so proudly on the dainty stem of her slender neck. Even the walls betrayed him, echoed back her lilting laughter, so healthy and impatient, so out of character for her class and culture and heritage. He should have taken that as a warning. She was too vengeful. Too passionate.

Unopened, the package she had pressed into his hand lay atop his traveling chest. He would not touch it. It would tear at his already bleeding insides.

Toy hobbled into the room.

"Please, Son of Autumn, you must save us," she whispered in Chinese, touched her throat, and bowed.

"What has happened?" he asked, also in Chinese.

"A white boy has taken opium."

Gil nodded. White men would march up Rio Street and wreak havoc. The way they had marched into Los Angeles a few years ago and destroyed a section of Chinatown called Nigger Alley. Enraged by the killing of one white man, Caucasians had burned many buildings and left hundreds without homes or possessions. Before that afternoon ended, twenty-one Chinese, including a twelve-year-old boy, had been hanged, and dozens had been killed in other ways.

Like a vicious Chinese bear crawling out of his winter cave, something dormant within Gil crept slowly, sluggishly, into life. Pretending normalcy, Gil came cautiously to his feet.

"You will go?" Toy asked.

"Yes, I will go."

Toy bowed low. "Thank you, Son of Autumn. Thank you for saving us."

Gil shook his head. He wanted to tell her that he had not saved her—probably could not save her—but he lacked the energy for words.

He had moved into the house to be near Lily and to escape the ghosts of her that haunted the spot where they had lain together so many nights.

Toy backed out of the room. Gil dressed himself carefully. He took off his silk garments and put on a cotton tunic and trousers. He stopped before his traveling chest. His gaze fell on the carefully wrapped package from Lily—the envelope he had avoided as if it were cursed.

Reluctantly Gil tore the paper. Inside, wrapped in tissue paper, lay a broken mirror—the mirror he had given Lily. No Chinese would ever deliberately break one unless…

Gil looked at the sharp splinters of glass and knew irrevocably that Lily would die. She had emptied the small bag of poison to be sure of that. With trembling hand he lifted the parchment and read:

> My dearest soul,
>
> Thy Lily is nothing without thee, as useless and wasted as a broken mirror. I told thee in secret, in the quiet midnight world, that I wished for us to fly in warm skies, two birds with the wings of one, and to grow together in the thirsty earth, two branches of one tree. But it could not be in this world.
>
> I forgive thee for thy unwillingness to save me from marriage to Chih-peh. I know it was impossible. In secret, even I am Chinese. I love thee with my dying breath. Please forgive me for the pain I now inflict upon thee. I would not wish it so, could I choose otherwise. Please do not grieve for me. I am better dead than married to another.
>
> I wait only for thee…
>
> Thy Lily

Her words stabbed at his heart. He sagged onto the floor.

Slowly he became aware of men yelling outside the house. *Fan quai* are coming. The Chinese had truly accepted Gil. Their voices yelled for Son of Autumn. Gil cared not. *I forgive thee for not saving me. I forgive thee for not saving me. I forgive thee for not saving me.*

Her words echoed and slashed inside him. Through a fog of despair. He realized suddenly and irrevocably that he had been wrong. Lily had every right to her own life. Lily was a different Chinese woman, bolder, more alive. The old rules would not work for her. He, Gilbert James Lee, had been the fool—sanctimonious about being one Chinese thread. He was not a thread; he was a man.

Crying hard and silently, Gil bent forward. Lily lay dying because he had forgotten that people were not threads. He had become old and sterile from trying to fit into societies that barred him. He had forgotten. Lily had been right to beg him to take her away. It had not been an impossible thing to ask. Liang would have survived her departure far easier than this final loss.

Gil stared at the broken mirror. His eyes blurred, and he could see

Lily, her black eyes glowing with love as she handled the mirror. *Thank thee. Thank thee. Thank thee.* She had pressed kisses on his face and tumbled him back onto his sleeping mat. *Take me away with thee. Please. Take me away with thee, my soul, my very own soul. I love thee. I want thee. Only thee. Thy Lily cannot live without thee.*

His head bowed down to his chest and he fought back the impulse to howl his pain to the heavens.

Gil threw the mirror shards against the wall. Panting, he stalked over and stomped his heel on the largest piece and twisted it hard, grinding it between shoe and lacquered floor. It crunched under his foot, but that was not enough. Enraged, he looked around for something else to destroy.

Breathing like a maddened bull, he stomped other pieces and ground them under his heel.

"Son of Autumn?"

Panting and dazed, Gil stared at his reflection in a small mirror hanging next to the Chinese language characters. His face was unrecognizable, terrible. He picked up a chair and smashed it into the mirror. Panting, he turned and strode to the front door.

He was ready to face *fan quai.*

Gil gathered every able-bodied man in the Chinese quarter and led them to a point south of the southernmost edge of Chinatown. He would make his stand here, surrounded by buildings owned by white men, so that if they started fires they would be burning out their own kind. If he and his countrymen were successful, they could save their possessions. If they failed…

It didn't matter. Only the fighting mattered. Only the dying.

The sun was at a forty-five-degree angle from the horizon. And hot. Traffic had virtually stopped. No vehicles or horsemen moved on this end of town. Some complaining, some silent, Chinese men waited behind Gil.

Within minutes, Caucasians left the street in front of the Baquero and walked north. Clotted together, they carried torches and waved ropes and guns to announce their intentions. Grimly Gil looked around at the pitiful weapons of his countrymen. Some had sticks, pike poles, swords, a few had knives. Gil had no weapon except himself.

He had fewer than a hundred men at his back. In China, when

he had fought in the Tai Ping Rebellion, at least there had been equal weapons on each side—if not equal numbers. Almost two hundred armed Caucasians walked toward them. In Los Angeles, during the riots there, angry whites had dragged helpless, screaming Chinese out of their homes and hanged them for no reason. Chinese who could afford it had offered bribes for their lives. The whites took their money and hanged them anyway. Gil prayed that his countrymen did not disgrace themselves by trying to bargain with their enemies.

When the Caucasians were a half block away, Gil stepped forward and yelled, "Halt! Go no farther!"

"Who's going to stop us, chink? You think you can do it with them sticks?" Laughing and shouting taunts, shaking their guns at the Chinese, the white men pushed forward.

"Halt!" Gil shouted.

"Go to hell, chink!"

The crowd of white men surged around Gil and cut him off from his compatriots. They prepared to move in for the kill. Gil could have avoided the trap, but he chose not to. Flatfooted, he crouched in the middle of the suddenly quiet mob. With a slight gesture of his hand Gil motioned to the biggest man, urging him to try his luck.

"I done never seen such a flimsy little chink in my life. Hold this whilst I swat this little fly." The man summoned by Gil passed his torch to another man and advanced on Gil. The man looked as if he expected to crush Gil easily.

Exultation rose up in Gil. For the first time in weeks he felt in control again. He toyed with the man, letting him jab clumsy blows past Gil's calculatedly negligent defenses, and then, when he had the crowd yelling for the man to kill him, to *tear his yella head off*, Gil knifed upward with his right hand and sliced with killing force into the man's diaphragm. The white man turned at the last second, and Gil's fingers broke his ribs. Gil went down on one knee, caught the man, gasping for breath, and flipped him over to send him crashing into a number of yelling, dodging, stunned whites.

Gil singled out another of the most belligerent and motioned to him. The grin faded on his hamlike face. He advanced more cautiously than his friend had. They circled for a few seconds, then Gil moved in close. Part of Gil knew this was insanity, this baiting of defenseless cattle, but it didn't matter. He could not stop himself. Within seconds he controlled his opponent. The poor devil did not stand a chance. He probably did not see the palm-heel strike that felled him.

A murmur went up from the crowd. Glancing at one another, five men in the front row advanced on Gil at once.

Joy leapt in him. He gave a loud yell of triumph, spun around, kicked with his heels, struck with his hands, and felled them one at a time—before any one of them could touch him.

The novelty was over. Men yelled their outrage. Seeing that they could not take him one on one, or even five on one, the crowd pushed in upon Gil from all sides, pressing in so tightly that his skill in the martial arts could not save him. Men hit him with fists and clubs. Even so, he struck one after another. The feel of their bodies connecting with his hands sent joy racing along his veins. Gil moved through the crowd like a razor until his strength failed him. Rough hands grabbed him while others hit him with fists and clubs.

Lance watched the men pummel Gil Lee, and he felt no desire to intervene. The only desire he felt was to help them. Even Gil Lee, with his spring-steel body and his consummate skill, could not last against a couple of hundred angry men. Lance wanted to be down there, pummeling Gil's hated body, but instead, he stood on the roof of a building that overlooked the crowd whose yelling had summoned him here against Sam's pleas.

A thought formed in Lance's waiting brain. *Gil Lee deserves to die, but I need to be the one who kills him.* Lance sighed, raised the barrel of the shotgun, and fired into the air.

The crash of it stunned the merging, yelling men into silence. Lance fired the other barrel of the shotgun to be sure every man there saw him. When all eyes had seen his badge and his shotgun and recognized him, he picked up another shotgun from a pile next to him and dropped the empty one. The roof he stood on sloped so gently that the shotgun did not slide toward the edge.

Lance leveled the shotgun at the white men nearest him and shouted at them to stand back. He counted on them to look at the pile of shotguns and remember his reputation for ruthlessness. Men shouted and backed away. Testing, Lance waved the barrel of the shotgun. Like tall wheat before a stiff wind, the mob swayed to avoid the ominous twin barrels.

"Gil! Can you hear me?" Lance yelled. He did not relish being the one to save the bastard, but he could not sit in the hotel while these idiots killed and burned out men, women, and children.

From the midst of the crowd Gil stood up. "Over here."

Lance used the shotgun like a pointer. "Make way! Let him through!"

Bleeding from cuts on his head and face, Gil pushed and limped to the edge of the crowd.

Lance tossed a shotgun down to Gil. A murmur of protest came up from the crowd, but no man pointed a gun at Kincaid.

"Any of your people know how to handle a gun?" Lance asked Gil.

Gil yelled in Chinese, and two Orientals stepped out of the crowd. Lance took shotguns off the stack and tossed them down. The two handled the guns like soldiers. Satisfied, Lance turned his full attention to the crowd again.

"What's this all about?" Lance demanded.

A man in the crowd cupped his hands and yelled. "These damned chinks got Atillo drunk on their damned opium."

Lance looked at the hundred or so Chinese. "It took *all* of them?" Lance asked, pretending surprise, waving his hand to include all the Chinese in the street.

Scattered whites laughed.

"Don't matter!" another man yelled. "They're all the same! They gotta leave this town. They don't belong here!"

"That's not for me or you to say! The United States and its territories have a treaty with China that allows Chinese to work here," Lance yelled. "And Arizona has laws against rioting and burning people out!" He paused. "Before I left Phoenix," Lance yelled, "McNamara said if I found myself in a situation like this, I'm supposed to kill as many troublemakers as necessary to restore law and order in Durango."

Lance raised his arm. "*Ready*..."

Gil and his countrymen lifted their shotguns and aimed them at the crowd. A murmur of fear and angry dissent rose up from the mob. "Hold on thar, Kincaid!"

"*Aim*..." Lance shouted.

Gil cocked his shotgun and spoke in Chinese to the two beside him who followed his lead. Men yelled and backed away in heightened alarm.

"Before I obey those orders," Kincaid yelled, "I'm going to wait *one minute* to allow *honest, law-abiding citizens to go home*, where it's safe. When I've counted to sixty, we're going to open fire on the criminal types and the troublemakers still standing in this road!"

Before he had finished speaking, men started leaving. They picked up their wounded and disappeared into the surrounding alleys and side streets. By the time Lance had counted to forty, Gil and his countrymen stood alone in the street.

Lance climbed down from the roof. "You okay?" he asked, eyeing Gil. Even the civility of the question grated on Lance. He shouldn't be talking to this bastard.

"One cannot beat oil out of chaff," Gil said, wiping the blood from his forehead.

Lance grunted. That had to be Chinese for no.

Elated Chinese babbled and embraced one another. Third Uncle walked over and touched Gil's sleeve.

Lance had not expected this to be so easy. He rubbed his chin. Gil sank down on the sidewalk next to Lance's boots. Gil bled from cuts on his forehead. Even Son of Autumn could be damaged. If the mob were big enough. Lance closed his eyes.

"How's Lily?" Lance asked. He did not intend to socialize with Gil Lee. He hated the bastard's guts, but Gil's pain was a palpable thing and he knew its source was not this confrontation but the dying girl.

Liang raised a hand to his head. Pale and shrunken, as if the juices in his body had receded, Liang sank down on the ground facing Gil.

Gil spoke quietly. "Comatose. Dying."

"Anything I can do?" Lance asked.

Gil's dark eyes were bitter. "Answer me this—when Lucinda died, did you feel anything…at that time?"

Jolted by the question, Lance looked away. He had never discussed this with anyone. He scratched with a fingernail at a spot on his trousers. He did not want to discuss it with Gil, but somehow, by asking the question, Gil had tapped into the part of Lance that remembered the friendship they had once shared. "At first I felt nothing. Later I felt rage."

"How did you get past the rage?"

Lance scowled. "I didn't," he said, his voice a rasp that was so irritatingly familiar to Gil that in its own way it comforted him.

"So what do I do, just smash things?" Gil asked, making a fist, tension evident in every line of his face.

"Don't use me as an example…" Lance's words drifted off. How many lives had he smashed before he gave up trying to live among civilized people?

He shouldn't be here, talking to Gil as if they were friends. He should have let them kill him…

"Guess I'll go," Lance said.

"What happened to Miss Logan's brother?" Gil asked as if only moments ago he had walked out of the courtroom where Laramee had been tried.

He'd forgotten about Laramee. Could he really leave Durango with Angie's brother in a precarious situation? Could he abandon Angie? "He's waiting to be tried a second time for the murder of the three Chinese brothers."

Liang blinked rapidly a number of times, looked from Lance to Gil, covered his face with his hands, and sagged forward into the road.

Solicitious, Gil touched Liang's sleeve. "Are you unwell, Honorable Father?"

Shakily Liang uncovered his face. "I am tired."

Lance stood up. "As I am. Good afternoon, Mr. Liang. If there is anything I can do for your daughter, let me know."

Gil stood and helped Liang to his feet. Lance walked tiredly back toward the hotel. He had never felt worse in his life. He needed rest desperately. But something nagged at him. Something about Liang's reaction.

Inside the Liang house, Liang stood up and walked into the bedroom where Lily lay. Unnoticed, Mei-ling wept in silence; only her tears moved. Toy, who had tended Lily tirelessly since they had brought her home, looked up. Her eyes filled with tenderness as she saw him.

Liang stood by the bed and gazed at Lily's still form. A white man sat in jail for the deaths of the three brothers. His daughter lay near death because of his cowardice. And all for naught. Liang knelt beside his daughter and took her hand in his. Toy stood up, bowed over her templed fingers, and scurried from the room.

Liang had never told his daughter that he loved her. It was not seemly. Now his heart ached with pain. He lifted Lily's limp hand to his lips and pressed a kiss to her warm flesh. He reverently put his head down on Lily's sleeping mat and touched his forehead to her warm shoulder. Life flickered in her now. Soon it would be gone. He must tell the white friend of Son of Autumn how the three brothers had died. That would atone in some fashion for the damage he had done with his greed for the white man's silver. But there was no need for haste. His secret would keep a little longer. He would face the white men's wrath after Lily died. Then it would not matter.

CHAPTER TWENTY-ONE

Wednesday evening, June 2, 1880

Angie didn't expect to see Lance again. He had taken Winchester to the hotel instead of the jail. He'd have to keep a close eye on him there. The thought of Lance being killed in his sleep by the evil Winchester terrified Angie. She wished she could see Lance, to be sure he was safe. He'd looked so angry. So filled with unaccustomed hatred.

Samantha was in town. Had Lance sent for her? Had she patiently waited for her fiancé to return to her in Phoenix this whole time? Angie remembered Samantha as a serious student. She had worked harder than anyone else, almost compulsively harder. Perhaps she worked that hard at all her relationships. Perhaps that was why she was engaged to Lance Kincaid, and Angie wasn't. Maybe God gave the good men to the girls who worked hardest in school. If so, she was doomed. School had bored her, except the classes that somehow related to photography and fine arts.

Angie walked from the kitchen into the parlor. She opened the front door and stepped out onto the porch.

Usually the desert soothed her, made her feel an unselfconscious connection with nature. Usually the night was her friend, but tonight was different.

Angie sighed. She'd known from the night of the celebration in Phoenix that Lance belonged to Samantha. Angie'd known it and ignored it as if it would somehow go away. Now the only thing that would go away was Lance, and Angie was so devastated about Lily that she barely noticed. She glanced north and wondered how Lily was. Had she died? Angie sat down on the porch. Gil would come tell her if Lily died. Or send someone. He knew she waited too.

• • •

Gil walked slowly up the hill. From the beating he had taken during the riot, he ached from the top of his head to the soles of his feet. Every step jarred him, but he had to restrain himself to keep from running. He had given Lily the medicine Kang Chou mixed for him, and nothing had happened. He had walked back to the pharmacy to see Kang Chou again, but the old man had been asleep or away or had refused to answer the door.

From his earlier visit, Gil saw Kang Chou's ancient face as the old man sniffed the decoction in the paper bag Gil had found in Lily's jewelry box. *Ahhh. Ahhh. Good possibility ancient mind played trick on old Chou. This smell like sleeping potion. You say Lily took this? Hummmm.*

Chou had tapped out a tiny amount of powder into a tin box. *Give her this. If that all she took, and I right about it, perhaps she wake up.*

Gil did not believe the old man's act for a second. Kang Chou was a wily old bird. He knew every ingredient in every jar in his shop. He did not make mistakes. He had known or guessed that Lily planned to kill herself and had deliberately substituted the harmless sleeping potion. Or he hadn't known, and she would truly die. Or she had bought something in the white man's store as well, and she would still die.

Afraid to go inside, Gil stopped at the front door, dreading what he would learn. The chill breeze whipped around the eaves of the house and made a low mournful sound. His heart pounding, cold from the wind and from his own weakness, Gil stared up at the sky full of bright stars, praying for the strength to bear whatever had to be borne, praying for the strength to help Mei-ling and Liang bear it, but praying most of all that Lily would live. And wondering, crazily, if this was his punishment for hurting Lance Kincaid so soon after Lucinda's death, but believing in his heart that the universe did not work that way. The universe always provided for growth even from death. As unknowable and unpredictable as the universe was, perhaps this would somehow constitute growth.

With his hand on the knob, he stopped. Something irrevocable was about to happen to him; he could not bring himself to turn the knob.

A low sound alerted Gil. His ears straining, he waited. Then it came again: the sound of Mei-ling crying. From long ago the sound of Lance Kincaid's voice recited a phrase he had particularly liked at the time: *As our life is very short, so it is very miserable, and therefore it is well it is short.* They had been discussing philosophy.

Gil sagged against the house, sick unto death. Lily was dead then. Her stubborn little eyebrows would never again lower in that special way. Her dainty, graceful hands would not touch him again. Gil slid down into a sitting position, covered his face, and doubled over with grief, too sick to move.

He had not cried since he had watched his eleven-year-old half-brother die aboard a slave ship headed for America. For men, crying was not condoned, but nothing mattered to him now.

Inside, at first Lily did not recognize the low moan as something human. "What is that?" she asked, leaning away from her mother, who had finally stopped her own pitiful crying.

They all listened. Lily walked toward the front door. Then the tone became recognizable to her. "Gil!" Lily said. "It is Gil."

Lily found him huddled beside the front door, his strong hands covering his face. She knelt beside him, pried his hands away, and replaced them with her lips.

"Lily? Lily!" Too strangled by emotion to say more, Gil gathered Lily into his arms and held her tight, his heart bursting with happiness.

Lance had a hard time getting to sleep that night. Too much had happened too quickly. Samantha's arrival had probably been the most unsettling. He hadn't figured out how to cope with Angie Logan, and now Sam was here, demanding his full attention. Fortunately Sam was safe ground. The need in her was so great he'd never have to surrender himself to her. But Angie…She'd demand every ounce of his soul. Her price was too high.

Physically he was almost recovered. This healing had been quite dramatic under the circumstances. His kidney seemed to be working. Doc Amberg said the dull ache in his back would pass with time. Lance's eyes opened, and he realized he had been asleep. In the next second he realized that some sound had awakened him. His gaze flitted around the room, probing the shadows. Carefully Lance stood up and walked into the next room to check the ropes that tied Winchester to the bed.

Winchester's eyes were closed, but he didn't look asleep. A warning tingle raised the hairs on Lance's neck. He dropped to the floor. A crash of gunfire reverberated through the room. Drawing his gun, Lance rolled under the bed and fired in the direction of the shot. A streak of gunfire pinpointed his target, and Lance fired again. A thud told him that the man had been hit or he'd tripped himself. Lance didn't move. A foot scraped the floor, and a soft sighing sound escaped, then nothing. Slowly Lance rolled out from under the bed and stood up. Outside, the sound of boots running along the hall told Lance that others had heard as well.

The man was dead. Lance didn't know his name but he had seen him drinking with Ramo a time or two.

Virgil Field yelled from the hall. "Kincaid?"

"Shootin's over. Come on in."

Summoned by Virgil Field, ten minutes later Ramo and Smalley walked slowly into the room.

Lance, his feet resting on the bed beside Winchester's bound feet, waved an arm at the dead man in the corner.

"Your friend is going to need help to get home."

Ramo glared from Kincaid to the dead man to Winchester. "Think you're pretty smart, don't ya?" Ramo and Smalley walked over, picked up the dead man, and turned to leave.

"Your cousin almost got killed a minute ago. If you or another one of your cronies tries again, the first thing I'm going to do is put a bullet in Johnny's head."

"That's murder, Kincaid," Ramo said tightly.

"Depends on your point of view. From where I sit it looks like insurance."

Tight-lipped, Ramo glanced from Winchester's watchful eyes back to Kincaid's. "You're not going to get away with this."

"Hell, it's only Johnny's life," Lance growled. "We're not talking about anything important."

In angry silence, Smalley and Ramo carried the dead man out. Lance checked Winchester's ropes, then spent twenty minutes reassuring a shaky, pale Samantha.

Lance locked Winchester's door, tucked Sam into bed, and returned to his own room. The only solution was to take Winchester to Phoenix and hold him in the jail there.

And that would mean taking Sam with him and saying good-bye to Angie. A small voice suggested he write to her, but he shrugged it off. He had to be sure she had not suffered any ill effects from her brush with Winchester. The act of thinking her name, which he had not allowed himself to do since he dragged Winchester out of Liang's house, evoked instantly, on some secret surface of his mind, a small, precise replica of Angie's face, complete with emphatic dark eyes. A flame ignited in the darkness of his belly, tingled for a moment, and leapt quietly.

The rest of the night, he struggled with the need to sleep. But Winchester's accusations about 'Cinda and about Angie had opened the floodgates. Lance saw Angie slipping out of her blouse for Winchester, and somehow, the image of Angie turned into the image of 'Cinda. *You like it this way too, don't you?*

Lance gritted his teeth. He should have killed Winchester. He should have killed the bastard…

The experience today had left him with the same feeling as his damned recurring dream about the drowned boy. He felt sick in his soul, and the awful sickness stayed with him. Downstairs footsteps sounded on the wooden sidewalk in front of the hotel. They stopped. A woman laughed, a low sultry sound. It sounded like 'Cinda. Unable to stop himself Lance spiraled back into that old memory.

Across the street from the Boston pier, he sat opposite 'Cinda at an outdoor café popular with students of Harvard and Radcliffe. Seagulls screeched and dived at the wrinkled surface of the ocean. 'Cinda laughed softly and leaned forward. As she did her lovely hand reached up and patted at the elaborately decorated hat he had just bought for her. The height of fashion, it sported flowers, a stuffed bird, and a ribbon on its jaunty brim. Her hand was soft and slim as a child's. Her nails were chewed to the quick. "I'll have lobster," she said to Hastings, the waiter. Lance smiled at the way Hastings always tried to appear unaffected, but his nervousness near 'Cinda showed in the jerky attentiveness of his eyes. They darted from her eyes to her lips to the swell of her hard little breasts. Lance had the playful urge to tell poor Hastings that they were as beautiful and as provocative as they looked. But of course he didn't.

"And extra butter, please," Lance added to her order.

"Ohhh!" she breathed the word as if horribly disappointed in him. "I thought I could have yours again."

"You can have anything you want," he said quietly, meaning it.

'Cinda sighed as tragically as an opera prima donna. "Bring extra butter, Hastings. I don't think he loves me anymore." She wore a white gown—a fresh thing with ribbons and lace with embroidered eyelets. Her soft blond hair was fine and clean and shiny. Individual strands were different colors—some gold, some silver, some honey-blond, some almost brown.

Lance reached out and touched her forearm. Even her skin fascinated him, caused his heart to pound, his mouth to go dry. "How could any man love a woman who takes his butter?" he teased.

"That is not all I will take," she said, reaching to brush his cheek.

"I love your eyes. When you look at me like that. I know you want me. I can almost feel how much you want me." Her hand caressed his cheek and his neck. Lance was aware, on the periphery of his vision, that heads turned, mouths opened, but as usual 'Cinda ignored them. She had no patience with propriety, with wagging tongues, with raised eyebrows.

"I want you to make love to me here," she whispered.

"Before or after Hastings brings our lunch?"

'Cinda laughed. "You always surprise me, you know that? No matter how outrageous I am, you always surprise me. I guess that is why I cannot quite give you up."

His heart constricted. "Cannot *quite* give me up? Are you trying?"

"Of course, darling. If I could give you up, I would be an extremely rich woman. I'm sure your father would be so pleased that money would be no problem."

Lance controlled the mixture of fear and anger that boiled up. "My father is too smart for that. Only a fool would interfere in that way." But Lance was not completely sure he would not. His father was implacable in his unfair assessment of 'Cinda. He had said quite firmly that a young man was allowed to make any number of mistakes. But he was not allowed to marry them. 'Cinda of course would not even listen to talk of marriage.

'Cinda leaned back in her chair. Her pink tongue darted out, waggled itself at him. A woman nearby gasped in amazement and shock, and 'Cinda laughed. "Kiss me, Lance. Lean over here and kiss me. I want to feel your tongue in my mouth."

She spoke loud enough for the gasping woman to hear. The chatter in the outdoor café ceased.

He reached across the table and picked up her hand. "I've given you everything: extra butter, lobster, a new hat, a headache on occasion, a ride in the park. If you behave I will take you to the beach."

"I'm not a child to be bribed so easily. We are at the beach. All of Boston is at the beach."

"You see. You have only to say it, and I do it." He shrugged with apparent nonchalance, but inside he writhed. 'Cinda seemed almost self-destructive at times, and it frightened him, caused him to wonder if he had fallen in love with a woman who could not manage the careful balancing act required to maintain a lengthy relationship. At times like this…

They walked on the beach, and she was sweet and loving and teasing and pouty. Her hair smelled of lilacs. She carried one of those frilly white parasols. At her door, while his buggy waited at the curb, she teased him again. "Make love to me here."

Lance reached for the door.

"No, not in there. Out here."

"Some things are better in private."

"Some things, yes, but not everything. Are you afraid?"

"Yes. Attorneys are trained to be afraid of the law. I am content with my fear of being tossed into a cell full of cutthroats."

"Coward."

"Tease."

"Coward. Spineless coward."

He turned to leave.

"Wait." Her hand on his arm stopped him.

"I work for a living. I have to get back."

'Cinda sighed. Her eyes were suddenly bleak. "I'm sorry. I don't know why I torment you." Tears pooled in her eyes. She dragged in a breath and shook her head hard and angrily. Her tears jetted away. She smiled up at him. Her hand, so smooth and childish, wiped at her cheek. "Don't leave angry."

Her tears unmanned him. The tension in him relaxed.

She leaned against him. "I do love you, Lance. I really do."

His own love was so intense, so gripping that he could barely speak. "I love you, 'Cinda."

"I love your voice, the way you say my name," she whispered. "Kiss me good-bye. I promise I will behave myself."

He was sure her mouth was like none other ever kissed by mortal man. He touched her lips, and he was lost. He could not remember anything except the taste and smell of her soft, hot, open mouth, her darting tongue. He fed openly and shamelessly on her tantalizing mouth.

That night after work he drove to her house to see if she would have dinner with him, but she was not home. Disappointed, he wrote her a short note telling her he would wait for her at his apartment if she wanted to see him, drove home, and spent the evening researching precedents for a lawsuit his father wanted to bring against a competitor. Shortly after midnight, a knock sounded on his door.

Manfred, his manservant, was asleep by now. Lance grinned. 'Cinda had changed her mind about seeing him tonight. He strode quickly into the entry hall and opened the door. 'Cinda—her face bloody and bruised, her gown badly torn—fell into his arms.

Lance carried her to his bed and yelled for Manfred to go for the doctor.

Lance knelt beside the bed. "What happened? Who did this?"

"I'm cold, Lance. It's so cold in here."

Fear paralyzed him. The temperature was probably eighty degrees. July was not cold in Cambridge. He jerked the counterpane and sheet from the other side of the bed and pulled them over her.

'Cinda's eyes opened, focused on him. "Don't be mad at me. I shouldn't have come here."

"Who did this to you?" he asked urgently.

Her eyes closed. "Sailors, three sailors…"

"'Cinda, can you describe them?"

With an effort she opened her eyes, but they didn't quite focus on his face. Her hand fluttered at her face, came away bloody. She smelled of semen and blood.

"The doctor will be here soon. You'll be fine. I need more information. Anything."

"You're mad at me, aren't you? It wasn't my fault."

"God, 'Cinda, I love you. How could you think I would think this was your fault?" She had been badly beaten, probably raped repeatedly. She was delirious.

"…they mentioned a ship. *Mabel Gray*, I think," she whispered. "*Mabel Gray…*"

A tiny spot of blood appeared on the coverlet. Alarmed, Lance uncovered her to check. Blood had caked on her legs. More seeped steadily from between her legs into the coverlet. Beneath her slim white hips, a bright red puddle spread out faster than the bed could soak it up. Lance cursed the doctor for taking so long.

He wanted to pack her with something to stop the flow, but she wouldn't let him touch her. Groaning in helplessness, gritting his teeth against the need to do something to stop the bleeding and relieve her cold and fear and pain—anything—he covered her again and ran for another blanket.

"I'm cold, Lance. Hold me."

He lay down beside her and held her as gently as he could. He wanted to clean her wounds, to wipe away every bruise, every trace of the beating, but he was afraid to touch her. Afraid of hurting her more.

"I'm scared, Lance. Don't let me die. Please don't let me die."

"I won't," he whispered. "I promise I won't." Dr. Hartman arrived sometime later. He examined 'Cinda and pulled the counterpane over her head. "She's dead, son."

Lance pushed the coverlet off 'Cinda's face and pulled her back into his arms. "She's not dead. We had lunch together today. We sat at a table in the sun and ordered lobster, with extra butter for her, and we walked on the beach…" He could see her in that white gown. He could smell the lilac perfume in her hair.

"I'll call your father."

"My father? What can he do? You're the doctor. Do something, goddammit. Don't just stand there. *Please…*"

Lance tracked down the three sailors from the *Mabel Gray.* It took days of surreptitiously checking alibis and leaves that coincided with the date of 'Cinda's murder. He finally narrowed the suspects down to three. It took another week to be sure he had the right men. Then one night he followed Sid and Morris to a sleazy waterfront pub and waited for them to come out. In the alley behind the pub, he confronted them with his proof and killed them with his bare hands, the way Gil had taught him to kill, except he hadn't known it would be so personal, so indelibly etched into his soul. He had been too sickened by what he had done to pursue the third man.

• • •

Thursday, June 3, 1880

A singing night bird joined the cacophony of crickets. Somewhere out on the desert, a panther screamed. It must have wandered down from the hills. Lance shivered. Above Durango stars looked like bright pinpricks of light in the dark fabric of the sky. They burned with fiery brilliance—alive, vital, intense. He turned onto his side so he wouldn't have to look at them. He wouldn't sleep because he did not want to have that dream again, and he knew he would.

He moved to the chair by the window. At dawn, still sleepless, he rang for a bellhop and instructed him to find out when the stage left for Phoenix. Lance washed, shaved, and dressed. When the boy came back with his answer, Lance sent word to Samantha and went to find Angie. Samantha would pack. Atillo would keep Nunca until he could return for him or send for him.

With all his chores done, all his excuses out of the way, he walked to *The Tea Time News.* The door was locked, and no one answered his loud knock.

Riding a rented horse, he headed east toward Angie's house. He would tell her that he would do his best to convince the governor to pardon Tan

Lin. Frémont was a friend of his father's. Seven years before Lance was born Lieutenant Colonel John C. Frémont led sixty well-armed civilians and soldiers into California in late 1845. Chantry Kincaid II was one of the civilians who had accompanied Frémont. They became friends during that fall and winter while the conquest of California went on, at least officially without their help. And John Stapleton was a friend also. As Arizona Territory's secretary of state, John probably wielded more power than Frémont simply because he did all the routine paperwork it took to run a territory. Things Frémont wouldn't bother with.

Lance knocked on Angie's door, waited, knocked again. The house had an empty feel to it. Lance cursed himself. He should have known that when he needed her she would be out taking those damned pictures that she prized more highly than life itself.

He watched for her all the way across town and didn't see her. He walked to Sarah's house. Sarah answered the door.

"Is Angie here?"

"No."

"You know where I might find her?"

"Did you try her house?"

"Yeah."

Sarah sighed. "Maybe Lily's house or *The Tea Time News*. If she's neither place, I don't know."

"Thanks." Lance turned to leave.

"You're leaving town, aren't you?"

"I haven't had a single secret since I came to Durango."

Sarah shrugged. "Small town."

"In case I don't find her before the stage leaves, will you tell her I tried?"

Disapproval clouded Sarah's eyes. "Certainly."

Virgil stepped out of the hotel and motioned Angie into the shade provided by the awning of the store next door to the hotel. "Ramo got a wire from the prison at Yuma telling him they're going to send the wagon for Tan Lin."

Angie grimaced. "When?"

"Monday."

"Only five days." And she hadn't heard from the governor in answer to the wire she sent yesterday.

Angie went immediately to tell Gil. He looked surprisingly well in spite of small cuts and bruises on his handsome face. Lily beamed in happy silence at his side.

"Monday?" Gil sighed. "That gives us some time to prepare."

"What will you do?"

"Resist. How I do not know."

"I've wired the governor, asking him to pardon Tan Lin. Why don't you wait for that to work? We *will* prevail. I know we will. I'll see the governor in person if he fails to grant Tan Lin's freedom. I'm not going to give up."

"On principle, I am not willing to let them imprison the boy. Even if I were willing, the others are not. They are immovable on that point."

Angie turned to Lily, pale and lovely beside Gil. "How are you feeling, Lily? Are you fully recovered now?" Gil had sent a messenger the night before to tell Angie the good news.

"Thou art very kind to ask. As thou canst see, thy friend, Lily, has recovered, except for some slight exhaustion."

"We give thanks to Kang Chou for his foresight or his lapse," Gil said.

Except for the problem of Tan Lin's impending move to the prison at Yuma and the danger that represented for all Chinese, the couple were ecstatically happy, barely separable. Chung Tu had made his demands to Liang and was told emphatically that Lily would not marry Chih-peh. All the wedding gifts had been returned to Tu's house.

"Have you seen Lance Kincaid since the trouble here?"

Emotion clouded Angie's lovely eyes. "I saw him for one moment at the hotel with Samantha Regier. Did you know she was here in Durango?"

Gil shook his head. "Do not judge Lance too harshly; perhaps he finds himself without choice," he said.

"What do you mean?"

"Never mind. I talk too much."

Angie left Gil and Lily standing beneath the scorched tree. Next she called on Du Pon Gai. She asked more questions than an eastern reporter, and wrote Gai's answers in her notebook. A plan was forming in her mind.

From upstairs in the photography studio Angie watched Lance and Samantha and Johnny Winchester board the stage. Before Kincaid stepped inside, he glanced up and down the street, and his narrowed eyes probed the shadows. Fearing he would see her, Angie stepped back. She could not bear having Kincaid tell her goodbye in front of Samantha.

The prison officials were coming for Tan Lin in four days. Monday. That information alone would have kept Kincaid in Durango, but her pride would not let her tell him. Besides, there would be a terrible confrontation. If he stayed, Kincaid would be in the middle of it and might be killed.

Dazed with heartache, Angie put her head down on her small table and cried.

In the midst of her crying Angie suddenly remembered the morning she woke up alone under the porch. Kincaid had slipped out sometime during the night. Like a thief. Or like a man who couldn't handle the weight of a woman's love. She had been so blissfully happy and so preoccupied with her picture book and the newspaper that she hadn't noticed. She should have known there was something wrong with him. He had known he would fail her, that's why he couldn't hide his conflicts about her.

He'd tried to warn her, but she had been too blind to see the warnings. She'd seen only what she wanted to see.

What do you want a poor woman to do? Want her to hang on kinda loose-like. Is this loose enough? That might be a tad too loose, Kincaid had said.

He'd almost come right out and told her not to get attached to him. He *had* told her he was engaged to Samantha. But even that hadn't stopped Angie Logan, the woman who'd been too stupid to see a freight train headed right for her.

She'd proceeded as if she and Kincaid would end as these things usually ended, with comfortable indifference on both sides. She hadn't imagined her heart would ache so.

It took a great effort to rouse herself. Brute will. Weighed down with frustration and pain, she managed to lift herself out of the chair about twelve o'clock. And only then because she had a great deal to do before the prison wagon arrived. Taking pen in hand, using the information she had garnered from Tan Lin's mother, Angie wrote what would probably be her last flier. She had taken enough pictures to fill three picture books. As soon as Laramee was free and the conflict with Tan Lin was settled, she'd return to her job with the *Weekly*.

She finished her third draft, read it, and sank back in her chair. It was as good as she could make it. A loud knock sounded on the door below. Knowing it could not be Kincaid this time, Angie walked to the window and leaned out.

"Up here, Atillo."

Atillo squinted up at her. "You have a telegram, Miss Angie."

"Be right down."

Unfolding it, Angie read quickly.

> TO A. B. LOGAN STOP GOVERNOR REGRETS UNABLE TO ACT ON REQUEST FOR PARDON STOP JOHN STAPLETON SECRETARY OF STATE

Angie crumpled the paper. The urge to kick the doorjamb was overwhelming. Only her habit of restraint saved her. "Wait one moment, please." She rushed over to Sarah's cluttered desk, picked up a pencil, and wrote out a telegram on a sheet of paper.

"Atillo, take this and have George send it to John Stapleton immediately. Then come back and tell me how much I owe. Will you do that for me?"

"*Sí, señorita,*" Atillo said, beaming.

Three hours later, the answer came.

> TO A. B. LOGAN STOP GOVERNOR WILL MEET YOU TOMORROW 7PM IN PHOENIX AT PIONEER HOTEL STOP FORMAL ATTIRE STOP STAPLETON

An audience with the governor! Angie frowned at the the telegram. Formal attire? Would the governor see her at some social function?

Anger swelled in her. *He was too busy playing the debutante to attend to business. The fop!*

Angie allowed herself only a moment to be furious. If she were going to make the morning stage, she had no time to spare. She would double the guards protecting Laramee to be sure Ramo didn't try anything while she was away. She would tell Sarah what needed to be done to finish the next edition. And she would tell Gil where she was going so he could forestall any drastic moves until she returned.

Lance helped Samantha check into the hotel in Phoenix, carried her bags up to her room, and then turned to leave.

"Wait," Sam said quietly. "I have to ask you something."

A muscle bunched in his cheek. His eyelids drooped to half mast as if to protect himself from her. "What?" he asked, his voice grim.

"I'm not intimidated by your surly manner, Kincaid," Samantha challenged him.

"I know," Lance said, smiling in spite of himself. In the stagecoach she had not been intimidated by Winchester. When he'd dropped his prisoner off at the jail, she hadn't been intimidated by twenty prisoners yelling their appreciation of her slender young body. It would be a blessing to find something that did intimidate Samantha Regier.

"That's better. The first sign of life since we left Durango."

"I'm tired, Sam. I'm going home to collapse."

"How did you find Angie?"

All expression on his thoroughly masculine face disappeared behind a mask. Finally he sighed. "Are you trying to get me in trouble?"

Samantha gazed at Lance fondly. He had learned that answer from Uncle Chantry. Anytime Aunt 'Lizbeth accused him of something he shouldn't have done, he countered with that question. At least Lance had not completely lost his sense of humor.

"You can tell me. I promise I won't tell anyone," she said, responding with the answer Aunt 'Lizbeth always used.

"I didn't *find* Angie. McNamara sent me to Durango on business. She was just there."

"So what are you going to do about her?"

"I did it. I left her in Durango." Muscles already darkened with beard stubble bunched and writhed in his lean cheeks.

"That doesn't have to be the end of it."

"But it is."

The look in Lance's cornflower-blue eyes stopped Samantha. She'd pushed him as far as he could be pushed. She knew what happened when she overstepped herself. Weeks ago he had volunteered for an assignment long before he was supposed to because she kept talking about things he didn't want to discuss. She hadn't realized that until Uncle Chantry commented on his son's eagerness to get back to work.

Sam stretched up on tiptoe and kissed him lightly. "Go get some rest, lawman. I'll see you later."

Word spread rapidly throughout the Chinese community that the prison was sending a wagon for Tan Lin.

Son of Autumn's face hardened with determination, and fear knifed into Lily's heart. "What wilt thou do?"

"Stop them."

"Canst thou wait? Our friend, Angie, hast sent a telegram to the emperor—"

"Governor," he corrected her. "He did not reply."

"Surely he will," she said, pressing her nose to his chest. He smelled wonderful to her—a clean, manly smell that made her weak.

Gil touched Lily's lovely, curving cheek. "Nothing is certain, beautiful flower. Sometimes it is not politically expedient to interfere with local justice."

"So he would sacrifice a small boy?"

"Better Tan Lin than himself…"

Lily turned away, already hating this governor who would not save a boy who should never have been tried in the first place.

A loud knock on the door interrupted her angry thoughts. Lily opened it. Flushed from her long walk, Angie Logan sighed. "Thank goodness I found you here," she said.

• • •

Friday, June 4, 1880

At nine o'clock Angie and Gil caught the Butterfield stagecoach to Phoenix. She had been prepared to make the trip by herself, but Gil had insisted on accompanying her, using the excuse that in this instance two would be more persuasive than one.

The Pioneer Hotel was the nicest hotel in Phoenix. Gil and Angie checked into separate rooms and agreed to meet in the lobby at six o'clock.

Angie had packed an elegant new gown she had bought in New York. The event she had bought it for was superseded by an opportunity to do a portrait sitting of Lady Randol, a visiting English noblewoman famous for her charitable works.

Unable to rest, she tried the gown on. It was entirely too extravagant for Phoenix. Perhaps a night at the Met in New York City, but the thought of being in the same town as Lance Kincaid and Samantha had made her a little competitive. She had imagined herself wearing this gown for his benefit. So he could look at her and be sorry he had chosen Samantha instead of her.

Angie turned to admire her profile. Gold cashmere flattered her tawny coloring. The fine feel of the fabric would have delighted her at any other time. It was the most sensuous gown she had ever owned.

And Lance Kincaid would never see her in it.

Angie bathed and dressed. The thought that perhaps by some miracle Kincaid might see her inspired Angie to pile her hair in elaborate curls atop her head.

Gil Lee was busy as well. He located Secretary of State John Stapleton and asked numerous questions. Then he borrowed a piece of stationery from the desk clerk and wrote a short note. He found a youngster playing in front of the hotel and gave him specific instructions for the note's delivery to Kincaid. His arrangements made, he shopped for a gift for Lily.

At six o'clock Angie found Gil talking to a strange man in the lobby. Gil excused himself and walked to her side. Admiration gleamed in his black eyes. His bruises were less noticeable. He bowed deeply and held out his hand.

"I located John Stapleton. The affair you have been invited to is a formal dinner in the hotel's Oregon Room. The governor will be receiving an award for his works in establishing educational facilities for children." He spoke so softly that Angie had to strain to hear him over the commotion in the lobby.

Elegantly dressed couples converged on the lobby. Seeing so many people, Angie prayed that she would have a few moments of the governor's undivided attention. Tan Lin's very life hung in the balance.

"Do you think Governor Frémont will give me an audience?"

"What man could resist you?" Gil held out his arm to her. "You are exquisite—a star too bright and lovely to ignore."

"Thank you, sir."

"Are you ready, *mademoiselle?*" he said, affecting a French accent quite successfully.

"You are a man of many voices," Angie said, smiling.

Once inside the banquet room, Gil pulled Stapleton aside and presented Angie to him with great care, speaking her name as if she were a person of high station. Angie smiled demurely. Gil certainly knew enough about politics for both of them. Any man hearing his introduction would assume she wielded great power in some circle. She sounded like the publisher of the *Weekly* and *The Tea Time News* or *The New York Times*. She couldn't be sure which. Gil left that a little vague.

"Angela Brianna Logan? Not A. B. Logan?" Stapleton stammered, flushing from the top of his wing-tip collar to the roots of his blond hair.

"How kind of you to remember," Angie murmured, unable to resist the opportunity to torment the embarrassed Irishman.

"I beg your pardon, Miss Logan. I had no idea. I assure you that I would never have addressed such curt replies to a woman of your beauty."

"I wish no special treatment because of my gender, sir."

"Even though it would be literally impossible to withhold it?" he asked, his tone earnest.

Hoping that the governor would be as easy to captivate, Angie blushed at the heated look in Stapleton's eyes.

John Stapleton was taller and broader than Gil, with coarse pinkish skin, heavy freckles, and jaunty hazel eyes that twinkled with good humor. His strawberry-blond hair fell across his forehead, and was repeatedly swept back by a freckled, impatient hand. No amount of hair tonic could tame that unruly mop. He had the handsome look of an outdoorsman going soft from drinking too much alcohol.

Another couple joined them, vying for John's attention. He easily disengaged the interlopers and turned back to Angie. He took her hand and nodded to Gil. "May I introduce you to our guests, Miss Logan?"

The guests nearly filled the small, high-ceilinged ballroom. One crystal chandelier sparkled overhead. Hardwood floors gleamed beneath the shine of patent slippers. The banquet room lacked the elegance of hotel facilities in the East, but it was adequate for Phoenix.

"Miss Logan, may I inquire…if I may be so bold…are you married or engaged?"

Angie stiffened. "No, I am not."

"I did not mean to offend, only to determine if you are already taken. In which case I would have asked you to excuse me so that I might kill myself."

"Thank goodness you are not the least melodramatic, sir."

"Melodrama would indicate some lack of sincerity. I assure you that if you were already spoken for, death would be an easy fate in comparison to no hope, Miss Logan."

John Stapleton's performance was reminiscent of Angie's school days at South Hadley, where the young men were both melodramatic and unpredictable. There they often vied with one another to make the most outrageous comment. "You are most refreshing, Mr. Stapleton. I thank you for your efforts to amuse me."

"I am wounded to the core, Miss Logan, that you could dismiss my admiration so lightly."

With a shrug of acknowledgment at Gil, Angie surrendered to Stapleton's extravagant attempts to keep her entertained.

The entire room buzzed with excitement. Each time a new figure appeared in the doorway, heads turned.

Twisting his handkerchief in trembling fingers, a frail, unconvincing man in a black frock coat rushed over and whispered into Stapleton's ear. The man's face splotched with agitation as he continued his frantic delivery.

"He's been late before," Stapleton reassured his companion. "I suggest we seat our guests, no sense in starving them. Just act as if we expected the governor to arrive late."

"Thank you, thank you," the splotchy-complexioned gentleman replied, and rushed away.

A murmur went up from the group of people standing next to Angie and Gil. Angie glanced at the door, and the blood stopped pumping away from her heart. A tall figure, his clean lines strikingly familiar, paused in the doorway. With a slight lift of his hand, Lance presented Samantha Regier for the crowd's admiration. Pausing, Samantha curtsied, nodded to her escort, and they moved forward in unison. Lance Kincaid wore the black frock coat that was *de rigueur* for men. Samantha was breathtaking in scarlet satin.

Every couple who had walked through that door had duplicated that small ceremony, but when Kincaid and Samantha paused there, the crowd fell silent and stayed that way for an inordinate period of time. If a man could be beautiful, Kincaid was. He had the unique ability to project the menace and power of the gunfighter and the smooth, easy intelligence and self-confidence of a Philadelphia lawyer—a mesmerizing combination. Just inside the door Lance bent toward Samantha to say something, and grim amusement twitched the corners of his mouth, deepening the already deep lines there. The sturdy handsomeness of his neck, the rebellious dark hair curling there, made Angie's pulse race. Beside her, she felt Gil Lee's attitude change almost imperceptibly.

The splotchy little man returned and pulled Stapleton aside.

Trembling, Angie turned to face Gil. "Did you know he would be here?"

"Yes."

"Thank you for the warning."

"You could not be more breathtaking if you had worked for six hours on your wardrobe. You are without rival."

Kincaid saw Angie and Gil and stopped. His bottom lip flattened.

The deeply etched grooves beside his mouth deepened into grim tracks that accented the appealing planes of his lean tan face. Sam's eyes widened, took on a look of distracted alarm, then cleared almost magically. She looked at Angie and offered a smile.

"Excuse me, please," John said, walking quickly to where Lance stood. They talked for a few seconds and then walked slowly toward where Gil and Angie waited.

"Miss Logan," Stapleton said, stopping with Kincaid and Samantha in tow. "No one could be more useful in your suit with the governor than my friend, Lance Kincaid."

John started to introduce them, but Lance stopped him. "We've met." The familiar husky grating of Kincaid's tenor accelerated the disarray in Angie's body. It took an enormous effort to nod coolly while her heart pounded as if she were being chased by a six-hundred-pound grizzly.

Kincaid's stunning blue eyes never left her face for an instant. She felt bathed in blue fire. Stunned by it. Unable to either look away or breathe. People talked around them. But they did it without Angie's knowledge. The hidden throbbing of Kincaid's blood contaminated her mind. She felt jangled by so much intensity. In formal dinner clothes he looked stronger, even more dangerously male. A rush—a wild pang of genuine pleasure—suffused her mind and body. Though only two days had passed, it seemed years since she had seen him.

"Evening," Gil said smoothly.

Kincaid glanced at Gil, and his eyes narrowed with rage. Gil must have sent him that note. It had arrived this afternoon and had stated simply that Governor Frémont would be available this evening to hear in person his request on behalf of Tan Lin.

Angie felt the throb of hatred in Kincaid and wanted to retreat. Gil didn't flinch. He met Kincaid's gaze with a carefully hooded expression that said next to nothing, but Angie believed, looking from Lance to Gil, that Gil neither feared Lance nor hated him. What did Lance see?

Lance felt blinded by rage. He cursed Gil Lee and planned horrible, prolonged deaths for the bastard who had summoned him here without warning him of Angie's presence.

A waiter stopped next to Lance, and he lifted a glass of wine off the proffered tray. As he sipped the wine he tried to ignore the urge to kill.

He turned his attention to Angie. She had gone all out for this occasion, whatever it meant to her. The gown revealed the sleek, slender contours of shoulder, breast, and waist to perfection. Cut low in front and even lower in back, it left her round, tender, golden arms exposed from mid-shoulder. Strands of gold ribbon lifted the shining mass of curls and left the sweep of her lovely neck provocatively exposed, silken, and vulnerable. The effect was crippling.

Place cards were quickly rearranged to put Stapleton next to Angie. "Let's take our seats," Stapleton said, flustered by the two beautiful women.

Gil held his breath while Kincaid located his and Samantha's place cards. He'd forgotten to check that.

Lance sat down across from Angie, and Gil sighed. A hefty tip had worked again.

Lance glanced between gleaming silver candelabra at the golden vision of Angie Logan and sipped at his wine. Pearls caressed the cleft between her small, firm breasts and enhanced the peachy-gold translucence of her skin. He had never seen her dressed in formal attire before. She was beautiful. In his mind's eye Lance saw her tantalizing, erect nipples jutting out at crazy, impudent angles, and almost felt the butter-smooth texture of her skin against his lips. A furnace of lust warmed Lance's body. He tossed down a glass of wine.

Gil made polite table conversation with Sam. Lance stopped a wine steward.

His glass full, Lance looked around for someone to attack. "Are you proud of yourself?" he rasped, leaning forward to be heard over the buzz and hum of the other diners.

Gil shook his head, more in warning than in answer. This was not the time or place for them to settle their conflict.

Lance's expressive, dark eyebrows lifted imperceptibly. One corner of his mouth quirked with cynicism and anger, but he seemed to agree. He sat back in his chair, apparently satisfied that Gil would give him satisfaction at the proper time.

Angie saw the exchange between Lance and Gil, but she had no time to wonder about it. Around her, a constant stream of banter left little time to think. Seated between Stapleton and Gil, Angie slowly relaxed in spite of Kincaid's smoldering, unsmiling face across the table from her. In spite of the air between them that seemed to shimmer like sunlight on a hot road.

"Miss Regier, are you enjoying your stay in Arizona Territory?" Stapleton asked.

"Why yes, thank you. I'm fascinated by Arizona's wild beauty. I love everything about it."

"And you, Miss Logan?"

"I don't find it quite as fascinating as Miss Regier. Perhaps because

I lived in the territory years ago, but of course one never stops learning. I've seen facets of Arizona that I never suspected before. This visit has been most enlightening."

"Oh, really? Because of your picture taking? I was most impressed with the quality of the photographs you sent with your letter."

"People live in quite primitive conditions on any frontier—Arizona is no exception. Did you know that some people actually sleep under porches on occasion?"

"Why no. I never heard that."

Lance choked on a mouthful of wine. Samantha turned solicitously and patted him on the back.

"Oh, but they do," Angie continued. "If you don't mind the smell of onions, or sand in your clothes…"

Kincaid flashed her a look and raised his glass to salute her. Seated to Kincaid's right, Samantha frowned from him to Angie. Somewhere between the *trout au bleu* and the boneless royal squab, while Stapleton and the banker seated next to Samantha monopolized the conversation with speculation about the stock market, Samantha's long black hair became tangled in a brooch pinned high on the shoulder of her gown.

"Lance?"

Kincaid turned toward Samantha and draped an arm over her chair to catch her whispered words.

Kincaid's clean profile obscured half of Samantha's lovely face. She smiled at something Kincaid said—some gravelly comment for her ears alone. Then Samantha turned her head slightly and kissed his cheek. His broad hand, draped on the back of Samantha's chair, casually brushed her slim white shoulders.

Angie's stomach clenched like a fist. Nothing she had endured in Durango matched this for sheer misery.

Kincaid glanced up, caught Angie's look and held it.

The blood rushed into Angie's head and pounded there. Kincaid's eyes darkened.

"Lance, my brooch?"

Lance turned back to his task, and a fresh storm raged in Angie's breast. "I declare," Angie said, dropping deliberately into the dialect. "That has to be the prettiest little trifle I've seen in a coon's age."

"Why, thank you," Samantha said.

Involuntarily, Lance's body reacted to Angie Logan's teasing comment. He visualized the slenderness of a downy limb and felt the heat of her ardent tongue.

Lance's hand dropped away from the brooch.

Angie smiled sweetly into Kincaid's frustrated eyes. "I do believe I could a untangled that little ol' mess by now," she said to Kincaid. Then to Samantha, "You really should stay in Arizona until you've experienced one of our desert storms. They're really quite powerful. People absolutely forget themselves in a storm."

Stapleton leaned forward and whispered something in Angie's ear—she would never know what—and she let out a husky laugh, pretending to be engrossed with John.

Thus encouraged, John Stapleton gave Angie his undivided attention. Lance freed the brooch and busied himself with emptying the wineglass that a crew of waiters seemed determined to keep full. Poor, splotchy Mr. Filbert came back to Stapleton, twisting his handkerchief in his hands. He whispered into John's ear; John sighed and begged to be excused.

Angie nodded, grateful. Her nerves jangled from so much tension. If the evening continued in this fashion, she would collapse before she saw the governor. If she could sit quietly for a few moments with no distractions perhaps she could get control of her unruly flesh. If Kincaid would disappear or stop his body's maddened signaling to hers…

Angie felt hopelessly and intensely attuned to him. She felt his every move reverberating inside her, as if some deep well of knowledge within her received and decoded signals from his lean, hard muscled body. Moments ago she had been famished. Now her stomach felt aglow and useless, like the rest of her.

"Angie." Lance leaned forward, commanding her attention with his piercing eyes.

"Yes?" Her heart leapt once and raced sickeningly.

"I tried to find you to say good-bye before I left, but I couldn't. I didn't expect to be leaving. I had to bring Winchester back here."

"You don't have to apologize. You were free to leave Durango anytime you liked."

"I know that, dammit," Lance said, his voice gruff. "I just want you to know that I didn't intend to leave without saying good-bye."

Looking at his empty wineglass, Angie shook her head. "Would you like my wine? I'm sure I won't drink it."

"Forget my wine. Did you hear what I said?" He reminded her of that first day in Durango, when he had scared the men who tried to start a fight after the barn burned. He had been louder and more profane than rioters. Now he was angrier than he had any right to be.

"I heard you the first three times," Angie said, her voice sweetly instructive.

John Stapleton sat down beside Angie. "Governor Frémont is still not here. If he doesn't show up soon, Mr. Filbert is going to need to change his trousers."

Kincaid leaned back and pulsated in stony silence. A pain started to swell in the back of Angie's head. When Kincaid pulsed, her head pulsed. She felt dazed by the beat of his blood. The thought of the extremely proper Filbert having an accident in his trousers caused Angie to giggle. This was too much to bear in silence. Once started, she giggled until she felt weak. She blamed the tension. Anything would have made her hysterical. People looked at her. Kincaid looked mad as hell. Samantha glanced quizzically from Lance to Angie.

Stapleton flushed with pleasure that he had had such an effect on her. Angie knew she was leading Stapleton on. It didn't matter. She would deal with the consequences later, just so she did not have to sit across from Kincaid, thinking about his marrying Samantha while he mouthed polite words of apology to her for not caring enough even to say good-bye to her.

After the meal's last course, Stapleton introduced the after-dinner speaker, a portly senator with a sickly pallor. The senator droned on and on. Stapleton leaned close to Angie. "I told him he has to talk until the governor arrives. Maybe I had better rescind that piece of bad judgment before we all die of boredom."

"A shame," Angie whispered. "He's just getting warmed up."

"That caps it." John stood up and walked over to where Filbert was becoming progressively more agitated and whispered into his ear, then stepped close to the podium. "Thank you, Senator." Loud applause accompanied the senator all the way back to his seat. Filbert presented the governor's plaque to Stapleton. John made a short speech apologizing for the governor's unexpected delay due to important territorial business and accepted the award on his behalf.

The crowd applauded, exclaimed in disappointment at not seeing the governor, then began to disperse.

Gil Lee sighed. Lance Kincaid handled himself so well, his manners so negligently correct, his control so complete, his hands so steady, only Gil knew Lance was drunk. Some intoxicated men had a tendency to become sloppy, others meticulous. Kincaid's drinking didn't appear to affect his intelligence or his ability to function. But once drunk, he was vulnerable, capable of making a mistake, and Gil was not certain whether that fact would serve or condemn Angie's cause.

The crowd milled toward the door. John Stapleton remained seated next to Angie. Kincaid and Samantha and Gil also remained seated. Samantha continued talking to Gil, while Lance stared morosely into his wineglass.

Stapleton leaned close to Angie. "Governor Frémont will be in Prescott tomorrow for a banquet. So that you don't miss this opportunity, I'll take you there in my own coach. You won't be inconvenienced too much. You and I can discuss the pardon for Tan Lin on the way there."

A wave of revulsion started in Lance's toes and swept upward, engulfing him. Lance set his wineglass down.

"That's very kind of you, Mr. Stapleton," Angie said softly, "but we have to be back in Durango tomorrow."

Though disappointed, John focused on the problem at hand. "Then I'll take all the particulars tonight after we get rid of this crowd, and I'll speak on your behalf to the governor when I see him, if that is agreeable to you."

Angie looked at Gil. Gil remained inscrutable. She turned back to John and said, "I guess we have no choice."

Surprising himself, Lance stood up. "I just came back from Durango, John. I have information that the governor will find crucial in making his decision."

Lance turned and helped Sam to her feet. "Gil can take you back to your hotel room, Samantha. I'll be up a little later to say good night."

Gil politely held out his arm to Samantha. Kincaid had to be drunk to ignore the look in Samantha Regier's eyes as she turned away. Gil felt Sam's anguish and was grateful he hadn't caused it. He quickly escorted Sam out of the room.

Angie didn't know what to think. Stapleton flashed a warning at Kincaid but said nothing. Angie's heart gave a small lurch. She didn't know whether to be grateful for or resentful of Kincaid's offer to help Tan Lin.

As the crowd continued to thin out, John led Angie and Lance into a smaller chamber next to the ballroom.

"Now," John said after they were seated around a small circular table. "Tell me about this pardon you want."

Angie told Tan Lin's story clearly and concisely. John interrupted twice to ask questions. He glanced at Lance from time to time, and Lance nodded, verifying the truth of Angie's statements. She showed him pictures of Tan Lin behind bars. He looked so thin, pitiful, and resigned that Stapleton shook his head. "This is incredible."

"Do you think the governor will grant a pardon for Tan Lin?" Angie asked.

Stapleton grinned. "I've been in politics too long to answer a direct question with a direct answer. I will relay exactly what you have told me, Miss Logan. The governor is a reasonable man. I can see no reason to keep an eight-year-old boy in Yuma Prison." He lifted the photographs. "The entire episode boggles my mind. Cadwallader must have been pi—upset about something. Since his resignation, we're having a devil of a time finding a replacement."

"Cadwallader resigned!" Angie glanced at Kincaid. A small smile twitched the corners of his mouth. He probably assumed that Cadwallader's bout of illness in Durango had precipitated his resignation.

John stood up and held out his hand to Lance. "Thanks, old man. Glad you stayed. I'll take care of Miss Logan from here on out."

"I promised Gil I would see Miss Logan back to her hotel room," Lance said, surprising them both.

"That won't be necessary," Angie said, her voice tight.

"I'll be glad to cover for you, old man," John said.

"I have a matter I need to discuss with Miss Logan. I wouldn't dream of leaving a beautiful woman alone with you, John." Lance took Angie's arm above the elbow and steered her forcefully away from the thunderstruck young man.

"What on earth are you doing?" Angie whispered.

"Saving you from a fate worse than death, I suspect. John Stapleton is a notorious rake and a womanizer."

Kincaid's warm fingers bit into Angie's arm, hurting her. "And you are not? Oh! Will you turn me loose?"

"No."

"You have no right—"

"I owe you an explanation, and I'm damn well going to give it to you!"

In the lobby Angie faced him angrily. "Then give it and be gone!"

"Are you so eager to be seduced by Stapleton that you can't wait until tomorrow night? Make him wait…" Lance took her by the arm and led her outside. A young black man saw Kincaid and brought his matched set of chestnuts and surrey to the front of the hotel.

Lance thanked him and slipped a coin from his pocket into the youth's hand.

"What are you doing? My room is in the hotel you just dragged me out of."

"We are going to discuss this now, Angie."

"Gil is expecting me."

"He'll keep."

"I have had a long day."

"This won't take long."

"We have nothing to discuss," Angie said.

Lance lifted her into the buggy. "A ride will do you good. Smooth the rough edges off your temper."

Angie waited in grim silence while Kincaid gathered up the ribbons and started the team.

A few lone horsemen and a couple of buggies moved through the main street. "Beautiful night," he said, glancing up at the sky.

"I'll take your word for it."

Angie looked straight ahead. Her profile was as clean and pure as a crystal medallion, her tone chilled with silvery precision. Lance had the wild impulse to reach over and slip his hand into the bodice of her gown. He wanted to feel her hard little nipples, to remind her that she had lain naked in his arms and had given every indication of liking it. He wanted to remind her of the times when she had allowed him to feed on her open mouth and of the way she quivered when he touched her just so. He was in a wild state of exasperation from too many unfulfilled yearnings.

"Where are you taking me?"

Lance hadn't thought beyond getting her into the buggy. "Where would you like to go?"

"Back to my hotel."

"As soon as I have my say."

He didn't know where he was taking her until he was there, and by then it was too late.

"Why are you stopping here?" she demanded.

"This is where I live."

CHAPTER TWENTY-TWO

The two-story house shone pale and luminous in the moonlight. One of those solid, sturdy houses with a wide, proper eastern veranda spanning its front.

"Does Samantha live here with you?"

"She does not." His gravelly voice sounded vaguely stunned; its rich tones disturbed every fiber of Angie's being so deeply that she shivered. Why had she come here?

"How thoughtful you are of Samantha's reputation," Angie murmured.

Kincaid tied the reins to the brake handle, jumped down, and held up his hands to her. It was madness to willingly slip into Kincaid's arms. The sheerest insanity, but the mind that had been grinding out suitable responses all evening refused to think of any way to avoid his outstretched arms.

His hands were warm and strong. His touch jangled her entire nervous system, and he seemed to have no desire to release her once her feet were on the ground.

"Why won't you let me explain?" he asked.

Kincaid was too close to her. The huskiness of his lean, raspy tenor invaded her and plundered whatever resistance she still had left. The inviolate, manly quality about him, the gruffness and testy humor he used to armor himself, even the dark, magnetic comprehension between them were all apparent to her now.

"On the contrary. You explained any number of times," she said, her own voice strangely breathless—afflicted, no doubt, by the throbbing tension in him. "I'm certain I have memorized your explanation. Winchester had to be brought to Phoenix…You had no time…Was there more?"

He turned her roughly. His steely fingers bit into her waist; he fairly propelled her across the lawn and up to his front door. Too impatient to look for his key, he banged on the door with the side of his fist.

A short, wiry Oriental with an alarmed look on his face opened it cautiously. He had thick black hair that looked trimmed under a bowl, tortoiseshell spectacles that gave him an owllike appearance, and a smile of relief that snapped into place as soon as he recognized it was Kincaid who shoved Angie past him with a low-voiced request. "Would you put the team away, Yoshio?"

"Yes, Kincaid-san." Yoshio hurried down the porch steps.

Once inside, Kincaid became more responsible and remembered his duties as host. "Would you like something to drink? Tea? Wine?"

"At least here you will not have to worry about running out," Angie said grimly.

Lance steered Angie into a room decorated and furnished as a library. He deposited her in the center, stalked to a buffet, and fiddled with bottles. Groping toward the appearance of normalcy, Angie walked slowly around the large study, touching objects here and there, too dazed to wonder about the man who had chosen them: a small black polished box inlaid with milk-white jade, a cloisonné bowl on a lizard's skin, a little mud god with a painted face, books in leather and gold—all dusted and well-handled—and on one wall an oil painting of a windswept sea with flying scud and waves whipped white. She almost felt the sea spray on her face.

Angie turned to face him. Lance stiffened. He lifted his chin and looked at her from beneath hooded lids, his eyes the color of a clear lake on a sunny day. He took a deep breath and shoved his hands into his pants pockets, as if willing his taut body to relax. Angie twisted the gold chain on her reticule, overwhelmed by the giddiness that ached in the back of her head.

How long were they suspended there, gazing at each other? Lance turned back to the buffet and picked up two glasses. Still watching her, he walked slowly across the room. Was this the way an outlaw felt when *hombre de verdad* stalked him in the middle of some dusty street? Like a sacrifice?

He held one glass out to her. Angie's hands trembled behind her back. She shook her head.

"Take it," he said. "Yoshio usually holds the woman down while I rip her clothes off, but he's outside right now. You'll have time to enjoy your drink."

"This doesn't make sense."

"Why change now?" he asked grimly.

"You've had enough wine."

"I thought you were trying to give me some of yours."

Exasperated, Angie took the glass, praying that he didn't notice her shaking hand. Quickly she sipped from it, set it on the bookcase next to her, and clasped her hands behind her back. "Would you please hurry. I'm tired. I've had a very long day. I neither want nor need an apology."

"You keep saying that, but you treat me like a leper."

To hell with you, Lance Kincaid. It didn't matter to her that she had no right to be angry. It didn't matter that he left her to marry another woman, and she was so furious with him that he would be lucky to escape with his worthless life.

Kincaid's lids lowered, and he looked away, his eyes bleak, and she knew. He was as miserable as she, but it was still over. There was nothing she could do to change anything. He was engaged to marry Samantha. A pain started in her stomach.

"You have a charming home. Is this where you and Samantha will live?"

"Don't you want to know why I brought you here?"

"Did Samantha furnish your house?"

"I furnished it myself. Don't you want to *know?*"

"You have excellent taste. This room suits you far too well."

"*Angie*..." His raspy voice grated with emotion.

Angie stopped. The tone and timbre of it moved into her very marrow, worked its strange alchemy there. She felt dazed.

"I left Durango without saying good-bye because I'm a coward. I didn't want to hurt you, but I can see that I did anyway. I feel like hell."

"Thank you for the apology," she said sweetly and insincerely. Her voice was clear and pleasant and anonymous, and it refused to produce that throaty, sensual tone he had heard on other occasions.

Frustrated, Lance put his glass down and grabbed her by her tawny arms; he shook her with restrained violence. "You don't give a damn for my explanations, do you?"

"Show me the value, and I would be happy to cherish them. I have a saying: I don't listen to excuses because I don't like red."

"At least it makes sense."

"When you don't give a woman what she wants, nothing matters except what you didn't give."

Lance flinched. She was too honest. A flame started in his bowels. His only chance was not to remain silent. He couldn't give her what she wanted, and he couldn't let her go. After an evening of watching her flirt with John Stapleton, he shouldn't have touched her, but he pulled her toward him. Now it was too late.

Angie closed her eyes. All her resolutions about how she would play the role of platonic friend—sophisticated and aloof—tapered to a quivering point and dissolved from her memory. He kissed her, and she lost all track of time, other people, and reasons. The next thing she remembered was Kincaid holding her close, whispering her name.

She tasted the salt of her own tears, felt his warm breath on her cheek, and relaxed against him; her body accepted his touch as the desert sand accepts water.

The throbbing heat of his body created a hungry urgency in her. Something unexpected passed between them. An unspoken understanding. It stirred within her, creating an almost tangible jolt between them. Instinctively she tried to pull away from him.

"Don't," he whispered.

She felt helpless against him, scalded by the heat and weight of him pressed against her belly. He groaned and lowered his head to brush burning lips against her throat. His hand cupped her needy, tingling breast.

One languorous stretching movement and her entire body flamed up. One hand slid up to tangle in her hair, to free those curls she had worked so hard to arrange, then slid warmly, slowly, down her spine, to press her close to him. His tongue plundered her mouth, summoning her desire, calling it home.

Her mouth was open and seeking, open and demanding, open and taking. His lips slid away, and, as if from a great distance, she felt him murmur against her cheek. His words were husky and demanding. They soaked into her dazed brain—unintelligible except for the message of need they conveyed. He groaned incantations—words of love and despair. She lifted her mouth willingly, and his hard, suddenly angry lips ground hurtfully into hers. And it was not enough.

Lance swung her up into his arms and carried her up the stairs to his bedroom.

Angie didn't know he undressed her. She was aware of his hands touching here, burning there, until thankfully they freed her of her stifling garments, freed her to press aching, feverish flesh against the warm, damp length of him.

She was alone with him. Woman to his man. Caught up in the mysterious merging of love. She was one long pain that only the feel of him could assuage.

His hands responded to her need for him by pressing her thighs apart, and entering her quickly, taking her with that intent, masterful movement through a doorway that disappeared behind her. Then it was only him, controlling her and the rising tide of her feelings, slowly and endlessly until her body crested in crashing peaks that seemed to go on and on like waves exploding inside her.

Little sounds of stillness gave way to small realities. The ticking of a clock on the dresser, the chiming of a clock downstairs, Westminster chimes. Did all grandfather clocks sound the same? Singing night birds chirped in the trees near his window. Outside, the wind would be chill. A tree limb rustled against the side of the house. Had Gil waited?

Lance opened his eyes and closed them. His ragged, quickened breathing had begun to return to normal. He hadn't meant to make love to her, but he couldn't remember why.

Then Johnny Winchester's face flashed before his eyes. *You're just like her, aren't you?* Another flash of memory, of Angie reaching out to touch Atillo's lips knifed through him. And just as it had happened at Gil's, rage swelled in him. Lance felt smothered suddenly and filled with rage. He started off the bed. Angie's warm hands reached out to him. He looked down at her, but her image was suddenly intertwined with those other hurtful images.

Angie didn't know what caused Lance to turn from lover to stranger.

The second time he took her, even the explosion of feeling that seized and held her in the grip of passion couldn't shield her from the knowledge that this time he pleasured himself with no regard for her.

She lay beside him afterward, spent and shaking. Still driven by things too raw to remember, she clung to him, pliant and submissive in the tangle of arms and legs. She was not yet humiliated by the memory of his warm hand against her convulsing belly, or by knowing he knew that even when he took her in the most selfish way that she still loved him, responded only to him.

When Lance realized what he had done, he turned away. His chest ached. A throbbing pain started in his temple. *Don't think about the way her eyes look when she's hurt. No point in thinking about that. Kiss her good-bye, keeping it light, teasing. You'll be doing her a favor—in the long run. She'll get over it. And so will you.*

It was too late to do anything else. Lance trusted his instincts in this. He looked at her tawny gold skin, felt its silk beneath his hands, and knew despair. Losing her was going to hurt him. But not as much now as later.

He didn't want to hurt her, but he had never been easy on himself.

So he could not start now.

Angie turned over at his urging. He pinned her down and stroked her belly and thighs, but the look in his eyes had changed.

"Listen, buttercup, you're damned good in bed. They don't come any better, but I'm really not interested in playing second fiddle to your camera or your young lovers. There are some folks who'd say I might just as well keep making the same mistakes all the time as new ones, but I don't see it that way. Oh, I probably wouldn't mind for a while. Us Texas boys always did have a weakness for big-eyed skinny girls. Guess that's durned obvious, though, isn't it?"

Thankfully Angie blotted out Kincaid's speech from that point on, barely remembering the rough way he'd taken her.

Later, at her hotel, Angie started to speak. She opened her mouth, but words would not come. In the gaslit corridor in front of her room his face looked pale. She reached out her hand to him, to steady herself. As if his body were reacting to another injury, a burst of light flashed deep inside his pupils. This time it happened only once, but she understood. She turned and stepped into her room. Tears cascaded down her face.

Had she only imagined that one moment when he looked at her and seemed to be crying inside? Or the other when they were still in bed, still panting from all the things he'd done to her, all the things she had enjoyed in spite of herself. His voice had turned suddenly harsh, oddly ragged, and his lean fingers hurt her as he forced her chin up. *Go back to Durango. You may think you care for me now, but you won't for long. I can't fall in love. There's something wrong with me. Go back where you'll be safe.*

Quiet words, killing words, like daggers, stabbing ruthlessly into her already bleeding heart. She sagged on the bed, holding her stomach, fighting off the dreadful feeling of nausea that threatened to engulf her.

Lance stepped into his entry hall and knew instantly Samantha waited for him. Her perfume preceded her voice. "Are you trying to convince me what a bastard you are?"

Lance sighed and looked at her, his own tiredness weighing on him like lead. "I didn't know there was any doubt about that."

Samantha's lips trembled. Her eyes filled with star shimmer. "Are you trying to make me stop loving you?" she whispered.

Lance's tiredness was a heavy weight in his chest. He didn't have th[e] necessary cruelty to tell Sam the truth. He was just trying to survive. H[e] hadn't remembered until this moment that she even existed.

Instead, he asked, "Did it work?"

Samantha looked at Lance for a long time. She sighed tiredly and shook her head. "No."

For her he forced himself to grin. "Trick you every time, don't I?" he asked, struggling for just the right tone, the teasing tone a triumphant kid would use on a vanquished foe.

Unable to help herself, she smiled shakily. Lance held out his arms, and she came slowly, hesitantly, into them. He held her trembling body close. Sam needed him. It was time to settle down. That would make someone happy, even if it was only his mother.

Gil watched Angie covertly during the trip back to Durango. He wanted to ask her what had happened, but they were surrounded by other passengers.

At the second stop to change horses, the station house served lunch. Angie ate almost nothing and walked away from the table, too agitated to stay amid the other travelers. Gil followed her from the rustic building.

"Are you unwell?" he asked softly.

"No."

"A malaise of the spirit?"

"A definite malaise." Angie stared out across the endless expanse of cactus, mesquite, and sand. Nothing appeared to move, though she knew from past experience that the landscape teemed with small insect and animal life.

"Is there anything I can do?"

Frowning, Angie shook her head. "Is there something wrong with me? Something about me that would keep a man from…falling in"—she shrugged—"love with me."

Gil shook his head. He had suppressed a great many things after watching Lance Kincaid with Angie Logan during the dinner. "Perhaps I should tell you a story about Lance."

A dreadful apprehension awakened in Angie's belly, but she stayed still. "Please do."

"By telling you this, Angie, I am abandoning any hope of friendship with Lance."

Angie turned away. "Then you should not tell me."

"Do you care for him?"

A hard lump came up into Angie's throat. Last night she had hated him, but the anger had died before morning, leaving her with only the sick feeling in her stomach. And a question: Was Lance Kincaid being deliberately cruel to her for some obscure purpose of his own, or was he merely being himself?

"In truth, there's probably nothing to jeopardize. Lance Kincaid hates me so thoroughly now that there is almost nothing I could do to soften his hatred. Listen carefully, Angie. There is little time. When he was fifteen, Lance Kincaid fell in love. The woman was twenty-five. He loved her with blind devotion and with no hope that she would ever see him as anything but a child. On his seventeenth birthday, more as a lark than anything else, the woman, Lucinda, invited him into her apartment for a drink. She was beautiful, exciting, and sophisticated. She had divorced her rich husband because he drank to excess, and, when drunk, he beat her. She had been given a comfortable pension by her father, but she was not acceptable to the Kincaid family. They opposed Lance's infatuation with her quite strongly. I sidetracked myself. Where was I? Oh, yes. On his birthday she invited him into her apartment. They drank champagne to celebrate his acceptance at Harvard Law. They became slightly tipsy, and somehow Lance found himself in her bed. They became lovers."

"The following fall Lucinda followed Lance to Cambridge. He could see no other woman. Lucinda was the beginning and the end of love for him. He loved her with complete innocence and total passion. The passion of an eighteen-year-old man who had coveted one woman since fifteen."

"Lance and I graduated from Harvard in 1874. Within three months of graduation Lucinda was murdered. In a rage Lance tracked down two of the three sailors responsible and killed them with his bare hands."

Angie reacted with horror. Gil let her recover and continued. "I must explain. I worked my way through Harvard Law teaching the martial arts to rich young Americans. Lance was my most apt student. He was a crack shot with rifle or hand pistol. One on one, he has the courage and the fearlessness of the warrior. He was the only Caucasian I knew or taught who developed *ting jing*, the ability to hear with one's skin…but I distract myself. My purpose in telling you this is that I wanted you to know that he was thoroughly capable of killing them in any number of ways. He killed them in rage, with his bare hands, and he suffered horribly for it."

Looking out across the heat-seared desert, Gil continued. "Months went by, and Lance did not seem to recover from his tragic loss. He served as an attorney for Kincaid Enterprises. He worked long hours, with desperate determination, as if the work were his punishment; perhaps in truth it was. He grew to hate it. Finally, in desperation, his parents sent him to Paris."

"He had an unfortunate relationship with a young woman there that caused him to banish himself into the most fatal occupation possible for a man. An Arizona ranger does not last long, but he lived a charmed life until shortly after he met you. A lesson could have been learned in that seeming coincidence, but Lance refused to learn it the same way he has refused to learn other lessons. Watching him last night, I realized that Lance loves you, and he does not know it. He hurts you to keep himself from being hurt."

Angie turned away, not daring to breathe. "So, is there a happy ending to your story?"

"That is entirely up to you. Lance is not capable of providing it. You must demand it. You must break through his resistance. Only then can you hope to restore him to himself. Only then will he be capable of loving you."

"His will seems impenetrable."

"He is very strong. A lesser man would have chosen death. He chose to challenge death, but he is too strong to willingly give in to it. It must take him by force. It must be so overpowering that it will be obvious to all that he resisted with typical Kincaid stubbornness."

"That does not explain why he resists falling in love."

"He is confused. He thinks that falling in love caused his pain."

"Didn't it?"

"Losing Lucinda to tragedy hurt him terribly. Love was seven years of intense feeling—joy, exultation, ecstasy. Lance Kincaid loves deeply and passionately. This ability is a two-edged sword, allowing him to hurt himself and others."

"Love," he continued softly, "is an affirmation of the will to live. When he decides to live, he will be capable of loving again."

"You speak of Lance as your friend. And yet…he—"

Gil shuddered. "That is true."

"May I ask what happened?"

"I made a mistake. It caused him great pain at a very bad time."

Angie bowed her head. Whatever had happened had not been resolved. She touched Gil's arm. "I'm sorry. I didn't mean to pry."

In Durango Gil escorted Angie to her house. At the door she stopped. "Thank you for being my friend, Gil. I can't tell you how much that means to me."

Angie Logan walked inside, and Gil turned away. He had given her hope where none might exist. Lance Kincaid had been a loner so long that it had become a part of him. Lance had never been able to change a path he set himself.

Gil dragged in an exhausted breath. There was a good chance he himself had just done Angie Logan a terrible disservice.

Late Monday morning Angie finished her printing job and gathered her fliers in her arms. Virgil had said yesterday that the prison wagon would probably get to Durango about five or six.

She wiped the ink off her hands, locked the door of *The Tea Time News*, and walked quickly to the livery stable. She paid Atillo to distribute fliers on the west side of town. She took the east side.

Each time she saw a woman on the street, she stopped her and gave her a flier. Angie stopped at each house and talked to each woman who would listen to her. She left a flier whether anyone was home or not.

By two o'clock people talked of nothing else. Some men were openly outraged that Angie lobbied their womenfolk. They viewed it as a highly political and totally unacceptable act. Few confronted her face-to-face, but, according to Charlie Miller, who heard just about everything worth hearing, condemning rumors spilled through town like a passel of tumbleweeds.

Sarah read the flier slowly:

> My name is Tan Lin. I am eight years old and Chinese. My honorable father has supported our family since I was born. Always, he has worked very hard. We were poor, but we always had food until both his legs were broken by an angry white man. He did nothing to deserve this. He only delivered towels to the saloon. My honorable mother lost her job because the association pressured employers not to hire Chinese.
>
> I went to the store for rice, but the man at the store would not give us credit because my honorable mother had no job. As I walked back to our house, a chicken stepped into my path. He seemed to be the answer to my prayers. I tried to capture him, but he squawked very loud and escaped.
>
> I was captured and taken to jail. At my trial the owner of the chicken, Ezra Wilkins, said that the chicken died

because of me.

I was tried and sentenced to five years in Yuma Prison. I know I have done wrong, and I am willing to go to prison, but my countrymen are prepared to fight. The guards will resist. Others may come to the aid of the guards. Men may die. I carry much guilt for what I have caused. I do not know how to stop what has already begun. I ask nothing for myself, but please stop them before others die.

Tan Lin

P. S. Please come to a meeting at 3:00 this afternoon at *The Tea Time News* office to hear how you can help stop your men and others from killing one another.

Sarah gave the flier back to Angie. "It's wonderful. How could any woman ignore a plea like that from a little boy?"

Angie lifted her chin. "I guess we'll find out."

Three o'clock came and went. Angie and Sarah waited at *The Tea Time News*, praying that women would come. Three-fifteen arrived, and only five women stood uncomfortably in the office.

Angie decided to proceed as if hundreds of women had responded. She led the reluctant five upstairs into her studio. She had borrowed chairs for a crowd. They sat down and Angie stepped to the front of the room.

"I want to thank each of you for coming here today. Your presence sets you apart from the majority of the women in Durango."

The women looked at one another uncomfortably, and Angie could have bitten her tongue. She hurried on before they could get up and leave.

"I guess you're—"

"What do you think we can do about any of this?" Ellen Smith interrupted. She was a brown-faced woman with prematurely graying hair pulled back in a severe bun.

"That's a very good question. I have appealed to Governor Frémont on Tan Lin's behalf. I went to Phoenix to talk with him, but he wasn't there. My appeal will be delivered instead by Secretary of State John Stapleton as soon as possible. Unfortunately I have not heard from him. The prison wagon is coming this afternoon, so we can't wait any longer."

"As you all know, the Chinese have been in Durango for many years now. They are as engrossed in the struggle for survival as any of us on this desert, and yet they alone are blamed for unemployment, stealing, and many other things they have no control over and no more propensity for than we do."

"At the national level, unscrupulous politicians use the Chinese as scapegoats in their attempt to cover their own inadequacies. It's a smoke screen of lies. They wave the Burlingame Treaty like a red flag before a bull, hoping we'll believe that unemployment, corruption in government, poverty, inadequate education facilities, unsafe trains, and high prices are caused by the Chinese. And like parrots, newspapers like *The Gazette* repeat the rhetoric, and people who don't know any better think they must be right."

"These are lies! How could fewer than forty thousand Chinese wreak such havoc on a nation that numbers more than fifty million?"

"The Chinese are not trying to tell us how to run our town. They're not trying to take over our schools and churches. I talked to Tan Lin's mother. You know what she told me? That Tan Lin went to school one day a week last year. You know why? Because he shared a pair of shoes with four other boys. On Tuesday it was Tan Lin's turn to wear the shoes to school. The teacher made a rule that no one could enter his school without shoes. The Chinese didn't do that. We didn't do that. One man did it. The Chinese suffered in silence. I asked the teacher why he made such a rule. You know what he said? Because it kept the riffraff out."

Angie paused and looked at each woman. "I wrote the flier and asked you here because there is going to be a terrible confrontation today. When the prison wagon comes at five or six, the Chinese are going to try to stop them from taking the boy. If we do not intervene, many will die."

Angie looked from face to face. "A terrible injustice is about to be perpetrated on a little boy, on a whole town. You've each had children. You know what an eight-year-old is like. He is like your Daniel, Ellen. He cries when he's scared. He gets dirty. He runs in the house. He talks too loud. He has an endless appetite."

"I'm asking you to follow me to the jail, to stand with me against the officials who would take a small boy to a prison facility where grown men die of the heat and the terrible conditions."

The five women looked from Angie to Sarah and then at one another.

"I wouldn't be willing to do that," Ellen Smith said, crossing her stout arms across her chest. She was a plain woman with one boy and three girls of her own. She worked hard without complaint and minded her own business.

"He's only eight years old," Angie said incredulously. "He's a *baby*. He doesn't belong in prison. No eight-year-old *child* belongs in prison."

"He should have thought of that before he stole."

Before Ellen Smith spoke, there had been hope. Now every face hardened against her except Sarah's. Hope died, and Angie filled with bitterness and frustration. She had failed.

"Thank you for coming," she said quietly. "I'll do what I can by myself."

She turned away. Bitter tears tried to flush hotly into her eyes, but she fought them back. The sound she had geared herself to listen for—the rumble and creak of the prison wagon—penetrated her pain. She rushed to the window and groaned. The rusty caged prison wagon lumbered in from the south, followed by a long, hovering red dust cloud.

The Tea Time News sat across the street from the jail at an angle. Warned no doubt by the lookout Gil had posted far outside of town, Gil and the Chinese huddled in the alley behind the jail. Angie searched for Gil, found him, and her throat constricted. He would be at the forefront. One of the first to die.

Women joined Angie at the window. The wagon passed the school and headed north on Rio Street. Two burly guards sat atop the wagon, one in front and one in back, both carrying shotguns and wearing two guns around their hips. Inside the prison wagon a bald, bearded man slept on his back. His head rolled from side to side as the wagon rattled down the street. Beside him a dirty man with a bright red scar across one cheek sat propped against the back bars. Children ran out of the schoolhouse and chased the wagon. The prisoner snarled at them, and they picked up rocks and threw them at him. He spat at them and cursed them. They squealed in glee and darted away.

The driver, C. J. Farlow, slowed the wagon in front of a saloon south of the jail. His throat fairly ached for a cold beer. Dust had caked so thick in his mouth, a sharecropper could grow peanuts there. Just thinking about a cold beer, his mouth started to water.

"There'll be time for that after we get our prisoner. No sense taking any chances," Simmons, the senior guard, yelled at him. Farlow cursed and slapped the horses, urging them on toward the jail. He pulled the team up in front of the jail and closed his eyes so he wouldn't have to stare ahead of him at the Baquero, filled to the brim with cold beer just waiting to be claimed.

Hidden in the alley beside the jail, barely out of sight of the driver, the Chinese lifted their rakes, shovels, rocks, clubs, knives, and guns into position. They waited until the two guards stepped into the jail. Then, noiselessly, they slipped into place between the wagon and the jail.

Gil stepped into a position of leadership and waited to confront the guards when they tried to return to their wagon.

Eyes closed, humming a tune to himself, Farlow spat a brown stream of tobacco onto what should have been the street. It landed on the back of one of the Chinese standing behind Gil. Muttering quietly in Chinese, the man shook his fist at the driver. Farlow opened his eyes. A hundred blue-coated Chinese surrounded his wagon.

"Holy shit!" he bellowed, reaching for the shotgun in the sheath next to his calf.

Gil raised the barrel of his gun and pointed it at Farlow's forehead. "Please do not make me kill you," Gil said, his voice so low that Farlow barely heard it.

"Good idee," Farlow whispered, nodding, raising his hands above his head. Gil took the shotgun.

All silent, the Chinese waited for the guards inside the jail to notice them. Seeing the way the men were armed, Gil figured that he and his compatriots had about one minute of life left to them. As soon as the guards turned and saw them, they would open fire. Except the Chinese had the ultimate advantage. No two men could kill a hundred of them. That was the advantage the Chinese always had. Sheer numbers. If the townsmen didn't rush to the aid of the prison guards, a possibility existed that they might get the boy out of town alive. Toward that end, horses purchased that morning waited beside the jail for Tan Lin and his armed escort. All the guns owned by the Chinese would go with them.

If he were not so superstitious, Gil would have prayed to the Tao of the ancient kings. But Tao did not like bargains offered from a position of weakness.

Inside the jail, Hank Simmons and Eddie Lathrop stopped in front of the marshal's desk. Del Ramo stood up.

"Got a warrant here for your prisoner, Tan Lin," Simmons said, handing the warrant to Ramo.

Ramo took it and laid it on his desk. A movement on the street caught his eye. He stopped. "You feel real strong about this, do you?"

Simmons shrugged. "It's a job."

"Ever thought about retiring?" Ramo asked, looking past them to the crowd slipping into place between the guards and their wagon.

"Hell. Ever damned day!" Lathrop snorted.

"If'n you're planning on actually doing it someday, maybe you might want to leave without the boy."

"What?" Simmons growled.

"Talk sense, Marshal," Lathrop cautioned.

"Turn around real slow and take a look at your wagon."

Simmons and Lathrop spun around. "What the hell?"

"I think they came for the boy."

"Jesus Christ! All the goddamned chinks in the world!"

Lathrop looked at Simmons. "Now what the hell do we do?"

Simmons shrugged. His position was clear. If he lost a prisoner, he served the man's time. He cocked the shotgun in his hand. "We go out there and kill about a hundred chinks." He turned back to Ramo. "Get the boy out of that goddamned cell."

"I'm on your side, boys. Just thought you might like a choice." Ramo took the key and unlocked Tan Lin's cell. He led the boy out. Men crowded in the other cells watched in silence.

Simmons and Lathrop looked at Tan Lin and then at each other. The boy's thinness and smallness astounded them.

Laramee stood up and walked to the front of his cell. "Jesus! Next you're gonna be carting away titty babies."

Lathrop looked at Simmons.

Laramee shouted his disgust at the jailers. "You see that scrawny little kid? Hope ta hell he don't hurt y'all none."

"Shut up, Logan," Ramo warned, leading Tan Lin to the two guards. With his left hand Simmons grabbed the boy by the back of his shirt, put his shotgun to his head, and gave him a shove. "Walk real slow. Don't make any funny moves, and you might survive this."

"Won't do a damned bit of good," Laramee yelled after them. "He'll slip right between them bars."

"Like hell he will. I'll cuff him around both legs if I have to."

Gil saw, but there was no way he could move quickly enough to stop them. The shotgun was already aimed at Tan Lin's temple.

A murmur went up from the Chinese. Seeing everything from atop the wagon, the driver shook his head. "Holy shit." He wiped his forehead with his sleeve, leaned forward, and spat down between the horses. He wished to hell he had gotten drunk last night and they'd left Tucson without him.

Simmons pushed Tan Lin along in front of him until he reached the open door to the jail. He was hot and tired and in no mood to mess with a bunch of damned chinks.

"Get back!" Simmons yelled at the Chinese. "Do these slit-eyed pigtails speak English?" he yelled at Ramo. "Get back or I kill the boy!"

The Chinese looked from the guards to Gil.

"Let the boy go and live," Gil countered, his low voice soothing and well-modulated.

"Dead or alive, the boy goes with me."

Neither backed down. Gil wouldn't, and Simmons couldn't. Terrified, Tan Lin trembled between them.

From the upstairs window of *The Tea Time News*, women peered down on the impasse. It had all happened so fast.

Ellen Smith could not tear her horrified gaze away from Tan Lin's trembling form. He could not be as old as her own Adam. She had read the flier and suspected it was only a ploy to engage her sympathy for a dirty criminal. Because of that, she had been alternately unmoved, vaguely uncomfortable, and irritated by Angie's impassioned plea, but Tan Lin in person looked so painfully thin, so doomed and pathetic in his baggy blue tunic and pants, her heart went out to him. She looked down at the flier, then at the scrawny boy. Now it was possible to believe he had stolen a chicken so his family would have something to eat. Ezra Wilkins always had been a damned skinflint. He probably ate that chicken himself.

"Men can be as stupid as warts on a boar," Ellen Smith said, shaking her head.

"What?" Angie asked, turning. Ellen's face flushed with heat and color.

"They could go have a nice cold beer in any one of the saloons, come back an hour later, and be in a better mood. I think Angie is right. We'd better do something." Shaking her copy of the flier, Ellen walked to the stairs. She waved Angie in front of her.

Her heart lifted by the first ray of hope, Angie moved into position, not daring to look back. She rushed down the stairs and out the front door. Footsteps clattered behind her, but she didn't know if the women were with her or just going down onto the street to watch.

• • •

Among the Chinese on the street a murmur went up. From behind, soft hands pushed them aside. A path opened to allow the women to walk through. Women who hadn't been upstairs, who had watched from stores and shops, spilled out onto the street and through the opening, filling the space between the two warring factions. Angie stopped next to Tan Lin. She took Simmons's shotgun barrel and pushed it down.

"We'll keep the boy in jail here," she said to the guard.

"What the holy hell is going on here?" Simmons sputtered.

Angie ignored him, knelt down beside Tan Lin, and took him in her arms. Trembling wildly, the boy clung to her with surprising strength. Ellen and her mother stopped beside Simmons. The elder woman was stout and buxom with a voice accustomed to issuing orders and having them obeyed. "You take your wagon back where it came from. We'll take care of the boy. And you tell your dang blasted governor that we'll have his job for this. We don't need outsiders coming in and taking our children off to some filthy prison."

A man who had stepped out of the Baquero recognized his wife among the women and lifted his fist. "And you better not smart-talk our women either, or you won't make it out of town." A chorus of shouts rose on the air. Men, who only days ago had marched against the Chinese, now sided with their womenfolk.

Simmons looked at Lathrop. He had been willing to take on a few scraggly celestials, but he wasn't willing to take on an entire town. "Let's get the hell out of here."

Lathrop nodded. "Suits me fine."

The crowd melted back, and the two guards climbed up onto the wagon. Farlow yelled, "Giddyup! I told you we shoulda had them beers first. Giddyup, you bastards!" The wagon lurched forward. The bald man's head wobbled from side to side without waking him.

Dust lifted on the hot air. A cheer rose up from Chinese and whites alike. Then, self-conscious, as if their feelings of benevolence were too fragile, they fell silent. Embarrassed, Chinese and Caucasians began to disperse.

Gil stepped forward. "Glad you came," he said to Angie. She stood up, still holding Tan Lin's hand.

"You have a way with understatement."

Gil chuckled. "I suppose I do."

"Do you think they'll come back?"

Gil shaded his eyes against the hot sun. "They have no choice. Next time they will be better prepared."

That night Angie had nothing to stand between herself and a whole slew of memories she didn't know how to handle. Tan Lin was safe temporarily. Lily was alive and well and no longer engaged to Tu's son. Gil had been spared. Atillo no longer smoked opium. Laramee chafed at his incarceration, but, at least for the moment, he was safe.

A fragile, new awareness of mutual dependency existed between the Chinese and Caucasians. Except for herself and Johnny Winchester, who awaited trial in Phoenix, things were getting back to normal.

Restless, Angie climbed out of bed and walked to the window. Off in the distance, singsong girls wailed to the screech of a Chinese violin. Angie imagined Chinese men watching them, sipping their warm wine, sucking on their sweet opium pipes, or eating their rice, fried chicken livers, and salted fish.

A crescent moon rode low in the eastern sky. The same moon that had been in place when she rode out to the Chinese quarter that night with Lance...

A sick feeling gripped her stomach. Lance would marry Samantha, and they would have beautiful, well-mannered children...valedictorians... sturdy and precocious...dark-haired, blue-eyed, polite, benevolent children who would look attainable but would not be.

Her throat ached suddenly. She would never see him again. Never hear his husky, whiskey-tinged voice...never touch him or kiss him.

Her throat flushed with heat. Her eyes burned. She sagged onto the bed. But she didn't cry, she lay in a paralysis of self-pity.

Minutes or hours later she woke up slowly, hesitantly. Fully clothed, she huddled on top of the covers in a dark room. Chilled.

She slipped off the bed and changed into her nightgown, ripped the covers back and slipped underneath them, hating the sudden coldness of the sheets.

She should have married James and stayed in South Hadley among those sane, genteel people who would never hurt her in this way.

To James she had been a crystal goblet of a woman, a delicate, costly, fragile heirloom to be treasured in its original condition.

To Lance she was a body to be seared with passion, a body to accommodate him in any way he chose—an unprotesting, selfish, eager body, pulsing with desire, filled with the same hunger she had seen in his hot, discerning gaze, felt in the heat of his throbbing body—a hunger that would never be satisfied between them.

It was better this way. What they felt for each other could not be contained within the proper bounds of marriage—it was too wild and sweet and profane. Their passion could not be tamed or domesticated for any useful purpose.

In silent agony Sarah watched her friend. Angie worked from morning to night, barely stopping to eat. She worked endlessly. Sarah sighed. Emotionally Angie was as strong as piano wire, but Sarah still ached for her, still wondered what had happened between Angie and Kincaid in Phoenix.

CHAPTER TWENTY-THREE

Tuesday night, June 8, 1880

Samantha stepped out of the buggy and paid the young man from the livery stable who had been kind enough to drive her here in the dead of night. She walked around back and woke Yoshio. He staggered to the back door and let her in.

In the hall in front of Lance's open door she stopped. She shouldn't be so needy. Lance's diamond sparkled on her finger. But he had made no effort to kiss her or make love to her. He'd made no effort to do anything at all except satisfy her need to feel his commitment, and somehow that had not satisfied it at all. She had the ring. She had set the date, but she felt empty. She needed him.

Samantha stepped noiselessly into Lance's room. At his open window, thin curtains waved out into the middle of the room. The room sweltered in spite of the breeze. She could never adjust to this heat. In New York, even in the summer, the nights were bearable. Here, almost nothing seemed bearable. She didn't know how Lance stood it. He had always been hot-blooded.

Silently she moved to the side of his bed. In the dim light from the moon that shone on his floor, she could make out his outline on the bed. She slipped out of her gown and undergarments and scooted under the covers with him. She could barely breathe. His broad back faced her. She scooted across the bed and fitted herself into the crook of his body spoon-fashion. His deep, even breathing continued without a break. She gave him time to adjust to her presence next to him and reached around his belly and found his manhood. She had been raised in a family of boys, so she'd seen men's privates before, only never Lance's. He'd been old enough to guard his privacy. Stuart, her own age, had been less inhibited.

Just as she had suspected, Lance's was wonderful to hold. It was smooth and heavy; her hand felt good around it. He'd be mad as blazes if he knew, and if she were successful, he would know, but she hoped he wouldn't wake up yet.

She pressed her cheek against his back. His heart beat a little faster now. His member swelled in her hand. She was so scared she was almost nauseated. She'd never done anything like this in her life. Well, almost anything. Once she and Stuart had played touch-and-tickle, but they had been five years old.

Lance started to turn over. She scooted out of his way as quickly as she could. Her heart pounded so hard she feared it might burst. She had been in love with Lance so long and he had given her so little encouragement that she was almost crazy with longing. It was his fault.

Lance blinked and tried to put it all together at once.

"What the hell?"

"I was hoping you would stay asleep."

"Until what point?"

"Until I figured out some way to get you to make love to me."

"You know many men who can do that in their sleep?"

Samantha grinned in spite of herself. "I don't know."

"Are you trying to get me in trouble?"

"No. I want you to make love to me. Is that so much to ask? Men have gone to great lengths to get me to make love to them, and I didn't."

"That is obvious."

"How?" She felt insulted.

"If you had, you'd know men don't do it in their sleep."

"Well, I thought you would at least…"

"Dammit, Sam."

"Well, it isn't fair. I want you. I love you. Why won't you make love to me?"

"Because the time isn't right." Lance turned onto his back. *And because you're not Angie Logan.* The thought seeped out of some traitorous wrinkle in his brain before he could stop it. He'd nearly made love to Samantha then, just to prove to himself that he could, but even with that impetus, he couldn't. His need to purge Angie from his life did not entitle him to misuse Samantha.

Lance stood up and walked across the room to where he had left his pants.

"Where are you going?"

"To pee," he lied. "You sure you don't want to come watch?"

Samantha giggled. "You can't make me mad, you know."

"I know." He started to say, *that's why I love you*, but he didn't.

Lance forced Samantha to put her clothes on, bundled her onto the back of his horse, and took her back to her hotel. He rode back to the house. In the moonlight the house looked exactly as it had the night be brought Angie there; he stopped. A longing came out of nowhere. A longing to feel Angie's butter-soft skin under his hands. It was so powerful his throat ached. The ache spread downward until his body was aflame. Lance dismounted and sat down on the front porch.

A vision of Angie Logan filled his mind—her great, dark eyes glowing with warmth and passion. Lance closed his eyes. Need raged in him. He put his head in his hands. Angie Logan had almost ruined him. It was a good thing he was finished with her for good.

A messenger came the next morning at eight o'clock with a note from McNamara to Kincaid. Still bleary-eyed from lack of sleep, Lance unfolded it and read:

> Kincaid:
>
> Are you alive? If so, get your butt in here. If not, consider yourself fired. Frémont wants full report immediately.
>
> McNamara

Lance crumpled the cryptic note.

"What the hell did you do in Duarte?" McNamara demanded, tossing a copy of the Durango *Gazette* on the desk in front of Kincaid. Lance sat facing his captain, his long legs crossed at the ankles in front of him.

Coiling forward, he picked up the paper, scanned the editorial circled in red, and sat back, folding his arms over his chest. "Durango. Looks like I walked into a nest of anti-Frémontites. I was in Durango, sir."

"Do you know where I got this? I got it from Frémont. Not hearing a goddamned word from you for over a month, how the hell do you think I felt when he asked me what we were doing in Duarte? I thought I told you to stay the hell out of Mexico."

"Durango, sir."

"Is that in Arizona?"

"Yes, sir."

McNamara had more to say, but Lance barely listened. Retired U.S. Army, from upstate New York, McNamara talked fast, with a hard edge to every word.

Samantha had awakened something in him that she should have left sleeping. Lust reminded him of Angie. There was no reason why it should. *She was not the most beautiful woman he had ever seen—no need for him to be sick about leaving her. And there was something in her emphatic brown eyes—a certain confidence and female ruthlessness—that terrified him. She was too aware, too instantly responsive. He hated the way her flashing dark eyes could turn soft—like the underbelly of a three-day-old kitten. She hated him now. It was better that way.*

Red-faced, McNamara paused for breath.

"You want my resignation, sir?"

"Hell no! And don't get smart with me. You know damned good and well I don't want your resignation. If I didn't fire your ass for leading twenty goddamned civilians into Mexico, I'm damned sure not smart enough to fire you for pissing off Frémont." He leaned back and surveyed his young lieutenant.

"What the hell's the matter with you?"

"Nothing, sir."

McNamara shook his head. "I love those southern boys. No matter what you say to them, they'll *sir* you. Don't lie to me, Kincaid. Why the hell don't you have a southern accent?"

Without waiting for an answer, he continued. "Any day you sit here and take a goddamned tongue-lashing without so much as batting an eye, something's wrong."

She's probably got her head under that canvas, getting her hair all frayed out so it looks like a halo around her face. Her face would be composed, her mind filled with a thousand things she planned to do next.

"Frémont got another telegram from that Logan bastard."

Lance straightened in his chair. He hadn't bothered to tell McNamara that that *Logan bastard* was a woman. "He did?"

"It's refreshing to finally have your attention, Lieutenant Kincaid. Logan's asking for a pardon for a damned thieving chink. He's gone so far as to threaten the governor. Can't be all bad, I reckon," he said. McNamara had nothing against Frémont personally. The two of them just always seemed to come out on opposite sides.

He waved the telegram. "A damned three-page telegram. I never heard of anything like it. At least the bastard has money. Or he did. Telegraph office's probably got it now." McNamara sighed heavily.

"What kind of threat?" he asked, starting to grin.

"Something about selling the story about the kid to some syndicated columnist, muckraker, or some damned thing."

Angie'd do it too. "The Chinese boy you're talking about, sir, is eight years old. Sentenced to five years in Yuma Prison for *trying* to steal a chicken that was probably eaten by its owner."

"Seems fair to me," McNamara said, mostly to irritate Kincaid, who had a tendency to take things too seriously. McNamara resented the Chinese. They were nothing but trouble to him. Their foreign ways made them walking, talking targets for every kind of abuse. They were a law enforcement problem plain and simple. He resented the work they caused. He had children of his own, grown now, but he remembered how helpless eight-year-olds could be. "So, did you save the kid?"

"No, sir."

Irritated, McNamara sighed. "Well, you're going to get another chance. I have a warrant here for a man by the name of Del Ramo who's supposed to be in Duarte. Wasn't he the marshal there? Anyway, there's a warrant on the books for a killing in Flagstaff. They'll be coming for him as soon as you let me know he's in custody. You might as well get packed. If you're feeling up to it."

He wasn't, but the thought of going back filled him with unexpected energy. He and Ramo had a pact. One of them would leave Durango in a pine box. He didn't particularly care which one.

Lance stood. "Yes, sir. I'll catch the next stage."

They shook hands. McNamara watched his usually testy young lieutenant walk to the door. "I want you back here as soon as you finish there."

Something flickered in Kincaid's eyes. "Yes, sir."

Kincaid closed the door quietly. McNamara sat down at his desk, frowning. *Something is wrong. Didn't get a rise out that boy once. Not once. Made at least three outrageous demands, and nothing.* He had rangers who could talk till they didn't have enough breath left to bend a smoke ring. Kincaid wasn't one of them, but usually he said something memorable to let McNamara know how he felt about the situation.

McNamara picked up the Durango *Gazette*, wondering what had happened in that goddamned town to gut one of his best rangers. *Why do I have the feeling that he won't be coming back?* Was Ramo so fast with a gun that he could beat Kincaid? Or was Kincaid so off his feed that he was a sitting duck for a man like Ramo?

A vague sense of loss pervaded McNamara. *Damn! I've sent men to their deaths before.*

Now, why the hell did I think that?

• • •

A buxom older woman, outrageous in a wasp-waisted gown and enormous puffed sleeves, had Samantha cornered in the lobby of the hotel. Samantha saw Lance and excused herself gently. Cool and lovely in a simple peacock-green gown, Samantha stopped smiling at the look in his eyes. "What's wrong?"

"Nothing. I need to talk to you," Lance said.

"We can leave the door of my room open…"

Once inside her room, Lance fidgeted. His usually purposeful hands picked at the coverlet and the sash hanging beside the door. His eyes avoided hers.

"How did it go with McNamara?" she asked, her heart beginning to ache. Something was wrong. His eyes—the fires inside them were banked.

"Like a visit home. Father could take lessons from him. I have to leave. McNamara ordered me back to Durango to arrest Ramo."

Samantha paled. "He won't come peaceably."

"Probably not."

"How long will you be gone?"

"As long as it takes."

"I want to go with you."

"No." His lips cemented into a look that would brook no argument.

"Then I'll stay here until you come back."

"I don't want you staying here alone. It's not safe."

"I don't get everything I want. Neither do you."

"Did it ever occur to you that I might want to marry a woman who knows how to take orders?"

Samantha laughed. "Not once. But I do remember that you are the one man in the world who has always told me that I can occupy any station in life that my conscience dictates."

Lance sighed. "I always lose these fights."

"Not always," she said archly. "I changed my mind. I'll wait here." Actually she did not relish the thought of bouncing around in a hard-bottomed Butterfield stagecoach for eight or ten hours, and she could see he meant it.

Lance had already missed the one stage going the direction he wanted to go that day, so he had to wait until Thursday. He stayed busy the rest of the day. Samantha barely saw him. Early Thursday morning, filled with anxiety, she walked with Lance to the stage. "I guess this is good-bye," she said softly.

Lance pulled her close and kissed her, and the magic of him—

his sturdy chest, his singular masculine fragrance, his animal vitality—worked together to push her to forgetfulness, but this time his kiss did not soothe her.

Samantha moped around the hotel all morning, knowing in her heart that in spite of all his protestations about leaving Angie Logan in Durango and its being final that somehow she had lost him. She went to her room and read until her eyes closed, too miserable to do otherwise.

Then Samantha woke up. What had awakened her? The sun streamed in the window of her hotel room. She felt inexplicably anxious.

Something was wrong. She sat up in bed and squinted into the sunny room, searching for whatever it was that had awakened her. The town was noisy. Lance would be halfway to Durango by now. Unless something had gone wrong.

Then it came to her. He hadn't said it. She'd said good-bye…*I guess this is good-bye*, and he hadn't responded. Every Kincaid knew the ritual. They used it like a good luck omen. *No good-byes, no good deaths.*

Lance wouldn't be coming back. Ramo was going to kill him.

She leapt off the bed. She could rent a carriage or a buggy or even a buckboard. Somehow she would get to Durango before Lance faced Ramo.

Thursday morning Ramo sought out Cort Armstrong at the Baquero. He found Cort in his office, sitting alone, nursing a beer.

"What the hell's wrong now?" Cort demanded, not bothering to hide his anger about Ramo's handling of the "chinklet." Yesterday Tan Lin had almost unified the town at a time when unity would keep Cort from getting what he wanted. 'Course a dim minion like Ramo wouldn't have been able to predict what had happened yesterday. Almost no one could have. *Or* that Kincaid would arrest Johnny Winchester and put him out of commission. That had put things into a cocked hat.

Ramo sat down heavily.

"With Cadwallader resigned, no judge is gonna come until the governor appoints another one. That could take a long time."

"So?"

"Set lower fines so's the bastards can afford to get out. As a matter of fact, I could appoint you interim police court judge right now. I think I could get the selectmen to ratify that little action. Set lower fines, empty the jail, and then…" Cort leaned back and contemplated the wall for a moment. Getting a new district judge could take weeks. Those damned chinks could blow hell out of his plans in two weeks. One wrong word… an idea formed. Why not? He sat forward. "What would happen if a mob tried to lynch Logan?"

"His big-mouthed sister would probably pull half the town down around our necks," Ramo groused.

"What if it came up real sudden like? And she didn't have time to do anything except just run down to the jail to try to stop them?"

Ramo sat down again. Cort was thinking out loud now.

"And she had a gun in her hand? And you accidentally shot her, not knowing it was a woman and all? And then Logan died in the mixup? Then both of them are gone. Then when my friend at the county seat just happens to divide that parcel of land on the books so I can buy it cheap, we're home free, aren't we? The Logan ranch goes to any heirs that might be around. That strip I want slips off the side, so to speak, and we get what we need. Can you think of anyone outside of Angie and her brother who knows where their property line is?"

Ramo scowled. "Hell, *nobody* knows anything about property lines for sure. 'Course Logan's been mouthing it around that the chinks are on his property."

Cort reached out and patted him on the back. "You finally said something that makes sense. Nobody knows anything for sure about property lines. There might be hope for you yet."

Actually, Cort thought, they were lucky Angie *had* come home. With her out of the way, no one would ever know what had happened. Whereas the other way, they would have always had to worry that someday she'd come home and discover what they'd done. Then she'd have opened up all the circumstances around her brother's death and no telling what would have come out.

This would be much cleaner.

"So when we gonna do this?"

"What's wrong with tonight? You think you can set low enough fines to clean that jail out?"

"Yeah."

"Good. I'll run this past the rest of the selectmen today just so we don't embarrass ourselves. Get the boys ready."

"At least we don't have to hope the next judge don't get the shits,"

Ramo chuckled.

Cort started to reply. He blinked. Now he knew what had been bothering him about that. "Damn that Sarah," he blurted out.

"What?"

"I'll wager she did it."

"Did what?"

"Put something in Cadwallader's coffee. Or had Ben do it. He'd do it for her."

"Great kid you got there."

"Wait till I get my hands on her."

Grinning, Ramo sauntered out.

Sarah walked into the house. Cort sat in his favorite chair, not reading the paper like he usually did, but facing the front door purposefully. Sarah stopped; a sense of alarm filled her at the look on his face.

"Took you long enough to get here."

"What's wrong?" she asked, her throat dry.

"Someone sweet-talked Ben into putting something in Cadwallader's coffee," he said, his right hand balling into a fist. "You're the only one who could get Ben to do a thing like that…with a good reason to want him to."

Sarah swallowed. What was he going to do to her?

Cort slammed his fist onto the arm of the chair. Sarah flinched. A small tic started in her left eye. Her almond-shaped green eyes remained wide and expressionless, reminding him of one of those damned forest creatures. Unexpectedly he had that cursed feeling again, as if it were him standing there in front of his miserly stepfather, having to account for eating an extra hunk of bread.

Irritated, he slammed his fist on the wooden table next to the chair, sending her knickknacks flying off the table, knocking the doily askew. He smashed those damned gimcracks she collected into a dozen pieces. Sarah flinched again, more noticeably this time.

"Did you do it?" he demanded.

As if he had smashed something else, Sarah cringed inside. If she were Angie, she'd have the courage to stand up to Cort. Her knees felt about to buckle. Her heart pounded so hard she could barely breathe.

"Yes."

Both Cort's fists clenched. His face contorted with fury. Sarah expected him to rise out of the chair and throttle her, but he only sagged backward, shaking his head. "Dammit, girl, *what* are you trying to do to me?"

"I was…trying to…save Laramee's life," she whispered, her heart drumming hard in her trembling chest.

"And what about mine?" Cort yelled, furious again.

Shaking so hard she could barely stand, Sarah shook her head. "You're in no danger."

"That's not for you to say!" he yelled. "You're supposed to mind your own damned business!"

"Laramee *is* my business," she said, her voice breaking with the fear that almost made her speechless. She had almost said, *I love him…*

"Bullshit! Laramee Logan is nothing to you. He may want to get into your drawers, but he wouldn't give you the time of day, girl! Don't you see that? He's a Logan! When he's ready to marry, he'll find him a fine lady like his sister! He won't marry a goddamned bartender's daughter!"

"He proposed to me!" she cried.

"To get you in the sack! Nothing more! You're not married to him. He didn't speak to me! He didn't show up here with a ring in a velvet box, girl! Anything short of that is just to get into your drawers!"

Cort stopped, looked at her through narrowed eyes. "Did he make it?"

Sarah's gaze wavered, dropped.

"God damn that bastard. I'll kill him!"

"No!"

"I'll be damned if that bastard is going to screw my daughter and live to tell about it."

Sarah blinked. She imagined Laramee in the cell, helpless and trapped, and Cort storming into the jail and shooting him. The room went dark with fear. "He didn't!" she screamed.

Cort stood up and strode across the room. "Liar!"

"What do you care?"

"You're my daughter! You belong to me, dammit!"

Sarah barely heard him. Her only thought was to distract Cort so he wouldn't kill Laramee. Surprising herself, she shouted, "I don't belong to you. I'm not a slave."

"No. You're a goddamned bartender's daughter, and don't you forget it. Men like Logan don't marry the likes of you! We're trash! Poor white trash who just happen to have money. We don't fool them! Men like me don't get invited to the Ellingtons'! Girls like you don't marry

Laramee Logan!"

Cort shook his head. He wished to hell she wouldn't look like he gutted her when he yelled at her. What the hell.

"You can't talk to me like I'm something you bought for the saloon!" she screamed. Strangely, with her newfound determination, her fear had peeled away, leaving only anger.

"You can't go around ruining my plans," he yelled in her face.

"Plans that include killing an innocent man!"

"I'm going to be somebody in this town, dammit! When I walk by, they're going to stop and tip their goddamned hats! And then you'll be somebody! Somebody even Logan would be willing to marry! Proud to marry, by God!"

"You *are* somebody," Sarah said more softly. "Everyone knows how powerful you are in this town."

Shamed that he had blurted that out about wanting to be somebody, Cort walked toward the kitchen.

"What could you possibly gain by killing Laramee?" Sarah asked, following her father.

"None of your goddamned business," he threatened.

Sarah moved in front of him so he had to look at her. "So now that I know, you'll have to kill me too."

"You'd rat on your old man?" he asked.

"Yes. I'll tell everything. Unless you promise me you will give up your plan, whatever it is."

Filled with consternation, Cort glared at his daughter.

"Promise me."

"I should have left you at that damned orphanage."

In the Baquero Ramo found Smalley talking to a friend. "I need your help a minute." They stepped outside and walked out aways so no one could hear them. "I want you to let Angie Logan overhear you planning a lynch mob to take her brother."

"What?"

"You heard me."

"We going to lynch him?"

"No, we're not. We're going to let her get herself shot trying to save him. Now, you got that?"

"How do I let her overhear me?"

"She's always at that damned newspaper office. Stop by there tonight and let her hear you talking to someone."

"Why me? What if she tells everybody in the world?"

"She ain't going to tell anybody. She'll be dead."

Sarah walked back to *The Tea Time News* and stayed there the rest of the day. She didn't dare go home. Cort might reconsider and decide to actually kill her. She didn't really think he would do anything to Laramee now, after what had happened, but she wasn't one hundred percent certain.

Angie had been out all morning taking pictures. She had developed them this afternoon. While they dried, she wrote stories for the children's section and set type. She should have been tired, but Sarah guessed that Angie was so numbed by her misery within that she didn't notice.

Just like she didn't notice that Sarah was terrified. Sarah was glad for that because she didn't want to betray her own father. Cort wouldn't really hurt anyone. She knew him that well. She was glad for Angie's distraction. Glad her friend couldn't see anything wrong outside her own body.

Angie straightened the office and prepared to lock up. She swept the floor with such concentrated attention that Sarah was vaguely appalled. Angie looked too thin, too big-eyed and bruised inside. Guilt caused Sarah to walk over and hug Angie.

Sarah held Angie's stiff, unyielding body away from her and tried to make Angie meet her gaze. Angie's dark, usually flashing eyes were quiet—nothing moved in them.

"He'll come back," Sarah whispered.

"Who? Oh." Angie shrugged. She had spent too many nights thinking about Lance Kincaid. Her reflections on the lawman had resulted in a striking realization: anytime she weakened she could seek Lance Kincaid out, and he would be as lost as she, as trapped in the temporary mindless joy of their doomed love as she. In some fashion this knowledge had given her the strength to go on. It was not as good as being loved, but as long as she kept busy she didn't have to think about Lance. Fortunately she had so many things to do that she would always be busy. This misery would pass. She trusted that absolutely.

"What do you think we could do to bring him back here?"

Angie shrugged again. "I don't want to discuss it."

"To tell you that he—"

"Please!" In spite of everything, a thin streamer of hope waved like a banner within. She could not bear having Sarah hold it up to the light of day and her own ridicule.

Defeated, Sarah sighed. "I'm sorry. I didn't mean—"

Angie turned away. "I just need to be left alone so I can get something done...Since that isn't possible here..." Angie looked around the office without seeing it. "I think I'll go home now. I have to fix Laramee some dinner. I promised him something special for tonight. I'll see you tomorrow."

Sarah watched Angie leave, and her heart ached. Angie was suffering and there was nothing she could do about it. Cort was mad as hell at her, and she didn't know what to do about that either.

Sarah worked until it started to get dark, then stood up to light the oil lamp beside her desk. She stopped herself. No need to light it. She would just make a target of herself in case Cort decided to kill her. Sarah stopped herself. That was nonsense. Cort would never shoot her. He might threaten to shoot her, but he never would.

Sarah sighed. She was too tired to stand up and light the lamp now. She sat at her desk and watched the light fade and the lamps flicker off in store after store. Men locked up and went home. Others rode into town to drink and visit.

Finally she realized that she had to go home. She was tired, and she sure couldn't sleep at her desk. If she didn't come home, Cort would have another reason to be mad at her.

She put on her hat, locked the door, and stepped out of *The Tea Time News*. Tired, she glanced up and down the sidewalk. The street was dark.

Two men stopped a few yards away from her. Sarah glanced at them to see if she knew them, but it was too dark. They didn't appear to have seen her anyway.

"That gal keeps a twenty-four-hour guard on that brother of hers," one gruff voice complained. "If this is gonna work, we'll have to silence them bastards first."

Sarah's heart flipped over in her chest. Were they talking about Laramee?

"I'll take care of that. You just see to it that when I give the signal you have the mob ready to slip in there and take Logan," the other man said. He slapped his thigh with his hat, and the two of them walked past her without seeing her.

• • •

Gil waited until he could speak to Third Uncle alone. He sat down beside where his foster father read his newspaper and waited a full minute before he spoke.

"I wish to discuss Lily."

Third Uncle lowered his newspaper. "Please continue."

Gil felt the urge to stammer and restrained himself. He was not a child. "I would like to ask your permission to marry Lily."

Third Uncle blinked. Somehow he had thought Gil had already done that. "Can you provide for her?"

"Yes, sir. I have been offered a partnership in a law firm in San Francisco. I will make a substantial salary from the beginning. It will be better later if I work hard."

"Why so far away?"

"That is the second thing I would like to discuss with you. Lily would like her family to accompany us to San Francisco."

Third Uncle nodded. He felt suddenly lighter, less burdened. "There is something I must tell you," Third Uncle said softly to Son of Autumn. "It is very important."

Sarah's head spun with confusion. Should she find Angie? What was most important? Was there time to save Laramee's life?

The guards from the Logan ranch were the most important link. They were Laramee's main hope. Sarah turned and ran toward the jail.

She stopped beside the shadowy figure who watched the jail from the alleyway next to the jail building.

"Excuse me," Sarah said. The man turned and looked down at Sarah. He was not one of the Logan riders posted there by Angie. Sarah had never seen this man before.

"I'm sorry. I thought you were…excuse me…" Sarah turned and veered away, but not fast enough to keep the man from realizing that she knew he did not belong there.

"Hey! Wait!" he yelled, and ran after her.

Sarah ran as fast as she could toward the Baquero. Two men loitered in front of the billiard parlor. They looked at each other, but neither moved to intervene. Closely pursued, Sarah threw herself through the swinging doors and raced to the bar. Music and laughter stopped.

"Where's Cort?" she demanded. Men and women—their expressions of merriment and rowdy boisterousness slowly fading—gaped at Sarah.

"Went home about an hour ago," Jack said, frowning, looking from Sarah to the man who had stopped at the door.

"Will you help me get to Angie's house?" Sarah asked, glancing from Jack's careful face to the man outside.

Sarah's heart almost stopped at the thought that flipped into her mind. Jack might be working with the men trying to hang Laramee. Jack worked for her father. She searched the surrounding men's faces, praying for one man she trusted.

These men were strangers. Jack seemed her only hope. "Will you walk with me? I stayed later than I should have." Surely Jack would not harm her or allow anyone else to. She had known him since she was fifteen.

"Let me get someone to watch the bar…"

"Could we go out the back way?"

Jack glanced quickly at the man waiting on the sidewalk. Sarah covered her face with her shaking hands, and Jack nodded to the man and signaled with his thumb at the back door. Grinning, the man nodded and headed for the back alley.

In the jail, Ramo stretched and stood up. Angie Logan had delivered Laramee's dinner, visited too damned long, and finally left. Her two guards had been disposed of within minutes after her departure. He had followed Cort's suggestions and cleaned out the jail except for Logan and the kid. He'd be sleeping by the time Smalley and his friends made their move.

"If anyone wants me, I'll be out of town for a few hours. I got to serve a warrant over in Silver Bell," Ramo yelled at no one in particular.

"You don't mind," Laramee drawled, "I'll just wait here."

Ramo chuckled. "You just do that," he said, in a good mood for the first time in weeks. "Try to be here when I get back."

Footsteps on the front porch brought Angie's head up.

"Angie! Angie! Let me in!" Sarah screamed.

Angie opened the door to find Sarah sagged against the door-jamb, her gown torn, her hair disheveled. Angie pulled her inside and slammed the door. "What on earth…?"

"They're going to take Laramee from the jail! The guards you put there are gone! Ramo is gone!" She sagged against Angie, her strength gone. "If Jack hadn't tricked the man into waiting for me in the alley, then slipped me out of the front door, I'd be dead."

Angie ran into her bedroom and pulled her drawer open. She found her gun under her chemises and loaded it. Angie turned with the gun in her hand just as Sarah walked into the bedroom.

Sarah drew back. Revulsion contorted her face. She gagged and doubled over.

"There's no time," Angie cried, tugging at Sarah. "We must hurry!"

Smalley watched the street from the deep shadows of the building across from the jail. Except for the saloons and their music and noise, the town was quiet. Ramo had cooked up a phony warrant to serve out of town so he wouldn't be suspect. Only the two phony guards loitered near the jail. They'd made a mistake letting Sarah overhear them instead of Angie, but he couldn't think what difference that would make. She'd grabbed Jack and made him take her to Angie's, so everything would still be okay. They'd made her think they tried to stop her from getting there, so even she didn't know what was really going on. Angie would come tearing over here any second now. All he had to do was wait.

Logan would be dead the way he should have been a week ago, and he himself would be that much closer to having what he wanted. Cort Armstrong would be pleased as punch when he found out that he, Neville Smalley, had taken care of all the details. Cort didn't think much of his or Ramo's ideas, but this would show him.

Two women running north toward the jail moved into the cone of light at the corner. Recognizing Angie as one of them, Smalley stepped out of his hiding place.

Gun in hand, grateful he had stayed so close at hand, Smalley ran across the road. He didn't realize he would have to kill Sarah, too, until he was halfway there. But Cort would be better off without Sarah. She had sabotaged the trial. She'd always cramped his style.

Jack Millicent banged on Cort's door. A light burned inside, but Jack didn't really expect him to be there. Cort was almost never home.

The door opened. The lamp inside outlined Cort's heavy frame. Jack sighed with relief. "Thought you ought to know. Sarah came running into the saloon all upset. She said she'd overheard a couple of men planning to take Laramee Logan out and hang him."

"Damn that bitch." Cort grabbed his hat. "Where is she? I'm going to kill her myself."

Sarah saw the man coming toward them, and even though she wasn't carrying the gun, she realized for the first time how difficult it was to decide whether to shoot or to wait. She didn't recognize the man closing on them, but he probably wasn't interested in them, wasn't going to do them any harm. Another part of her was terrified. If they failed, Laramee would hang. With her heart pounding so hard that she could barely breathe, Sarah held out her arms and stopped Angie to drag her back against the wall.

The man angled across the street, and the dim light from the jail illuminated his face. Neville Smalley. Terror rose up in Sarah. Angie lifted the gun. From behind Angie a man stepped out of the alley, hit Angie's arm, and the gun slid across the sidewalk and skidded out of reach.

The man's strong arms encircled the women and dragged them back. "What the hell do we do with them?" Joshua Bell demanded of Smalley.

"Kill 'em!" Smalley whispered.

"Jesus! Women?" Bell whispered.

"They was trying to break Logan out of jail. They almost shot me, a deputy marshal. Don't matter whether they're women or not."

"I ain't going to kill no woman," Bell muttered.

Smalley realized then that he was going to have to kill Joshua too. 'Course, that wouldn't be all bad. With Angie dead, he could say she killed Josh. He cocked his gun and aimed it at Angie.

Cort was badly winded. As he ran past the Baquero, he saw Neville Smalley cross the road toward the jail. In the same breath Cort saw Sarah and Angie. Smalley's gun came up, and Cort realized that the bastard was going to kill both of them. Sarah as well as Angie. At first Cort's brain did not know how to react to that, but something started in his bowels and surged upward.

"No, goddammit!" he roared. "That's my daughter!"

• • •

Sarah struggled free and threw herself between Smalley and Angie. Angie clawed at Sarah, found a hold on her skirt, and tried to pull her aside. Instead, she knocked Sarah into Smalley. His gun discharged and flew out of his hand. Smalley dived for his gun; Sarah threw herself in the direction Angie's gun had gone skidding out of reach.

Smalley staggered and cursed. He leaned down and scooped up his gun. Sarah's hand groped in the dirt and found Angie's gun. Smalley fired. Sarah saw the flash of his gun, but barely felt the fiery, stunning pang as the bullet hit her. The gun bucked in her hand. Angie screamed.

Darkness enveloped Sarah. She stumbled backward off the sidewalk and into the dirt.

Clive ran out of the Baquero, saw Cort, and stopped. Cort grabbed the gun out of Clive's holster and ran forward.

Gun in hand, Sarah lay in the road. In the light from the jail, her blouse was red with blood that pumped from her in a steady stream. Cort turned toward Smalley, lying on the sidewalk.

"*You bastard!*"

Smalley groaned. Cort aimed the gun at Smalley's chest and fired until the hammer clicked on an empty chamber.

CHAPTER TWENTY-FOUR

Thursday Evening, June 10, 1880

Third Uncle finished speaking, and Gil remained seated. His mind would not all at once take in the impact of Third Uncle's words. He knew the seriousness of it. He felt Third Uncle's guilt and pain, but he could not quite believe that so much trouble had been caused so simply.

In deep pain, Third Uncle touched Gil's sleeve.

"Forgive me, Honorable Father," Gil said, shaking off the lethargy. "I will find Miss Logan and tell her what you have told me."

Gil walked to town and then south on Rio Street. A crowd stood around the jail. From the north a stagecoach pulled by eight lathered horses passed Gil and stopped in front of the hotel. Three strangers leapt down, and then Lance Kincaid stepped out. Lance looked south at the crowd clustered around the jail and strode off in that direction. Gil followed.

"Kincaid, wait for me."

Lance stopped, turned, and looked for one split-second as if he would draw his revolver and shoot Gil, but he ignored the hostility. He stopped in front of Kincaid.

"Aren't you pushing your luck?" Lance asked. Anger rushed into him, unbidden and uncontrollable.

"Laramee Logan could not have killed the three brothers," Gil said quietly. "They smothered when the mine shaft they were digging collapsed on them."

Lance forgot his anger for the moment. "Did you just find this out?"

Gil nodded. "Third Uncle kept the mining a secret because he did not want *fan quai* to take the silver he had discovered. He was tired of living in poverty."

• • •

Lance shouldered his way through the crowd around the jail. Dr. Amberg knelt over a body. Lance saw women's shoes; his knees went weak.

Inside the jail Laramee strained at the bars of his cell and yelled at no one in particular. "Let me out of here, goddammit."

Lance stopped beside the sprawled female form, recognized Sarah's pale face, and his heart lurched and began to beat again. Angie knelt beside Sarah, crying quietly.

"She going to be all right?" he asked, looking from Angie to Doc Amberg, who lifted Sarah's arm, his hands covered with blood. He pressed a pad into her armpit.

Amberg glanced up at Kincaid. "Yeah. I can stop the bleeding. The bullet severed one of the veins under her arm. Been bleeding like a stuck pig. Gonna have to sew it up."

"Where's Ramo?" Lance asked.

"Don't know. Smalley's dead," Amberg said. "Reckon you're the ranking lawman in town at the moment. And I'd say you've got a mess to figure out." Amberg stood up. "I need two strong men to carry her. You and you," he yelled, pointing at men from the crowd.

"What the hell is going on here?" Del Ramo growled. He rode his horse almost onto the sidewalk. He'd seen the crowd and Logan in the jail, straining at the bars. Ramo realized their plan had failed. Josh Bell was nowhere to be seen, and sight of that bastard, Kincaid, caused the bile to rise in Ramo's throat. Hatred swelled in him.

Doc Amberg looked at Kincaid, then at Ramo. "Reckon you two lawmen better figure this one out. Just be sure you don't open any more bleeders. I've got my hands full already."

Grumbling, Amberg turned away. "All's I ever wanted was a nice quiet practice: a couple of babies to deliver, a case of croup ever' now and then…"

Ramo stepped down from his saddle. "What happened here? Where's Smalley?"

Amberg grunted. "Dead."

"Who the hell killed him?"

A hush fell over the watching crowd. Cort stepped out of the crowd. "I did."

"You! What?"

"He shot my daughter."

"So?"

"You son of a bitch," Cort growled, looking as if he were going to climb over Sarah and tear into Ramo.

Ramo stepped back. This was getting out of hand. He shouldn't be fighting with Cort. He should be establishing his own innocence. "What the hell happened here?"

Angie stood up. "We came to save Laramee."

"Jailbreak, huh? Reckon I'm gonna have a jail full of Logans."

Hands on hips, Angie yelled at Ramo. "*No!* Protecting *your* prisoner from *your* deputy and *your* friends who tried to hang him."

Ramo sneered. "That's a damned lie. You killed a deputy while trying to break your brother out of jail. And you ain't gonna get away with it!"

"You lie! We overheard you planning it."

"That's another damned lie! I just this minute got back," Ramo yelled, shouting Angie down.

Sarah waved the men away who tried to pick her up. She struggled up onto her right elbow and sat up. "I heard two men planning it. They had to be doing it with your knowledge. You knew Laramee was innocent. You knew, in a fair trial, he'd go free."

"That's hogwash! A damned lie! What the hell would I gain from doing anything of the sort?"

"Silver," Kincaid said firmly. "You and Cort Armstrong found out that Liang's cousins had discovered silver on Logan land near the creek. The three brothers suffocated when the tunnel they dug to mine the silver collapsed on them. No one killed them. The only murder that needed to be solved was who killed Rufe Martin the day of the barn fire. And we already know that was Johnny Winchester."

Ramo paled. He took a step backward. "You're all lying. Even if every damned lie you told was true, I wouldn't gain anything by killing Logan."

"I'd be willing to bet that someone has made an offer for that land lately."

"You're damned right they have!" Laramee yelled. "Cort Armstrong has made me three offers for that strip of land."

A murmur went up from the listening crowd.

"I hope nobody here is real surprised by his saying that. Any man facing the gallows would say that," Ramo sneered. "Lying bastard. Logan killed them chinks hisself for trying to build on his land."

Kincaid turned to Cort. "Did you offer to buy Logan's land along the creek?"

Cort looked at Sarah. "Yeah."

A murmur went up from the crowd. Kincaid looked at the men surrounding the jail. "There's one way to find out if anyone is guilty of murdering the brothers."

"How's that?" Ramo demanded.

"Open the graves. See how they died."

Excited by the prospect of opening graves, the men all talked at once.

"You doubting my word?" Ramo demanded, backing up. He had testified in court that the three were stabbed with Laramee's knife.

A hush fell over the crowd. Kincaid nodded. "I am."

Ramo sneered and spat on the sidewalk. "Don't know what the hell you hope to gain by this."

"A fair shake for Logan," Kincaid said.

At the prospect of a shootout between the two lawmen, a hushed murmur rippled through the crowd. A path opened behind the two.

Sweat popped out on Ramo's forehead. Kincaid might be the faster on the draw. He'd be crazy to die here just to protect Cort Armstrong, who looked like he'd changed sides. Ramo shook his head. "I ain't going to be stampeded so's you can kill me the way you done them others. I ain't done nothing wrong. Even if there was some kind of plot against Logan, I wasn't in on it."

"Either draw or get into that cell next to Logan."

"What?"

"You heard me. Draw or walk into that cell. I have a warrant for your arrest."

"For what?"

"For killing Hank Neufeld in Flagstaff."

"That was self-defense."

"That'll be decided by a judge and jury. Draw or walk," Kincaid ordered.

Ramo expelled an angry breath. "I'll be damned if I'm going to be the only one to take the blame for this. Cort Armstrong planned it every step of the way."

"I didn't plan for you to kill my daughter," Cort interrupted.

"Well, I don't know how the hell she got involved. You should have controlled her."

"You and that asshole deputy of yours should have used some sense."

Ramo flushed with anger. "You son of a bitch." Ramo's hand flashed downward.

In one part of his mind Cort knew Clive's gun, tucked into the top of his pants, was empty, but when Ramo drew, Cort's hand grabbed for the gun anyway. Too late, he tried to abort the motion, but Ramo cleared leather and fired. Cort didn't feel anything, no burning, no tearing of flesh, but he was spun backward faster than his feet could balance him.

Sarah screamed, and Angie moved to put herself between Sarah and the men shooting. Angie wanted to cover her face, but she crouched there and watched in spite of herself.

Once he had started, Ramo could not bring himself to stop. He swung his gun around toward Kincaid.

As Ramo turned, Kincaid drew and fired. Ramo staggered backward, a red spot spreading over his shirt. Lance checked him, then Cort. Ramo was dead.

Amberg turned to Angie. "Can you hold this pad in place so she don't bleed to death?"

Angie nodded, and Amberg stood and walked to Cort's side. Cort was conscious and shot in the hip. Nasty hole, but only a flesh wound. It would be a long night.

To Angie, Kincaid looked pale. He had healed fast, but with the constant demands on him, it was a wonder he could stand at all. He started to turn and walk away.

"What about me?" Laramee yelled.

Kincaid holstered his gun and ran his hand through his hair. "I'll release you tomorrow."

"You know damned good and well I didn't kill them," Laramee yelled, furious at having to spend another night in jail with Sarah out there bleeding to death.

Lance hesitated. He probably could let him out. No one would object, but it wasn't legal. He couldn't let a man out of jail on hearsay evidence without a judge to take the rap for it. "One more day isn't gonna kill you."

Lance walked back outside and singled Gil out from the crowd. Laramee took off his hat and threw it at the floor.

"Gil, can you find the graves of the three brothers?"

"Third Uncle will know."

"It's too dark tonight. We'll meet at seven o'clock tomorrow morning here at the jail. Bring men to dig—"

"And a couple to verify," Amberg said.

"Good idea," Kincaid said. "Who wants to come?"

Twenty men stepped forward.

• • •

Samantha leaned out the window of her hired coach. Scattered lights of a small town blinked on the horizon. That had to be Durango. At the last stop to change horses, the stage hands had told her that the stage Lance was on had left there only minutes before. It had rolled in with a broken brake lever at two-fifteen and they'd had to lay over for repairs.

Samantha pulled out her watch and tried to read it in the dark. No use. She leaned back against the seat. Money was a wonderful thing to have. Five hundred dollars had enabled her to divert the Flagstaff stagecoach to Durango with her as its only passenger. Probably some law prohibited her from bribing drivers, or whips, as they were called, but she didn't care. She would face whatever had to be faced after she saved Lance. He could personally put her under arrest.

The stagecoach rocked to a stop and Samantha leapt down.

"Here, now, let me help you thar."

Samantha barely stopped to thank the driver. She located the hotel and ran toward it. A gaunt, balding man dozed behind the desk. She shook him awake. "I'm looking for Lance Kincaid."

The man blinked, "The ranger?"

"That's right."

"He's probably over at Miss Sarah's."

"You mean Miss Angie's?"

"No, ma'am. Miss Sarah got shot. Pretty sure they took her on home."

"I need someone to take me there."

"Don't have anybody here who could do that this time o' night."

"For fifty dollars."

The man rubbed his eyes and stood up. "Well, I could probably break away for a little while."

A knock sounded at the front door. Angie left Sarah's side and walked to answer it. She opened the door and blinked.

"Is Lance here?" Samantha asked.

"Yes, he is. Won't you come in?" A diamond solitaire sparkled on the ring finger of her left hand.

Angie stepped back. Samantha walked into the parlor and stopped. Lance stepped out of the bedroom.

"What are you doing here?"

Samantha walked across the room to his side. "I couldn't help myself," she whispered. "I thought you were going off to be killed. You didn't *say* it."

"Say what?"

"You k-know…" she stammered with embarrassment. It was too childish to say aloud, in front of someone who hadn't grown up with the silly custom.

Lance realized what she meant and shook his head. "Aren't we ever supposed to grow up?" he chided her.

"I guess not," Sam replied, subdued.

"Come in and meet Sarah."

No matter how hard she tried to control it, Angie's eyes tracked Kincaid's lean form. Samantha looked subdued. Her beautiful face, so vividly colored, was vibrant with life. Angie writhed inside.

Sarah lay in her own bed looking strangely relaxed. Lance, Samantha, Gil, and Angie stood at the foot of the bed. Lance and Gil ignored each other.

Angie shuddered over how close she had come to losing her dearest friend. She could not quite believe the nightmare had ended so abruptly. It had seemed insoluble. She knew absolutely that Liang and Gil spoke the truth.

Samantha spoke to Sarah, her voice lovely and concerned, and Kincaid turned to watch her. Both dark-haired, Lance and Samantha were a handsome couple. Next to his brick-brown skin, Samantha looked exceedingly fair and lovelier than any woman had a right to be.

Lance paid no undue attention to Samantha or Angie, but Angie felt his irresistible nearness. The room throbbed with his smoldering presence. Even when he did not acknowledge her with his eyes, she felt the very air between them charged with emotion.

"I'll be going now," Gil announced.

Samantha walked him to the door. Kincaid held back, unable or unwilling to encourage his ex-friend in any way.

"In the excitement I forgot to ask about Lily," Samantha said softly. "How is she?"

"Fully recovered, thank you. Third Uncle waits to hear how his confession was received. I must leave now."

Samantha went up on tiptoe and kissed Gil's cheek.

"Let us know if we can do anything," Samantha said.

"Thank you," Gil said. "Will you be leaving now?"

"Whenever Lance is ready."

Gil turned to Angie. "It grieves me that your brother was abused in this fashion because of my people."

"Your people did nothing. Ramo, Smalley, and Cort put Laramee in jail."

Gil turned to Lance. "I would like to talk to you tomorrow."

Courtesy kept Lance from speaking his mind. Lance did not want to talk to Gil. Tomorrow or ever. "We'll be at the Orlando."

Gil left, and Angie turned away. It was remarkable how painfully that *we* stabbed into her vitals. *We'll be at the Orlando*...Lance and Samantha. A couple. Engaged. We.

Angie wished *we* would leave. She felt herself dueling with Kincaid—she felt alarmingly aware of his every move, his every word, his every look. Her heart beat much too fast. She felt exhausted from the events of the evening and yet strangely invigorated. Part of her seemed to be grieving; part of her refused to believe he was really lost to her.

Eleven o'clock. The clock on the mantel confirmed that everyone should leave. Holding up extremely well for a man shot in the hip and openly accused of trying to kill an innocent man for personal gain, Cort called out from his bedroom.

"Kincaid, don't take that crap seriously. Even if everything the girls claimed was true, which it ain't, I broke no laws. Ramo tried to implicate me to save his own neck. Hell, nothing even close to that came off—"

Kincaid raised an eyebrow. Two Logan riders standing guard at the jail had massive headaches; men who had replaced them and the man who had grabbed Angie and Sarah were gone. But there might not be anyone left to testify against Cort. And for the moment Lance was a guest in Armstrong's house, and nothing said here tonight would change anything. Accusations against Cort would be investigated and turned over to the new district judge. He would make the decision whether or not proof existed for a trial.

"Yes, sir," Lance said, his tone noncommittal.

Satisfied, Cort asked Sam questions about her trip. Out of courtesy Sam walked into Cort's bedroom to answer.

Ready to leave, Kincaid shifted from foot to foot. Tension emanated from every surface of his body and filled the room. Lamplight from the low desk in the parlor illuminated shadows and hollows on his face.

At last he looked into Angie's eyes. She had thought he'd never face her again.

Lance wanted to say something to comfort Angie, but no words came. Her dark eyes avoided his. She wore a yellow gown with tiny white ruffles around her throat. Pleasingly frayed wheat-blond hair had been braided and coiled around her head. Her tender neck tempted him. He knew how her skin would smell, how it would taste, how smooth and soft it would feel under his hands. A pulsing started in his loins. He took Angie, who had volunteered to stay with Amberg's two patients through the night, by the arm and walked her to the far side of the bedroom.

Sarah had already fallen into sleep.

Angie turned to face him. His eyes were neutral, evasive. Her heart lurched sickeningly.

To forestall whatever he was going to say, she tried to speak first, but so did he. They both stopped and waited for the other to speak. "Go ahead," she said.

"No, you," he said.

"What were you going to say?" she asked instead.

A quick, impatient gesture of his hand, like a man tossing a cigarette away, told her little. He was a man of abrupt movements and sometimes scowling impatience.

"Nothing," he growled.

"Was she waiting for you in Phoenix the whole time you were in Durango?" The question surprised them both. Angie wanted to take it back, but it hung in the air between them until Kincaid shook his head. And she knew, looking into his startled eyes, that she'd been right about him. Anytime she wanted she could look for him and he would oblige her by becoming as insane as she. Anytime. As long as he had breath in his sturdy body, he would be available to her for an hour or two.

Lance saw her frustration and felt it from his heart down to his toes. All Angie had to do was look hurt. Thank God he wasn't marrying *her*. She would keep him in turmoil. "Sam left with my father the day after you left Phoenix. But she came back."

Angie tried to turn away. Kincaid's hand caught her arm and turned her. A radiant light blazed once in the blue depths of his eyes and disappeared. In Phoenix he would take her to his house, if Samantha wasn't home, and make love to her there if she liked. Angie had the mad impulse to grab the gun out of his holster and shoot him.

"They're waiting for you," she whispered, her voice husky, breathless with rage.

"Are you going to the newspaper office tomorrow?"

"I don't think so. I'll take care of Sarah…she'll need me…"

"I wanted to thank you for taking care of me."

"You already thanked me for that."

A forbidding wariness tightened his lips and deepened the lines on either side of his mouth, making more of a grimace than a smile. Reluctantly his hand released her arm.

His voice sounded controlled, husky. "Good night."

"Good night."

"If you need to go to your house to get anything…" he volunteered.

"No, thank you…" she murmured.

Lance rejoined Samantha at the door. With a perfect proprietary air and the grace of a woman who had never made even the tiniest *faux pas*, Samantha slipped her hand into the crook of Kincaid's elbow absently, sweetly, maddeningly.

"If you need anything at all," Samantha said, and turned to Angie. "Please let us know. We owe you so very much."

Angie felt that *we* like an iron weight slammed against her heart. Kincaid flashed a look at Angie but smoldered in silence. Lance Kincaid was a warlord. A destroyer. He cared about nothing except himself and perhaps taking her and using her for a time. A short time. His hooded eyes masked an emotion Angie could not identify. She lifted her chin. She *did* hate him. Her hatred almost choked her.

"In case I don't see you before you leave, have a pleasant journey," Angie said sweetly, and struggled to control the shaking inside her.

Kincaid turned Samantha and propelled her out of the house. Angie had the feeling that memory of his hand—broad, brick-brown, and powerful on Samantha's slender waist—would haunt her as long as she lived. Carefully Angie closed the door and walked with measured step into Sarah's room.

Angie slipped into bed beside Sarah. She felt both angrier and more hopeful than she had in weeks. Tomorrow Laramee would be free, cleared of all charges. Sarah would live. Lily was alive and well. Kincaid would marry Samantha Regier and live happily ever after…

A sharp pang pierced Angie's heart. She fought it down with the only thing she had at her disposal. She had seen into Kincaid's soul in Phoenix, that night when he took her back to her hotel. Even if he didn't love her, they had shared something. He had been as torn and twisted by it as she. His soul had signaled her that much. She knew it irrevocably. No one could take it from her. Not Lance. Not Samantha. Not if Lance and Samantha were married a hundred years.

Angie held the pulse points in Sarah's temples and feet. Sarah woke twice during the night. Each time Angie forced her to sip water. By morning Angie was exhausted from lack of sleep, but Sarah was better.

Fifty men waited at the jail. Kincaid walked across the street to join them at seven o'clock. The sun glowed relentlessly hot already.

Gil led the party to the bank of the creek less than five hundred feet behind the Liang house. Firecrackers popped incessantly. A dozen Chinese clustered around the graves. Smells of incense and gunpowder hung heavy in the clear morning air.

"What the hell are they doing?" one man asked.

Gil smiled. "They burn spirit money and incense. Opening a Chinese grave is very serious. They must follow specific rituals in the Chinese Book of Rites."

Lance watched Gil Lee. Mrs. Lillian had been right about Gil and about him. He had to finish with Gil before he could get on with his own life. Unfortunately Mrs. Lillian would not get her wish. The only peace he could make with Gil would be with a gun or a knife.

As if he had heard Lance's thoughts, Gil turned and looked into Lance's eyes.

"Are you ready?" Gil asked.

Lance knew he did not mean to begin the digging. Gil Lee knew too much for that.

"I'm ready. Are you ready?"

"Yes," Gil said softly. "You'll be in town today and tomorrow?"

Lance nodded. He would have to get rid of Samantha first. She would have a hissy fit if she knew he intended to kill or be killed by an old friend of hers.

Firecrackers continued to explode. White men watched as if they were at the theater. When the rituals were finished, Gil motioned for the men with the shovels to begin.

Lance walked into the jail and stopped. Laramee Logan stood up and glared at him.

"Well?"

"Next time you decide to stab three Chinaboys, don't do it with sand. It gets in their throats and suffocates 'em to death."

Laramee breathed a sigh of relief. He had spent the night worrying. If they had been stabbed by anybody, he was all set up to take the blame for it.

"Well, blame it, Kincaid. You took your time coming back to tell me."

Lance walked to the hook and took the keys down. "Knew you'd probably want to sleep in."

Laramee walked out of the cell and stopped. "Want to thank you, Kincaid." Laramee stuck out his hand.

Grinning, Lance took it. "Just doing my job."

Angie opened the door. Laramee stood on Sarah's porch, his face a picture of restrained emotions.

Angie surged into his arms, crying his name. The nightmare had truly ended. Laramee hugged her hard. She cried and laughed and kissed him. He spent an hour sitting beside Sarah's bed, holding her hand. Sarah smiled sleepily at him. He whispered into her ear and kissed her cheek, and Sarah did not protest.

Laramee left. Angie and Sarah slept off and on all day. Kincaid did not come. But Angie had not expected him to come. He had no business here.

Samantha stuck like a saddle burr to him all day. Lance finally despaired of getting rid of her and relaxed. Tomorrow would be a better day for it. He would be rested. And so would Gil.

"You want to go home today? You could probably buy us a stagecoach line," he said.

"I would not get back into another one of those contraptions today if my life depended on it." The coaches Butterfield used were not nearly as heavily sprung as the ones she had grown accustomed to back east.

They ate dinner in the hotel dining room. Lance read the paper while she played gin rummy with a Bible drummer. At bedtime Lance walked Samantha to her room on the second floor of the Orlando. He kissed her on the forehead.

"Are you going to spend the rest of our life together kissing me as if I'm still four years old? I had no idea you were such a fuddy-duddy."

"Sleep tight."

That night, with every important task accomplished, he could not sleep. He wanted to end it with Gil. He felt trapped. He hated Gil. Gil had known all along that 'Cinda was meeting another man. Gil had known. He hadn't saved her.

Lance hated everyone. Visions of Angie Logan haunted him. Sleep would not come. A small replica of Angie Logan tortured his mind. Her skin glowed as tawny and lustrous as her shiny wheat-colored hair; her eloquent, richly lashed dark eyes flashed as hauntingly as the elusive flowery fragrance she wore.

He paced, and Angie's image was replaced by that of Lucinda, whom he had not thought about in a very long time. Previously, when her memory tried to surface, he had punched it down by sheer willpower. Now he allowed it to speak to him. Allowed himself to look closely at her, to delve into the mystery of her.

Near dawn he finally slept. He dreamed about Gil and the boy who had drowned.

Lance woke slowly, haltingly. Furious and sick, he struggled into a sitting position on the side of the bed. The dream slipped out of consciousness. He groped for it. It had been so unsettling, so unfair. It needed to be examined in the light of day, purged so it would not come back to torture him again.

Bright sunlight streamed through the window. Yoshio must have opened the drapes. Lance smelled bacon. Then he realized he was in Durango, in the hotel.

Filled with turmoil and a paralyzing sense of loss, he closed his eyes. Over a stupid dream. It wasn't even a fresh dream. It was the same terrible dream he'd had two times before. He didn't even know the boy. He didn't know the woman. Gil shouldn't have let the boy slip outside like that. Gil knew the creek was there.

The dream had spilled over into the waking realm and filled him with grief. Lance punched his pillow into a more accommodating shape. To hell with breakfast. He would sleep. To make up for the dream that had been a waste of time and energy…

Lucinda was good for you. She taught you to be more careful in love. The next time you will give your heart to a woman worthy of it. When did Gil say that? The day they fought. The day Gil tired of watching him suffer. *I'm sick of watching you beat yourself over something you had no control over…* Thanks for caring, Gilbert Lee. Go to hell. *You're already there. One sacrifice to Lucinda is enough.*

Tired of his own thoughts, Lance forced himself out of bed. The smells of breakfast cooking downstairs made his stomach lurch.

Samantha expected him. She would wait to have breakfast with him. Lance got as far as the hall and ran out of steam. He walked back into his room and sat down in the chair next to the window. The dream still nagged at him. What the hell did it mean? He felt as bad as if the boy had just died. As furious with Gil for letting it happen as he had been when they fought the day Johnny Winchester almost killed Angie and the Liang family. He hadn't felt this bad since right after 'Cinda was killed…

Lance closed his eyes. Exhausted, he half-dozed. A noise woke him. Surprised, he opened his eyes. *Hell, it wasn't Gil's fault. The kid had a mother. The mother was supposed to take care of her own child. Gil and I just happened to be there. That didn't make either one of us responsible.*

Relieved, Lance sighed. A great weight lifted off his shoulders. *Why the hell didn't I realize that right away? Why did I even have such a senseless, unsettling dream?*

He felt so much better, he almost couldn't believe he was the same man who awakened that morning.

He had the urge to tell Gil about the dream. Like a two-year-old he wanted to run up to Gil and say, *It wasn't your fault. I just realized, it wasn't your fault. It was her fault. The mother's. She should have been looking after her own kid…*

Hell, what was wrong with him? It was only a dream.

Lance sagged in the chair. Now he knew what the dream meant. At first the meaning was still fuzzy to him, but he could feel it taking shape in his head and heart.

"Ohhhh, shit!"

Lance closed his eyes. His heart pounded. He shook his head and leaned back. And the rest came to him. *'Cinda was responsible for herself.* Gil didn't cause her to die at the hands of those three men. *Nobody could have stopped her. It was her choice. Hers alone.*

By the morning of the second day Sarah sat up in bed and received visitors. To her surprise, she learned that she was considered a heroine by many.

Angie languished almost as rapidly as Sarah bloomed. Laramee came several times that day. Sarah held Laramee's hands, and they talked and whispered until Angie ran him off.

"Looks serious," Angie said after Laramee took his reluctant leave.

Sarah blushed prettily.

"Sarah Elizabeth Armstrong, you've changed!"

A new look of confidence shone out of Sarah's pretty green eyes. "Think so?" she asked.

"I know so. You haven't tried to run Laramee off a single time. What happened?"

"Since I was eight years old, I'd wake up screaming with nightmares about being shot." Sarah shuddered at the memory. "Then I was really shot. When that happened to me—being shot the way I had been in all my nightmares—it should have killed me, but when I woke up alive—not dead—I felt wonderful. How is it possible that having the worst thing in the world happen to me could turn the world so sweet? I feel so happy to be alive. So glad that Laramee loves me, that Cort didn't want them to shoot me."

"You two set a date?"

"Sort of…If Cort is okay by then."

"Hallelujah," Angie breathed. "You've always been my sister, now it's finally going to be official."

Sarah hugged her. "I'm so happy. I just wish Cort didn't have this hanging over his head."

Looking into Sarah's eyes, Angie saw none of the shadows, none of the conflict. "You've changed so much."

"After I was shot, I realized you were right. All men carry guns. Laramee was unlucky. He *had* to defend himself. He did such a good job of it that I didn't stop to think that perhaps he didn't want to. When I shot Smalley I realized that Laramee was just doing what he had to do to survive." Sarah sighed. "I've been so mean to Laramee."

A wire came for Angie. Atillo delivered it to Sarah's house. Without speaking or looking at Sarah, Angie read it, folded it, and put it in her pocket.

"Well?" Sarah demanded, walking out of the bedroom and stepping up beside her.

"The governor granted Tan Lin a full pardon."

Squealing, Sarah hugged Angie as hard as she could with one arm.

CHAPTER TWENTY-FIVE

Saturday, June 12, 1880

Lance found Samantha in the lobby.

She glanced up, her lovely blue eyes focused on him, and her face lit up, brightening the whole lobby with her own special radiance.

"Lance!" She ran to meet him, and her feet barely touched the floor.

He hugged her in full view of the horrified, disapproving matrons in the lobby.

"What's wrong?" She searched his face. Tears pooled in her lovely eyes. "I waited breakfast for you. What's wrong. You look—"

Her chin trembled with her tumultuous thoughts.

Shamed to the core, Lance took her by the arm. "Let's take a walk. We need to talk…"

Sarah no longer needed a full-time nurse. Her injury had been mostly a bleeder. She had suffered little damage to her arm or side. And Angie was sure Cort would be happy to have his home to himself. Apparently he was going to get off scot-free. Laramee was so happy to be engaged to Sarah that he wasn't going to encourage anyone to pursue the charges against Cort. Angie had mixed feelings about that, but since Cort didn't appear to be a real danger to anyone now, except possibly as a selectman, she remained silent. Sarah was about to become her sister-in-law. Maybe having a landed daughter would satisfy Cort.

Laramee brought over and fixed Sarah and Cort lunch, while Angie gathered and packed her things.

Sarah touched Angie's sleeve. "You want me to go home with you?"

"I do not want you to leave this bed."

"I have an idea. You could ride me on your bicycle. Why don't we go to the creek and hang our feet in the water?" Sarah asked. There was one place along its meandering path where the water pooled. Even in midsummer it would be three or four feet deep. "You could swim. I'd feel better just watching you."

The thought of undressing and trying to swim with Lance Kincaid in Durango—if he were still in Durango—raced through Angie's mind. What could Sarah be thinking of? "I think I'll go home and lie down. The heat is really tiring me."

Lance walked slowly up the gentle incline. Gil lay on his sleeping mat in the shade of the singed tree. Bruises on his face had faded to pale green and purple. Lance stopped about ten feet away from Gil. Gil did not stand, but with the quiet unobtrusiveness that had characterized Gilbert Lee as long as Lance had known him, the energy to fight began to build. Lance waited until Gil was fully ready.

"Why didn't you just come right out and tell me there was nothing either one of us could have done to change anything?"

Relaxing slightly, Gil sighed. "I tried, Kincaid, but you weren't ready to hear it. You were furious with me—"

"You said only that she met them at the apartment…"

"Some things a man has to figure out for himself."

Gil had sacrificed their friendship to tell him that Lucinda had had another lover. Only Lance hadn't believed him, he hadn't accepted the out Gil had given him. He had insisted on blaming someone for Lucinda's death.

It had been less painful to blame Gil.

Gil held up his hand and waited for Lance to take it, to help him to his feet. Gil had never needed anyone's help before. Never asked for it. Never accepted it. Gilbert James Lee's body was a ribbon of spring steel. Effortlessly, within a fraction of a second, he could go from complete prostration to a fighting position. Gil's waiting hand blurred out of focus and then in again. A wave of emotion flooded Lance. He swallowed. Slowly, Lance reached out and clasped Gil's hand, pulled Gil to his feet. Gil held out his arms, and Lance stepped into his embrace. A rush of warmth swept over Lance, and for one ragged moment he felt tears well up.

"Start over," Gil said quietly. "Make a new life with Angie Logan. She loves you."

Regret darkened Lance's eyes. Twin dimples fired in unison in his lean cheeks. "It's too late."

Gil leaned against the tree. "You have wronged her, and now you feel unable to approach her…"

Looking away, narrowing his eyes at the horizon that shimmered under the hot sun, Lance agreed. "That's about it."

"Since you have wronged her once, why must you wrong her again? Could this be another mistake, my friend?"

"Angie wouldn't have me now."

"Instead of deciding for her—why don't you ask her?"

Gil couldn't resist another gentle barb. "Or haven't you learned that lesson yet?"

"You don't know what I did." His voice was taut with contrition. "A man can't deliver that much hurt to one woman and have any hope of ever seeing her again."

"If she loves you, perhaps it doesn't matter."

"How could she love me after—" Lance turned, rubbed the edge of his fist on a low tree limb. "I wasted six years of my life."

"You have accomplished a great deal, my friend. You built a life that protected you against unnecessary involvement. You were able to do some tasks that needed to be done. Who is to say that you were not doing exactly what was needed for yourself and for your country?" Gil moved around until he faced Lance. "We are each given a special energy from the universe. It is our job to take it and do the best we can with it."

"It seems like I did the worst I could."

"Perhaps that might have been your intent, at some moments, but it matters not. You learned a great deal from Lucinda about love. She was neither all good nor all bad. Because of your loss of her you are one of the finest lawmen in the territories. You are part of history. You champion those who are unable to help themselves. You are neither all good nor all bad…Angie Logan does not expect sainthood."

"No, she probably expects a man to act like a man, not a beast…"

"All men make mistakes, my friend. Mistakes are necessary. There are no accidents in life. Trust this. I myself have learned a good lesson in Durango. All my life I have been the outcast, the half-breed who was never good enough. I have been uncomfortable among whites and Chinese alike. As a result of this I learned to conform. I became accustomed to living in this way and did not realize that there are times when one must defy all rules. You were right about Lily. I should have taken her away. I should not have let them desecrate our love."

Gil could never have said these words before, but Lily had taught him that life was to be lived and savored, and sweated over and struggled with, not accepted like a dead fish in a newspaper.

"Sometimes, a man is given the grace and mercy of another chance. It would be a cowardly act not to accept it."

Clenching his fist, Lance rubbed the side of his hand against the rough bark of the tree. "I doubt if Chane would agree that I deserve another chance."

"You are wrong. Chane loves you. He and Colette could have overcome your interference if their love had been true. Life is not a constant state and we are not fixed like threads in a tapestry, we are always reacting. Some actions must be taken quickly, sometimes without adequate information. Mistakes are not a sign to give up life, only proof of our fallibility, our humanity—a small reminder.

"You must have had a good laugh on me."

"Because Lucinda betrayed your love? No. That was Lucinda's shame, not yours. No person's private shame is ever a laughing matter. Lucinda hated what she did to you. To herself."

And to you, Lance thought. He kicked the tree trunk with his foot. "How'd you get so damned smart?" Lance asked, feeling he had posed this question years before.

Gil leaned against the tree. "Lily taught me what I know today, what I did not know before."

"I never stood a chance," Lance growled darkly.

"On the contrary, you are very powerful. You can do anything you wish."

A wry smile flickered in Kincaid's eyes. "I suspect I can."

Angie walked home slowly. It was too hot. Once there, she felt both exhausted and too nervous to lie down. She found a book and began to read, but her attention was too fragmented. Finally she sat with the book on her lap.

The knock on the door startled her. It was Kincaid. Even through the door, she could feel the throb of him. Panic flooded through her like water breaking through a dam.

He knocked again, harder this time. More commandingly. The sound rattled her, vibrated through her intensely, just the way he did. Dazed, Angie stood up and walked clumsily toward the door. How should she compose her face? How should she act? She was too straightforward to plan so much.

Lance Kincaid—finely sculpted, appealing features in his thoroughly masculine face. His eyes—luminous blue against the bronzed richness of his skin—were filled with something she did not recognize. Uncertainty?

Neither of them spoke. Wearing rough clothes, dusty, hot, and probably tired, he met her gaze and ran an impatient hand through his dark hair, pinning her there with a look from his piercing eyes.

"May I come in?"

Angie stepped back. He walked to the center of the room, then turned to face her. His gaze held hers. His chin lifted slightly in a mannerism that was singularly his, firing a question with a slight movement of eyebrows and bottom lip that she'd never noticed before. The look seemed to say, *Am I wasting time coming here?* But she'd been wrong about Kincaid too many times to trust her perception. The look in his eyes wavered. She turned away.

"I want to thank you for getting Laramee out of jail," she said to fill the space.

"You're welcome." Silence stretched out.

"Did you hear from the governor?" he asked. The attractive raspiness of his voice moved into her, loosed butterflies within her.

Treading her traitorous emotions as frantically and as unobtrusively as she could, Angie smiled. "Yes, he gave Tan Lin a full pardon."

"I'm glad it worked."

The awkward silence lengthened. Angie Logan had the tender look of a bruised daisy. It wrenched Lance. Part of him was too dazed to know how to proceed with this uncowed yet frightened young woman. He had hurt her, but he hoped not so badly that it could not be corrected.

"What's Laramee going to do about the silver mine?"

"It takes capital to work a mine. He has no money and he isn't willing to borrow it. He doesn't trust the offers that have been made to him."

"Maybe I could make him a reasonable offer."

They had never talked about money. She had assumed he had none. Suddenly remembering what Winchester had said about money, she quirked an eyebrow at him.

"Why would you?"

Lance shrugged. "Why not? For an interest in the mine. Whatever Laramee and you think is fair."

To be near Angie Logan was almost as good as touching her. Being close to her again awakened all the needy parts inside him. He had startled her. With a curious, quick uplifting of her flashing eyes that Lance felt sure would never lose their charm, she answered.

"Talk to Laramee. It's his mine. His ranch…" A quicksilver rippling of emotion crossed her lovely face.

"Would you object to his having me for a partner?"

Angie felt her stomach lurch. Lance Kincaid watched her the way a hawk watches a pullet. Everyone in town was out trying to strike it rich. They ran from spot to spot with pick axes and shovels. It sickened her that Lance Kincaid had come here to talk to her about the silver.

Anger was quick and hot inside her. It urged her to be honest. "Yes. I guess I would."

"Then I guess marriage is out of the question?" His whiskey-tinged voice was harsher than gravel now, finer than silk.

"That would depend entirely upon who you wished to—" Angie said, carried by her anger, her own voice breaking as she realized what he had said. "…marry?"

"You. I want to marry you."

Shaken to the core, Angie turned away. "Does Samantha know you want to marry both of us?"

"You know better than that." His warm hands encircled her arms, turned her, forced her to face him.

Heart pounding, Angie lifted her chin, looked at him through slightly narrowed eyes. "Is this a trick?"

"I don't know. Why would you want to trick me?"

Angie lifted her eyebrows at him. How neatly he had turned that around.

Encouraged by her near smile, Lance continued. "I'm not good at tricks. I have a past. You have a future. Perhaps we could turn that combination into something useful."

"If this is supposed to sweep me off my feet—"

"Hardly…"

"Then why bother? You owe me nothing." Furious, she tried to jerk away from him, but the firm pressure of his warm hands stopped her.

"I love you, Angie."

Angie stopped struggling in mid-tantrum and searched his tense face. Appealing in a way that no other man could ever hope to match, his eyes looked deep inside her with no attempt to mask anything.

His hands dropped away from her. Lance ran an impatient hand through his disheveled hair. "I know that doesn't seem possible, the way I treated you…"

Remembering the evening she had spent in his bed in Phoenix, Angie flushed. "No, it doesn't."

"I was afraid."

"And now you're not?"

"No. Now I'm scared to death, but too miserable to care."

Angie mustered a small shaky laugh. He loved her. Her heart swelled with love for him. But she wasn't ready to concede everything yet.

"How can I be sure that you are not always so abusive to the ones you love...?" The look in his eyes was answer enough, but the agony she had been through in the last week demanded its own redress.

"I don't suppose my word would be worth much?"

Part of Angie was giddy and blinded by his declaration of love. Another part of her still needed to be soothed and coaxed. "Maybe I need to know more..."

Lance spread his hands in surrender. "Whatever you want."

"I want to hear about everything. About you and Gil. About you and Lucinda. About all the women in your life. How you treated them. How much you loved them. Everything."

Lance expelled a short explosive little breath. "Glad you're not going to pamper me," he growled, pinning her with a fierce frown. "Where do I start?"

Angie took him by the hand and led him into the kitchen. She took tea out of the icebox and poured two glasses, then sat down across from him so she could watch his face.

"Start with Lucinda. How do you feel about her now?"

"Now?" Frowning, leaning back in his chair, Lance stared at the wall behind Angie. The clefts on either side of his mouth deepened into a scowl. "I guess I feel bad about some of the things I've been thinking about her for the last few years." He looked down at the table and crossed his arms over his chest. "I loved 'Cinda. When she died I was pretty broken up about it. Then Gil got tired of seeing me in such bad shape and told me the truth."

Lance clenched his fists, jammed them back into his pockets, and glowered at the floor. "I didn't take it very well. I had assumed she was murdered by strangers—" Muscles in his lean jaws bunched and writhed, "—and she wasn't. They were friends of her lover's. Gil knew she was meeting Winchester at an apartment across town. He didn't say anything about it to me until six months after she died. I blamed Gil for letting her die when he knew what the hell was going on. I blamed 'Cinda for being a cheating little bitch. I blamed myself for not being able to keep her happy." He pulled in a tortured breath. "I blamed everybody. I don't remember a hell of a lot about those first two years after she died. I look back on it now, and I have this image of myself floundering like a beached bass."

"A few months after 'Cinda's death, Gil and I moved to Paris. I saw a girl who interested me. I worked for my father. On my way to work I walked past her dress shop. She flirted with me. One day I walked into the shop and led her out to my carriage. I took her to a château I had rented that morning on the outskirts of Paris. She was the first woman I had wanted in six months. We made love, and she tried to tell me her name. I told her if she did, I wouldn't see her again. I didn't even want to know where she worked so I would have no way to ever get back to her again, but I couldn't trick myself. I went back for her a number of times. She stopped trying to find out who I was, and, finally, she stopped threatening to tell me who she was."

The grooves on either side of his mouth deepened in a look of disgust. He expelled another angry breath. "There were times when we'd stay in bed for three days running. I don't know how she explained her repeated disappearances."

"You certainly don't lack in energy."

"No, I don't."

"And then what happened?" She knew what Gil had told her, but she needed desperately to know how honest Lance could be with her.

"I found out my lover's name was Colette and that she was engaged to my very own brother, Chane. I drank until I thought I was blind, and when I recovered enough to drag my body down to the telegraph office I wired my father that I had resigned. Gil's romance had just ended, so he offered to go home with me. We landed in Boston and when I realized my folks had assigned Gil as my wet nurse, we fought in Cambridge. I was angry and bitter and tired of being the fool. I said something insulting to Gil and he was just mad enough to finally tell me the truth about 'Cinda. We were parted in just enough time to keep from killing each other. I stopped in New York long enough to say hello and good-bye to my family and took a ship to San Francisco. I cut all ties with my family and their money. I decided that if I couldn't earn my keep I'd die, and that would be fine. I took odd jobs until I wandered into Arizona and John Stapleton tricked me into becoming a ranger."

"How did he do that?"

"I got drunk playing poker with him. I bet him three years of my life against his horse. I lost. He turned me over to his friend, McNamara, who gave me a tongue-lashing about hard work, sobriety, gambling, respect, and lots of other things I've forgotten. When he wore the hide off his tongue, he gave me a badge. When my three years were up, I stayed on."

"And what about your brother, Chane?"

"Two years ago, on a visit home, I told him I was sorry." Twin muscles clenched his jaws.

"And what did he say?"

Lance scowled at the wall opposite her. "Colette gave him back his ring, wouldn't see him again. He said he understood." Lance sighed. "Blood is thick. What else could he say?

"Chane was my idol when I was a kid. I would have done anything in the world for him. I would have died for him. Instead, I took the one woman in the world he loved, and I destroyed her as surely as Winchester destroyed 'Cinda."

"I don't believe that for one minute, Lance Kincaid. You broke her heart for a time, but you didn't destroy her. She's alive, isn't she?"

"I don't know."

"Of course she is. She's probably married with three beautiful children. Of course, I don't want to talk you out of doing something you enjoy, like feeling bad, but…"

Lance looked at her, and a grin spread across his face. "Naw, me?"

Angie turned serious. "The first time Gil saw me, he mentioned that I looked like someone he had known. After hearing Winchester, I realized that I must look like 'Cinda. I have to know…" She hesitated. "…how you can be sure you love *me?* And not her?"

"'Cinda?" His blue eyes penetrated her with a look that caused her heart to leap. "I'm confessing to being a son of a bitch, not to being stupid. I've been in love. I know what it feels like. You look a little like her, but you're not her."

"Is this going to be one of those relationships you mentioned in which a woman is in love, and you are grateful?"

The swell and curve of his lips arranged themselves in a look of sardonic amusement. "Lord, I hope so."

Angie controlled the urge to laugh. This was too important. "How do you know you can trust me not to take my gift of love back?"

A wry look came into his eyes. "I don't."

"Then why are you willing to risk getting hurt again?"

"No choice."

"I don't understand."

"We walked out into the desert a few days ago, then all hell broke lose, right?"

"Yes."

"I've lived through more misery in that short time than I did in the last five years. I missed you every waking moment. It was getting worse, not better." Grimacing, Lance shook his head. "In upstate New York, at my folks' country place, we had these endless winters. It felt like one of those had set in and would never end."

Joy leapt in Angie's heart. She felt exhilarated by it, but the part of her that had been hurt was still bruised and sensitive. "Why were you so cruel to me?"

Lance grimaced. "I wanted you, and you scared hell out of me."

"What happened with Samantha?"

"I told her the truth."

"Where is she now?"

"Packing to go back to New York. She'll be fine. Buffy and Maggie will take care of her until she bounces back. Sam was like a little sister to me. She lived with my family from the time she was four. Sam was a big piece of the puzzle for me. Because she loved me so much, I realized what it must have been like for 'Cinda being loved so much by me and having to betray my love to keep peace with herself."

"What about Winchester? How does he fit into all of this?"

"Winchester was 'Cinda's lover. I don't think he killed her. At least he claimed he didn't, but he knew the men who did. He covered for them." Lance's voice turned rough. "I guess that explains why he fought me in Nogales. Probably explains why he set the barn on fire with you in it."

"It does? How?"

"You rattled him, looking so much like 'Cinda." Lance shook his head. "Liang *was* in the barn. He escaped through a tunnel covered up by the corn crib. They took thousands of dollars in silver out of that tunnel. I guess your brother's got a claim against them."

Angie envisioned Chinese, their knees bending deep under their heavy loads. Dirt? Instead of laundry? "The money is gone. I don't care about the money. What I care about is that you'll end up seeing 'Cinda in me—because of the resemblance…"

Lance quirked expressive black brows. "You ever look in the mirror? You have everything a woman needs to be loved for herself."

Angie smiled. "I know that, but how can I be sure you know it?"

His lean form shimmered the air between them. "Trust me. I know."

Angie did trust him. She sensed the strength in him; it seemed bottomless. The swell and curve of his smiling lips, the warmth and openness in his cornflower-blue eyes were such clear signals. He had finally dropped his mask.

"How do you feel about 'Cinda now?"

Lance expelled a short breath. "Bad. I expected too much from her. I was only fifteen when I fell in love with her." He stopped. His lips tightened, and he looked away.

"How were you able to make up with Gil?"

Lance's breathing was shallow and fast. "I came to my senses. I realized that neither of us had been the cause of her dying."

"You can accept it? That simply?"

Lance's eyes darted from side to side as if checking some unseen authority, then he dragged in a breath and relaxed. "Yeah."

Angie felt the unmistakable release of tension from within. He *had* gotten over 'Cinda. She held out her hand to him. Cautiously, he took it in his own.

"What about Atillo?"

Lance shrugged, but Angie knew. Atillo had reminded him of his own passion for 'Cinda. He had wanted to keep the boy from making the same mistake he'd made.

Love for Lance Kincaid almost overwhelmed Angie. To hide her surrender, she laughed. "You were dreadful to me!"

"Angel, I'm on bended knee, proposing to you. How could you accuse me of anything except excellent taste in women and terrible timing?"

"Because I know *all* your faults." Angie said, feeling suddenly girlish, a happy smile spreading inside her.

Seeing the banter in her dark eyes, hiding the relief he felt, Lance scowled. "All of 'em?"

"Your faults? Heavens! I hope so. I'd hate to think there are more."

Lance feigned perplexity. "I didn't give you the list, did I?"

Angie widened her eyes at him. "Someone has taken the time to actually *list* your faults?"

Grinning, Lance pulled Angie to her feet. His arms encircled her and held her close to him. The dry, tingling heat of his body moved through her like an invasion. Her blood raced.

"It could be done," he murmured against her cheek.

"A formidable undertaking…I'm sure." She forgot what they were talking about before the words left her mouth.

Lance lifted her chin, leaned down, and touched her lips with his own, brushing softly. A small tremor moved through her body. Lance tormented her. He didn't really kiss her—he teased her lips, her eyes, her cheeks, her throat.

Groaning, she reached up to take his face in her hands, to find his mouth with her own. "You're dreadful to me—" She sighed, capturing his lips at last, going blind in the sweet fire that surged through her at the warm, adhesive pressure of his lips as he took control and kissed her the way she needed to be kissed.

Angie floated in a near swoon. He finally relinquished her mouth. "You probably noticed I came without references," he breathed, stirring the wispy hairs near her ear.

"A wise move," she whispered. "Forgeries are very easy to detect."

He kissed her long and thoroughly. "Do I have nothing to recommend me?" he murmured against her cheek, his warm breath tingling her sensitive skin.

"Nothing I would want to see mentioned in a letter of reference."

He dropped his teasing banter and held her away from him. "I love you, Angie. Will you marry me?"

She touched one of the buttons on his shirt. "I'm not a good cook."

"That's probably the least of your flaws."

"And I hate housework."

"Maybe you can figure out some way to get Yoshio to do it. Lord knows I've tried…"

"Liar." Angie pinched him.

"Ow!"

"And I have a great number of things I want to do. I'm going to publish my picture book about Durango, and then one about San Francisco, and then one about Mexico City…"

"Can I pull your wagon?"

"You can pull the perambulator."

"Is that anything like a baby buggy?"

They laughed. He nuzzled her neck. The heat of his lean body sent a flush of pleasure searing through her. He lifted her chin to kiss her, and she trembled with the same quivering intensity she had felt that night under the porch.

His dizzying kiss was a confirmation. Everything had changed and nothing had changed. "I love you, Angie. I've probably loved you from the second I saw you, irritating me with that damned camera."

"Am I supposed to believe all this?"

"It'll make things easier if you do."

"Okay, then."

Lance leaned down to nibble her ear and swung Angie up into his arms. He carried her into her bedroom, lowered her gently onto the bed, and then grasped her gown at the bodice as if he were going to rip it off.

Seeing the alarm on her lovely face, he sighed.

"Guess I'll have to pretend at least until I get you married, won't I?" Cornflower-blue eyes twinkled with laughter and reassured her more thoroughly than the teasing tone of his husky voice.

Angie let out a wicked little laugh. "No." She grabbed his shirt, ripped it open, then slipped her hands around his lean waist, and pulled him close. The need to tease was gone, replaced by a sweet fire, urgent and breathless, the evolution of heat into light. Whatever existed between them—disguised as fierceness and hunger—took hold, and she remembered nothing except the feel and taste and touch of him. She would never know what their bodies did that day. Whatever it was, it had to be right, because she wanted it, because he wanted it. Once she moaned and was rewarded with a burning flash from his blue eyes. Every emotion she had ever wanted to see in him was reflected in the blue depths of his eyes: fierce possession—passionate and consuming love.

A bird sprinkled the air with a shrill, gay tune. Angie opened her eyes, amazed to see the sun shining outside. She had thought…

He rolled over and pulled her on top of him. His hands stroked her back, buttocks, thighs. Her cheek pressed against his. Their breathing was still much too fast.

"Lance…"

"Hmmmmmm."

"I love you. I forgot to tell you."

A sideways look from his eyes, as merry as bluebells in a light breeze, was accompanied by a husky chuckle. "No, you didn't."

"You're very observant."

Lance's hand stroked her smooth round buttocks. Smoother than butter. "A compliment at last…"

"Don't get cocky, Mr. Kincaid."

Effortlessly, Lance lifted her body higher so his face nestled between her breasts. Her hair fell forward, brushing his cheek. Sighing, he rubbed his cheek against the shiny tresses and her soft skin. "I used to have a softee I carried around with me," he said, nibbling first one sensitive peak then the other. "A silk shimmy of my mother's. They said I would sit on the floor, rubbing my softee on my cheek, sucking two fingers of my left hand…" He turned her, positioned her right nipple to his lips, and sucked it into his mouth, sighing. "I think I've finally found an acceptable substitute."

Angie giggled. "Man marries softee."

"Is that a yes?"

"How can I resist? It's a headline."

EPILOGUE

Calling out to Mrs. Lillian, Elizabeth rushed down the stairs and opened the front door. She had seen the cabriolet stop in front of their town house on Fifth Avenue and recognized Samantha as she leaned out to look up at the building.

Samantha's eyes widened at sight of her in the doorway, and she abandoned her bags and flew up the steps into Elizabeth's arms. Elizabeth held Samantha's trembling body close. Finally Samantha sighed and leaned back in Elizabeth's embrace. Samantha's eyes were dark.

"I guess you heard."

"Yes. We received your wire." Elizabeth sighed. How had she gone so wrong in raising Lance that he could hurt her baby in this fashion? Hadn't Samantha suffered enough? "Come inside, darling."

Swallowing, not yet ready to face the family, Samantha took Elizabeth's hand and held her there. "I had a nice trip. I mean, I hated the heat and the misery of travel, but I accomplished a great deal actually…"

Samantha tugged on Elizabeth's hand and sat down on the stone balustrade next to the steps. The driver assembled her luggage at the front door and received his tip from Mrs. Lillian who took in the situation with a glance, stepped back inside, and quietly closed the front door. The man tipped his hat at Samantha, climbed back into his cab and departed.

As if dazed, Samantha watched him drive away. Elizabeth sat down next to her.

Samantha twisted at her gown. "I mean, Lance is fine…he's really fine…and he's completely healed now."

"What about you?"

Samantha lifted her chin. She sighed and looked into her aunt's eyes. "You remember the puppy Buffy had when we were about nine?"

"Big Foot?"

"Big Foot loved Buffy. He would sleep beside her bed, follow her anywhere and eat anything she gave him. I was so jealous of her. I loved

Big Foot, but he didn't know I existed. One day when Buffy was away somewhere, and I was home, I took him out to the barn and held him prisoner all day. I petted him and fed him fresh raw chicken breasts I stole from the kitchen. I told him over and over how much I loved him, and he seemed to accept me, but when Buffy came home, he almost went crazy to get away from me. I hated Buffy all that summer." Her lovely chin crumpled. Sam looked from her hands, gripped together in her lap, into Elizabeth's eyes. "You can't force a puppy to love you just because you're the one who needs to be loved."

Sam was right. Lillian had warned Elizabeth in her gentle way that Lance would have to choose his own replacement for Lucinda. Men rarely accept volunteers.

Elizabeth reached out to touch Sam's hand.

Samantha glanced up at the town house. In the late afternoon sun, its red brick walls gleamed amid the trees that surrounded it; the people inside waited to greet her. How she hated the thought of facing them…

"Is everyone home?"

"No one is home except Mrs. Lillian, and she was about to take her afternoon nap. Your uncle Chantry went to Chicago to meet with the Republicans who nominated Garfield. You know how he loves a dark horse. The girls are playing tennis on the Vanderbilts' new clay court. Stuart is riding."

"Thank goodness," Samantha breathed.

Understanding perfectly, Elizabeth helped her with the luggage.

All that week Samantha allowed Maggie, Buffy, Elizabeth, and Mrs. Lillian to shower her with their love. At the end of the week Samantha went shopping and came back with a puppy. Elizabeth met her at the foot of the stairs.

They exchanged surprised looks.

"How adorable he is!" Elizabeth exclaimed.

"Be careful. I've trained him to bite everyone except me."

Elizabeth drew back in alarm. "What?"

Samantha laughed. "I'm only joking. I think."

At the end of the week Samantha decided that perhaps Europe was not such a bad idea. As soon as she felt strong enough to leave the nest again…

At the end of the second week, on July 2, 1880, Samantha sailed for London on the White Star Line's *Oceanic.*

Elizabeth came home alone. Buffy and Maggie had stayed in town to shop. She stopped in the entryway and took off her bonnet. On the sideboard a box waited. Sighing, Elizabeth leaned over and peered down at the familiar handwriting. Her heart gave a small leap. It was from Lance, addressed to Mr. and Mrs. Chantry Kincaid II, marked personal.

"You're home," Lillian said, stepping into the entryway. "How was the bon voyage?"

"We all cried as if someone had died. It was wonderful. Three young men were vying for her attention before the ship left the pier. She will be fine."

"Samantha is strong—she *will* be fine."

Elizabeth quietly turned her attention to Lance's package and quickly untied the strings, opened the box, moved aside the tissue paper, lifted the topmost photograph with a soft sigh, gazed at it for a moment, and then slowly passed it to Lillian.

"This looks serious," she said, spreading the remaining cardboard-backed portraits on the rich mahogany table beside the library doors.

Lillian studied the photograph. The young Lance she remembered with such fierce motherly love shone up at her from the portraits, the same intensity and exuberance coupled now with fierce love. She had waited so long to see that again. The blond bride's face—so much like Lucinda's that it gave Lillian a start—shone with adoration as she smiled up at Lance. Lillian searched the girl's face. Yes. It *was* different. A great deal showed in that dark-eyed, sensitive face that she had not seen in Lucinda's face: character, strength, and self-possession. Lucinda had been a child-woman, a careless lover, an adventuress. This young woman appeared thoroughly conscious and passionately involved with life.

Lillian glanced sideways at Elizabeth, silent and enthralled.

At the bottom of the box two envelopes rested: one addressed to Mother and Father and one to Mrs. Lillian. Elizabeth rushed to her sitting room for a letter opener. Lillian slipped hers into her pocket and went to her room at the back of the house.

Lillian sat down carefully at her writing desk, where she had a view of the garden, and tore off the end of the envelope. A ten dollar bill fluttered onto the smooth mahogany desktop. Mrs. Lillian smiled at sight of Lance's bold, fast-paced handwriting and fingered the bill as she read his letter.

> Dear Mrs. L.,
>
> You were right, of course. The universe works just as you directed it to work. Within days of our discussion I found Gil Lee.

A great deal has happened since we talked. Gil is my friend again, and I am married.

My wife, Angela Brianna Kincaid née Logan, graduated in Sam's class at Mount Holyoke. I met her in Nogales. Our story is remarkable. Angie is an amazing young woman, stronger and braver than a dozen badmen. She is a wonderful photographer, as you can see from the photographs she managed to both shoot and be in.

Please take care of Sam for me. I know I hurt her, but there did not seem to be another way. I hope someday she can forgive me.

My father will be happy to learn that I have resigned from the ranger unit. I've bought a quarter interest in a silver mine that I'm going to operate. I've hired some professionals and laborers, and I'm up to my eyebrows in books about engineering and mining. Fortunately I have a strong back and natural talent with a shovel and pick axe. Chane and Stu should get a laugh out of that.

The ten dollars is for a final favor. The next time you're in Cambridge, would you please take a bouquet of flowers to 'Cinda's grave? I realize now she did the best she could. She loved me, but she had her own demons to deal with. Tell her to rest in peace. That I have forgiven her and myself.

Thanks for not giving up on me.

I love you,

Lance

MORE FROM JOYCE BRANDON

THE LADY AND THE ROBBER BARON

Jennifer Van Vleet is a woman who knows what she wants out of life and won't let anything stand in her way. She's dedicated herself to the art of ballet and becomes the prima ballerina for her company. When her costume catches fire during a performance, Chantry Kincaid III—a rakishly charming Texan builder whose family has as many enemies as it has properties—saves her. Jennifer finds herself drawn into a whirlwind romance with Chantry, where the passion between the two is undeniable, until she learns of the Kincaid family's hand in her parents' deaths years ago. Now she has a decision to make, one that will decide whether she can let go of the past and move forward from tragedy.

THE LADY AND THE OUTLAW

Leslie Powers has every reason in the world to hate Ward Cantrell, the devilishly handsome outlaw who kidnapped her. Instead she finds herself head-over-heels in love with him. When prompted by the sheriff to testify against Ward, Leslie firmly states that she was never Ward's hostage. Now a free man, Ward courts his way through the young ladies of Phoenix society, appearing to seduce them with wanton abandon. Leslie believes he is a rogue and worse, but she can't get him out of her mind or her heart. She's seen behind his mask and knows there is more to him than meets the eye; something in him has captured her heart.

ADOBE PALACE

After the deaths of her parents, Samantha Forrester was raised with the Kincaid children. She fell in love with Lance Kincaid as he protected her from childhood bullies. Now they've both grown up and Lance has married another. When the devilishly charming Steve Sheridan rides into Samantha's life, she sees her chance to build the house of her dreams, save her son's life, and claim Lance's heart for her own. But life doesn't always go according to plan, and fate will take them all on a journey as wild as the land they live on.

AFTER EDEN

Teresa Garcia-Lorca was raised as the favored daughter of "El Gato Negro," the infamous Mexican revolutionary. She lived in sheltered bliss until the day the truth of her paternity comes out, and her former "father" becomes furious. Teresa and her mother are forced to flee for their lives to escape El Gato's murderous rage. Her only hope lies in the home of her biological father, Bill Burkhart, but nothing could have prepared her for the treachery of gringo/white greed. Her new-found father's bastard daughter, Judy Burkhart, has had everything—and every man—she's ever wanted. Her indulgent world shatters when Judy learns she's been disinherited in her father's will. She and Teresa must learn to fight for all they have lost—and only one of them will end up with the man they both love.

Printed in the USA
CPSIA information can be obtained
at www.ICGtesting.com
JSHW031706140824
68134JS00038B/3538